No Brakes

On the Wing

Ellen Ann Callahan

PARKS WELLS PUBLISHING, LLC
Gaithersburg, Maryland

While the author strived for accuracy, sometimes it gave way to storytelling. The Office of the Baltimore City State's Attorney does not have a gang unit. With the exception of Patterson Park, the specific locations of crime scenes do not exist.

Cover design by Jera Publishing

Follow Ellen on Twitter at https://www.twitter.com/ECallahanAuthor
Like Ellen on Facebook at https://www.facebook.com/EllenAnnCallahan
Visit Ellen at http://www.ellenanncallahan.com

ISBN 10: 0996252800
ISBN 13: 978-0-9962528-0-5

For Ron, my husband and best friend

Part One

Chapter 1

May 1

S ometimes it's the most unlikely person who screws up.

Lucy sprinted up three flights of stairs, two steps at a time, and yanked open the glass door to the entrance of Jones & Hart. She tried to ignore the crying woman behind the reception desk. There was no time for sympathy. Minutes meant the difference between a day's profit and loss. "I'm here for a pick-up. Are you the lawyer?"

"Yes."

"Where to?"

"Civil office, courthouse. By four thirty."

"Lady, it's four fifteen!"

"Please." The woman wiped her eyes with a tissue, smearing mascara across her cheekbones. "The statute of limitations. I'll get sued, lose my jo—"

Lucy felt sorry for the woman. How could she have gotten into such a mess? The lawyer didn't seem like a drunk or a stoner, but Lucy knew what it was to screw up and to screw up bad.

She snatched the envelope from the lawyer's hands. "I'll get it there. No matter what."

Lucy rushed out of the office building and unlocked her bike from the nearby light pole. It was a *Wabi Lightning SE* fixed-gear. Aluminum framed, it weighed less than eighteen pounds, making it swift and easy to maneuver. Learning to slide-stop the bike took a few weeks; it didn't have any brakes. Only rookie couriers and wimps rode with brakes.

She strapped the document pouch across her chest and checked her leg and arm pads. While tucking her hair into her helmet, she looked down St. Paul toward its intersection with East Baltimore Street. She noted the construction near Saratoga. Traffic was the usual rush-hour mess, complicated by something going on in the city. No Orioles game this afternoon, maybe a concert tonight at the Royal Farms Arena.

She mounted her bike and inserted her mouth guard. She made it a practice to wear one ever since Pringles, her friend and competitor, lost his front teeth in a crash. Her teeth weren't straight or particularly white, but she wanted to keep them.

It was time to launch. Tingles ran up her spine—the adrenaline rush was the sweetest part of her job.

Fifteen minutes. Piece of cake.

She pedaled down St. Paul Street, scanning for hazards and obstacles in her path. The most dangerous hazards were the parked cars—doors could fly open at any moment. That's what happened to Fireball. He ended up with a broken arm and a wrecked bike.

Deathtraps lurked everywhere. Floater had pedaled into a nearly invisible rope closing off a parking lot. He now sported a nasty rope burn scar across his throat, worse than anything he'd gotten in Afghanistan. Crackhead earned her nickname when she'd fractured her skull after the front wheel of her bike caught in a grate.

Lucy concentrated as she careened down St. Paul through traffic, darting in and out between cars. As she neared the road construction, she diverted onto the sidewalk. The maneuver cost her precious seconds. She pedaled faster. A cluster of tourists meandering down the sidewalk occupied so much space she couldn't bike around them on either side.

"Coming through!" she yelled. Startled people jumped in all directions, opening a crack in the cluster.

Lucy zipped between them and heard the usual "Fuck you, asshole!" as she whizzed toward East Baltimore Street.

Cross Lexington, cross Fayette, left on Baltimore, left on Calvert. Lock up bike. Get through security. Run up stairs. Get to civil office.

The light on East Lexington turned yellow. The flashing *Don't Walk* signal began its ten-second countdown. She bent her body low to minimize wind resistance and pumped the pedals with all of her strength. There were no pedestrians, no hazards, and no obstacles.

The day was sunny, and the balmy wind felt good on her face. Baltimore's Inner Harbor was less than a half-mile from the courthouse. She inhaled the Patapsco's fragrance of water, salt, and diesel fuel. The river emptied into the Chesapeake Bay—the glistening, lovely bay. She could almost taste the blue crabs.

She loved Charm City. Baltimore was her hometown and was beautiful, despite its nickname, "The City that Bleeds." Baltimore didn't bleed that much—things were getting better. Besides, that was just a nickname some joker used to mock the mayor's promotional slogan, "The City that Reads."

Lucy glanced at her speedometer. Twenty-two miles per hour.

A seagull cawed above her, and she looked up. For a moment, they soared together—the seagull in the sky and Lucy on her bike. When the moment was over, she looked ahead and saw the light on East Lexington had changed to red.

Cars were entering the intersection. So was she.

Oh, shit.

Lucy regained consciousness in the middle of East Lexington. At first, she couldn't hear anything. The quiet in her head gave way to the noise of crying and screaming. A voice hollered something about her being dead. Maybe she was dead—she wasn't sure. She thought she heard someone yell, "Call 9-1-1!"

She made out a blurry figure, rushing around the front of the car, coming toward her. A male. Angry. She only understood bits and pieces of what he was shouting. His car. Fucked up. Asshole. Escape was impossible—her arms and legs refused to budge. She squeezed her eyes shut and braced herself for whatever was coming.

A man knelt beside her, his face inches from hers. The scent of a fresh shower and shave rose from his skin. She risked a peek at the man. When their eyes met, he gave her a slight smile. He was talking to her. The words made no sense, but his voice was low and his warm breath soothing. He brushed a lock of her hair from her face. The gentle touch left a hot spot on her cheek.

Lucy lay in the street, mangled in the remains of her bike, unable to comprehend the commotion going on around her. She faded into darkness.

Sirens quieted. The man's clean scent disappeared. She floated on the sidewalk until she sank. Was she lying on the bottom of the Inner Harbor?

Something wet was running down her face. It had to be water from the harbor. The man dabbed her forehead. His handkerchief turned red. He was handsome. Very handsome.

I guess I'm dead. No one is this handsome in real life. Like Adonis, only Latino. Oh, I know—he's a merman! Who knew Latino mermen lived in the Inner Harbor? Wow.

Lucy reached for his left hand and stroked his fingers. No ring. She smiled and slipped back to unconsciousness.

She awoke again a few minutes later. Someone was strapping her to a backboard. A woman with soft, chestnut eyes was holding her hand.

"I'm Rosalie. I'm a paramedic, and I'm going to take care of you. Understand?"

Lucy tried to answer but couldn't because of her mouth guard. She struggled to point to it. Rosalie understood and removed it from her mouth.

"Good thing you were wearing this," Rosalie said.

She swept her tongue across her teeth. They were still there, all of them.

"Time?" she mouthed to Rosalie.

"Almost four thirty."

Her eyes widened as she jolted to alertness. "Where's my pouch? I need my pouch!"

"It's right here, hon. Relax. We'll take good care of it."

"Get me up! I need to get to the courthouse!"

Rosalie patted her arm. "You're not going anywhere. You stay tight while we get you ready for the hospital."

"No! No! This has to get there by four thirty."

Lucy tried to get up, but she was strapped to a backboard. "Get me off of this fuckin' thing. Right now!" She yanked at the neck brace.

"Don't do that! You're hurt. Settle down."

"I'll settle down after I make my delivery. Get away from me." Lucy swung her fist at Rosalie. She tried to kick free from the backboard. A searing pain in her left ankle made her scream.

Desperate, Lucy choked out, "Get Pringles! Get Fireball!"

The handsome man walked over to the ambulance. "I'll deliver it."

"No, no!" she protested.

"Look, honey, that's the best deal you're going to get," Rosalie said. "If he's willing to deliver it, let him."

Lucy relented, tears falling down her face. "You have to deliver it before the court closes. Someone's job depends on it. Please, please."

Rosalie handed him the pouch.

A female police officer said to the man, "Hold it! You can't leave. I need to take your statement."

Lucy's heart sank. The stranger gave her a look, then the cop. He turned and took off running with the pouch.

Chapter 2

May 1

Lucy awoke to someone nudging her shoulder. "Lucy, wake up! Wake up!" When her eyes opened, the bright overhead lights made them squint and water.

"She's awake."

A petite woman wearing a white lab coat said, "Hello, Lucy. I'm Dr. Kelsey. You're in the emergency room. How are you feeling?"

Lucy's raspy reply was inaudible. The doctor leaned in close. "Tell me that again."

She was anxious to talk to the doctor; she had something terribly important to say. "Doctor, there are handsome mermen living in the Inner Harbor."

The doctor nodded matter-of-factly. "Get her up to X-ray as soon as we're done here for CT-scan of head, back, neck, pelvis. X-ray left ankle."

The doctor spoke to Lucy. "Can you tell me your name?"

"Lucy Prestipino."

She shined a light into Lucy's eyes. "Pupils good. Heterochromia."

Lucy whispered, "What's that?"

"Your eyes are different colors. One's brown, and the other's blue."

"Oh, I didn't know it had a name."

Dr. Kelsey listened to Lucy's heart. "Do you know why you're here?"

She drew a blank. "No."

"You've been in an accident."

"Where am I?"

"Maryland Shock Trauma."

Lucy scanned the room without moving her head. "I didn't recognize it. It's changed a lot since I was here."

"When was that?"

"My thirteenth birthday."

"You were treated here?"

"Uh-huh."

"For what?"

"Car accident. Drunk driver."

Dr. Kelsey shook her head. "I'm sorry you went through that. Did the police catch the driver?"

It was me.

"Yes."

"I'm glad. We see a lot of drunk-driving trauma here." The doctor continued her examination. "What's your date of birth?"

"May first. Today's my twenty-first birthday."

The doctor raised her eyebrows. "You certainly have bad luck on your birthdays."

"Maybe today my luck will change."

Dr. Kelsey looked at her a long while without comment. Finally, she said, "Your luck *has* changed. Your protective gear saved you from catastrophic injuries. I've ordered some tests just to be sure. It will take some time to set up. Are you in pain?"

"My left ankle really hurts."

The doctor made a note on Lucy's chart. "We'll have it x-rayed. I can give you some pain medication."

"No! No pain medication." Lucy looked at Dr. Kelsey, embarrassed. "I'm an addict. I've been sober for five years. I don't want to screw up."

"What are you addicted to?"

"Alcohol, cocaine, but I stay away from everything."

"I'll write an order for something you can take, if you want it. It won't be as effective as a narcotic, but it'll help you get by. You'll be staying overnight for observation. Is there anyone you want us to call?"

"Am I going to die?"

"No. You're not going to die."

"Then I don't want you to call anyone." She grabbed the doctor's wrist. "Promise me."

"I promise. Try to relax until we can get you up to X-ray. It'll take a few minutes."

The doctor left the room, but returned within seconds. "You have a visitor waiting to see you. Shall I send him in?"

"A visitor? Who is it?"

"I don't know. I believe he was at the scene of the accident. He said he wants to return your courier's pouch."

"Is he smokin' hot?"

Dr. Kelsey nodded and, for the first time, smiled. "I see your vision hasn't been affected and your memory's returning."

"Send him right in. You see? My luck has changed."

The man sauntered into the examining room. She didn't need a heart monitor to tell her she liked what she saw. He was tall and broad-shouldered, with shiny white teeth and hair as black as the nighttime water in the Inner Harbor. Cocoa butter skin complemented deep, brown eyes. The only imperfection were the scars—an extensive one on the left side of his neck and a tiny nick under his right eye.

"I'm Romero Sanchez. I met you on East Lexington Street."

"I'm Lucy Prestipino." She held out her hand, along with all the IV's attached to it. "I noticed you when I flew over the hood of your car."

He shook her hand. "There are easier ways to introduce yourself. You could've just knocked on the car window."

Lucy laughed. A bolt of pain shot through her ankle. A tear trickled down her cheek.

It was all coming back to her. She remembered the all-important question. "Were you able to deliver the papers before the court closed?"

"Yes. I put the court filing receipt inside your pouch." Romero placed the pouch by her feet on the gurney.

Lucy could feel every muscle in her body relax. "Thank you."

"Is there anything you need?" he said. She noticed he had dimples.

"That *I* need? This was totally my fault. I tried to beat the light. I was flying more than twenty miles an hour. I thought I had a few more seconds to cross the intersection. A serious miscalculation."

"A serious understatement. It's refreshing to hear someone accept responsibility. But what I actually wanted to know is whether you needed some water or something. I'd be happy to get it for you."

She smiled, feeling rather sheepish. "A *Baltimore Sun* paper would be nice, or a *New York Times*. I also need you to tell me how much it'll cost to fix your car."

"Just a few scratches. I can fix them myself with touch-up paint. Don't worry about it."

There was a knock on the door. An attendant announced he was taking her to X-ray. Romero stepped aside while she was wheeled away.

It was just after eight thirty in the evening when Lucy settled into Room 624. She stared at the cast that began below her knee and covered all but the tips of her toes. The ankle pain was manageable—the medication worked better than she thought it would. To pass the time, she practiced saying the diagnosis, "Fractures of the medial malleolus and calcaneus." It sounded a lot sexier than "broken ankle." The orthopedist told her she'd wear the cast for at least six weeks. The doctor expected full recovery and complete mobility.

Romero walked into her room without knocking. "Hello, again," he said.

For a fleeting moment, she fantasized he was lying in the hospital bed on top of her, naked. Her tongue was sliding across his straight, white teeth. Lucy blinked the fantasy away.

He handed her a *Sun* paper and the *Times*. "Your wish is my command."

"Thanks, I love reading the paper."

He held up a take-out bag from El Mariachi's. "Do you like enchiladas? I thought you might be hungry."

"I'm starved. You're an angel of mercy."

Romero laughed out loud. "I'll tell my homies you said that."

He moved the adjustable table over her bed, set out the food, and put a rose in a water glass. "I tried to sneak in some wine, but a nurse caught me."

Lucy's sexual fantasies surged again. This time her legs coiled around his waist, embracing him, squeezing his nakedness deep inside her body.

Lucy's cell phone sang out "Mamma Mia." The call history showed three missed calls and two text messages, all from her mother. She inhaled deeply before answering.

"Hey, Mom."

Her mother sang the first few notes of "Happy Birthday" and said, "Are you having a happy birthday, sweetie?"

The volume on the cell phone was loud, allowing Romero to hear both sides of the conversation. He didn't leave the room.

"I'm having a great birthday."

"Why didn't you call me back? I was so worried."

The familiar annoyance rose in her chest. She was tired of reporting to her mother.

"Sorry, Mom." Lucy didn't want to argue. "Been busy celebrating my birthday." She caressed the rose in the glass. "I got flowers. And a friend is treating me to dinner at El Mariachi's."

"I thought you hated Mexican food."

Lucy glanced at Romero and winced. "For some reason it tastes fantastic tonight." Romero was chuckling. His good-natured reaction made Lucy laugh. Suddenly, a vise of pain squeezed her ankle. She gasped.

"What happened?" her mother said. "Are you all right?"

Tears rolled down Lucy's face. She struggled to answer. "I accidentally bit into a jalapeno pepper. Give me a second to recover." Lucy sniffed and wiped her tears. "Okay, I'm better." She forced a laugh. "I forgot Mexican food is spicy." She covered the phone and stifled a sob.

Romero said loudly, "Hey, Lucy—how about a birthday dance?"

"I didn't know El Mariachi's had a dance floor," her mother said. "I didn't even know you danced."

Lucy choked out, "Can I tell you all about it later? I don't want to be rude talking on the phone in front of company."

"Of course. Go dance! I just wanted to wish you a happy birthday. Love you."

When they disconnected, Lucy burst into tears. Romero left the room and returned within minutes with a nurse.

The nurse handed Lucy a pill. Before long, Lucy was feeling a little better. The medicine took the edge off.

"Thanks, Romero. I feel like I've been thanking you all day."

There was a short, assertive knock on the door. A police officer walked in and introduced herself as Sylvia Marlow. She was large and muscular and looked like she'd seen a lot of mileage on the Baltimore streets.

"Dr. Kelsey said you were well enough to give me a statement about what happened today." Marlow glanced at Romero as she took a small notebook from her front pocket. "Please excuse us. This'll only take a few minutes. When I'm done, I'll take your statement as well. You didn't wait at the scene like I instructed you to."

"I don't talk to cops," he said. Romero glanced at Lucy and walked from the room.

The officer asked Lucy her name, address, and date of birth. "Ms. Prestipino, tell me what happened."

Lucy paused for a long while. "I'm sorry, Officer. I don't remember much."

The woman responded with an aggravated look Lucy knew well—she'd seen it on her mother's face whenever she caught Lucy in a lie. Lucy considered her inability to tell a good yarn as one of her worst faults. Sometimes she could get away with a fib if she spiced it up with a little truth.

"Try your best to remember," Marlow said.

"I ate Cocoa Puffs this morning. The next thing I remember is waking up on East Lexington. That's all I know."

"Witnesses said you were biking at a high rate of speed down St. Paul before the collision. Why didn't you slow down or stop?"

"I don't remember."

"Ms. Prestipino, is your bike equipped with brakes?"

"My bike! I completely forgot about my bike! What happened to it?"

"It was destroyed, totally. The pieces were taken to the scrap yard."

"Pieces? My thousand-dollar bike is in pieces?"

Marlow nodded.

"Yes, my bike was equipped with brakes."

Romero hooted a laugh from the hallway. Lucy didn't realize the door was ajar, and he was listening to the conversation. The officer slammed the door shut.

"You could've killed someone! And that guy out in the hall…take my advice and lose him. I don't know who he is, but I've been around long enough to know he's bad news. Don't mess with him. He'll hurt you a lot more than this accident did."

The warning hung in the air until Marlow said, "Is there anyone I can call for you?"

"I'm supposed to testify in court the day after tomorrow. I don't want to testify when I'm hurting, I might start crying and mess up. Can you tell the State's Attorney's Office where I am?"

"Who's the prosecutor handling the case?"

"I don't know. One hadn't been assigned the last time I called."

"Who's the defendant?"

"Jason Coopersmith."

The officer's eyes opened wide. "You're the messenger who took down that strong-arm robber, aren't you?"

The media had hailed Lucy a hero. Everyone else, except her courier friends, told her she was a reckless, adrenaline junkie. Bicycle messengers were an adventurous breed, and Lucy fit right in. That was one of the reasons she loved her job—she'd found her people.

"So will you call the prosecutor for me?"

"Yes."

Romero walked in as soon as the police officer left, his black eyes twinkling. "I must say I enjoyed the interrogation session. I couldn't have done better myself."

Lucy didn't want to talk anymore. She was feeling guilty about lying to Officer Marlow.

"You're tired," Romero said. "I'll tuck you in and say '*Buenos noches.*' I'll come visit you tomorrow."

He found a blanket and kissed Lucy on the forehead, leaving another hotspot. As he placed the blanket over her, he whispered, "Happy birthday, *mi amada.*"

That's when she saw it.

Roach—tattooed across his knuckles. Everyone knew Roach, the notorious gang that plagued the city with drugs, prostitution, and guns.

Lucy grabbed his hand. "You're a gang member?"

He pulled his hand away.

She waited for his answer. As slow seconds passed, she pictured the corner boys—the middle-school children who stood on street corners slinging Roach's drugs. She pedaled past them every day. Romero and his ilk recruited them.

"Romero, don't come back tomorrow."

"You're tossing me? I looked out for you. Are you afraid of me?"

"Shit no, you don't scare me." She glared into his eyes without blinking.

"I thought you liked me." He seemed hurt.

"I used to like Irish car bombs, but whenever I drank 'em, bad things happened. So I don't drink 'em. You need to leave."

He didn't move.

"I don't hang with criminals. Get out or I'll call security."

His expression turned dark, dangerous. "I want the money to fix my car."

"You just said you could fix it yourself with touch-up paint."

"I want a professional paint job. It'll cost two thousand."

"Two thousand? Good luck with that. The only valuable thing I own is now in a scrapyard. I'm a turnip, and you can't get blood from me."

Romero grabbed her hair and shoved his face within inches of hers. "I can get plenty of blood from you, Lucy. Believe me." Before she could scream, he released her and stormed from the room.

Chapter 3

May 2

They were swaying in tandem with the curves of the road. Best friends, drunk on adventure and alcohol. "Go faster," Amber shouted. Lucy stretched to press the accelerator with the tip of her big toe. Suddenly, they were rolling, rolling. A tree. Glass shattering. The dashboard crunching toward them. Screaming.

"Amber!"

Lucy bolted upright, sweating and afraid. Where was she? The eerie room had walls painted with the surreal cast of a distant florescent light. There were mechanical sounds, low voices, and soft footsteps. Antiseptic smells filled her nose. Several seconds passed before she remembered she was in a hospital. It was just a dream, she reassured herself.

She lay in the bed, perfectly still. Her heart pounded, and her knees shook. It took several minutes of deep, controlled breathing before the fear passed. She hadn't had that nightmare in over six months. It had been that long since she'd needed the relaxation exercises, but she remembered how to do them. Just like riding a bike.

A nurse rushed in. "Is everything all right?"

"I had a bad dream, that's all." She rubbed her eyes. "What time is it?"

"Four thirty in the morning."

"I'll never get back to sleep. Can you help me to the window? I love watching the sun come up."

"Sure I will, hon. If the weather cooperates, you can see a gorgeous sunrise from this room. The sun comes up right over the Inner Harbor."

The nurse assisted Lucy to a large, comfortable chair by the window. She moved the adjustable table nearby so she could reach her water and personal items.

"Anything else I can do for you?"

"No, I'm good. Thank you."

Lucy stared through the window at the moonless night. She was ashamed of herself. She'd lied to Officer Marlow. Her mother raised her better than that, and she didn't want the officer to think otherwise. Marlow was right—about everything. Lucy knew she had to apologize. Amber never accepted her apology; maybe Marlow would.

In her mind's eye, she was thirteen years old again. Her head was resting on her mother's lap, and she was weeping. Her mother was stroking her head, kissing her, shedding her own tears into Lucy's hair.

"Lucy, sweetie. You made a mistake. Don't let it ruin your life. You're more than this mistake. You're allowed to be happy. You have to forgive yourself."

"How can I do that if Amber won't forgive me?"

"Pray for Amber when you think of her. Do good things for her when you can. Learn from your mistake. That's all you can do."

A teardrop splashed on Lucy's hand, startling her back to the present. The only way to stop her nipping conscience was to call Marlow and 'fess up.

She grabbed the *Sun* paper from the table and, as usual, flipped to the obituary section. That's how her mother read the paper—obits first. Her mother said you could learn a lot of life's lessons by studying other people's lives. Today, there were no interesting obits. No celebrities, no gang members, no Medal of Honor recipients. Just regular people who'd died in a regular way.

She read the paper until the sun peeked over the harbor. The nurse was right; the window presented an unobstructed view of a glorious sunrise. Today was a brand new day. She made her daily to-do list. The first item was to call Marlow.

Lucy reached her on the first attempt. The officer re-interviewed her over the phone and said she'd stop by with some traffic citations.

Next on the list was figuring out how to pay her bills. It'd be at least two months before she could get back on her bike. One thing for sure; she wasn't going to ask her mother for money.

Lucy opened her smartphone and began job hunting. She needed money right away and focused on jobs nobody in their right mind would want. One job prospect seemed possible. It was in Crisfield, on Maryland's Eastern Shore. K.T. Crockett's, a seafood processing plant, was looking for crab-pickers. The sit-down job came with room and board. The pay was low, but she could probably negotiate. Lucy called and was immediately hired. She'd start as soon as she could get herself to Crisfield.

As Lucy worked through her list, a young man entered the room carrying a long, white box. Inside were a dozen roses and a handwritten note, "Please forgive me for my poor behavior. Let's start over. RS." She tore the card into bits and tossed the roses into the trashcan.

"How are you feeling today?" The voice belonged to a courteous, but frosty, Officer Marlow.

"I'm much better, thank you. I'm sorry for the way I acted yesterday."

Marlow handed Lucy a single ticket—operating a bicycle without brakes.

"Only one ticket?"

"You've paid enough for this accident. No sense piling on." Marlow's tone became stern. "Listen up. If you go back into the courier business, you have to ride a bike with brakes. At this morning's roll call, the sergeant instructed everyone to keep a lookout for you. Thanks to Mr. Coopersmith, every cop in the city knows who you are. If anyone sees you riding without brakes, you'll get a ticket. We'll ticket you right out of business, got that?"

"I got it. You don't have to say any more."

Marlow saw the long, white box. "Flowers?"

"Yes. They're not wanted." She looked at the box. "You were right about that guy. He turned out to be a Roach gang member."

The cop didn't look surprised.

"How'd you know?" Lucy said.

"The way he looked at me, the way he held himself. I knew he was a wrong guy. Just because a man is nice-looking, doesn't mean he's nice."

"You sound like my mother."

"Where's your mother?"

"She lives in the city, in Highlandtown."

"Why isn't she here with you?"

Lucy shrugged.

The officer held up her hands, palms out. "Sorry, none of my business. My kids accuse me of being a mother hen."

"A mother hen with a gun. Wow."

Marlow smiled. She was warming up to her.

Lucy shifted gears. "Were you able to catch up with the prosecutor?"

"Yes. It's Sean Patrick McCormick, goes by 'Rick.' He's getting a continuance. He'll call you to let you know the new trial date."

"What's he like?"

"Young guy, early-thirties, smart. He's rather intimidating. Defense attorneys are scared of him. So are police who screw up. He has no tolerance for sloppy work."

"Is he a good trial attorney?"

"He's better than good. So good he's heading up the new gang unit for the State's Attorney's Office. Your case is Rick's last one as a prosecutor in the violent crimes unit. I'll be working with him." Marlow patted Lucy on the arm. "Okay, I need to get back on the street. Get better soon. And remember—get a bike with brakes."

After the officer left, Lucy pulled the florist's box from the trash and selected a long-stemmed rose. She sawed off the flower with the plastic knife from her breakfast tray. The next eleven roses met the same fate. She stewed as she hacked. Romero was a total psycho. At first, he'd been nice to her—delivering the court papers and buying her dinner. Then he threatened her. *He messed with the wrong girl.* Next time he bothered her, she'd spray him with a can of Raid—that was the best way to kill roaches.

After each beheading, she returned the decapitated stem to the long, white box. She was scooping the rose heads into the trashcan when she heard a soft knock on her door.

"Come in."

In walked a smartly-dressed woman, not much older than her mother— forty years at most. It took Lucy a few minutes to recognize her. It was the crying lawyer, only now she looked more like an ass-kicker than a crier.

"Ms. Prestipino, I didn't find out what happened to you until just a few minutes ago. I came right over. Thank you just isn't enough. There are no words."

The lawyer handed her a business card. *Minerva Wilson James, Attorney at Law.* Lucy had forgotten her name.

"I hope you don't mind my asking—how'd you get into a fix with the statute of limitations? I saw another lawyer blow it, but he was a total stoner. You seem so together. What happened?"

Minerva flushed pink. "May I sit?"

Lucy patted the bed. Minerva sat.

"I don't mind you asking, you're entitled. You saved me from a terrible mistake. A new client called me right before the statute was about to expire. She had a good claim, worth a lot of money. Right after I took her case, my mother died. A car accident. Afterward, I simply stopped function—" She closed her eyes and took a breath. "It was such a shock, still is. I pick up the phone to call my mother at least three times a day. I can't get used to her being gone."

Lucy teared up.

"I didn't mean to upset you." Minerva pulled tissues from her purse and handed one to Lucy. The women wiped their eyes.

"If you ever need a lawyer, you call me, all right? I owe you."

Lucy gave her a smile full of mischief. "Okay, but I get in trouble all the time."

Thirty minutes later, the hospital phone rang. It was Rick McCormick. He spoke with the commanding voice of a television anchor.

"The trial has been postponed until June fifteenth. I trust you'll be able to attend."

"You trust right."

"Good. It begins at ten in the morning. I'd like you there at nine fifteen so we can review your testimony."

"We're not going to talk before then?"

"Another prosecutor will call you and prepare your testimony. You're tasked with describing the robbery and identifying the defendant. Do you have any concerns about that?"

"No."

"Good. I'll see you then."

The doctor discharged Lucy at noon. A few minutes later, Pringles arrived to take her home. He pointed to the cast on her leg. "Geez, how'd this happen?"

"I should've stopped at the red light."

He rolled his eyes.

"Pringles, you speak Spanish, right?"

"I understand it better than I speak it."

"Do you know what '*mi amada*' means?"

"Did someone say that to you?"

"Uh-huh."

"You've been holding out on us!" Pringles winked. "It means 'my beloved.'"

Chapter 4

May 2

Lucy stopped by the patient information desk as she left the hospital. "If a hot Latino guy stops by to see me, please give him this." She handed the receptionist the long box of beheaded rose stems, re-tied with the red ribbon.

Pringles drove Lucy to her home in Canton, a revitalized neighborhood near the harbor, and waited while she packed her suitcase. She'd return on June fifteenth to testify in the strong-arm trial. If all went well, her cast would be removed two weeks later, and she'd get back to her courier job. Pringles agreed to babysit her courier business, just as she'd done for him when he was getting his mouth restored.

Her final task before heading to Crisfield was to talk to her mother. She had to tell her about the accident, and worse, explain the lie. She was dreading it. At this very moment, her mother was baking a birthday cake and expecting an afternoon of girl-talk. They were going to watch re-runs of *Xena: Warrior Princess,* just like they'd done every Saturday when Lucy was little.

Lucy was proud of her mother, but doubted she would ever understand her. They couldn't be more opposite. At thirty-six, Debbie Prestipino was beautiful—a tiny brunette with dark eyes and olive, flawless skin. Lucy inherited the flawless skin, but everything else came from her father. She was tall and lean with wavy blonde hair and fair skin. She'd been born with two blue eyes. The car accident injured her right eye, turning her iris into a mottle of muddy browns, rimmed in blue—like a Jimmy crab. She called it her "crab eye."

Lucy didn't mind that she hadn't inherited her mother's beauty. It was a fair trade for not being saddled with her mother's fearful nature. Her mother ran from every fight. Except for the time she whacked the guy with a pizza pan. That was a surprise.

As soon as Pringles pulled into the driveway, Debbie opened the front door and began singing "Happy Birthday." He pulled the crutches from the trunk. She stopped singing, mid-sentence, and tore down the steps.

"What happened?" she said. A tiny, white dog flew out of the house and took the three steps with a single leap. When he landed, he began yapping, spinning, and jumping.

Pringles helped Lucy out of the passenger seat and handed her the crutches. The dog halted his greeting to sniff the crutches.

"Hi, Mom. Just a little mishap. I'm fine." She bent down and patted the dog. "How ya doing, Steppie?"

Debbie stared at the cast. Pringles said his good-byes and disappeared.

Lucy climbed the front steps and settled into a green and black plaid living room sofa. She admired her mother's spotless home, but not the décor; early-American maple furniture, over-sized landscape pictures, and brass Stiffel lamps. The fragrance of a baking cake filled the house. Her mouth watered.

"The cake smells great. What kind did you make?"

Debbie sat next to her, with the perfect posture that told Lucy she was in big trouble. The deep wrinkle etched across her mother's forehead betrayed the appearance of inner calm.

"What happened?" Debbie said.

"I ran into a car during a delivery. My ankle's broken. No big deal."

"You got hit by a car?" Debbie threw her hands in the air. "I knew this was going to happen."

"No, I was the one who hit the car—ran right into the side of it."

"When?" Debbie checked her watch. "It's only one o'clock. How could you make a delivery, break your ankle, and get a cast already?"

Lucy steeled herself. The interrogation was about to start.

"It happened yesterday."

"Yesterday? I talked to you at nine o'clock last night. You were eating dinner at El Mariachi's. What did you do? Make a delivery after dinner? At night?"

"I was eating El Mariachi's food at the hospital. It was take-out."

"What?" Debbie paced around the living room. "I don't believe this. You were in an accident, went to the hospital, and didn't bother to call me?"

Lucy didn't answer. Her mother had described the situation exactly right.

"Who took you to the hospital?"

"An ambulance."

The oven timer went off. Debbie ignored it.

"Mom, the timer."

"Fuck the timer!"

"Please don't burn up my birthday cake."

Debbie marched into the kitchen with pounding feet. Lucy could hear the oven door slam shut and cake pans clank on the counter. Her birthday cake was going to be as flat and dense as a manhole cover.

Her mother returned to the living room, her eyes tearing with fury. "Why didn't you call me?"

When Lucy saw her mother's eyes, her own eyes watered. "I didn't want you to get another call from a hospital on my birthday."

"So you kept this a secret for my benefit?"

Lucy winced. "Partly."

"Explain the other part."

"I met a man at the hospital. I knew if I told you, you'd come flying down, have a meltdown, scold me about my job, tell me to go to college, move back home with you, and on and on and on. I didn't want that. I wanted to spend my birthday with him, without my mother haranguing me about my life."

Debbie was silent, her posture no longer perfect.

"If it was bad, I would've called you, I swear." Lucy held up her right hand as if she was taking an oath. "I asked the doctor if I was going to die and she said 'no.'"

"Imminent death is your standard for calling me?"

"Mom—"

"You lied to me."

"It wasn't really a lie. I was going to tell you. I just wanted to put it off a little bit, so it wasn't on my birthday, that's all."

Debbie pulled out a cigarette from the pack laying on the coffee table.

"Mom, please don't smoke that. Fireball's mother died of lung cancer, and it's a terrible way to die."

Debbie shrugged and headed for the back door, off the kitchen. Within a minute, puffs of smoke wafted by the kitchen window. Lucy hobbled to the door and opened it.

"I don't want to fight with you," she said. "Either we make up or I'm calling a cab."

Debbie crushed out the cigarette and flicked it to the ground. "It's not like you to run from an argument."

"I wonder who I learned it from."

Debbie shot her a look before returning to the house. She sat at the dining room table. "Lucy, sit down."

She sat.

"I don't run from arguments." Debbie fixed her eyes on Lucy's. "I'm not as quick as you, especially when you ambush me. Sometimes I need time to think. I needed to consider your concept of postponed truth. I want you to explain it to me."

Lucy thought a while before answering. Her mother wasn't quick, but she was cagey. "Sometimes the timing of telling the truth is all wrong. There could be good reasons to put it off. Not always, but sometimes."

"You think under certain circumstances, it's all right to lie as long as you plan to tell the truth at a better time."

The question was a trap. There was no good answer. Her mother should've been a lawyer.

"Sometimes, under certain circumstances, depending on the truth and the reason why the person wants to put off telling it."

Lucy was hedging as best she could, not sure why. She couldn't read the expression on her mother's face. Debbie wasn't angry or upset; oddly, she seemed relieved.

"One day you'll face postponed truth from the other side of the coin," Debbie said. "I hope when that day comes, you'll remember this conversation."

Lucy nodded with vigor. "I'll never forget it. Believe me."

"Let's talk practicalities. Obviously, you can't work. Now'd be a good time for you to get your GED. Then you can go to college, get back on track. You can live with me. I'll give you a loan so you can keep up with your bills."

"Thanks, but I'm set. I got a temp job."

"Doing what?"

"Picking crabs in Crisfield."

"Oh, for God's sake!" Debbie put her head in her hand. "Picking crabs? What kind of a job is that?"

"The kind that'll pay my bills so I don't have to live in your basement." Debbie's wounded expression pricked Lucy's conscience. She softened her tone. "You have to let me live my own life, don't you see?"

"All I see is the cast on your ankle, the one you got doing your dangerous job. I know you want your independence—you can have that with a job at Home Warehouse. You'd do very well there. It's a steady job, with benefits. You could do that while you're going to school."

Lucy leaned back in her chair, deflated. The argument would never end; maybe there'd be a truce today, but the disagreement wouldn't end until Lucy caved or one of them was dead. Why couldn't she make her mother understand? She'd give it one last try.

"I love my messenger job. I need it."

"You may love it, but you certainly don't need it."

"I do need it." Lucy fiddled with her hair. "You think I'm not an addict anymore, but I am. Every day, when I wake up, it's the first thing I think about. Where can I get a joint? A Bloody Mary would taste good with breakfast. Then I worry if today's the day I'm gonna slip. The thing is, I can't think about drugs or alcohol while I'm pedaling. I have to stay focused, that's the only way to keep from getting hurt or killed. Pedaling keeps me alive."

Debbie's eyes were wet.

"Mom, don't cry."

"I'm not driving you to Crisfield. I can't take time off."

"You don't have to. I'm taking a bus, and I already have my ticket... That reminds me, I want to get my driver's license. Can you give me my birth certificate?"

Debbie stared at her, wordless.

"I've been sober for five years. I'm tired of taking buses and bumming rides. I won't hurt anyone again."

"I know, sweetie, I know. I'm not worried about that. It's just that I don't know where your birth certificate is. Give me some time to find it, okay?"

Lucy didn't want to talk any more. She'd had enough arguing, asking, and appeasing.

"Okay. Want to watch Xena? I packed my DVDs."

"Sure."

After setting up the DVD player, they sat together on the sofa. Debbie clicked on the remote and put her arm around Lucy's shoulder. Lucy cuddled against her. Their size difference made it awkward, but she didn't care. Steppie snuggled between them.

Lucy caught a glimpse of the cigarette pack on the coffee table. Minerva's grief re-played in her mind. She'd always expected to outlive her mother; that's the natural order of things. By the time her mother died, Lucy would be married and have her husband and children to comfort her.

What if it didn't happen that way? Her father died when she was little. She didn't have any brothers or sisters. There were no relatives anywhere. If her mother died, she'd be all alone. The idea was so painful she blocked it out by kissing her mother's cheek. "Love you, Mom."

Chapter 5

June 15

Lucy was exhausted by the time she arrived at the entrance of the courthouse. Her travels from Crisfield began the day before. There was an accident on the Chesapeake Bay Bridge; the bus ride took six hours. Her fellow passengers peppered her with questions about her boot cast. By the time she arrived in Baltimore, she was sure she'd heard enough broken bone stories to get a license in orthopedic medicine.

She sat on a wooden bench near Courtroom 5 and waited for Assistant State's Attorney Sean Patrick McCormick. The hallway was quiet. Too quiet. She fretted about her testimony. How detailed was she supposed to get? Should she describe every street and corner she'd pedaled while chasing Coopersmith?

By far her biggest concern was her juvenile record. It was supposed to be sealed, but what would she say if asked about it? She couldn't lie. Her stomach felt like it was crawling with stinkbugs. She wanted to ask McCormick for advice. During the last month, she left three messages for him. He didn't return any of them. This morning she arrived at nine fifteen, just as he'd told her, but he was nowhere to be found. What a jerk.

She looked around. The courthouse was old and traditional, with shiny tile floors. The atmosphere was solemn and dignified—a place that looked like it belonged in the justice system.

A few attorneys trickled into the hallway and took seats on the benches. They read files, took notes, and talked softly into their cell phones. Lucy opened her purse and pulled out a list she'd compiled from her research.

> *Sean Patrick McCormick, 31 years old*
> *multi-lingual*
> *Duke*
> *Georgetown Law School*
> *Baltimore City State's Attorney's Office, Violent Crimes Unit.*
> *Incoming Chief, Gang Unit.*

Her confidence grew as she read the prosecutor's credentials. McCormick would be a fierce warrior who'd protect her from the ravages of cross-examination. He'd be her hero, even if he was a jerk.

The hallway was now crowded. Lawyers consulted with their clients. Police officers mingled about, chatting with one another. A frail woman, in her seventies, walked with a cane toward Courtroom 5. She appeared out of her element, as if she found herself draped around a pole in a strip bar. A dark-skinned man, wearing a polite smile, stood from a bench and approached the elderly woman.

The man had been sitting there all along, but Lucy hadn't noticed him. He wore an ordinary summer suit. The tie could have come from anywhere. His appearance and demeanor were so nondescript he'd simply blended into the surroundings, like one of the tiles on the floor. An average man.

After the average man spoke to the woman, he helped her sit on a bench. He then turned to two nearby police officers, no longer wearing the smile. He was focused, intense. The police officers, who'd been chatting together a few minutes before, became alert. They deferred to him and listened closely to what he said.

The bailiff unlocked the courtroom door from the inside. The average man entered the courtroom accompanied by the police officers. Her jaw dropped.

Sean Patrick McCormick?

She was so astounded she needed confirmation. She called to a nearby police officer, "Was that Rick McCormick?"

The officer nodded.

Disappointment replaced her astonishment. McCormick was not the prosecutor she imagined. She expected a tall, attractive man with a commanding presence. McCormick couldn't be more forgettable.

A frazzled, young woman hurried over to Lucy. She was wearing a precision haircut and designer suit. She'd rolled up her skirt at the waist to make it shorter.

"Ms. Prestipino?" The woman extended her hand. "Good morning. I'm Penelope Lundt, Assistant State's Attorney. I'll be second-chairing the trial today with Mr. McCormick. Stay nearby until you're called. There's a rule on witnesses, so you're not allowed inside the courtroom until you testify."

"I have a lot of questions," Lucy said. "Can you—"

The bailiff announced from the courtroom door, "The judge is taking the bench."

Lundt dashed into the courtroom without another word.

Lucy fished a magazine from her backpack, *Biking Today*, and perused the ads for GPS bike trackers. She became vaguely aware of a man sitting next to her.

"Hello, Lucy," a silky voice said. "You're looking much better than when I saw you last."

Her jaw went slack for the second time in ten minutes.

Romero Sanchez.

"Romero, get lost."

"I wanted to thank you for the headless roses." He smiled, showing his twinkling eyes and dimples. "I must say, you have a very creative way of expressing yourself."

"Get away from me or I'll make a scene even Martin Scorcese can't top."

"As you wish." He strolled into Courtroom 5.

Thirty minutes ticked away. Lucy caught the flinty eyes of a massive man lumbering down the hallway, wearing biking shorts and carrying a helmet. His name was William Holiday. He'd served with the 101st Airborne, parachuting into Afghanistan under cover of night. A Nightstalker, special ops. Lucy lovingly nicknamed him "Floater." He was her new AA sponsor.

Lucy speed-limped in his direction, delighted to see him.

"Slow down, kiddo." He hugged her. "Thought you might need some moral support. Nervous?"

"A little…but now that you're here, I've got something I've been meaning to ask you. It's kinda personal."

He gave her a *go-ahead and ask* look.

"What's bigger? One of your thighs or my waist?"

Floater guffawed, deep laugh lines sprouting at the corners of his eyes.

"Don't know," he said. "This is what I do know—under your usual sweaty mess, you're actually quite pretty."

"Awww…thanks." She smoothed the plain, navy shift dress she found at the Goodwill retail store.

They waited together on the bench. Lucy was grateful for Floater's company. Bantering with him kept her mind off her worries. She watched Lundt shuttle in and out of the courtroom collecting a witness with each trip. Two police officers came and went, followed by the elderly woman.

At last, Lundt requested her presence in the courtroom. Lucy fiddled with her hair and re-pinned it into a soft bun. Wisps of loose hair framed her face.

"Do I look okay?"

"You look like a million bucks."

She took a deep breath and sent a prayer heavenward.

Daddy, don't let me fuck up.

Chapter 6

June 15

Lucy hobbled into the courtroom with her boot cast and cane, wearing her backpack. She accidentally clunked the cast against a gallery bench, causing echoes to bounce around the courtroom. She thanked the bailiff as he helped her to the witness chair.

"Good morning, everybody," she said to the courtroom-at-large.

The jurors seemed surprised and returned her greeting. The attorneys and the judge did the same. She waited for the first question. Her heart was clamoring and her stomach woozy.

The courtroom clerk said, "Do you swear to tell the truth, the whole truth and nothing but the truth, so help you God?"

"Yes."

With that oath, it all became simple. She'd tell the truth, no matter what.

McCormick stood, all seriousness. Lucy guessed he was about five-ten. Straight, black hair, parted on the side. He introduced himself and Penelope Lundt, sitting beside him at counsel's table.

With the first words out of his mouth, he appeared large and powerful. He had a physicality about him that was compelling. His movements were as graceful as a dancer's. She looked past McCormick and spotted Romero sitting in the last row of the gallery. He was watching McCormick's every move.

"Please state your name and occupation." McCormick's voice resonated with authority.

"Lucy Prestipino. Right now, I'm a crab picker."

He glanced at Lundt and then back at Lucy. "What was your occupation in March of this year?"

"I'm the President and CEO of Star-Spangled Bicycle Courier Service Corporation. In March, I was working for the company as a bicycle courier." She pointed to her left leg. "Due to an occupational mishap, I'm on a medical leave of absence."

"I direct your attention to March sixth of this year. Do you remember that day?"

"Like it was yesterday."

"What was the weather like?"

"Clear, sunny. It was a great day for biking."

"Did you see anything unusual happen that day?"

"Yes, I did."

"Tell the jurors exactly what you saw."

"It was around noon. I was between courier runs. I was starved and craving a Faidley's crab cake so I biked up to Lexington Market. I was pedaling down West Lexington, eating my crab cake, when a black Schwinn Hornet Cruiser bicycle zipped by me on my left."

"Describe the biker."

"I could only see him from behind. He was a skinny, white guy. Wearing an Orioles T-shirt. No jacket, even though it was kinda chilly. On the back of the T-shirt was a number eight and the name *Ripken*. He had a purple and black bike helmet, with a small mirror on the left side."

"What did you see after the man passed you on the bike?"

"I saw him reach over with his right hand and snatch a purse off of a woman's shoulder as he went by. The woman fell down. I followed the biker until he crashed, and the police arrested him."

"Were you ever able to see the biker's face?"

"Yes, after he crashed. I stayed with him until the police came."

"Do you see the biker in the courtroom?"

Lucy looked at the defendant for several seconds before answering. "Yes." She pointed to the defense table. "He's sitting at that table, wearing a white, long-sleeved shirt and black tie."

McCormick said, "Let the record show that the witness identified the defendant, Jason Coopersmith."

"Thank you, Ms. Prestipino. I have no further questions."

"Mr. Stonegate, you may proceed," the judge said.

The attorney sitting next to Coopersmith stood, grasping a pen and a yellow pad. He was a man in his thirties, with cup o'joe eyes and a pleasant face. His dreads were pulled into a ponytail. "Ms. Prestipino, my name is Alexander Stonegate, and I represent the defendant, Jason Coopersmith."

At that point, Officer Sylvia Marlow entered the courtroom. Lucy's fear of cross-examination vanished.

"Ms. Prestipino, at the time of the purse-snatching, did you see the perpetrator's face?"

"No, sir."

"You testified you didn't see the face of the perpetrator until after he crashed. Could you describe the crash?"

"Where do you want me to start?"

"Just describe the immediate events leading up to the crash."

Lucy shifted in her seat to get comfortable. The answer would take some explaining.

"Okay. Right before the crash, we were on Greene Street. Greene is all downhill at that point, and we were going pretty fast. Greene turns into I-95, so I figured he'd turn onto West Lombard. There was construction on West Lombard, still is. Lots of sand on the corner. I thought the sand would surprise him because it sure surprised me the first time I ran over it." She gave the jury a knowing half-smile.

"Anyway, Mr. Coopersmith was pedaling fast to get away from me. He turned onto West Lombard just like I thought he would." Lucy slid her hand along the railing in front of the witness chair. "Then…bam! He wiped out." Her hand smacked the railing for emphasis. The jury jumped.

"He slid under a delivery truck that was double-parked. I hopped off my bike and looked under the truck." Lucy tilted her head as if she was looking under a truck. "Mr. Coopersmith was trying to crawl out. I told him if he didn't stay put, as soon as he got out from under the truck, I was going to park my bike on his spine and sit on it." She shrugged. "So he stayed put. Then the police came. And that's what happened with the crash."

The jury was leaning forward, taking in every word.

Stonegate flipped a page on his yellow pad. "When the police pulled out the biker, that was the first time you saw his face, correct?"

"Yes, sir."

"How many miles did you chase the perpetrator?"

"A little over two."

"How long did this pursuit take?"

"About twenty minutes. The traffic was pretty heavy."

"Did you ever lose sight of the biker while you were following him?"

"Yes, sir."

Lundt clenched her teeth. McCormick appeared unperturbed.

"How many times did you lose sight of the perpetrator?" Stonegate said.

"Eight times."

"Eight times?"

"That's right. After a block or so, he figured out I was following him, so he took off fast, and I began chasing him. Whenever we went around a corner, I lost sight of him."

Lundt frantically thumbed through her file. McCormick wore a poker face.

Stonegate paused until he had the jury's full attention. "Ms. Prestipino, isn't it possible that during at least one of those eight times you lost sight of the perpetrator, the real perpetrator disappeared from your sight, and when the biker appeared again, it was not the perpetrator but my client?"

Lucy paused and considered the question.

"There's no way that happened. He was never out of my sight for more than a split second. When I saw him after each corner, he was wearing the same clothes, on the same bike. He kept looking over his shoulder at me. Right before the crash I saw him toss the purse over his head like this." She demonstrated. "I told the police about the purse and later I saw an officer holding it. I never lost sight of him after he threw the purse."

McCormick grinned with the side of his mouth not facing the jury. Lundt looked as if she would collapse with relief.

Stonegate flipped another page on his yellow pad. "Ms. Prestipino, how far did you go in school?"

"Tenth grade. I'm studying for my GED now."

"How did you get here from Crisfield?"

"I took the Greyhound bus."

"How long did that take?"

"I came yesterday. There was a big accident on the Bay Bridge. It took about six hours."

"That must have been difficult with your cast and cane."

McCormick objected. The judge gave a slight backhanded wave and said, "Move along, Mr. Stonegate."

"After my client was arrested, you became somewhat of a celebrity, isn't that right?"

"What do you mean?"

"You got your name in the paper, got a lot of attention, treated like a hero. Didn't that happen?"

"Yes."

"I want to understand this. You chased the perpetrator for over two miles in noonday traffic. You risked life and limb, yours as well as others, to capture him. You made a six-hour bus trip from Crisfield, wearing a cast, carrying a cane. You have a great deal invested in getting Mr. Coopersmith convicted, don't you?"

McCormick objected. The judge overruled him. "Answer the question, Ms. Prestipino."

"No, that's not true. It's not about Mr. Coopersmith, it's about me. I—"

"My point exactly." Stonegate sat down. "No further questions."

Lucy's adrenaline leaked away. She berated herself for screwing up. Like always.

The jury was no longer leaning forward, but sitting all the way back in their seats. None of them were looking at her. McCormick wasn't looking at her either—he seemed to be studying the jury.

"Any re-direct, Mr. McCormick?" the judge said.

"Just a follow-up question. Ms. Prestipino, defense counsel didn't allow you to complete your answer. Was there more you wanted to say?"

She sat up straight and took a deep breath.

"After the robbery, everyone on the sidewalk rushed to help the victim. It was a violent snatch. I knew she'd been badly hurt. Since everyone was helping her, no one went after the robber. Nobody could, really, because I was the only one on a bike. It was up to me and only me to catch him.

"So I chased him. I hated the attention I got afterward. My mother had a fit. She was so angry that I didn't even tell her about coming to court today. Anyway, after the police arrested Mr. Coopersmith, I thought I was done.

"Then here comes the trial. It turns out that I was the only one who could identify Mr. Coopersmith. Again, it was all on me. Justice depended on me stepping up and testifying. Now that I've done that, it's all on the jury. They have to decide if Mr. Coopersmith is guilty or not, and whatever they decide is fine by me. I can go to bed tonight knowing that I did everything I was supposed to do, the best way I knew how. That's all."

Lucy heard hands clapping. All faces turned toward the spectator's gallery. The clapping was coming from Romero Sanchez.

The judge banged the gavel. "Silence in the courtroom!"

McCormick stiffened. He scribbled a note and handed it to Lundt. She delivered it to Marlow, who left the courtroom.

"Do either of you have any more questions for this witness?" the judge said.

When the attorneys responded in the negative, the judge excused Lucy, thanking her for her service. The bailiff accompanied her through the courtroom. As soon as she was on the other side of the courtroom door, Marlow and two armed sheriffs surrounded her.

Chapter 7

June 15

"What's going on?" Lucy said.

No one answered. The law enforcement officers hustled her onto the elevator, whisked her to the fourth floor, and escorted her to an empty witness-waiting room. There was a sheriff posted outside the door.

"Officer Marlow, am I in trouble?"

"No, hon. Something came up during the trial. Attorney McCormick wants to talk to you about it."

They chatted for a bit. Marlow handed Lucy a *Sun* paper. "Let the sheriff know if you need anything."

After Marlow left, Lucy occupied herself with the newspaper, beginning with the obituaries. The last obit was headed, "Kyle Abernathy, Bigamist." *Wow.* Was that his most noteworthy accomplishment? The ridiculousness of it made her laugh.

Rick McCormick paused at the waiting room door before opening it. There were some parts about his job he hated; telling a young woman she might be the target of gang retaliation was one of them.

She was a terrific witness. The jury was bored and disinterested. The robbery was routine—it happened all the time—nothing dramatic or compelling. In the midst of a sleeper trial, Lucy Prestipino appeared, surprising everyone. He expected a hulking Amazon woman. So did the jury; he was sure of it.

She hobbled into the courtroom, full of spunk. Pretty. She charmed the jury with her Highlandtown accent. They loved her. She stumbled a bit with her testimony, but in the end, placed the responsibility for justice squarely on the shoulders of the jury. Right where it belonged.

He heard Lucy laughing on the other side of the door. She had a light-hearted laugh, full of life and fun. He lingered at the door for a few seconds, procrastinating. The words he was about to speak would dissolve the laugh into angry tears. He straightened his tie and knocked. He found her reading the *Sun*.

"Good afternoon." Rick took off his suit jacket.

Her smile threw an electric current through him. He hadn't experienced that kind of jolt since he was five, when he'd poked a paper clip into an electrical socket. Lucy was even more attractive up close than on the witness stand—smooth skin, muscular, nice shape. Her clothes and hair were simple. He didn't smell any perfume or hairspray. No makeup. No nail polish. He found her natural look incredibly sexy.

Rick sat across from her. For the first time, he noticed her eyes. They were odd.

"After your testimony, Mr. Coopersmith pled guilty."

"Why didn't he plead guilty in the first place?" A lock of hair strayed from her bun. She tucked it behind her ear. "It would've saved a lot of trouble."

"His attorney hoped to poke holes in the identification part of the State's case, but that didn't happen, thanks to you. Maybe he was also going for the 'shit happens' defense."

"What's that?"

"Something unexpected happens—the witness doesn't show, the police make a mistake, evidence gets lost." Rick cracked a smile. "I just have to ask you. Why in the world are you picking crabs? You couldn't get a better job than that?"

Lucy's jaw clenched, and the smile vanished. She looked pissed. He'd just made a big mistake.

"Mr. McCormick, I know I'm not here so you can ask me about crab-picking. Just spit it out."

"I don't want to alarm you, but we learned today the robbery was gang-related. I need to talk to you about witness protection."

He expected her to gasp in horror, to lash out at the prosecutor who failed to warn her prior to her testimony.

"Gang related?" She burst out laughing. "What have you been smoking?"

"Ms. Prestipino—"

"There's no way this was a gang—"

"There was a known gang member in the courtroom watching you."

"You mean Romero Sanchez?"

Rick raised his eyebrows. "How do you know Sanchez?"

"I had the misfortune of running into him, literally." She lifted her left leg to show the cast. "It was his Escalade I crashed into."

"What's your relationship with him?"

"Relationship? The only relationship we have is one of mutual irritation."

"Explain."

"After the accident he couldn't have been nicer. He made a courier delivery for me, visited me in the hospital, brought me dinner. Then I saw the Roach ink on his knuckles. I told him to leave. And just like that," she snapped her fingers, "he turned into a prick. The next day he sent me roses. I was so mad I hacked their heads off."

Her left hand held an imaginary rose while her right hacked at it. She finished re-enacting the mutilation with a grin. "I wish I'd seen his face when he opened the box and found the stems."

"You beheaded his roses and gave him back the stems?"

"I left them at the hospital. He came back to see me—I knew he would—but I'd been discharged by then. I heard all about it later." She giggled. "He kicked the box across the lobby. I didn't hear another word from him until he sat down on the bench beside me while I was waiting to testify."

"Did he say anything to you?"

She shrugged. "He said 'hello.' I said 'get lost.'"

Rick leaned back in his chair, silent, and toyed with his pen. How could anyone so smart be so stupid? No, she's not stupid—she's immature and naïve. A bad combination.

"Mr. McCormick, I don't mean to be flippant about this, but gang involvement doesn't make sense at all."

"Why not?"

"For starters, Coopersmith isn't a gang member. When he crawled out from under that truck, the first thing I did was look for gang tats. He didn't have any, and no jump-in scars either. Second, if the gang was going to do something to me, wouldn't it make more sense to do it before I testified?"

She pulled out her cell phone and checked the time. "I need to go. I have lots to do before I go back to Crisfield, to *pick crabs.*"

"We need to talk about witness protection."

She stood, holding the back of her chair for balance, and grabbed her backpack. "No, we don't. Thank you anyway."

Rick jumped to his feet and leaned over the table toward her. This foolish bike messenger was not going to blow him off, even if he had to scare the wits out of her. "What're you doing, getting into it with a gangster? Gang life is a macho culture, respect is everything. Any sign of disrespect gets a person killed. And it's worse for a woman, especially a pretty girl like you. Exercise a little common sense, will you?"

She zipped her backpack as if she was telling him to zip shut his mouth. "And by 'common sense' do you mean 'be respectful' to these lowlife gangbangers?"

"No, I mean 'be circumspect.'"

"Explain 'circumspect.' I don't have a high school diploma, you know. That's why I'm *picking crabs.*"

"Lose the sarcasm and listen. When a gang member sends you flowers, don't cut the heads off and send him back the stems. Just toss the flowers. When a gang member says 'hello,' don't respond with 'get lost.' Just ignore him."

"Thanks for the tip." She grabbed her cane and hooked the backpack over her free arm.

"Let me arrange for the police to take you home," he said. "An officer can check your residence before you enter it. At least let us do that."

"No, thank you."

She headed for the door. He followed. After a few steps, she paused and turned to face him.

"I just realized something. Romero followed you into the courtroom. And while I was testifying, he wasn't watching me, he was watching you. What's he do for Roach?"

"We have our theories, but I'm not at liberty to share them with you."

"Here's my theory. I think he was there to watch you, you being head of the new gang unit. Maybe he was evaluating you."

Rick hadn't thought of that. It made a certain amount of sense. He forced a cordial smile.

"What grade do you think he gave me?"

Her eyes narrowed. "He probably gave you an A-plus. You looked good."

His smile turned genuine. "Thanks."

She continued toward the door. As she turned the doorknob, she looked over her shoulder. "Want to know what grade I'd give you?"

"Sure." It'd be nice to get a compliment from her.

She turned and locked her gaze onto his eyes. "Capital F. I think you stunk."

"What? Are you kidding?"

"All style, no heart. When I was at the hospital, you said someone would call me. Nobody ever did. I left you three messages. You never called me back. So rude. You've forgotten what it's like for a witness facing cross-examination. Or maybe you don't care."

He remembered the messages. He'd handed them off to Lundt. Told her to return the calls. Why didn't she? Shit.

"I came early to court so we could talk," he said hoping this would appease her.

"So did I, just like you told me to. With a name like Sean Patrick McCormick, I expected someone who looked...well, not like you. You could've mentioned that you're...you're...so what are you anyway?"

Rick was taken aback. No one had ever asked him the question flat out. Actually, it was refreshing to have someone ask directly. She seemed sincere.

"I'm Latino, born in Colombia, South America," he said. "Colombians are many races. I'm a mix of Amerindian and black. Now can we get back to business? You're right, I could've done better. Sometimes things slip between the cracks."

"So seal the cracks."

"I will, I promise. Thanks for reminding me to be sensitive to witnesses' concerns. I'm sorry." He paused a beat. "Are we good?"

"Yeah, we're good." She handed him her business card. "Just in case you ever need messenger service."

"What're you going to do if Sanchez shows up again?" He held up his cell phone.

"I'll get a carry permit for my gun."

Chapter 8

June 15

Lucy admired her home from the street as the cab pulled away. It was no more than fifteen feet wide; the nameplate she attached to the brownstone front read *Twiggy*. The summer weather had been kind to her flowers. A large pot of red geraniums sat on the front stoop, matching the newly painted front door. Orange and white nasturtiums bloomed profusely from the window box.

She opened the door, and her mouth watered. She had the foresight to throw some ingredients into her slow cooker before leaving for court. The inside of the house was hot, but not nearly as stifling as K.T. Crockett's—and it smelled of stew, not crabs. The tiny house was hers, and she was proud of it. Not bad for a high-school dropout.

It took her months to buy the row house through a Baltimore City tax sale. The house was structurally sound, but had been abused by a long string of renters, and eventually abandoned by the owner. She titled the house in the name of her business, used it as a home office, and treated most of the improvement costs as a business expense.

As soon as Lucy closed the front door, she plopped onto a small love seat in the living room. Beads of sweat covered her forehead. The house was suffocating. The windows had been locked shut since the morning and were now sticking in the heat and humidity. Installing new windows was on her ever-expanding to-do list.

She made her way to the front window, and tugged on it with all her strength. It wouldn't budge.

The kitchen window was smaller. She hobbled to the kitchen, avoiding the ceiling fan resting on the floor. She'd begun installing the fan in April, but her efforts were waylaid by her bike accident.

A small puddle of water had formed on the kitchen counter by the slow cooker. She glanced at the ceiling, looking for a leak from the upstairs bathroom. No leak. She looked at the faucet. No leak there either. She'd investigate further after mopping up the water.

As she reached for a dishtowel, she lost her balance. Grabbed at the counter. Missed. Knocked over the coffee pot. Tripped on the ceiling fan. She fell with a loud crash, and a louder curse. She lay on the floor in a heap.

"Lucy, are you hurt?"

Startled, she looked up. *Romero Sanchez!*

He squatted beside her. "I'll help you up."

She answered by swinging the coffee pot at his face. He dodged the makeshift weapon with little effort.

"I'll take that," he said. He put the pot on the counter.

After moving the ceiling fan, he held out his hand to assist her. She smacked it away—whatever Romero had in mind, she wasn't going down without a fight.

"Come on, let me help you. You'll end up killing yourself."

"Stay away from me."

Lucy crawled to a kitchen chair and used it to pull herself upright. "What're you doing here? How'd you get in?"

"I'm here because I missed you. And I got in by slipping a credit card between the lock and the door. You should invest in a deadbolt."

"Get out or I'm calling the police."

He showed her the cell phone he'd taken from her backpack. "You won't be calling anyone, babe."

Now what should she do? She kept a gun in her bedroom. The police wouldn't think twice if she shot a gangster who'd broken into her home.

"I'm hot and bothered, and I'm not your babe. I'm going upstairs to get out of this miserable dress. When I come back down, you'd better be gone."

After she'd struggled up five of the fifteen steps, Romero said, "If you're going upstairs to get your gun, don't bother. I have it." He opened his suit jacket and displayed her Sig-P232 semi-automatic pistol tucked in his belt. "I wouldn't want you to go through a lot of effort for nothing."

She spun around and threw her cane at him, more out of anger than fear. He caught it with one hand.

"Romero, *por favor páseme el recogedor de cangrejos!*"

He chuckled until his amusement gave way to a belly laugh. He pulled out a handkerchief and wiped the tears from his eyes.

He was still laughing when he said, "Lucy, Lucy—I gather from your tone that you meant to say something hateful to me. What did you say? In English, please."

"You know what I said."

"I know what you said, but I have no idea what you meant."

"I said, 'Romero, you're a mother fucking, piece of shit prick.'"

"Your Spanish needs some work." He smiled, showing all of his white, straight teeth. "What you actually said was, 'Romero, please pass me the crab picker.'"

"Oh."

"You've had an exhausting day. Sit down and relax a bit." He extended his hand to help her, but she refused to take it. Lucy climbed down the steps hanging on to the bannister. She limped to the dining room table.

He brought her iced tea from the refrigerator. The drywall caught his eye.

"Nice job. Who did this? I might want to hire him."

Lucy resigned herself to answering his questions. "My mother and I." She sipped her tea. "And we're not for hire."

"That's a shame. I'm very impressed with your work. Nice cutouts and finishing."

He removed his suit jacket and shirt, keeping Lucy's gun tucked in his belt. Fear swept through her. She scanned the room for her cane. Where did Romero put it?

A small step ladder leaned against the far kitchen wall. Romero positioned it under the ceiling electrical box and placed the tools and hardware on the kitchen counter. He put the fan on the kitchen table.

"Romero, what're you doing?"

"I'm installing the fan."

"No, don't. I can do it."

"I know you can, but you can't install it with a broken ankle. I don't want you breaking your other ankle by tripping over the fan again."

Lucy muttered profanities while she planned her escape. Screaming was useless; the windows were shut, and no one would hear her. Bolting for the front door was not an option—he'd overtake her in a moment. Her only weapon was the glass of tea she was holding. He was now on the step ladder examining the electrical box. She could smash the glass. Attack him with a shard. Make a run for it. She corrected herself—make a hop for it. But he had her gun. Even if he didn't shoot her, she'd have no chance at hand-to-hand combat because of her cast.

She studied him while he installed the fan, looking for anything she could turn to her advantage. His physique was as fine looking as his face. As he reached overhead, his arms and shoulder muscles reminded her of a system of pulleys and thick cable wires. Intricate gang tattoos covered his arms. His sleeveless undershirt barely hid the tats on his torso. Perspiration dampened his undershirt, and it stuck to his abdomen, displaying a ripple of defined muscles.

She watched Romero, fascinated. She'd seen other attractive men before, but the image of him installing the ceiling fan was compelling. Her mind drifted. She was lying naked on top of him, kissing the tattoos on his chest. The fantasy ran amuck until she saw the expression on his face. He was reading her mind.

God dammit! My face is just like Steppie's tail. Tells everything.

Romero installed the fan within an hour. As he tested it, Lucy made her way into the kitchen. She stood underneath the whirling fan. He pulled the fan chain, and the fan spun at its highest speed. The fan was quiet—no rattling or oscillation. Romero had balanced it perfectly. The paper napkins on the kitchen counter flew through the air. She closed her eyes, and the fan's wind blew her hair in every direction.

When she opened her eyes, she found Romero gazing down at her. She didn't understand his expression. Was it contentment? Satisfaction? No, he looked happy.

"Thanks for installing the fan." She re-clipped her hair to get it away from her face. "Tonight I'm bringing down a pillow and I'm gonna sleep on the kitchen floor right under this fan."

"Have you considered getting air conditioning?"

"It's on my list. I'll probably have to pedal five thousand miles just to finish off my current list."

"What's next on your list?"

"A deadbolt."

Romero threw his head back and laughed. "You tickle my funny bone, you really do. And whatever you're cooking tastes great. I hope you don't mind, I sampled it. May I stay for dinner?"

"Are you going to hurt me?"

"No, no, of course not." He picked up her right hand and kissed it. "I'd never hurt you."

"You can't sit at the dinner table wearing a gun. And I want my cell phone back."

He put the gun and the cell phone on the counter. There was no magazine in her gun.

"Nice gun," he said. "Where'd you get it?"

"My mother gave it to me as a housewarming gift."

He raised his eyebrows. "A gun is not the first thing that comes to mind as a housewarming gift."

"You're not my mother."

He walked around the house unsticking the stubborn windows. A cool breeze flowed through the house, drying the sweat from Lucy's skin and dissolving the tension in her muscles. An understanding swept through the open windows; Romero didn't intend to harm her. Within a few minutes, they were seated together at the dining room table.

She watched his eyes as they scanned the room. He saw the valances she'd built, the love seat pillows she'd sewn, and the pictures she'd needlepointed.

"You have a beautiful home. You've put a lot of love into it."

For reasons she couldn't understand, his compliments meant a lot to her. They were sincere—not the get-you-into-bed compliments she was used to hearing.

"Who taught you and your mother how to drywall?" he said.

"We took home improvement classes at Home Warehouse. In fact, we took so many classes that they offered my mother a job. Now she's the assistant manager."

He nodded, encouraging her to continue.

"We started when I was seven. After we learned the basics, we moved on to cars and took automotive classes. It ended up being pretty fun. After class, we'd come home, and my mother would read the newspapers to me, the *Baltimore Sun* and the *New York Times*. And then we'd watch Xena together. That was my reward for being good."

"What's Xena?"

"Xena's a 'who.' She's the Warrior Princess. It was a TV show. I used to pretend I was Xena." She took his right hand. "The tattoos on your knuckles are gone. Are you out of Roach?"

He pulled his hand away. "It'd be best if we have a 'don't ask, don't tell' policy."

Lucy sighed.

"Where's your father?" he said.

"He died when I was three."

"I'm sorry." His eyes showed honest sorrow. "Your mother must've been quite young."

"She was."

"A brave woman. Is she as beautiful as you?"

Out of habit, her tongue swept the inside of her mouth, feeling her crooked teeth. Getting braces was on her list. She'd never had a professional haircut. Cosmetics weren't in her budget. Her clothes came from the Goodwill store. She was a hot mess. Lucy didn't know how to answer his question other than to say, "Want more stew?"

He did.

Romero ate a heaping spoonful. "Did she remarry?"

"No…I don't think she ever will. My father was the love of her life. Do you think it's possible to love someone that much?"

"Yes, I do," he said in a wistful voice. "It's getting late. I'll help you with the dishes."

She washed and he dried. The fan blades whirled overhead, blowing Lucy's hair into her face. She kept pushing the hair away with her wet hands. Romero moved behind her and removed the clip from her hair. With both hands, he swept the hair out of her face, pulled it neatly to the back of her head, and secured it with the clip. A swell of sexual desire bubbled inside her.

"When do you go back to Crisfield?" he whispered.

"The bus leaves tomorrow morning."

He stood close behind her and brushed the top of her head with his lips. He caressed her neck and collarbone and finally rested his hands on her shoulders. Romero bent down and gently kissed the back of her neck.

"I'll take you, if you'd like."

She turned to face him. His expression was not one of domination, but of hope. She could say, "No."

An argument with her mother launched inside her head.

Just because you want to, doesn't mean you have to, her mother said.

I know I don't have to, but I'm gonna—just this once.

She put her arms around Romero's neck.

"Yes, you can take me."

He kissed her lips with a sweet, soft kiss.

"*Mi amada*," he whispered.

Chapter 9

September 20

It was eight o'clock in the morning. Rick was sweating. He walked the ten blocks from his condo on President Street to his office, believing the morning stroll would energize him for his meeting with Homicide Detective Ulysses Campbell. The air was thick with humidity. He stepped into the office elevator, wilted rather than refreshed. His first stop was the men's room. He rinsed his face in the sink, dried it off with a paper towel, and headed to the conference room to claim the only seat directly under the air conditioning vent.

The gang unit. Rick hadn't yet processed the fact the Baltimore City State's Attorney's Office now had a gang unit, and he was its chief. He'd pushed for a gang unit for years, arguing that gang crimes should be handled by prosecutors with expertise in gangs, not assigned to prosecutors according to the crime committed. His efforts went nowhere until Appoline Mercer was elected the Baltimore City State's Attorney. She believed as he did—gang crimes should be handled by gang prosecutors.

The unit was small, composed of two attorneys and two detectives, but it was expandable when necessary. Each of the city's nine police districts had a gang liaison. In the event of a surge in gang violence, Rick could call upon the violent crimes unit for additional prosecutors.

The gang unit was a stepping stone to the job Rick truly wanted—the U.S. Attorney for the Southern District of New York. It might take a

51 •

while and a lot of luck, but one day he'd be prosecuting high-visibility gang crimes in Manhattan.

The powerful air conditioning vent ruffled Rick's hair while he reviewed the agenda. The only action item was Campbell's status report on the surveillance of Romero Sanchez. Why the notorious Roach shot caller was in Baltimore was a mystery. Jill Sanders, Rick's counterpart in the Los Angeles District Attorney's Office, had requested help in solving the mystery.

Roach originated in Los Angeles as a Salvadoran street gang. Since the 1980's, it had grown into a fierce criminal enterprise, both in territory and scope. The gang's largest presence was in LA, but its cliques penetrated every State, Central America, and Mexico.

He'd gotten his first personal glimpse of Sanchez during the trial of Jason Coopersmith. Sanchez was spotted on Maryland's Eastern Shore later in the summer, and he now appeared in Baltimore at least twice a month. His comings and goings were no more suspicious than those of an ordinary tourist. Maybe Lucy Prestipino had been right—could Sanchez be evaluating Baltimore's nascent gang unit?

Detective Campbell entered the conference room wearing a Cheshire Cat smile, perspiration dripping from his bald head. "We've got a way to get to Sanchez." The detective took a seat, grabbed a handkerchief from his pocket, and mopped the sweat from his face, mustache, and scalp. "Jesus, it's hot out there. What the hell happened to fall?"

"How?"

"Give me that seat and I'll tell you."

They switched chairs. Campbell leaned back in his chair, closed his eyes, and allowed the air conditioning to blow its relief onto his face. He opened one eye, saw that Rick was waiting for his answer, and grinned.

"Trojan's got himself a Baltimore hon. An undercover first spotted her with Sanchez in Crisfield. He figured she was just one of Sanchez's many dalliances. We didn't think much about it at the time."

He handed four photographs to Rick. "Investigators took these in Canton in August and September."

Rick couldn't tell much from the first three photographs—Sanchez was entering the front door of a small row house. The last photograph was a full facial shot of the woman as she opened her door.

"We've identified her as—"

"Lucy Prestipino." Rick chucked the photographs on the table. "Fuck!"

"You know her?"

"She was a witness in a case I prosecuted. A bike messenger. Prickly, but she struck me as a stand-up citizen."

Rick's stomach churned. This was going to get ugly. "Dammit! Sanchez was in the courtroom during the trial. I met with Prestipino afterward. Asked her about him. She knew him, but convinced me there was no relationship. She even scoffed at the idea."

"Everybody lies," Campbell said. "You should know that by now. How do you want to play it? She's probably got some good intel on the guy. There's no better informant than a pissed-off ex-girlfriend. And she's going to be a *pissed-off ex* when she finds out why his street name is 'Trojan.' Let's bring her in and tell her."

"We need to be careful. The guy's a monster—you saw the pictures of his wife. Prestipino's not some gangsta hoodrat. She witnessed a strong-armed robbery, chased down the perpetrator, and testified. The People of Baltimore owe her."

Campbell shrugged. "And we owe the People of Baltimore our best efforts to get rid of that gangbanger. We may not get another chance."

Rick loved being a prosecutor, but deciding between conflicting interests always gave him a headache. He rubbed his temples with his fingers.

"This is why you get paid the big bucks," Campbell said.

The joke provided a moment of clarity. Lawyers didn't go into public service for the big bucks. He served the public and that included Lucy Prestipino. He intended to protect her.

"Prestipino's an immature girl who's in over her head," Rick said. "I'll get her in here and give her a reality check, but I'm not asking her to inform on Sanchez."

Campbell said nothing, but his eyes told Rick he disagreed. After Campbell left the conference room, Rick poured himself a cup of coffee.

He needed to calm his fury. How could she have sat there, ridiculing his concerns about Sanchez, and lie right to his face? That explained why she didn't want to hear about witness protection. How could he have believed her? He hurled his coffee cup against the closed conference room door.

A woman materialized. "What's going on in here?"

Appoline Mercer, the State's Attorney for Baltimore City, stood in front of him. His boss had rushed through the door. Rick's face heated. "Sorry, Mrs. Mercer. Feeling a little frustrated here."

He would've preferred calling her "Appoline," but no one had that privilege—not even the mayor. Mercer had been married for thirty-five years and was the mother of three successful, adult children. Her title—*Mrs. Mercer*—was a source of pride, and she insisted on being addressed by it.

Mercer gave him a sympathetic smile. "Don't worry about it. Sometimes this job can get to you. I've thrown a coffee cup or two during my career." She sat in the chair opposite his. "Tell me what's happened." Her voice was soothing, maternal. "It's my job to help you."

Relief washed over him. Mercer mentored him during his days as a freshly-minted ASA. He came with her to the violent crimes unit when she was promoted its chief. Her appearance and demeanor were deceiving. She was a beautiful woman, having once represented Louisiana in the Miss America pageant; she spoke with a slow and easy Cajun drawl; her mocha skin and blue eyes made her race indeterminate. Hidden beneath the charm and grace was a finely-honed killer instinct. She rarely lost a trial or negotiated a plea unfavorable to the State. Last November, she'd been elected the Baltimore City State's Attorney.

"I just learned that one of my witnesses has become romantically involved with Romero Sanchez."

He explained Lucy's role in the strong-arm trial, the conversation he had with Lucy afterward, and the photographs. Mercer listened without interruption, her mouth tightening at every word.

"Lucy Prestipino." Contempt dripped from her mouth. "Believe me, she's no innocent party. Don't get sucked in by her *sincere, innocent* act."

"What? Are we talking about the same person?"

"Peculiar eyes? One blue, one brown?"

He confirmed.

"I've known that girl since she was thirteen. I prosecuted her in juvenile court on a slew of charges stemming from a drunk driving spree. She almost killed her best friend. The victim was only twelve years old. At the end of the hearing, she kicked me! She spent the night in baby booking."

Mercer's mocha skin turned ruddy.

"That girl didn't learn a damn thing. Two years later, she was back in court on drug and theft charges. She'd gotten herself addicted to cocaine and was stealing to support her habit. By some miracle, she ended up in rehab instead of jail. She's never suffered a consequence in her life." Mercer leaned back in her chair, laced her fingers together, and held them to her mouth. "Maybe Sanchez is her drug connection...with benefits."

Rick was dumbfounded.

"This is what I want you to do," she said. "Bring her in. Convince her it's in her best interest to cooperate in the investigation. I don't care how—charm, intimidation, whatever it takes."

"You want me to turn her into an informant?"

"Of course." Mercer smiled. "I'm sure you can be a very charming man."

Rick shifted in his seat. "It could get her killed."

"That girl has a great talent for taking care of herself." She paused a moment. "Rick, don't let me down. Frankly, I thought you were tougher."

Rick stared at his boss, no longer seeing the Appoline Mercer he knew, but a callous and ruthless woman.

"I'll see what I can do."

She gave him a long, hard look.

Mercer stood. "You need some background information on that girl. I'll have her juvenile prosecution files brought to you. Review them before you talk to her. They'll be quite illuminating."

As Mercer exited the conference room, she paused in the doorway. She turned to face Rick. "I'll be disappointed if you don't have the stomach to do what needs to be done."

Thirty minutes later, an inter-office messenger delivered two files, each labeled "State of Maryland vs. Lucy Prestipino."

He read the charging document in the file marked Case No. 111213J. Driving while intoxicated, theft of automobile, reckless driving, speeding. The incident occurred on Lucy's thirteenth birthday. Lucy and Amber Anderson drank Irish car bombs at a friend's sleepover party. Lucy bragged she knew how to hot wire a car and offered to prove it. Amber took her up on the offer. They left the party and found a parked car Lucy could open and hot wire. Lucy drove with Amber in the passenger seat. She crashed into a jersey barrier on I-83. Both were transported by helicopter to Maryland Shock Trauma. Lucy escaped with an eye injury and a stomach pumping. Her blood alcohol concentration was .14.

Amber wasn't as fortunate. Her right leg was crushed and later amputated.

Appoline Mercer represented the State. Assistant Public Defender Sharon Krinsky represented Lucy. There was a plea agreement. Lucy pled guilty to the charge of driving while intoxicated and all other charges were dropped. Judge Charles Hartman placed her under the supervision of the juvenile court while remaining in the custody of her mother. Lucy entered an outpatient alcohol treatment program.

Rick reached for the second file, Case No. 670982J. Lucy was fifteen when she was charged with theft and possession of cocaine. Same attorneys, same judge. Krinsky did her best to introduce reasonable doubt, but the prosecution was a slam-dunk. During the disposition phase of the hearing, Mercer argued passionately that Lucy should be detained in a secured juvenile facility. Judge Hartman decided otherwise. He ordered Lucy to spend six months at the Mountain Lake Renewal Center in Western Maryland, a private rehab facility, at Mrs. Prestipino's expense.

Rick shut the file. He left his office, poured himself another cup of coffee, and went into the conference room. Sunshine streamed through the east window. He gazed toward the Inner Harbor, trying to reconcile the information in the files with his impression of Lucy. The rehab must've been successful—there were no additional criminal involvements of any kind.

He pulled Lucy's business card from his wallet and punched in her number. She answered immediately.

"This is Rick McCormick from the State's Attorney's Office. You testified in a case I pros—"

"Hi, Mr. McCormick." She sounded happy to hear from him. "What can I do for you?"

"I have a delivery. Can you come to my office around eleven this morning to pick it up?"

"Sure...and thank you for your business."

He disconnected, feeling like shit.

Chapter 10

September 20

Lucy was thrilled. It took her three years to cultivate a decent roster of customers from private businesses, but she couldn't break into the government sector. She was grateful to Rick for opening the door. Maybe he was a nice guy, after all.

It was ten o'clock. She treated herself to an iced latte from Café No Delay and pedaled to the corner of Charles and East Lexington. The city's messengers affectionately called the intersection, located in the center of Baltimore, "Ground Zero." It was here they waited between runs; sometimes eating, sometimes gossiping, sometimes sleeping.

Ground Zero was deserted. The temperature read ninety-seven degrees on the display above the entrance to Keystone Bank. Extreme heat didn't bother her—wimpy messengers stayed home, and she made money helping their customers.

A granite wall separated the front of the Charles Center from Charles Street. Normally, she would've perched on the wall, but today the granite was hot to the touch. She sat on a little patch of grass and sent a prayer of gratitude to her father. She had a house, her own business, and a job she loved. She also had Romero.

She'd see him tonight. The thought of him made her sweat more than the heat index. Their reunions were always the same; he'd sweep through her front door with his blazing smile and a sexiness that made her heart flutter. He'd pull her close. Graze her face with kisses and whisper, "I missed you, *mi amada*."

She'd fix dinner. He'd read the paper. Their dinner conversation was one-sided; he never spoke about himself. He listened to her prattle on with messenger tales and gossip about her posse. After dinner, she cleaned the dishes, and he tinkered around her house.

By nine o'clock, anticipation tingled in her private places. "C'mon, Romie—let's go to bed!" He'd answer with hot eyes, but wouldn't stop tinkering until she pleaded with him. He'd say, "It's been a long day. I need to take a shower." Finally.

She'd sneak into the shower. Wash his body. Slather the soap on all the right places. She'd kiss each and every one of his tattoos. He'd pin her against the tiled wall and give her a probing kiss. Her rapture would start. It would continue until she was spent, exhausted, and happy. Afterward, they'd watched *Xena: Warrior Princess* as they lay intertwined in her bed, her head on his shoulder.

Lucy's sexual fantasies halted when she spotted Pringles and Crackhead pedaling her way.

"A dollar says neither one of you can beat me today," Crackhead said.

Crackhead was referring to a *track stand* contest. The track stand event was part of every messenger competition; the winner was the biker who balanced longest on a stationary bike before putting a foot on the ground. Lucy practiced at every opportunity: red lights, traffic jams, and delayed pick-ups.

"I'm in," Pringles said.

"Me too," Lucy said.

While they competed, Pringles reached over and tapped Crackhead's helmet with his fingertips. "How's the skull?"

"Epoxy's still holding."

The distraction didn't cause Crackhead to put her foot on the ground. She always claimed a fractured skull improved her sense of balance. Before her accident, she'd never won a track stand competition; now she was world champion, having won the event three years in a row at the Cycle Messenger World Championships.

"Not bad," Crackhead said to Lucy. "Finally getting your mojo back?"

"I'm gonna beat you at next year's championships, you'll see."

While Lucy concentrated, she counted her blessings. She was back to messengering with all its benefits—the camaraderie, the freedom, and the movement. The odor of crabs no longer followed her. She swore she'd never look at another crab, either in the bay or on a plate.

Her mind drifted to Romero. He visited her in Crisfield throughout the summer. She loved how he looked deeply into her eyes. His tender touch electrified her. He was generous with his attention, his money, and his body.

"Crackhead, look at Lucy's face!" Pringles said. "She's thinking about her *mi amada*." Lucy put her foot on the pavement.

Shoot.

Pringles laughed. "Gotcha! When're we going to meet this guy?"

Her phone's alarm saved her from answering. It was ten forty-five, time to head to Rick's office.

Chapter 11

September 20

A gray-haired receptionist with long, blue nails escorted Lucy to the conference room. Rick was waiting for her. He smiled when she entered the room. She knew right away something was wrong—he was wearing a weird faux smile.

"Thanks for coming in." He gestured toward the chair. "Please sit down."

She took a seat and put her helmet on the chair beside her. He sat opposite her. A thick manila envelope sat on the table in front of him.

"I'm not here for a delivery?"

"No." He reached for the envelope. "Sorry for the pretense. This is crucially important."

He placed four photographs in front of her. She was quiet as she looked at them.

"Romero Sanchez has been under surveillance. When I saw these photographs, I called you."

Lucy's mouth tightened. "Why? What concern is it of yours?"

"I don't understand this. After the trial, you told me your relationship was one of 'mutual irritation.' Were you lying to me?"

"Of course not. Romero and I became friends later." She heard the edge in her own voice. "You didn't answer my question. Why do you care who I go out with?"

"We're investigating him for a murder, a vicious murder. I wanted to warn you, for your own safety. He's a bad guy, an evil guy. Don't you know—"

"Am I under arrest?"

"No, this is a friendly meeting."

"Don't treat me like I'm stupid. This is not a friendly meeting."

Lucy stood and snatched her helmet. As she walked toward the door, Rick grabbed her arm. He hauled her to the conference table and shoved her back into the chair. "Stay put!"

"If you touch me one more time, I'm swearing out a warrant."

For a moment, she considered backhanding the helmet across his face. She would surely knock out some teeth. Make a necklace out of them for Halloween. Nobody manhandled her.

"Please," he said in a voice now polite.

She stayed. There were two files on the table, each labeled with her name. They were her juvenile prosecution files. Nausea rose to her throat.

"Lucy," Rick began. "In retrospect, I should've just asked you to come in to talk with me. I was concerned that if I mentioned the reason, you'd refuse."

"Say what you want to say."

"About six months ago, Sanchez became a prime suspect in a murder that occurred in Los Angeles. We're working with the investigators in LA. When you and I spoke after the trial, I told you Sanchez comes to Maryland regularly. The investigators still don't know why, but that's the reason we were contacted by LA. The victim was Marcela Sanchez, his wife. She was killed in an unspeakably brutal way. I'm worried that he'll kill you, too."

Romero was married?

She shook her head vigorously. "I don't believe it."

"Marcela was killed shortly after contacting the LA police. She had information about Romero. The gang's law is 'You rat, you die.' Working with law enforcement is considered the ultimate betrayal. That's why Romero's the suspect."

"You're wrong!" Her voice was quivering. "You're wrong."

"I know this is hard for you to hear. Do you know his street name? 'Trojan.' In his younger days, he was a *babysitter* for Roach. Do you know what that is? Whenever the gang ordered a killing, he'd befriend the victim, make them comfortable, trusting. He'd lure the victim into a situation where the gang could make an easy kill. A Trojan horse—a charming, cunning, and ruthless Trojan horse."

Rick leaned in close.

"That's what he's been doing to you. Has he been paying you compliments? Telling you you're beautiful? Making you feel special? Acting as if he understands you? He's been luring you into his world for some nefarious purpose."

Lucy's eyes were streaming tears, but she wasn't crying. "I don't care what you say. He cares about me. I know it. Do you know his tattoos are disappearing? I think he wants to get out of Roach."

"You're so naïve! He's a shot caller—if a Roach clique wants to kill someone inside the gang, it has to get permission from a shot caller, a *green-light* to murder. The smart shot callers are removing their tattoos so they blend into society. It makes it easier for them to commit their crimes.

"There's another reason he's called *Trojan*. He's a man-whore, he goes through condoms by the case. The street name's a joke."

Rick reached across the table and covered her hand with his. His voice became a whisper.

"You're not the only one. He has women all over the country. Even when his wife was alive, he screwed every female who would lie down for him. You're no more than a sex doll to him. Want to see the picture of the woman he was with last night?"

She yanked her hand away. "He's been nothing but sweet to me, kind."

"Sweet? Kind? You must be a moron!"

He pulled another photograph from the envelope. Flicked it across the table. It landed in front of her. "Look at *sweet*. Look at *kind*."

It was a graphic photo of a woman hacked to death with a machete. She was nearly decapitated. Blood soaked the walls and floor of the room, giving it the macabre appearance of an Eastern Shore chicken slaughterhouse.

"Mrs. Sanchez lost over half her blood," he said.

Lucy vomited into the trashcan behind her. She put her head in her hands and wept uncontrollably.

"You're in a unique position to help us with Romero," he said gently. "Will you consider it?"

"Help you how?"

"Help us get information we need to destroy Roach. Remember what you said to the jury when you testified against Jason Coopersmith? You wanted justice. You can get justice for all the people Roach has hurt.

"It's not often we come across a brave woman like you. That's why I'm asking for your help. We want to put Roach out of business—put an end to its violence. Much of the blood that flows through our city streets can be traced back to Roach. It's a scourge on our community."

"What exactly do you want me to do?"

"Tell us everything you can about Romero. Who he talks to, where he goes, what he's up to."

Lucy wept, occasionally picking up the crime scene photograph between sobs. He began to slide the photograph from her line of vision.

"Wait!" She grasped the photograph with both hands. "Something's off. Something's wrong."

When he attempted to grab it from her, she swung her foot under the table and kicked him in the shin.

"Jesus! Do I need to call security?"

"You go ahead and do that. I have a friend at the *Sun*. Warren Hughes, the crime reporter. He'll write a story about how you tricked me into coming to your office. Ambushed me. Forced me to look at an obscene photograph. And called security on me."

She picked up the hem of her T-shirt and gagged into it.

"Let's go," he said. "Let me take you home."

"No! I need to think. Don't say anything."

They sat in silence for several minutes. She could see that Rick was distraught.

"Give me the photograph," he said.

"No." She looked at him with tear-filled eyes. "Give me ten minutes. Just ten minutes. Then I'll leave peaceably. If you don't, the only way I'm leaving is in handcuffs."

He glanced at his watch. "Ten minutes."

"Give me all the photographs." He handed them over. She wept as she examined each one.

The dead woman looked familiar, but Lucy couldn't place her. She scanned her memory. Who was she? If Lucy could figure out how she knew Marcela Sanchez, she could solve the puzzle. The gagging and tears slowed, but didn't disappear. Lucy wiped her eyes with the back of her hand.

Rick handed her a handkerchief. She blew her nose and gagged into it. The smell of her vomit filled the conference room. She didn't care; she was going to figure this out.

Lucy concluded she'd never met Marcela Sanchez. Why did the dead woman look familiar? The answer was floating in front of her—so close she could almost grab it. Rick reached over and touched her. She jumped, startled from her near-trance with the photographs.

"It's been ten minutes. Come on. Let's go."

"No, two minutes more. The answer is right there. I can see it, but barely."

Lucy twirled her hair while she studied the photographs. Without warning, she ripped a hunk of hair from her scalp. Rick gasped. She placed the torn-out hair on top of one of the photographs. She studied the woman's face. One eye was covered in blood. The other was blue. It was telling her something. What was it?

Think. Think.

Rick interrupted her train of thought. "Time's up. Call the *Sun* if you want. It's over now."

Without saying a word, she grabbed her helmet and left the conference room. A sob of fury slipped from her mouth as she closed the door behind her. She needed to compose herself. Crying and pedaling don't mix; that's what Crackhead always says.

She found a women's room nearby. The water from the sink rinsed the vomit from her mouth. She rested her head against the mirror and began her relaxation exercises. Her knees stopped shaking. Her face remained blotchy and her eyes bloodshot.

The mirror revealed the answer. *Mi amada*!

Lucy sprinted from the women's room, yelling, "Rick! Rick!"

She tore down the corridor to the conference room. No Rick. A security guard confronted her. "Miss—"

"I need Rick McCormick!"

She ran past the guard. "Where's Rick McCormick?" she shouted to anyone within hearing distance. She opened every door in her path.

Rick stepped from the men's room, holding the trashcan. "My God! What is it?"

"I get it! I figured it out."

Rick led her back into the conference room.

"Give me back the photographs," she said.

He hesitated.

"Do it! It'll only take a minute to explain, and then I'll get out of here, forever."

He handed her the photographs.

"Look at the hair on Mrs. Sanchez. Blonde. Wavy. Her left eye is blue. I can't tell about the other. I'm betting it's brown. Romero didn't kill his wife—he's grieving. That's why he wants to be with me." Her voice trembled as she strained to control her emotions. "He's pretending I'm Marcela. You see, I remind him of his wife. Romero didn't kill her. Someone else did. He thinks the killer's in Maryland. That's why he comes here. He's here hunting for his wife's killer."

Lucy could see the skepticism in Rick's eyes.

"Do you have a picture of Mrs. Sanchez?" she said.

"None other than the crime scene photos."

"Get one that shows her features. You'll see I'm right."

Rick put the photographs back in the envelope. He stopped looking at her.

"You're not going to do anything about this, are you?" she said.

"No."

"Why not?"

"You've dreamed up a fantastic theory that allows you to deny reality. The fact is, you've been dating a brutal killer. If you don't wake up, you could be his next victim."

Rick would never be convinced. Time to leave.

She had to say one more thing. "Find out if Mrs. Sanchez had heterochromia."

Chapter 12

September 20

Lucy set the kitchen timer for an hour. Her mother said it's okay to cry over a disappointment—just don't wallow. An hour's worth of tears is enough. If that doesn't work, go to Loaves & Fishes and help people with real problems. Get your mind off yourself.

She dangled a Tiffany bracelet in front of her living room window so it would catch the rays of the afternoon sun. The result was a kaleidoscope of blues, greens, and browns cascading throughout the lower level. She performed this ritual every sunny day.

Romero had called her a week before giving her the jeweled bangle. "Babe, I'm coming into town on Friday. Be ready at seven—and dress up." When he arrived for their date, he was sharply dressed and handsomer than ever. She craved his touch.

"Let's have sex before we go out," she said. "I won't be able to think straight until we do."

He gathered her into his arms and kissed the hollow of her throat. His left hand gripped her buttocks while the right slipped beneath her blouse. He caressed her breasts until she moaned. His hand followed her body's midline, sliding between her breasts, passing her navel, and finding the hem of her skirt. His hand climbed upward beneath her skirt until it found the leg rim of her panties. He toyed with the lace while purring into her ear, "A dishwasher is coming tomorrow."

"Huh?"

He gave her a long, penetrating kiss.

"Romie," she said when she came up for air. "I don't need a dishwasher. I need sex!"

He laughed and pecked a kiss on her cheek. "You must wait, *mi amada*. Anticipation will make tonight that much sweeter."

The dinner was perfect. A deep-throated Latino man named "Peeps" drove them to a remote town in Pennsylvania. They dined at *Le Palais* Bistro. Romero was his usual charming self. He appeared fascinated with her every word, told her she was gorgeous with such sincerity she believed him. She remembered his elegant manners. And his easy, perfect smile.

Over dessert, Romero said, "Have you heard from McCormick recently?"

"No, why in the world would you ask that?"

"He was quite taken with you at the trial. He strikes me as a man who would follow up."

The idea hit Lucy as absurd, and she joked, "Are you jealous or something?"

"Will you tell me if he calls you? I want to have a fighting chance."

"A fighting chance at what?" Her little voice harped at her. "I don't understand this conversation."

"At winning you." He kissed the palm of her hand. "Promise me you'll tell me if he calls you."

"Okay, I will." She was still mystified. "Do you want to be exclusive? Is that what this is about?"

Romero only smiled and handed her the little box from Tiffany's. It was an anniversary gift; they'd met exactly four months before. She burst into tears when she saw the bracelet.

"The aquamarines and axinite reminded me of your eyes," he said.

Romero was right; their night together was deliciously sweet.

Now, as Lucy watched the colors flash around her living room, she analyzed the conversation. Was Romero cultivating her as an informant? He said all the right things from the beginning—she was pretty and clever, he liked her house, he complimented the drywall. He oozed sexuality while he installed her ceiling fan. She was mesmerized. Hypnotized. Aroused. Her desire for him flamed, even now.

Romero read her well. He probably did a background check on her. That would explain why he never drank in front of her, pulled out a joint, or offered her flake. Getting her using again would destroy her value as a snitch. He probably knew when he broke into her house how it would all go down. Soften her up with compliments. Admire her mother. Start doing a *manly* task. All so he could pretend she was Marcela, fuck her and turn her into his snitch. She rebuked herself.

McCormick was right. You're a moron!

She didn't understand how she could've been so wrong about Romero. He was a good friend, helped her out whenever she needed it. He painted her living room, fixed her running toilet, tiled her bathroom floor.

Once, when she was in Crisfield during her crab-picking days, he surprised her with a visit and found her crying.

"Tell me," he said.

"I want to get my driver's license. I signed up for driver's ed, but I need my learner's permit for the in-car instruction. I can't get my learner's without my birth certificate. I asked my mother half-a-dozen times to give it to me. She keeps stalling, saying she's looking for it. I finally gave up and went to Vital Records to get it myself. It was an hour's bus ride to Reisterstown.

"Some nice lady at Vital Records looked and looked, but she couldn't find it. She told me to go to Mercy Hospital and come back with something called a verification of birth. Then she could make me a birth certificate. I took the bus back to the city, went to Mercy Hospital, and guess what? There was no record of my birth…I guess I was born on Mars."

"That would explain a lot."

"Oh, Romie," she said as she pretend-hit him on the arm. "Anyway, I told this tale of woe to my mother. You know what she said? She didn't offer to help me get the birth certificate—she told me she'd drive me anywhere I wanted to go.

"What the fuck? I got angry. I told her I was sick and tired of bumming rides from people. I don't want to be a nuisance to my friends. It's embarrassing! Twenty-one years old and can't drive. Besides, it's my birth certificate, and I'm entitled to have it. I told her I wasn't going to talk to her again until she gave it to me. And I hung up on her.

"Right away, I felt awful. I called her back, and she was crying. She couldn't even talk."

Lucy wept again.

Romero wiped the tears from her cheeks with his thumb. "You make up with your mother, and I'll find your birth certificate."

"How?"

"I'm very resourceful." He smiled and kissed her cheek. "Tell me the details of your birth, and I'll find it."

She gave him all the information. Two weeks later, he handed her the birth certificate. "As soon as you get your learner's permit, I'll teach you how to drive." Her mother was astonished when Lucy showed her the birth certificate.

"How did you get—?"

"I have a very resourceful friend," she said, quoting Romero.

Yes, Romie was a good friend. He didn't want her as an informant. Rick was full of shit, just fucking with her mind, confusing her. The only thing Romero wanted was a substitute for his murdered wife.

The more she thought about it, the angrier she got. Rick believed Romero butchered his wife, that he was a Roach shot caller, and he had the power to green-light a murder. Yet Rick asked her to be an informant. Lucy was nothing more to him than fodder in his war against Roach. She burst into tears.

She stopped crying when she heard a knock on her front door. It couldn't be Romero; it was only three thirty, and he wasn't due until six. She ignored the knock. It became louder and more insistent until she opened the door.

Rick McCormick was on her front stoop. Now what? His tough-guy demeanor was gone. Had he come to apologize? To tell her she was right?

"May I come in?"

She opened the door but didn't invite him to sit down.

"Today was a rough day," he said. "I only wanted to check on you. Are you all right?"

"Dandy. And you?" Her voice sounded more snarky than she meant it to.

"I'm not dandy. I feel terrible about putting you through the ringer today."

"Go help out at Loaves & Fishes. It'll make you feel better. Get your mind off yourself. That's what my mother always says."

The oven timer buzzed. She went into the kitchen and turned it off. Afterward, she lingered at the stove, not wanting to resume the conversation with Rick. He'd interrupted her pity party. She decided she was entitled to a do-over on the timer.

When she returned to the living room, Rick was standing in front of her bookcase looking at her stack of *Xena: Warrior Princess* DVDs. He picked up the bracelet on the coffee table. His teeth were clenched.

"He gave you this, didn't he?"

"Put it down."

He tossed Romero's gift back on the coffee table. "Have you thought about what I said?"

"You said a lot. What in particular?" She knew exactly what, but wanted him to say it out loud.

"Helping us with Romero."

"Can't you just talk to him? Why do I have to be in the middle?"

"How do you suggest I approach him? 'Hey, Romero, wazzup? Want to talk about Marcela's murder?'"

Her blood simmered. "Cool your jets, McCormick. You're not in your office anymore. You're a guest in my home. Mind your manners."

"I didn't mean to…Lucy, tell me what I need to do to get you to help us."

"You don't need my help. Ask Romero straight out who killed Marcela. See if he wants out of Roach."

"For starters, I don't have a number for him. Give it to me, and I'll call him."

Lucy was sorry she'd brought it up. If she gave Rick the number, he'd probably put a wiretap on it. The truth was she didn't have Romero's number. He shielded her from the details of his work. He always called her from a pre-paid phone.

"Did Marcela have heterochromia?"

Rick raked his hair with his fingers. "You're still not getting this. You're living in a fantasy world. Romero isn't some redeemable guy out of a romance movie. He's a sociopath. A vicious animal who slaughtered his wife. How many times do I have to tell you that? We need your help. Please."

Her blood went from simmer to boil.

"Okay, I'll give you his number."

Chapter 13

September 20

Figure it out. Her mother said that all the time. Figure it out, everyone makes mistakes, just don't make the same mistake twice. Goddamn McCormick! He was all data, data, data. If you couldn't see it and hear it, it didn't count. What's wrong with intuition? What's wrong with knowing something because you feel it inside?

Lucy had to protect herself. No one else was going to.

Romero didn't kill his wife. That meant someone else did. That someone was in Maryland, probably watching Romero. Probably watching her. Whoever it was hated Romero enough to butcher his wife. Marcela's killer might be planning to do the same to her.

She spent the next hour cleaning her gun.

It was five thirty. Lucy strapped on her backpack and attached a note to the front door telling Romero to meet her at CC's. Compression Connection, nicknamed "CC's," was a popular downtown salsa bar. She selected the bar because it was Romero's favorite, and he considered Javier, the owner, a good friend.

She biked to the intersection of Redwood and South Calvert, turned left down an alley, and pulled up to a black decorative railing in front of CC's. Lucy locked her bike and entered the bar. It was quarter to six. She wanted to talk to Romero in a quiet, public place. CC's wouldn't get busy until at least ten.

The bar was empty, except for Javier, who was standing behind the polished, wooden bar taking an inventory of the liquor. He was as wiry as his glasses. He looked up when Lucy entered.

"I'm meeting Romero."

"Want anything while you wait?"

"A diet ginger ale. Thank you."

She found an out-of-the way table and sat down, hooking her backpack over the chair. The bar was familiar—she'd been there once before. She'd just gotten her cast off, and Romero wanted to celebrate. They arrived at midnight; the bar was jammed. The patrons were mostly in their twenties and thirties, all dressed to maximize their sex appeal. Couples were crushed together on the floor, salsa dancing. Their movements were intense, sensual. Lucy found the bar exciting.

"Let's test out your ankle," Romero said. "I'll teach you how to salsa."

"My ankle still hurts a little. You go on and dance."

She begged off, not because of her ankle, but because she didn't want to make a fool of herself. She didn't know how to dance. Her mother, who taught her everything, thought dancing was a waste of time and energy.

She didn't mind wallflowering while Romero danced. Watching people was fun. Before long, the people watching became very interesting. She nearly choked on her drink when she saw Rick McCormick step onto the dance floor. He moved like a professional dancer—smooth, self-assured, cool. His prosecutor intensity was gone. He was relaxed, happy. He almost looked handsome. The transformation intrigued her.

Romero returned to the table. "Let's go. You look bored." Before she could protest, he hurried her out the door. He was silent during the drive home. It wasn't until they were in bed together that he returned to his amiable self. Two weeks later, he gave her the Tiffany bracelet.

Lucy checked her cell phone for the time. Five minutes until six. Her knees were shaking under the table. She breathed deeply to regain her composure. It was important to be calm and collected—her life depended on it. She wasn't about to start sleeping with her gun under her pillow.

She was stirring the ice in her soda with a straw when she saw a silhouette come through the door. It was Romero.

"*Hola*, Javier," he said. The two men kissed each other on the cheek.

Romero strolled over to Lucy. He flashed his movie-star smile, the one that showed his dimples, twinkling eyes, and gorgeous teeth. The smile she couldn't resist. Her resolve melted. Lucy leaped from her seat and threw her arms around his neck. She hugged him tightly.

"Now you're talking my language," he said.

He kissed her on the forehead, slid his lips down her cheek, and rested his mouth on hers. His tongue greeted hers with the slightest of touches. "*Mi amada*," he murmured between kisses.

She flinched and pulled away.

"You're trembling," he said.

She returned to her seat, holding the edge of the table to steady herself. Javier came over and placed a Baja in front of Romero.

"Want another ginger ale, Lucy?"

She wondered how Javier knew her name. He couldn't have gotten it from Romero—they'd been discreet about their relationship. Was Javier undercover?

"No, thanks."

Romero watched Javier as he walked to the bar then turned his attention to Lucy.

"What's wrong?"

She didn't know where to start, or how. She wished she'd written down her speech so she could simply hand it to him. Her words had to be delicate, subtle. She was never any good at being either delicate or subtle.

"I want you to tell Rick McCormick who killed Marcela."

Romero fell against the back of his chair as if she'd pulled out her gun and shot him. He stared at her for ten interminable seconds before moving. She watched his expression morph from surprise to anger to rage. He slammed his fists on the table two inches from her soda. The glass flew off and spilled into her lap.

"Romie! I'm doing what you told me to do!"

Javier appeared at the table.

"It's okay," she said. "Can you give us a moment, please?"

She surprised herself. Instead of being afraid, she was angry. So angry she could feel it in her kicking toes.

Romero said something in Spanish to Javier. Lucy didn't understand what it was, but the tone was apologetic. Javier walked to the bar, glancing back several times. Once behind the bar, he watched them.

"I'm sorry," Romero said. "Tell me what happened."

He smiled. She didn't.

"You asked me to tell you if I was contacted by McCormick. I was. He called me on the pretense of a courier delivery. Once I got to his office, he told me about Marcela."

Romero's dark eyes blackened until she could no longer see his pupils.

"I'm sorry for your loss." Her voice broke. "I don't have the words to tell you how sorry I am. I just don't."

He was motionless, wordless.

"The LA police think you killed her. You already know that, don't you? Rick wanted to warn me. I know you didn't do it, I told him that."

"How do you know I didn't?"

"I do, that's all. I don't know how to explain it. There's no way you could do that."

"Do what?"

"Kill someone you love like that…with a machete. I knew it wasn't possible when I saw the photographs. The ones of the crime scene."

"That rat fuck showed you those photographs?"

She nodded, tears welling in her eyes. "When he told me you were the suspect, I defended you. That's when he showed them to me."

Romero took a drink from his Baja. He was gripping the bottle so tightly his knuckles were white.

"No one should see those photographs," he said. "No one should see Marcela like that—like a slaughtered pig. She was beautiful, good." His eyes glistened. "She deserves respect."

A sob escaped from Lucy's throat.

"How'd you know from the photographs that I didn't do it?"

"I could see that Marcela—" She stifled a sob. "Marcela looks like me. You've been pretending I'm Marcela. You wouldn't do that if you were the one who killed her."

Tears streamed down her face. She pressed on in spite of them.

"Romie, I've been with a lot of guys who wished I was different, but I've never been with a man who pretended I was someone else."

"You're wrong…I never pretended you were Marcela."

"I don't believe you." Her voice was steady, strong. "*Mi amada*. How many times did you say that to me? I was never your beloved. I didn't understand why you called me that until I saw those photographs. Those terrible, terrible photographs."

"No, Lucy. Maybe you look like Marcela, but you're completely different. I care about you. Not because you look like her, but because of who you are. "

"Prove it! Whoever killed Marcela is still out there. He could kill me."

She slid Rick's business card toward him. "You know who did it. If you really care about me, you'll tell McCormick."

Romero leaned away from her and crossed his arms in front of his chest.

"Romie, Romie." Lucy was pleading. "I'm not Marcela. I don't want to die like her. You don't want that either, do you?"

"Of course not. What kind of a monster do you think I am?"

"Tell Rick who killed her."

He sat without moving.

"Tell him! I know you know who did it. That's why you're in Baltimore—you're hunting him! Help the cops get him off the street...before he kills me."

"I don't know who killed her."

"You're a liar, a fucking liar! Tell him who did it!"

"I can't help you."

"You mean you won't. What would Marcela say if she knew you put another woman in danger of getting hacked to pieces, and you did nothing about it? What would she say?"

"Keep Marcela out of this."

"Marcela's right in the middle of this." Lucy stood. "Tell him!"

He stood, grabbed her left arm, and pulled her to him so that his mouth was next to her left ear. He whispered, "Revenge belongs to me. Only *me*."

The heel of her right hand slammed against his nose. She heard the cartilage break with a loud crunch. Blood flowed from his nostrils and dripped onto his white shirt. Romero held his nose with his hands.

"You fuckin' bitch! You broke my nose!"

Lucy shoved the table into his thighs, throwing him off balance and crashing to the floor. She grabbed the bottle of Baja.

Pain seared her scalp. She was being dragged away by the hair. It was Javier. He grabbed the beer bottle from her hand.

"I run a nice place. Keep your domestic bullshit out of here. You're *persona non grata*. Show up in here again, and I'll have you arrested."

"Let go of me!"

Javier released her hair. "Get the fuck out!"

Romero was on his feet. Javier stood between them.

"Romero, one day you're going to die." She grabbed her backpack from the chair. "It'll probably be sooner than later. And wherever your evil soul goes, it won't be with Marcela's. She won't want you. She won't want to spend her eternity with someone she's ashamed of."

Romero lunged for her. "I'm going to kill you!"

Javier grabbed him around the chest and restrained him.

"Romie!" Javier said. "Let her go. She's a toxic bitch. She's not worth it." Javier turned to Lucy. "Get out of here."

Lucy stumbled out of the bar, her vision obscured by rage.

As she pedaled away, she glanced over her shoulder. Romero was on the street, standing motionless, hands at his sides, staring after her.

"Well, Mr. McCormick," she said to herself. "How's that for circumspect?"

September 20

Lucy meant to go home, but the Tiffany bracelet was sitting on her coffee table. It would mock her. Tell her she was stupid. You deserve what you get, it'd say.

She couldn't face the bracelet. Not yet. When she was ready, she'd grind the damned thing into powder with the heel of her foot. Sweep it up. Dump it into the gutter drain in front of her house. The next rain would carry the remains to the Pataspco River. Eventually, the Chesapeake Bay would sparkle a little brighter.

For now, she'd pedal. Anywhere. Everywhere. It always made her feel better. She biked through Bolton Hill, Downtown, Inner Harbor, Fells Point, and Brewers Hill. It was time to take a breath. She discovered she was nowhere. The intersection was quiet. The streets were nearly vacant. The streetlights were few and far between. Where was she?

She heard drunken laughter. It was coming from down the street. She spotted three men, in their twenties, stumbling out of a corner bar. Now she knew where she was—Dundalk. She'd pedaled out of the city into Baltimore County. The bar was Poe's Poison.

Lucy'd never been inside the bar, but she thought about it occasionally—more out of curiosity than desire. Tonight, she could hear the bar speaking to her. It's okay to have only one drink, it said. You've been good, but you don't have to be perfect. A slip every once in a while won't hurt you. No one will know, but you. She walked her bike toward the Siren's call and stopped in front of Poe's entrance. The bar crooned its melody of seduction.

There was nothing Lucy desired more than a drink. A joint would do. Some blow would be even better. She hyperventilated at the thought of it.

She could go into Poe's. Get an Irish car bomb. She loved that drink. She hadn't touched one since the night she maimed Amber. Just one drink, then maybe a little weed. She could score that in Poe's, too. She'd pass a couple of drug corners on her way home. She could buy a half-gram of coke and snort it in the privacy of her kitchen. The corner boys would be happy to sell it to her. Hell, they'd even give it to her for free, knowing she'd be a repeat customer.

The craving was unbearable. She took her father's picture from inside her helmet. Held it against her heart. Prayed.

Daddy, don't let me fuck up.

Her left foot stepped onto the bike's left pedal. For some reason she couldn't push off. Her right foot was stuck to the sidewalk. No matter how hard she tried, she couldn't go forward. She began to cry. A man with thick, white hair stepped out of Poe's.

"Lucy?" he said. "Are you in trouble?"

She nodded, unable to speak.

"I'm Joseph. Call your sponsor. Right now."

She pulled out her cell phone.

Floater answered. "Where you at, Lucy?"

"Outside Poe's."

"I'll be there in five minutes. Don't move. Don't go in there."

Floater clicked off.

"Do I know you?" she said to Joseph.

"I saw you at the AA meeting last night. I was in the back."

She couldn't tell how old Joseph was. His hair was thick and wavy, but not completely white. There were a few strands of yellow mixed in with the white, like lemon-flavored salt-water taffy. It was the wrinkles that threw her. Deep, almost as if they were carved into his face. Souvenirs of a life lived fast and hard. She guessed he was younger than he looked.

"Follow me," he said.

Joseph walked her across the street to the corner diagonal from Poe's. He held onto the handlebars of her bike. "We'll wait here."

Lucy spotted Floater a block away, biking as if he were racing a freight train on its way to splatter her across the tracks. He slid-stopped his bike in front of her. Lucy hugged him. She turned to thank Joseph. He was gone. She pressed her father's picture against her cheek.

Then she told Floater everything.

Chapter 15

September 21

Now that Rick had Sanchez's cell phone number, he had to decide what to do with it. There were three choices: get a wiretap, give the number to the feds and the LA gang unit, or call it himself. One thing he wasn't going to do was involve Appoline Mercer. The last time he sought her advice, she ordered him to turn Lucy into an informant. He still hated himself for trying. He could've ended up like Sanchez—sporting two black eyes and a nose packed full of bloody gauze.

Rick knew all about Sanchez's injuries. Undercover officer Javier Rodriguez took Sanchez to Mercy Hospital's emergency room. Two hours later, Sanchez left with a pretty, blonde nurse coming off duty.

"How a guy with a broken nose and two black eyes can get a woody is beyond me," Javier said while giving Rick his report.

Rick decided to call Sanchez. Maybe a night of pain meds and nursing care had put him in the mood to talk. He dialed the number from his office landline.

"Yeah." The voice was gruff and nasal.

"This is Rick McCormick."

There was a moment's hesitation. In the background, he could hear the steady din of voices and activity. Was Sanchez in a bar?

"Do you know who I am?" Rick said.

"Of course. You're the gang unit chief of the State's Attorney's Office."

"Are you in a private place?"

"No, but I can get to one. Five minutes?"

Rick spent the next five minutes writing down talking points on a yellow pad. The phone rang.

"Mr. McCormick," the nasally voice said. "We've never spoken before, so we need to establish ground rules."

"Agreed."

"Most important, are we talking on or off the record?"

"Excuse me? Who am I talking to?"

"You called me, remember? This is Warren Hughes. *Baltimore Sun,* crime beat."

Rick felt the bile rise up his esophagus. Oh, fuck me.

"There's been an error here, Mr. Hughes."

Hughes sniggered. "I think you've been spun...who'd you mean to call?"

"Thanks for your time."

Rick almost threw his coffee cup at his office door, but thought the better of it. *Shit. I'm going to kill that girl.* What a total whack job. Assaults a gangster and spins an ASA—all within twelve hours. Who does that?

He had to get out of the office to cool down.

Rick sat on the steps of the Inner Harbor promenade, watching the crowd stroll in the bright sunshine. The Baltimore Harbor was bristling with paddleboats and water taxis. Seagulls danced overhead. It was a perfect September day—moderate temperatures and a sky as blue and clear as a sapphire. A tumultuous cold front crashed its way through Baltimore last night, taking with it the heat, haze, and humidity. Fall returned.

His phone rang, disrupting his peaceful moment. He answered with his usual cryptic greeting. "McCormick."

"Good morning. This is Romero Sanchez."

Rick snorted. "Whoever you are, tell Lucy to cut the crap."

The caller waited a beat. "Is our girl giving you a tough time?"

"Who's this?"

"I told you—Romero Sanchez. We've never had the pleasure of speaking. Perhaps you were expecting a man with a Latino accent. Unlike you, I was born in the United States. LA to be exact. You were born in South America. Adopted when you were a baby. Ironic, isn't it? I can be President of the United States, but you can't."

"You called me to discuss the U. S. Constitution? Let's talk about the Eighth Amendment. Is it cruel and unusual punishment for a murderer to live in solitary confinement for the rest of his life?"

"Good one, Mr. McCormick. May I call you Rick?"

"Why are you calling?"

"Lucy asked me to. For reasons I don't understand, Lucy has faith in me—she believes I didn't kill my wife. She pointed out to me she's in danger as long as Marcela's killer is at large. Lucy's one crazy bitch, but I don't want anything happening to her. She thinks if I tell you who killed Marcela, you'll act on it. I decided to test her faith in both of us. I'm calling to tell you who killed my wife."

Rick took a moment to calm himself.

"Who killed her, Romero?"

Fifteen silent seconds ticked by. Rick could hear deep breathing on the other end of the phone. Sanchez choked out the answer rather than said it.

"Luiz Alvarado."

"Why? Why did he kill her?"

"I fucked his wife. She lied, told him I raped her. Marcela was a revenge killing."

"I'm sorry for your loss." The expression of sympathy sounded lame, even to Rick's own ears.

"Are you really? Or are you thinking 'that gangbanger got what he deserved?'"

"No. Of course, not. No one deserves…"

"He should have killed me, instead."

"Tell me where he is," Rick said. "We'll get him."

"He's on the run. He knows I'm coming for him."

"You think he's in Baltimore?"

"His mother lives here, on Edmonston Avenue."

"What's her name?"

"Juanita Alvarado."

"Give me a description of Luiz."

"Five-eight, stocky build. Late twenties. Brown hair, brown eyes. Roach tats on neck, arms, hands. He's got one eyebrow. It's thick, dips down across the bridge of his nose. His street name is 'Sine Wave.'"

"How can I reach you?"

"You can't…question for you. Where'd Lucy learn to fight?"

Rick swallowed hard. There were only two people in CC's other than Sanchez—Javier and Lucy. If Rick knew about the fight, one of them must've told him. He had a split second to decide how much to reveal. It couldn't be too much or too little. Lives depended on it.

"What're you talking about?"

"A word to the wise, Rick. Don't make the lady mad." Sanchez dropped the pretense of civility. "Tell that lunatic I gave you Marcela's killer. And tell her to stay the fuck away from me. Next time, she might get hurt."

The phone clicked off.

Rick looked across the Inner Harbor, staring at nothing in particular. Suddenly, he gasped for air. He'd stopped breathing. His heart was still hammering, jaw still clenching.

A teenager jogged by. "Mister, you'd better get outta here."

The Inner Harbor was deserted. Clouds were blotting out the sun. Rick checked his cell phone for the time. How long had the call taken? He couldn't believe it was only noon. They'd spoken for less than ten minutes.

A cold wind blew through his hair. Thunder. Sheets of rain. Hail smacked him in the face as he ran to the Pratt Street Pavilion. Refugees from the storm packed the pavilion. Nervous laughter erupted with every thunderclap. Loud conversations. Deafening hail clacked against the glass walls. Rick was desperate to communicate the information he'd just received, but a phone call was impossible. He couldn't hear himself think, much less hear a voice on the phone. Rick sent a text message to Lundt.

"Assemble gang unit ASAP. Cola, Rodriguez too."

When Rick entered the conference room ten minutes later, the gang unit was already seated at the table. Lundt took one look at him and handed him the stack of paper napkins sitting by the coffee pot.

"Thanks." He mopped the water dripping down his face.

"What's going on?" Lundt said.

"A few minutes ago, I received a call from a tipster disclosing the identity of Marcela Sanchez's killer. During the conversation, the tipster led me to believe Javier's cover may have been compromised."

Glances were exchanged, but no words.

Campbell spoke first. "You think the tipster is credible?"

"It was Romero Sanchez."

The room erupted in collective disbelief.

Javier Rodriguez walked into the conference room, followed by Lieutenant Antonio Colafranceschi, both from the Violent Crimes Impact Section, Narcotics Unit. The lieutenant was a swarthy man with a blanket of black hair. He was nicknamed "Tony Cola" by a police academy instructor who could never get his name straight.

"Jesus!" Javier said. "I could hear the racket out in the reception room."

"It appears the investigations of our respective units have collided," Rick said. "Have a seat. Some of you may not have met."

Rick made the introductions. Afterward he detailed his conversation with Sanchez ending with, "There are two decisions to be made. The first, and most important, is whether Narcotics should pull Javier out of CC's. The second is whether we should pursue this tip about Alvarado. Do you agree, Lieutenant?"

Cola nodded.

"Question for you," Javier said. "What was it about the conversation that worries you? Maybe Sanchez only wants to know if getting his nose broken by a girl is public knowledge. If it's out there, he'd look bad. Hurt his status with Roach, make him look vulnerable."

Rick rubbed his forehead. "Maybe. I don't think so. You and Lucy were the only ones in the bar, correct?"

"Yeah, besides Sanchez."

"So if I knew about the fight, it'd mean one of you made the fight public, or told me specifically. Maybe he's trying to figure out if one of you betrayed him."

An eerie quiet settled over the group.

Marlow broke the silence. "Sanchez was fishing."

"Rick," Campbell said. "Do you think he caught you?"

"Honestly, I don't know. If it were anyone else, I'd say 'no.' We can't forget his AKA is 'Trojan.' He's gifted at deception, that's how he makes his living with Roach. In view of that, I can't be sure."

"You're overlooking another scenario," Lundt said. "Lucy could be Sanchez's informant. That fight could've been staged to flush Javier out."

Javier guffawed. "There was no way that fight was staged."

"Listen to me," Lundt said. She leaned on her elbows into the table. "Let's say Sanchez is suspicious of Javier. He and Lucy stage a fight. If someone outside the bar knows about it, they'd know it came from Javier." She looked directly at Javier. "We can't dismiss the possibility she's involved—just because she's pretty."

Javier threw his pen against the table. Rick caught it one-handed on the bounce.

"The girl's problematic, no doubt about it, but she's no gangster," Marlow said.

Lundt groaned. "She's got you fooled, too."

"We can't assume she's a criminal just because she's pretty," Marlow said.

Lundt shifted in her chair. "She's an addict with a slew of juvenile involvements."

"None of this is relevant," Cola said. "The decision to pull Javier out of CC's has already been made. Overtaken by events. Late last night, a call came in on the Crime Stoppers Hotline. The tipster said that Javier had been made." Cola turned to Javier. "I'm pulling you out."

Javier protested, but Cola stopped him with a slight flicker of his hand.

"Who called?" Lundt said. "Lucy Prestipino?"

"Ms. Lundt," Cola said with flashing eyes. "We don't know who called. It's an anonymous line."

"It must have been her," Lundt said. "We can subpoena—"

"Speculation can get a person killed," Cola said. "Keep your trap shut."

"Lieutenant," Lundt said. "I—"

Cola stood up, cutting her off. He shook Rick's hand. "Our business here is done. Good instincts, Rick."

Cola and Javier left. The gang unit stayed. Lundt glowered in her seat, huffing. Rick ignored her.

"Question," Rick said to Campbell and Marlow. "Do we pursue Alvarado? Sanchez's call could've been a pretense to fish about Javier. Do we want to risk wasting time and resources hunting down Alvarado?"

"Absolutely," Campbell said. "If for no other reason than to cover our asses. What would happen if we ignored his tip, and it turned out Alvarado murdered Marcela Sanchez?"

"Go find him, bring him in," Rick said. "Keep in close touch...and be careful."

As they moved to leave, Rick said, "Sylvia...hang back a second."

"What do you need?" she said.

"At the Coopersmith trial, I couldn't help but notice you have a decent relationship with Lucy. I need to tell her what Sanchez said. Can you come with me? Lucy and I are like oil and water."

Detective Marlow punched Lucy's number into her cell phone. "Mr. McCormick and I are coming to see you, hon."

Rick waited at his office until eight o'clock. There'd been no word about the hunt for Alvarado. There were plenty of words from Marlow, none of which concerned Alvarado. She'd ripped him a new one after learning Rick pressured Lucy to be a confidential informant. As he walked home, Marlow's words burned in his ears.

Lucy's proven she's a friend to law enforcement. We owe her. Instead of giving her protection, you took a vulnerable kid and tried to manipulate her into snitching against a vicious gang member. Were you trying to get her killed? If anything happens to her, it's on you, McCormick.

Then there was Lucy. "Romero always looked out for me," she said during their meeting. "He cares about me. You? You asked me to snitch on a shot caller who could *green-light* me. You're a despicable person, Rick, one of the worst I've ever met."

He pulled his dinner from the microwave and was about to eat when Javier called.

"I heard I blew my own cover. Is it true?"

"Probably. Marlow and I met with Lucy today. When we asked her what happened inside CC's, she mentioned you addressed her as "Lucy." She said Romero always kept her name out of things. If Romero didn't tell you her name, he knew you got it from somebody else. He probably put two and two together."

There was a long pause. "Oh, fuck me."

After eating, Rick fell into a restless sleep, awaking throughout the night to the sound of his grinding teeth. At five, he bolted upright, sweating. Maybe Romero's question to him wasn't about Javier, at all. Maybe he'd been fishing about Lucy, testing her loyalty. And she'd betrayed him with her call to Crime Stoppers.

Chapter 16

September 22

Rick's jaws ached, and his head throbbed. Shake it off, he told himself. A cold shower and fifty pushups cleared his head. He grabbed an espresso from Café No Delay and arrived at the office at seven. At eight, Marlow called.

"I have a status."

In a cool voice, she reported she'd found the home of Mrs. Alvarado. She knocked on the door, but no one answered. There were no signs of activity. No mail, no paper, no visitors, no Mrs. Alvarado. Patrol was keeping an eye on the house.

"Right now I'm canvassing the neighborhood. Maybe the neighbors know something."

"Keep me posted…uh, Sylvia?

"Still here."

"Thanks for setting me straight yesterday."

"You're welcome." Marlow paused a beat. "I have a bad feeling about this, Rick."

Her words shook him. They confirmed his worries had a basis, not drummed up by a fitful night's sleep. "Be careful, Sylvia."

He spent the next two hours addressing pleadings filed by defense attorneys in pending prosecutions. Motions to dismiss, motions to suppress evidence, discovery requests. All routine. All boring.

Marlow called with an update. Two weeks ago, Mrs. Alvarado fell inside her home and left by ambulance. The neighbors didn't know where she was. Marlow was waiting for transport information from the 9-1-1 Emergency Communications Center.

Campbell called an hour later. Mrs. Alvarado was at Bon Secours Hospital recovering from hip surgery. She had no visitors, but occasional telephone calls. When he visited Mrs. Alvarado, she was fearful and uncooperative. Campbell requested hospital staff to notify him if anyone came to see her.

"Luiz knows we're lookin' for him," the detective said. "He's probably on the wing by now."

It was nearly noon. There was no further word about Alvarado. Rick wondered how Lucy was holding up. During their meeting, Marlow did her best to convince Lucy to leave town.

"Do it for your mother, if not for yourself. If something happened to you, she'd be alone. I've seen the effect of murder on the surviving family. They never get over it. You know that yourself—you saw what happened to Romero. He lost his mind with grief. Spare your mother. She stuck with you during your worst moments. You owe her, Lucy. Start paying the debt. Stay out of Baltimore."

"Running away is not what I do," Lucy said. "I'll stay with my friend, Floater."

Rick's stomach told him it was lunchtime. He stood at the corner of Lombard and Saratoga, waiting in line outside a food truck, thinking about the steak and cheese sub he was about to order. The phone rang. It was Sanchez.

"Do you have him?" Sanchez said.

"No. Help us. Give us more to work with."

Sanchez disconnected.

"Fuck." Rick walked away from the food truck, empty-handed.

He watched the clock in his office. It was three thirty. Nothing new on Alvarado. He reviewed a stack of police reports and witness statements as he prepared for an upcoming three-day trial.

Campbell called. "We've got trouble."

"What is it?"

"Our CI's are telling us Sanchez put a $50,000 bounty on Alvarado. Weird thing is, the call went out to Roach's rivals—Crips, Bloods, Dead Man, Inc.—but not Roach. All the district stations have been alerted. Baltimore City is being torn apart by bounty hunters looking for Alvarado."

"Sanchez green-lighted the guy."

"Worse," Campbell said. "Terms of payment are delivery of Alvarado alive."

"He wants to kill Alvarado himself. Any intel on the site of delivery?"

"Not yet."

"We'd better have a warrant ready to go if Alvarado turns up dead," Rick said.

Rick's headache was back. What if Lundt was right? The whole city—gangs and law enforcement alike—was hunting Luiz Alvarado based solely on the words of Lucy Prestipino and Romero Sanchez. What if Lucy was a player in an elaborate scam to clear Sanchez by extracting a false confession from Alvarado?

Four o'clock. Campbell called. Mrs. Alvarado would be moved in the early evening to a rehabilitation center, which center yet undetermined. The hospital lobby was filled with Crips, all waiting for Alvarado to show up. Uniforms were on the way to clear the gangsters from the lobby.

Rick looked up from his desk when the office door swung open. There'd been no knock.

"What the hell are you doing, McCormick?" said Mercer. She was standing in his doorway, hands on hips. Her green suit clashed with the angry red blotch covering her forehead.

Mercer interrupted Rick's summary with a hand held up stop-sign style.

"I know the chronology. I want to know one specific thing. What's the basis for your belief Luiz Alvarado murdered Marcela Sanchez?" Mercer was using the voice of a parent dealing with a recalcitrant teenager. "Tell me it didn't originate with Lucy Prestipino."

"I can't tell you that."

"I knew it!" Mercer sat down in the chair facing Rick. She crossed her arms in front of her chest. "You'd better have something more to justify the cost and danger to our community and our law enforcement officers."

He showed her the autopsy report for Marcela Sanchez, pointing out the dead woman had heterochromia and was a ringer for Lucy Prestipino.

He described his conversations with Sanchez. Mercer frowned and shook her head with irritation.

"You're getting played. Don't you see—?"

Rick's office phone buzzed. The receptionist said, "I'm sorry to interrupt—I thought you should know. Attorney Stonegate from the Public Defender's Office is on the line. He's calling about Luiz Alvarado."

"May I take this?" Rick said.

"Keep it on speakerphone. I want to hear what Stonegate has to say."

"Hello, Alex. You're on speakerphone. Mrs. Mercer is here."

"Good afternoon to you both. I understand the police are looking for Luiz Alvarado for the murder of Marcela Sanchez. He's with me at the PD's Office. Mr. Alvarado wishes to turn himself in. Before doing so, he wants a plea agreement. Maryland doesn't have jurisdiction over the crime since it occurred in California. I'm calling for the name and contact information of the person in the LA District Attorney's Office who has the authority to negotiate an agreement. One of Mr. Alvarado's demands is protection, beginning the moment he steps out of the PD's office. Your office will have to be involved in that part of the agreement."

Mercer's eyes enlarged with every syllable she heard.

"What's prompted this?" Rick said.

"He knows about Sanchez's bounty. He believes that if Sanchez gets ahold of him, he'd be tortured. He's terrified."

Rick could feel the hair rise on his neck and arms, not so much for Alvarado, but for Lucy.

Mercer leaned toward the phone. "How do we know that Alvarado's confession will be reliable? He may give a false confession simply to get protection from Sanchez."

"Assuming an acceptable agreement can be negotiated, my client will provide corroborating evidence, including the location of the weapon. He believes that a forensic examination of the weapon will provide DNA corroboration."

Mercer looked at Rick and mouthed, "Get it done." She left the office, shutting the door behind her. Rick turned off the speakerphone.

"Mercer's no longer on the call." Rick exhaled his relief. "Hey, man, good to hear from you." He gave Alex the number for Los Angeles ADA Jill Sanders. "Set something up with Sanders. I'll come to your office, and we can Skype the negotiation. Once we've put this baby to bed, I'll buy you a beer."

Five hours later, Alvarado was incarcerated in a holding cell in the Central District Police Station, awaiting transport to Los Angeles by the LAPD. Rick and Alex sat in a bar in Fells Point, awaiting their third round of beer. Empty peanut shells dotted the floor by their feet.

"I don't mind telling you," Rick said. "I don't think I was ever happier to hear your voice than I was this afternoon. That whole bounty thing had me spooked." Rick toasted his friend. "Alex, may you live to be one hundred years, with an extra year to repent. *Sláinte!*" They clanked their mugs together.

Rick's phone sounded.

"Congratulations," Sanchez said. "You got my wife's killer."

"Despite your sick bounty," Rick said.

"Because of it. You asked for my help. I gave it to you. That bounty scared the little rat-bastard right into your arms."

"You hunted him for six months. Why didn't you issue a bounty earlier?"

"I wanted to kill him myself. A bounty would've left a trail to me. Then circumstances changed. I wanted him off the street."

"The circumstances being Lu—"

"Nice doing business with you, homie." Sanchez disconnected.

Rick spit out the word *homie* under his breath.

Alex took a few gulps and put his mug on the bar. "I recently heard a story about Sanchez. An eyewitness account. I won't say who told it to me because of the attorney-client privilege. Understood?"

Rick nodded.

"It happened about ten years ago. Sanchez was ordered by his clique's shot caller to find a rival gang's *primera palabra.* He used a tactic so savage it shocked the members of his own clique. When all was said and done, three people ended up dead, including an infant."

"Why are you telling me this?"

"Sanchez is one vile sicko. Watch your back, buddy. We go back a long time. I don't want to lose you."

Rick drained his mug and swept a handful of spent peanut shells onto the floor. The conversation with Sanchez replayed in his mind. The vile sicko called him *homie*.

A text message dinged on his phone. It was from Lucy.

"Just read *Sun* online," the message said. "Is it over?"

"It's hit the paper," Rick said to Alex. "It'll probably be in tomorrow's print edition."

The men clanked their mugs again.

"Excuse me," Rick said. "I need to answer a text message."

"Lucy," he wrote. "It's over. Your world is safe again."

Part Two

Chapter 17

September 29

Lucy kept to herself after Alvarado's arrest. She spent her days working and attending AA meetings. Volunteering at Loaves & Fishes was out, at least for a while. The people there needed food and fellowship—not some mope who felt sorry for herself. She distracted herself with home improvement projects, but the little nagging voice inside her head wouldn't leave her alone.

Getting involved with Romero was a mistake. A whopper. She needed time to think about it. Understand it. Learn from it. There were an infinite number of mistakes a person could make in a lifetime. No sense making the same ones over and over. The introspection made her gloomy.

She was about to hammer the Tiffany bracelet into powder when her mother called.

"I've had a brain storm," Debbie said. "Let's go to Deep Creek Lake. It'll be my treat. We'll have a long girls' weekend."

Lucy would've surfed the cellular radio waves to hug her mother if physics allowed it. She loved the resort, a 3900-acre man-made lake nestled in the Allegheny Mountains of Garrett County, Maryland. Deep Creek was only a few miles from the Mountain Lake Renewal Center, where she'd spent six months in rehab. Part of the curriculum was learning to sail, fish, and waterski.

"Yes! Yes!"

They decided to go on October sixteenth.

Mom always knows what to do. Her sadness lifted. She took an early afternoon bike ride, just for the fun of it. The cloudless sky was azure blue and filled with squawking seagulls. The sun sparkled on the Inner Harbor. Lucy decided enough was enough. Time to move on. She was free to do whatever she wanted. What she wanted was to volunteer at Loaves & Fishes. She called Sister Donna, the director, and asked to be scheduled as the dinner cook.

Lucy tasted the chicken corn chowder. The soup kitchen's recipes were pretty good, but not good enough for her. She always brought her own stash of spices and snuck them into the recipes.

"We missed you," Sister Donna said. "And bless you for sending me such a fine volunteer."

"Huh?"

The nun pointed to the server placing dishes on the long tables. It was Rick McCormick, wearing an apron. Lucy muttered a string of curses under her breath.

— ▲ —

Rick took a short dinner break. The chowder was the best he'd ever tasted. An elderly man sitting beside him said, "Tastes good, don't it? That's 'cause Lucy's in the kitchen."

She's finally here. He silently rehearsed what he'd say to her—something along the lines of gratitude for her assistance in obtaining justice for Marcela Sanchez. If she wanted to punch him in the nose, he wouldn't defend himself. She could wale away on him all she wanted.

Lucy was scrubbing a pot when Rick entered the kitchen.

"This is my turf," she said, glaring. "I want you gone."

"You're the one who suggested that I volunteer here, remember? So, Ms. Prestipino, I'm here at your behest. I'm staying."

"Then you can clean up."

Lucy snapped off her rubber gloves and left the kitchen.

Two hours passed without a word between them. Lucy returned to the kitchen and gathered her belongings.

"You leaving?" he said.

"Going to a meeting."

Rick followed her out the front door.

"May I walk with you?" The door shut behind him. "A peace-keeping gesture?"

"You need something warmer than that apron, knucklehead."

Rick retrieved his sweatshirt and returned, feeling hopeful. He offered his arm for her to take. She slid her hand through the crook of his elbow and rested it on his forearm, so lightly he could hardly feel it.

They walked together in silence until Rick saw a small crowd mingling in front of a red brick building a half-block away. A distinguished-looking man with white hair greeted Lucy by name.

"Hello, Joseph," she said.

Lucy turned to Rick. "Here's my stop. See you next time."

October 14

It was Thursday—Lucy's favorite day of the week. She loved the lattes at Café No Delay, but they were wicked expensive. The foamy coffees were her once-a-week indulgence. God bless grocery store coupons. She set aside the food money she saved to fund her latte craving.

On Thursday mornings, she could practically smell the treat the moment she opened her eyes. Yummy. She waited until the afternoon to buy her latte. Anticipation made the pleasure that much sweeter. Romero'd said that about sex, way back when.

She got over Romero faster than she expected. Rick's interest in her helped. They met every week at Loaves & Fishes. Afterward, they walked together to her AA meeting. He held her hand. She wasn't interested in more—this time she'd take it slow. Rick was a gentleman, and he wasn't pushing. She couldn't wait to introduce him to her mother. For once, her mother would approve of someone she was seeing.

The ordering line in Café No Delay spilled onto the sidewalk. It was unseasonably chilly. Customers stamped their feet and rubbed their hands together. Lucy ignored the cold by focusing on her latte. Her mouth watered with every step she advanced toward the barista bar. Five minutes passed before she was inside the door.

She spotted Rick sitting at a table. His back was toward her, and he was chatting with an exotic young woman. Lucy stole glances at the beauty. She was lithe, with fine facial features. Her hair was thick and black. Long eyelashes framed her soft brown eyes. Lucy guessed she was from India. Who was she? Maybe a witness. Another lawyer?

Lucy put on her helmet. She turned her back to the woman and watched her in the helmet's mirror. When the woman spoke, her hands fluttered, and her eyes danced. Lucy could hear Rick laugh. The woman affectionately touched his hand. A girlfriend. Shit.

She was now standing in front of the cashier.

"Hey, Lucy," the cashier said, "Your usual?"

"Yeah, thanks...and a *City Paper*."

She glanced at the couple again. Rick seemed smaller, like he was shrinking himself. His body was no longer relaxed. He radiated discomfort.

That asshole knows I'm here. He's trying to hide.

Lucy tried to skim the paper while she waited for the latte, but all she could see was Ms. Beauty smiling at Rick. That's it, no more hiding. She rolled up the paper, walked over to the table, and bopped Rick on the head with it.

"Hi, Rick." Lucy took off her helmet. Her hair crackled with static electricity.

He turned around and acted surprised. The woman stared at her with apparent fascination.

"Hey," he said.

An awkward silence ensued. The woman interrupted the quiet by extending her hand across the table to Lucy. "I'm Colleen, Rick's sister. Glad to meet you."

Sister? Lucy had an epiphany—siblings from different parts of the world. They'd been adopted.

"Of course! I should've guessed. You look exactly alike."

Colleen laughed so hard she snorted.

"Lucy Prestipino." She shook Colleen's hand. "I'd love to chat, but I've got a delivery. Nice meeting you."

Lucy wasn't cold anymore. The more she pedaled, the hotter she got—more from anger than physical exertion. With every downward push on the pedal, she hurled a curse at Rick.

She needed to sit in a quiet place, drink her latte, and figure out what just happened. Fuck! She forgot her latte. Now she was totally pissed off. She'd have to wait until next Thursday for another one.

Ground Zero was deserted of messengers. She parked her bike and hoisted herself on the granite wall. As she sat motionless, the cold air collided with her sweat, and she shivered. Why didn't he introduce her to his sister? There could be a lot of reasons, but it came down to only one. He didn't want to. He knew she was in the coffee shop before she'd ever said anything. It made her sick to think he was pretending not to see her.

One rebellious brain cell told her she shouldn't criticize him—after all, she'd done the same thing to Romero. She'd never introduced him to her mother or any of her friends. Why spend all the energy explaining a relationship that wasn't going anywhere?

The idea that she was on the receiving end was depressing. She liked Rick—in fact, she viewed him as a *potential.* Smart, hard-working, ambitious. She had a secret she'd never told a soul; she wanted to be a stay-at-home wife and mother. Lucy grew up with a mother who was never home. No judgments or complaints—her mother did a great job under terrible circumstances. It wasn't the life Lucy wanted.

Her phone sounded the melody of "Mamma Mia."

"Hey, Mom."

"What's wrong?"

Lucy let out a mournful sigh. How did her mother always know?

"I've known this guy a while and kinda like him. I bumped into him at Café No Delay. He was talking to a girl. At first, it was a little awkward—I thought maybe he was seeing her, but I said hello anyway. Then the girl introduces herself—she turns out to be his sister. He didn't introduce us."

"How long have you known him?"

"Since June."

"You've known this guy for four months, and he didn't introduce you to his sister?"

Lucy could hear the familiar inhaling and exhaling of cigarette smoke.

"Get away from that prick this second. Nothing I hate more than a man who mistreats a woman—lowest form of scum on this Earth. Just get away and don't look back, you hear me? A man like that—"

"Mom! Stop! All he did was not introduce me to his sister."

"Oh…I guess I got carried away."

"I guess so. Why'd you call me?"

Lucy heard another round of cigarette smoke consumption.

"I wanted to hear your voice, that's all."

"That's silly, Mom. You're gonna hear it all weekend. What time are you picking me up Saturday?"

"Sweetie, don't waste any energy on Mr. No-Manners. One day, you'll meet someone who'll appreciate how smart, beautiful, and talented you are. He'll jump over tables to be with you. You'll see."

After they disconnected, Lucy considered the conversation. Mom sure knows how to give a pep talk. Crap! Debbie didn't tell her what time they were leaving for Deep Creek.

I'll talk to her tomorrow.

Chapter 19

October 15

Maybe today was the day Lucy would finally pedal a century—one hundred miles in a single day. At least that's what she hoped when she saw the morning's rush hour traffic.

It was raining, but only enough to mix the fallen leaves and city grit into a concoction that slicked up the roads. She biked past a fender bender on West Conway Street, the main road into Baltimore from I-95. The resulting traffic jam cascaded throughout the city. There was total gridlock.

This was good news for Lucy. The heavier the traffic, the more calls she got. No matter what the day or circumstances, documents needed to get from here to there. Messengers could zip around the city, even when cars were jammed like logs in a stagnant river.

It was seven thirty in the morning. Lucy was at Ground Zero bracing for the tsunami of calls about to sweep her away. Thirty more minutes, tops.

She called her mother. They were heading to Deep Creek tomorrow and hadn't yet worked out the logistics. Lucy left a voice message. Even though her mother wasn't keen on texting, Lucy sent a text anyway. The phone rang. She lurched for it, but the caller wasn't her mother.

"Lucy—George, from Capital Title. Can you get some settlement docs over to Sheehan & Swann within thirty minutes?"

Here we go.

The calls were relentless. It was two o'clock, and Lucy had already pedaled seventy miles. She took advantage of the momentary lull to call her mother. No answer. A lump grew in the back of her throat. A worrywart, her mother called it. Lucy sent another text and left another message.

Thirty minutes passed. No response. Lucy called Home Warehouse and spoke to Debbie's boss.

"Have you seen my mother today? I haven't been able to catch up with her."

"No, I haven't. She took the day off, said she had lots to do. Aren't you girls going to Deep Creek tomorrow?"

"Uh-huh. If you see her, will you tell her to call me?"

He promised to do so. Lucy disconnected and resumed her fretting.

By three thirty, the worrywart had grown so large she could feel it in her mouth. She called it a day, short of her century by ten miles, and biked to her mother's home.

Lucy found Debbie's car in the driveway. She didn't know whether to be aggravated or relieved. She swore to herself that if her mother didn't have a decent reason for being *incommunicado*, she'd find a cigarette and puff on it, right in front of her.

Steppie didn't yap when Lucy knocked on the front door. She walked around the outside of the house to see if her mother was in the backyard. No Debbie. She looked in the windows of Debbie's car. No clues.

Her mother kept a spare house key hidden in the front garden. Lucy retrieved the key and unlocked the front door.

"Mom? Mom?" she shouted from the foyer.

No answer.

Lucy went upstairs and continued hunting for her mother. Nothing out of the ordinary, other than Debbie's unmade bed. Her father's picture lay in the rumpled blanket.

"Daddy, what should I do?" Lucy said to the picture.

Should she wait, hoping her mother would show up? No point calling Debbie's cell again—she'd left at least six messages. Call the police? They'd ask how long she'd been missing. It'd only been seven hours. They wouldn't do anything.

Maybe Debbie was walking Steppie. So why doesn't she answer her phone? Maybe it was broken. Maybe she was in a cell hole. Maybe this, maybe that. The worrywart had metastasized into Lucy's brain.

She remembered that her mother usually walked Steppie in Patterson Park. It took her less than two minutes to pedal to the park. Yellow police tape was strung across the Eastern Avenue entrance. She biked to the next entrance, and the next one. Yellow tape closed all the entrances. Patterson Park looked like a birthday present tied up with bright, festive ribbon.

Three police cars and a crime lab van lined Eastern Avenue. Pedestrians talked to one other, nodding their heads and pointing at the park. Five police officers crawled on hands and knees searching the grass on each side of the path leading to the boat lake, a tiny pond inside the park.

Lucy lifted the yellow tape and ducked under. She wouldn't be thwarted by two-inch tape.

"You're not allowed in here," said a baby-faced man with pink cheeks. "This is a crime scene."

"I need help, please help me. I don't know what to do."

"What do you need help with?"

"I can't find my mother." She could only gasp out the words because of the worrywart obstructing her air pipe.

"There's no one in the park now. Only police investigators."

"Could you ask them if they've seen her? She walks her dog here every day. Maybe they saw her."

The baby-faced man gave her a concerned look.

"What does she look like?"

"She's pretty, five-five, about a hundred and twenty pounds. She has dark hair, brown eyes."

"What's your name, Miss?"

"Lucy Prestipino. My mother is Debbie Prestipino. Who are you?"

"I'm a police recruit, Roger McMann. I'll go ask around, find out if anyone's seen her. You stay right here until I come back."

She watched the recruit jog up the path. He stopped when he reached four people, two men and two women, all wearing business suits. They were talking to each other. Now they were talking to the recruit. Lucy couldn't make out their facial features, but she recognized their physiques. The women were Sylvia Marlow and Penelope Lundt. One of the men was Rick McCormick. She didn't recognize the second man.

They kept looking her way as the recruit spoke. When he stopped talking, the group walked toward her, leaving the recruit behind.

"Hello, Lucy," Rick said.

"Hi." She didn't recognize her own voice.

She exchanged greetings with Marlow and Lundt. Rick introduced her to Detective Ulysses Campbell.

"I understand you can't find your mother," Rick said.

She nodded.

Marlow moved closer to Lucy until she was standing beside her. "Why were you looking in Patterson Park?"

"She walks her dog here. She's always walking that dog. He's spoiled rotten. I'll bet she walks him more than she ever walked me in a stroller." Lucy chuckled at her own joke.

"What's her dog look like?" Campbell said.

"He's little. White, curly hair. He's a bichon. Barks a lot."

"That sounds like the dog that was shot!" Lundt said.

"Lundt!" Rick said, his eyes glinting anger.

Marlow put an arm around Lucy's waist.

Suddenly, Lucy was back on East Lexington Street, lying in the middle of the road, believing she was underwater. Marlow and Rick were talking to her, but she couldn't understand them. Mouths moving, eyes staring. She was looking at the sky. There was a seagull soaring. Was it the same seagull she saw right before she crashed into Romero?

Something soft touched the tip of her nose. A butterfly.

An acrid smell sent a jolt through her body.

Lucy sat upright on the sidewalk parallel to Eastern Avenue. Marlow was kneeling beside her, holding smelling salts. Rick was kneeling on the other side of her, his hand on hers. Lundt was nowhere in sight.

"Oh, geez," Lucy said. "What happened?"

"You fainted," Marlow said. "How're you feeling?"

"Embarrassed. I've never fainted in my life." Her face was hot.

An officer came over and handed Rick a bottle of orange juice. He gave it to Lucy.

She sipped on the juice. "So what are you all doing here?" Her voice was chipper, as though she'd bumped into them on the boardwalk in Ocean City.

Rick squeezed her hand. "We're investigating a homicide."

"That's terrible! I didn't think that happened in Patterson Park anymore."

She saw Rick swallow air. "It happened early this morning. The victim was a woman. She was walking her dog, a little dog. White."

Lucy watched the bottle of orange juice shake in her hand. The juice spilled out right before she dropped it into her lap. Her knees were trembling. There must be an earthquake going on.

"We need to get away from these trees!" she said. "There's an earthquake!"

Rick squeezed her hand tighter. "There's no earthquake."

"Put your head between your knees," Marlow said.

That's stupid! It won't stop an earthquake.

Lucy did as she was told, just because Marlow told her to.

After two minutes, she picked up her head. "I'm better now."

"I'm going to ask you to do something that'll be very hard," Rick said. "The woman who died didn't have any identification on her. We don't know who she is. I want you to look at a photograph taken by the Medical Examiner's Office. Can you do that?"

Lucy nodded.

"We're waiting on the photo," Marlow said to Rick. "The ME said ten more minutes."

"Lucy and I will wait in my car. Bring it over when you get it."

"She's not my mother," Lucy said. "You'll see."

Chapter 20

October 15

Lucy gazed at the rush hour traffic through the windshield of Rick's car. She'd been to the ME's office a couple of times on courier runs. Once, while she was waiting for a package, she had a long talk with the receptionist. She learned the Office of the Medical Examiner performed autopsies on all suspicious deaths that happened in Maryland. One day, her courier business would cover all of Maryland, mountain-to-shore service—like the OME. She made a mental note to write an ad that excluded the delivery of dead bodies.

There was no trace of the rain that wreaked havoc earlier that morning. The sun was straight ahead, on its downward trajectory. In a few minutes, it would disappear behind Baltimore's skyline, but now it shined directly into Lucy's eyes. She swung down the visor, wishing she had her sunglasses.

"It turned out to be a pretty day, didn't it?" she said.

"Yes, it did," Rick said.

"Why were you in Patterson Park?"

She saw him take a deep breath.

"We got a call from the Southeast Police District that a woman's body was found there. We came to help with the investigation."

"Why you? You're not police."

"Prosecutors and police work together, especially on homicide cases." He looked straight ahead, avoiding eye contact.

Why wasn't Rick telling the whole truth? Of course, the police work with prosecutors—but there are a lot of Baltimore City prosecutors. Why Rick? She decided not to press him further. He was upset. She'd give him assurances.

"The woman who was killed wasn't my mother, you know. No one would kill her. She's a regular person. A mother. She has a house, a dog, a job. Did I ever tell you that she's the assistant store manager of Home Warehouse? Everyone likes her, she's wonderful with customers. She's not dead. You have the wrong person. We work on my house together. She's a talented drywaller. Even Romero thinks so."

Lucy glanced over at Rick. He was staring at her. "What's wrong?"

Rick turned off his stare. "When was the last time you spoke to Romero?"

"Not since that time in Compression Connection."

"Has he ever met your mother?"

"No, but I told him about her. He thinks she's brave." She grinned. "Probably because I give her such a hard time."

"Does Romero know where your mother lives?"

"He knows she lives in Highlandtown."

"Does he know about the dog?"

"Oh, sure. He always laughed when I told him Steppie stories."

Rick rubbed his fingers through his hair.

"Why are you asking so many questions about Romero?"

She noticed Rick's eyes were wet. Before he answered, Marlow approached the car carrying an iPad. The worrywart grew larger. It tasted like a meatball made out of stomach acid. Marlow slipped into the back seat.

"Are you ready?" Marlow said in a voice that was creamy and comforting, like mashed potatoes covered with gravy. Marlow passed the iPad to Rick. He opened it and positioned the screen for Lucy to see.

The photograph showed only the woman's face. The hair was matted, but the face was clean. Her eyes were closed. The mouth was peculiar—puffy and dark, sunk-in like the front teeth were gone. The left side of the woman's face was purple. It hardly had a shape.

Lucy heard heavy, erratic breathing inside the car. The breathing gave way to eerie moans. The moans weren't human sounds, and they frightened her. She spun around looking for the source of the sounds, but saw only Rick and Marlow. She tried to speak, but didn't have the saliva needed to formulate words.

The frightening sounds were coming from her. The worrywart was trying to scream. It could only moan through her dry mouth. Marlow handed her a bottle of water. She guzzled it down. The worrywart made high-pitched squeaking noises. Lucy didn't know if she was hearing them through her ears or from inside her head.

Rick's arm was around her shoulders, squeezing. He was saying something. So was Marlow in her mashed potato and gravy voice. Lucy couldn't hear them—the worrywart was drowning out their words.

"Shut up! Shut up! Shut up!" Lucy screamed at the worrywart, covering her ears with her hands.

There was silence.

She heard her mother's voice. *Think, don't cry.* Debbie always said that.

"Lucy," Rick whispered.

"Shhh...Mom's talking to me."

His arm squeezed her tighter.

Cry later. Now you have to take care of business.

"Rick," she said. "What do you want me to do?"

"Can you talk to the police investigators?"

A strong, clear voice replaced the moans. "Yes."

Chapter 21

October 15

Rick grasped Lucy's hand as they entered Police Headquarters. Debbie Prestipino, her mother and only living relative, was dead; killed by an act of skull-crushing brutality. Lucy's world had been crushed along with her mother's skull.

It was plain to Rick that Lucy hadn't connected her mother's killing with the presence of the gang unit at the crime scene. How would she react when she did? He remembered the reports in her juvenile prosecution files. After nearly killing her best friend, Lucy alleviated her guilt by medicating herself into addiction. Her mother saved her from self-destruction. Now her mother was dead. Would Lucy blame herself? There were plenty of people who would—some in his own office.

When they walked into interview room one, he saw the interrogation room through Lucy's eyes. The walls, floor, table, and chair were variations of beige, like the monochromatic colors on a paint store color strip. Even the box of tissues on the table was beige. The room smelled stale and institutional. Rick got her settled and brought her a cup of coffee.

"I'll be back in a few minutes," he said.

Rick found Detective Campbell in the homicide office studying photographs on his cell phone.

"Can you give me a run down?" Rick said.

"Sylvia's still at the crime scene. The techs are taking footprint impressions. Recruits are looking for shell casings. There was no house key found. I need to ask Lucy about that. If she can't account for it, we'll get a warrant and search Mrs. Prestipino's house—in case the perp took the key and used it to enter her house. Uniforms have secured the house pending my interview with Lucy. The blood found in the dog's mouth is being processed for DNA. So is the bandana. The stupid fuck left a bandana behind. Blue and black."

"Roach colors," Rick said. "A gang initiation?"

"Maybe. We'll see where the evidence takes us."

"What about Romero Sanchez?"

Campbell looked puzzled.

"Lucy talked about Sanchez while we were waiting for the OME photo. He knew quite a bit about her mother. Where she lived. Worked. The dog." He filled Campbell in on the conversation.

"This isn't his style." Campbell slowly shook his head. "I can't see him killing an ex-girlfriend's mother, no matter how bad the breakup."

"Remember the Crime Stoppers call? Sanchez might've guessed it was Lucy, just like we did. She was his girlfriend. Sanchez would've expected her to tell him if she thought there was an undercover at CC's. Instead, she called Crime Stoppers. She betrayed him. He punished her in return. Nothing would hurt Lucy more than the murder of her mother. He knows that."

"You think Sanchez green-lighted Mrs. Prestipino?"

"I wouldn't rule it out. Why else would there be gang colors left at the scene? You're right—only an idiot would do that. Roach assassins don't leave calling cards. That bandana was a message for Lucy and anyone else thinking about interfering with Roach's business."

Campbell leaned back in his chair. After a few minutes, he stood. "Let's walk and talk."

The men walked toward the interview room, but Campbell wasn't talking. He seemed preoccupied. When they reached the door, he turned toward Rick. "I'll ask her about the call."

Rick headed for the technical services department. He wanted to watch Lucy's interview through the closed circuit television. He took a seat in front of a row of television screens. The camera in the interview room was focused on Lucy.

Lucy sipped her coffee. It tasted scorched and smelled even worse. She held the cup of coffee for its warmth. She'd never experienced this bone-chilling cold before.

"I'm very sorry for your loss," Campbell said. "May I call you 'Lucy'?" She nodded.

He retrieved a small spiral notebook, with an attached pen, from the inside pocket of his suit jacket. He opened his mouth to ask a question, only to be interrupted.

"Detective Campbell, what happened to my mother?"

"We're still piecing it together. We believe she was walking her dog when she was accosted. The ME on the scene said your mother probably died from head trauma. That's all I can tell you for now."

She pressed the cup of coffee to her cheek. "I'm ready."

"There was no house key found at the scene. Do you know why?"

"My mother never carries a key when she walks her dog. She's afraid she'll drop it. She has this stone turtle in the front of her house, a hide-a-key thing. She puts the key in there. That's how I got into the house."

Lucy pulled a key from her hip pocket. "Here it is."

"That answers that. When you went inside the house, did you find anything unusual?"

"Her bed wasn't made. She's a neatnick."

"Anything else?"

"No."

He flipped through his notebook. "Did your mother carry a cell phone?"

"Always. Didn't you find it?"

"Not yet. Tell me about the phone."

"It was a dinosaur Motorola. She got it years ago. Text messages, no Internet. I keep telling her to get a new one, but she says she only needs it for calls."

"Who's the service provider?"

"Verizon."

Lucy twirled her hair. "Are you thinking someone robbed her for the phone?"

"We're looking into everything. We'll contact Verizon and find out if anyone's used it."

"Nobody would want to steal that thing. She probably couldn't even give it away."

Campbell wrote it all down in his notebook. Next came questions about Debbie's job, the people she worked with, her social habits, and daily routine.

"What was your mother's maiden name?"

"Debbie Tate."

"Was she seeing anyone?"

"You mean in a romantic way?"

"That's what I mean."

"No, there wasn't anyone. My father died. She never dated anyone after that. I tried to fix her up, but she wasn't interested."

"When did your father die?"

"A long time ago. I was three."

Campbell paused. He looked at her with kind eyes.

"How did he die?"

"He was an apprentice bay pilot. He was transferring from the pilot boat to a merchant ship and fell. It was raining. They didn't find him for two days. He drowned."

"I'm sorry. It must have been a terrible time for you and your mother."

"What does this have to do with anything?" Lucy's voice was cracking. "I don't understand."

"The more we learn about the victim of a homicide, the more leads turn up. We never know where information is going to take us in an investigation. I didn't mean to upset you. Can you go on?"

"Yes."

"When did you last speak to your mother?"

"We talk every day. I last spoke with her…" She closed her eyes and rubbed her forehead. "What day is this?"

"Friday."

She opened her phone and checked the call history. "Oh, right…here it is…Mom called me yesterday around three."

"Where was she? Do you know where she was calling from?"

"She had to be at work. I could hear lots of noise in the background—you know, people talking, rattling carts. She doesn't get off from work until five."

"What did you talk about?"

Silent minutes passed. Her eyes welled. "I don't remember. How come I can't remember the last conversation I ever had with my mother?"

"It's okay." Campbell pushed a box of tissues toward her. "You're under a lot of stress. Tell me what you did today, step by step. It might help you remember."

"What's today?"

"Friday."

"Oh…you said that. I got up at six, like I always do. Took a shower. Read the paper. It was raining. I hung out at home until the weather cleared up. It stopped raining around seven fifteen. I went to Ground Zero—you know, where the bicycle messengers hang out. I called my mother, but she didn't answer. Work got busy, but I kept calling her all day. She never answered or called me back, and that's not like her at all. I got worried. At about three thirty, I couldn't stand worrying anymore and went looking for her."

"Do you have a list of customers you saw today?"

"I have run sheets. How come?"

"It'll help establish a time line."

"Where's my mother now?"

"The medical examiner is taking care of her."

Lucy nodded, remembering.

"When was the last time you spoke to Romero Sanchez?"

"When we broke up in CC's. Do you know about that? I don't remember when that was. It seems like a long time ago. Can you ask Rick? He'd know."

"Not since then?"

She shook her head. "It was bad. But in the end he came through for me, didn't he?"

Detective Campbell paused a moment. "Yes, he did. Does Romero know where your mother lived?"

"He knows she lives in Highlandtown, but he's never been there, and I never gave him her address. Why are you and Rick asking all these questions about Romero?"

"We're looking into everything. Are you tired? Can you go on?"

"That's right...you said that...yes, I can go on. I don't want my mother's killer to get away."

"Do you know anyone who'd want to hurt your mother?"

She shook her head vigorously. "No, no one."

"Has she ever argued with a colleague or a customer?"

She sat motionless, with her hands around her cold coffee cup, scanning her memory.

"Five years ago there was something. Do you want to hear about that?"

"Tell me anything you can think of."

"I'd just gotten out of rehab. I was nearly sixteen. A few friends came over to my house. Tiffany Litofsky and her boyfriend were there. Lance was a big guy. Played defensive lineman for the high school football team. It was pretty outside, so we all sat on the front stoop. My mother was in the kitchen fixing us a pizza. Tiffany and Lance left and walked to his car. It was parked a little ways down my street. They got into a fight. He started hitting her. We ran to help Tiffany, but Lance was so big, we couldn't pull him off her.

"Mom must've heard all the commotion because she came flying out of the house screaming at Lance. 'I'm going to kill you! I'm going to kill you!' She hit him on the head with the pizza pan she'd just taken out of the oven. She began yelling, 'Lucy! Get the gun! Get the gun!'

"I didn't know what she was talking about. We didn't have a gun. Like a dope, I said, 'What gun?' Mom hit Lance in the knees with the pizza pan. I think she even bit him. All the time she was yelling for me to get the gun. He got out of there fast. I think her total craziness freaked him out. It sure freaked me out. I never saw her like that before, or since."

"What happened next?"

"She took Tiffany inside and cleaned her up. Tiffany was bleeding, crying. My mother was crying too and comforting her. After a while, she took Tiffany home. She lived about three houses down. We found the pizza in the front bushes. My mother had burns on her hands from the pan."

"What happened to Lance?"

Lucy shrugged. "Nothing, absolutely nothing. Tiffany didn't bring charges, even though my mother tried to get her to. They got married right after high school. Had three kids."

She stared into her coffee cup.

"What's Lance's last name and address?"

She gave Campbell the last name. "I have no idea where they are."

"Can you think of anything else? Any grudges?"

"Appoline Mercer."

Campbell did a double-take. "You mean the State's Attorney?"

"That's who I mean." Lucy looked at her hands. "During my first juvenile hearing, she was cruel to my mother. Called her incompetent, said she had no business raising a child. She made Mom cry. Even the judge got mad—told Mercer it was his job to judge, not hers."

Lucy pressed her fingers against her closed eyes, trying to force the tears to stay in place. "Excuse me...I need a minute."

Campbell was silent until Lucy nodded her permission to continue. "You think Mrs. Mercer killed her?"

"Huh? No, of course not! I was answering your question about grudges." She released a short giggle. He smiled.

"Detective Campbell, what happened to Steppie?"

He looked confused. "Who's Steppie?"

"The dog. His name is Steppenwolf, after her favorite band. She calls him 'Steppie.'"

Campbell spoke with a consoling voice. "Steppie was shot. He was a brave little dog. He died defending your mother."

"Is Steppie dead?"

"Yes. I'm so sorry."

She tried to fight back her tears, but couldn't. "Who would do that? Kill a little dog? Who would do that?"

Campbell waited until the sobs slowed. "Would you like another cup of coffee?"

Lucy looked at the primordial mix in her coffee cup. "No, thank you. I'm not suicidal."

He let out a soft chuckle. "Atta girl. Can you answer a few more questions?"

She dried her eyes with a beige tissue and nodded.

"Soon after your breakup with Sanchez, the Crime Stoppers Hotline got a tip concerning Javier, the owner of Compression Connection. Were you the caller?"

Her face fell. "I thought those calls were confidential."

"They are. I'd like you to answer my question anyway."

"Did I do something wrong?"

"No, no. You were very brave. Why'd you make the call?"

Lucy looked away from Campbell.

"Were you afraid Romero might hurt Javier?" he said, pressing.

She shivered. The coffee cup wobbled in her hand.

Campbell removed his coat jacket and placed it on her shoulders. She rubbed her arms and legs. The shivering continued. "Why's it so cold in here?"

"I'll be right back," he said.

A few minutes later, he returned with a blanket. "Let's put this around you."

An officer arrived with a steaming cup of tea. Lucy pressed it against her cheek.

"Are you warmed up now?" Campbell said.

"Warm as toast. Thank you."

"Good." He smiled. "So, tell me...why'd you make the call?"

She tightened the blanket around her.

"The meeting at CC's was my idea. I set it up. While I was talking with Romero, Javier called me 'Lucy.' Romero got this strange look on his face. It gave me the creeps. I wondered if Javier was police. The more I thought about it, the more upset I got. If something happened to Javier, I couldn't live with myself. I had to say something. So I called."

"I understand," Campbell said as he handed her more tissue.

"Is Javier police?"

"No, he's not. It was good of you to call anyway. You've been through a lot today. Try to get a good night's rest. We'll talk again tomorrow."

After Lucy left, Rick joined Campbell in the interview room. "Why didn't you tell Lucy that Javier was police?"

"Two reasons." Campbell returned the notebook and pen to his front pocket. "One, I don't disclose the identity of undercover officers. Two, it may have nothing to do with her mother's killing. That's a lot of weight for Lucy to carry. Let's not put it on her until we know for sure."

"I hope it doesn't come back to bite us."

Chapter 22

October 15

R ick sat at his desk, staring at the piles of files in front of him. "Fuck," he shouted to no one. With one hand, he smacked the files, scattering them to the floor. He knew all along that something like this would happen. He tried to stop it and thought he had, but the Trojan tricked him. Lulled him into believing he cared about Lucy. The snake had waited, coiled to strike, until he lunged at the equivalent of Lucy's jugular—her mother. His message was loud and clear—don't fuck with me or I'll kill someone you love.

Rick prosecuted hundreds of crimes, but this one was personal. He wouldn't rest until he put Sanchez away. He wasn't able to protect Lucy from this evil, but he'd give her the satisfaction of knowing her mother's killer would rot behind bars for the rest of his life. Too bad Maryland rescinded the death penalty. Rick imagined a toxic needle slipping into Sanchez's arm.

Appoline Mercer interrupted his fantasy.

"I heard." She took a seat in the chair across from Rick.

He didn't reply.

"Stop beating yourself up. This was inevitable. I saw it coming when Lucy was a kid. There was nothing you could've done to stop it. Remember your role here. You're a prosecutor—not a social worker. Forget that, and you'll second-guess yourself into paralysis."

She tapped her pointer finger on the desk. "Do your job. Stay on top of the investigation until there's an arrest. Then prosecute the hell out of it. Bring the motherfucker down and Roach too. Understood?"

"Understood."

Rick watched the door close behind her. He thought of nothing, until the Doppler effect of a police siren brought him to the window. It was dark outside. Streetlights cast a soft, buttery glow on the street. Traffic signals twinkled like multi-colored stars. Baltimore looked almost beautiful. Lucy was almost beautiful, too. Now she was grieving for her murdered mother. A sense of helplessness swept over him, and tears filled his eyes.

Stop it! Appoline was right. Focus on the job or be paralyzed. Tonight, there was nothing more for him to do. It was up to the police. Time to go home.

Rick made one last phone call. He dialed the number he rarely called, but knew by heart.

"Hi, Mom," he said. "Sorry it's been so long. How are you?"

———

The aroma of food mingled with the night air when Floater opened Lucy's front door. It was nine o'clock.

"Would you like to stay for dinner?" she said. "It's been in the slow cooker for way too long, it's probably all dried—"

"Yes, I would."

They sat together in silence except for the clinking of Floater's utensils on his plate.

"Eat something, Lucy."

She shook her head.

He took her plate and stabbed some meat with her fork. "Open up."

She obeyed, and he inserted the food. After she swallowed it, she said, "You're like a mother bird feeding her chick. A great, big mother bird."

"Take another bite."

She shook her head and smiled at him. "Know what? I tried to fix Mom up with you. You would've been perfect for her. I used to pretend you both fell in love at first sight, like it was with my parents. Then you'd get married, and we'd be a family."

Floater's eyes dampened.

She waved away the next fork of food. "I'll save it for Steppie. He loves this stuff."

"Go get some sleep. I'll be right here if you need anything. You'll be able to think more clearly tomorrow."

Without saying a word, Lucy followed his command and went upstairs.

She lay in bed, not moving, staring across the room at the window. The moon was so full and bright it cast shadows throughout her room. She ought to be crying. That would make her feel better. As hard as she tried, she couldn't conjure up any tears. Three hours passed. No tears. No sleep. There was nothing but an all-encompassing numbness—like her skin when she pedaled all day in freezing temperatures, only now the numbing cold was on the inside, next to her heart.

Deep snores boomed downstairs. Floater was asleep.

Lucy climbed from her bed to her desk and turned on her laptop. More police questions were coming tomorrow. This time she'd be ready. She needed to understand the direction and path of an investigation. That was the only way she'd be able give Detective Campbell relevant information. Why did she waste Campbell's time with that stupid story about Lance? It didn't mean anything.

Her fingers tapped in *homicide investigation.* The search engine led to *crime scene investigation, forensics, DNA, fingerprints, ballistics,* and *autopsy.* The science was fascinating. She found respite from her grief. Hours passed.

It was still dark when Lucy heard car doors slam as her neighbors headed off to work. After a while, the traffic stirred. Lucy heard the *Baltimore Sun* land with a thwack outside her front door. The next thwack would be the *New York Times.* She always read both papers. If you get two points of view, you can figure out the truth. That's what her mother always says.

She got another point of view today—about Rick. He could be an asshole, and he could be nice, like most people. She pulled up the research she'd done on him while preparing for the strong-arm trial. His background made her feel better when she was getting ready to testify. It would make her feel better now.

Sean Patrick McCormick, 31 years old
multi-lingual
Duke
Georgetown Law School
Baltimore City State's Attorney's Office, Violent Crimes Unit.
Incoming Chief, Gang Unit.

The biography sucked the oxygen from her lungs.
Gang Unit?
Is that why Rick was in Patterson Park? Was her mother killed by a gang member? Both Rick and Campbell asked her questions about Romero. Did they think he killed her mother?

Lucy couldn't breathe or blink or swallow or stop the gagging.
My fault, my fault, my fault.

She ran for the toilet with no results. Her stomach was empty. After rinsing her mouth in the sink, she stood in front of the bathroom mirror, staring at herself, her mind empty. The water dribbled down her pajamas and onto her feet. How did she forget to turn off the spigot? She was losing her mind, that's how. She cut off the water and mopped up the floor with a towel.

As she wrung the towel of water, she remembered the boat lake, Patterson Park, her mother, the gang unit. Why was this a gang case? She had to know. Lucy put on her shoes and crept past Floater, who was sleeping soundly on the floor. She slipped a long sweater over her pajamas.

Her plan was to pedal to police headquarters. Get the truth.

Chapter 23

October 16

Where was her bike? Lucy had no idea. The last place she pedaled was to Patterson Park. When was that? She couldn't remember.

It was five thirty in the morning—too dark to walk the three miles to police headquarters. Lucy took the transit bus from South Conklin Street. Thirty minutes later, she was standing in front of a glass window in the lobby of police headquarters. A uniformed officer, speaking from behind the glass, told her Detective Campbell wasn't due for another two hours. No, she didn't have an appointment. No, he wasn't expecting her.

"I'll wait for him." She took a seat in the reception area.

A few minutes passed. Bored, she called her mother. No answer. She let it ring. Her mother was an early-riser. *She's probably getting ready to walk Steppie.* Lucy remembered the dog was dead. So was her mother. Her hands flew over her mouth to stifle an outburst of sobs.

"Miss, are you all right?" said the officer behind the glass.

She couldn't answer. Within minutes, the officer escorted her to an interview room and gave her another cup of scorched coffee. This interview room was identical to the last, except for the beige metal table. It wobbled.

"I've called Detective Campbell," said the officer. "He'll be here as soon as he can."

The tears subsided. Lucy sent a text to Floater telling him where she was. She bumped her hand against the table and watched the coffee slosh inside the cup. Slosh. Slosh. At seven thirty, Campbell walked in. He sat on the other side of the table. His bald head was shiny smooth. She didn't notice that yesterday.

"How are you holding up?" he said.

"I'm losing my mind. I keep forgetting my mother's dead. I keep calling her thinking she'll answer the phone."

He handed her a beige tissue. She dried her eyes.

"How can I help you, Lucy?"

She had to suppress her gag reflex before she could answer. Her hands trembled. She held the edge of the table to keep her hands steady. "Detective Campbell…why do you think this is a gang case?"

"No one's saying this is a gang case."

"No one needs to say it. Rick McCormick's involved. Detective Marlow's involved. They're in the new gang unit. Don't treat me like I'm stupid. Tell me the truth—why do you think this is a gang case?"

He shifted in his chair. "I'm sorry. I can't disclose the details of a pending homicide investigation."

"Why not? I'm the victim's daughter."

"It's against public policy. Premature disclosures can jeopardize an investigation. It can lead to vengeance killings. Sometimes it even thwarts a criminal conviction when we bring the killer to trial."

"I read about investigations in the *Sun* all the time," she said. "How's this investigation different?"

"Those reports are the result of unauthorized leaks."

"My mother's not important enough to leak about?"

"Of course your mother's important." Lucy heard the exasperation in Campbell's voice. "Finding her killer is our top priority. I'll tell you whatever I can, as soon as I can. I promise."

"Do you think Romero did it? Is that why you and Rick were asking all those questions about him?"

"Everyone's a suspect until we rule them out."

"What about me? Am I a suspect?"

"You were ruled out."

"What? How?"

"We verified your alibi. With your run sheets."

She gasped at the implication.

"Please don't take it personally," he said. "I only told you so you'd understand we consider everyone a suspect, until they're excluded. When we exclude Romero, he'll be off the suspect list."

"How will you exclude him? Did you take DNA from Steppie's mouth?"

Campbell looked surprised. "We swabbed the dog's mouth. The swab's been submitted to the crime lab for processing."

"What happens then?"

"If the crime lab can get enough DNA alleles from the swab, it'll develop a DNA profile. The lab will compare the profile to the DNA profiles already in the system. If there's a match, we'll have a suspect."

"How long will that take?"

"Time varies—at this point it takes about two months."

"Two months! The killer could be long gone by then."

"We'll find your mother's killer, even if there isn't a DNA match. Most of the time, crimes are solved the old-fashioned way. We'll get him, Lucy. I promise."

"I want copies of the forensic reports—DNA, fingerprints, ballistics—anything you have. And the crime scene photos. When can I get them?"

He stared at her for a few seconds before clearing his throat.

"They're part of the pending investigation. We can't give you those, like I explained before."

"I can help you, I know it. I'm good at figuring things out. Ask Rick."

"I believe you, but I can't give them to you. I suggest you discuss it with Rick. He's the ASA prosecuting this homicide."

Lucy sized up Campbell. Sincere, smart, ruled by rules—like Rick. If Campbell and Rick thought Romero killed her mother, the investigation was going haywire.

She sprinted the six blocks to the State's Attorney's Office. Maybe she could persuade Rick that the police were on the wrong track. Maybe he'd give her some answers, or at least listen to her. The doors to the building were locked. She forgot it was Saturday.

Lucy banged her forehead against the locked door and screamed in frustration. A security guard opened the door. She took two steps backward, startled.

"May I help you?" the guard said.

"My mother's been murdered, and the police are screwing up the investigation…I know it…I want to see Rick McCormick, and his office is here, but the doors are locked because it's Saturday, and I keep forgetting it's Saturday."

"Mr. McCormick is upstairs. Wait here while I call him."

A minute later, the guard returned. "He's on his way down. Come inside."

She saw Rick exit the elevator. He led her to his office on the ninth floor. It was a small cubicle with a window facing east. Law books and files covered the floor. The calendar on the wall showed August.

"What can I do for you?"

She took a couple of deep breaths.

"Detective Campbell won't tell me why my mother's murder is being investigated as a gang case." She could hear her agitation seep into her voice. "He said I can't have any of the forensic reports. That's bullshit."

He registered no surprise. Campbell had given him a heads-up.

"The detectives are investigating everything, no matter how far-fetched it may seem," he said with his authoritative, courtroom voice. "We can't hand over the investigation reports to you. Keeping the investigation confidential is the only way we can be sure we charge the right person.

"There are a lot of whack jobs out there. Some will confess to anything just to get a little attention. Some prison inmates will claim to know information, so they can cut a deal. We're able to sort out perpetrators from the fakes by keeping the details to ourselves. The real perpetrators know the details, not the fakes."

She bristled. "I wouldn't tell anyone the details."

"Not on purpose, you wouldn't. But you could slip and accidentally sabotage the investigation. The killer could walk, or we could convict the wrong person. You don't want that, do you?"

She didn't reply. She wanted to think about this.

"I know you think Romero had something to do with this," she said, avoiding the issue of investigative reports. "Why do you think that? He told you about Alvarado because I asked him to. He made sure I didn't end up like Marcela. Why would he then turn around and kill my mother?"

Rick raked his right hand through his hair. "I don't want to hurt you."

"Fuck that! You can't hurt me any more than I already am."

"Lucy—"

"You're out to get him for the glory of it. The prosecutor who finally takes down the notorious Romero Sanchez. Your ambition is running this show."

Rick's brown eyes flashed fury.

"Jesus Christ! Is that what you think? I'll tell you why he'd kill your mother—that's the kind of shit gangs do. He's a babysitter, remember? *The Trojan.* He seduced you and made you feel special. Did he ever ask about me? He was grooming you to be an informant so he could keep tabs on Marcela's murder investigation.

"Only it backfired in a big way. You broke his nose. He kills your mother. Hurts you where you're most vulnerable. There are brave people who'll risk their own lives to confront a gangster, but not many will put their family at risk. That's the message he sent—'screw with me, and I'll kill the one you love the most.' He's a monster. Why won't you believe me?" Rick leaned across the desk. "Hear me on this, Lucy. Do not disclose anything to Sanchez about your mother's killing or this investigation. If you interfere or hinder us in any way, I'll come after you for obstruction of justice. Do you understand me?"

"Yes." Lucy didn't recognize the small, weak voice that came from her.

Rick looked tired, like the flash of anger had combusted the energy inside of him.

"The ME has released your mother's body. You need to make arrangements. Go home. Take care of your mother. Get some counseling. Let us do our jobs."

She walked out of Rick's office, exited the building, and looked around. *Where's my bike?*

Dazed, she sat on the street curb to think. Once she was on the ground, the location of her bike was the furthest thing from her mind. Rick's words wouldn't stop looping around her brain. After each loop, she said aloud, "This is my fault."

She put her palms on her knees and used them to cushion her forehead. All she needed was a little catnap. When she woke up, she'd be in her own bed, and she'd call her mother about the terrifying dream she'd had. Debbie would listen, and when Lucy was done, they'd go to Deep Creek. Have their girls' weekend. Maybe she'd tell her about Romero and listen to her talk about college. All that would happen if she could just go to sleep.

"Lucy, what are you doing?"

She looked up to see Floater hovering over her.

"I lost my bike."

He sat on the curb beside her. She collapsed into his arms, weeping.

"Oh Floater, I really fucked up."

Chapter 24

October 16

Patterson Park was no longer ribboned like a birthday present. The crime scene tape was gone, except for a lone strip fluttering in the breeze. Lucy sat on a bench by the boat lake, staring at the murky water in front of her, trying to remember why she'd come to Patterson Park. She was looking for something. Like yesterday when she pedaled to the park looking for her mother.

Her bike, that's what she was looking for.

She saw a police car make a U-turn on Eastern Avenue and parallel park against the curb. Marlow sat down beside her.

"I can't find my bike."

"It's at the station. I'll bring it to your house later this afternoon."

Marlow gave her a once-over. "You're still in your pajamas."

Lucy shrugged. So what? It didn't matter. Nothing mattered other than the fact her mother was dead, and it was her fault.

"I'm so sorry about your mother."

"Is it my fault?" Lucy folded over herself and wept into her knees.

Marlow hugged her fiercely. "This isn't your fault. You didn't do anything wrong. There's only one person to blame here—the person who killed your mother. No one else. No matter what anyone says, it's not your fault."

Lucy raised herself from her knees. "Will you at least tell me how it happened?"

Marlow hesitated, apparently weighing the pros and cons. "All right. You didn't hear this from me, understood? Follow me."

They walked together on the path toward the park entrance on South Linwood Avenue.

"What I'm about to tell you is based on what we saw at the crime scene. It's very preliminary. It was about seven yesterday morning. Your mother was walking Steppie down this path toward the boat lake. She was accosted by a single male, right here."

Marlow bent over and stroked the grass. Lucy squatted so she was eye-level with her.

"We found a lot of footprints. There must have been an argument. Your mother dropped the leash and ran down the path toward the boat lake." Marlow stood and signaled for Lucy to follow her. They moved fifteen yards down the path and stopped.

"The perpetrator chased her, but the dog intervened. Attacked him. This gave your mother a small lead. Steppie put up quite a fight. Bit the perp hard enough to draw blood. Steppie lost his front teeth."

Marlow pointed to the ground. "The perpetrator shot him right here."

She resumed walking, Lucy in tow, until they reached the bench at the boat lake. "The perp caught your mother here. There was a struggle. He struck her in the face with a hard object, presumably the gun. She died instantly."

Lucy stood frozen, seeing the killing in her mind's eye. She surveyed the park in all directions.

"Detective, why would she run to the boat lake? She should've run toward Linwood. She would've gotten to a traffic area faster."

"That's a good question."

"What happened to the phone? Has anyone used it?"

"More good questions, but I can't answer any of them. I've said too much already."

"But—"

"If I were you," Marlow said. "I'd get a lawyer."

Lucy returned home to a front stoop covered with flowers and casserole dishes. There was a bouquet from Joseph. It took her a moment to remember who he was—the taffy-haired man who rescued her from Poe's. Joseph's note simply said, "There are no words."

Somebody said that to her, a long time ago. It was Minerva Wilson James, the crying lawyer. She also said, "Call me if you ever need anything."

Lucy called her.

At four, Lucy was in Minerva's office choking out her sorrows. The lawyer listened and passed her tissues. When Lucy finished, the trash-can beside her chair was overflowing with physical proof of her anguish. "Can you help me?"

"I can help you with some, but not all."

Lucy was calm, exhausted from her spent emotions.

"Call Tyson's Funeral Home," Minerva said. "Tell them I referred you. You can trust them, they're good people. They'll contact the Medical Examiner's Office. You're entitled to money from the Maryland Victim's Compensation Fund. That'll help with the cost of the funeral. Does your mother have life insurance?"

"I don't know."

"When things settle down, we'll go through her files and set up an estate case with the register of wills. The court will appoint you as your mother's personal representative. That'll give you the authority to settle her estate.

"What I can't do is get information about the homicide investigation. It's confidential. It's a specific exception to Maryland's Public Information Act, *MPIA* for short."

"What's that?" Lucy said.

"It's Maryland's version of the federal Freedom of Information Act. It allows the public to get governmental information, but there are exceptions. Information about an ongoing criminal investigation is one of them."

"MPIA? How's it work?"

"It starts off with someone asking the appropriate governmental agency for information. If the agency refuses, the requestor files suit to force disclosure. Then the court decides."

"Can we try it?"

"I'm not willing to. The exception is clear. An MPIA lawsuit wouldn't pass the *red-face* test. The court would view the lawsuit as frivolous. I could be sanctioned."

"Red-face test?"

"Lawyer shorthand for whether a legal position is credible. Here's the test—is a legal position so ridiculous it's embarrassing to argue it? I don't file lawsuits that flunk the test."

Lucy was quiet for a long minute before she said, "I could try it myself, right? Not much embarrasses me."

"You could try, but you won't win."

"Shit happens in court. Rick told me that after the strong-arm trial."

The lawyer looked bemused. "I'm surprised Rick would say that to you. He's usually quite formal with witnesses."

"You know him?"

"I worked with him when he first joined the State's Attorney's Office."

"What was he like?"

"The same as he is now—smart, ambitious, formidable. Establishing a gang unit was Rick's idea. It took him years of advocating, but he got it done. The gang unit is his baby. Rick's got a lot on the line. He'll make sure the unit doesn't fall on its face."

Minerva trained her eyes on Lucy.

"Do not, under any circumstances, warn Romero Sanchez about the investigation. When Rick said he'd go after you, he meant it. Don't test him. Understand?"

Lucy nodded.

"This is going to be difficult for you to hear. Sanchez's name has been floating around the gang prosecution world for a long time. Corrupt, dangerous—he's one of the worst. You need to accept the possibility he killed your mother."

Lucy was silent.

Minerva thumbed through a Rolodex and selected a card. She took one of her own business cards, flipped it, and wrote on the back. When she was finished, she handed it to Lucy.

"This is the name of an excellent grief counselor. She has a wonderful reputation and, personally, I found her quite helpful. This is going to be a tough time for you. You need support."

Lucy took the card and put it in her backpack. *No way. I've had enough shrinkage to wrap all the chickens on the Delmarva Peninsula.*

Minerva gave her a comforting smile. "After the funeral, bring me your mother's files and any other information you can find. I'll prepare the papers you need to open your mother's estate case."

It was nearing midnight. Lucy had long ago given up her quest for sleep. On her nightstand was a Café No Delay cup, half-filled with coffee. It wasn't until after she'd guzzled down the remains that she wondered how long it'd been sitting there. Was it deadly? She wouldn't mind if it was. She could be buried right alongside her mother. Not have to face all this.

Lucy rifled through her desk and found two index cards. On one card, she wrote *Romero*. On the other, she wrote *Rest of the World*. She leaned them against the empty coffee cup.

"After the funeral I'll figure out which one to keep."

She lay in her bed and imagined aiming her gun at a faceless man. He was on his knees, his hands clasped behind his head. He was crying, begging for mercy, for forgiveness.

"Tell it to St. Peter," she said before blowing his head off.

Chapter 25

October 23

Coffee. Diet Coke. Red Bull.

Lucy couldn't decide. Her mind wouldn't focus. A line of impatient travelers stood behind her at the counter of the McDonald's, Concourse C, Baltimore-Washington International Airport.

"Miss, you need to order something or get out of line," the counter clerk said.

Lucy got out of line. She wandered over to Departure Gate 27 and joined a throng of passengers waiting for their flight to Los Angeles. What time was it? The clock on a far wall showed two in the afternoon. She panicked. Did she miss her mother's funeral? She grabbed a discarded *Sun* paper from the empty seat next to hers. Today was October twenty-third. No, she didn't miss the funeral—it was this morning. She'd been there.

The funeral was a blank except for brief flashes of memory—like an album filled with random snapshots. It was crowded. Her posse was there. McCormick and Marlow, too. There was a slew of people from Home Warehouse. She saw volunteers from Loaves & Fishes and friends from AA. Joseph had organized a carpool.

Lucy nodded in her seat until a loudspeaker blared the boarding instructions.

The Grand Canyon, the Great Salt Lake, and the Rocky Mountains came and went, but she had no interest in them. Her body was dull, lifeless. The numbness kept her from feeling fear. She was about to confront Romero Sanchez, the infamous gang kingpin. If Romero killed her mother, he'd kill her too. She wasn't afraid of that. What she feared was learning she'd set in motion a chain of events resulting in her mother's murder. She couldn't live with that.

Her mind drifted to the Golden Gate Bridge. Did it hurt much to hit the water from the bridge? She could see herself dead, floating in the water, as relaxed as a jellyfish, drifting this way and that, with no cares or worries.

A flight attendant asked if she was all right.

"I'm fine, thank you."

Her thoughts returned to the task at hand. How would she find Romero? She knew only three things about him for certain: he was a Roach kingpin, liked to dance, and lived in Los Angeles. What would she do when she found him? She didn't know.

Seven hours later, Lucy landed at LAX airport. She had no memory of collecting her baggage, exiting the airport, or taking the hotel shuttle. There was a man behind the reception desk wearing a red blazer with a tag that read "Melburn." He looked her over when she handed him cash.

"Are you okay?" Melburn said.

"I want to go out tonight. Can you recommend a nice bar? Some place where Latinos might go. Handsome ones, tall ones."

"The Havana Sky Bar is popular. I'll write down the address."

"I need the names of three more Latino bars." She glanced at the time on the lobby clock. "That's probably all I can do tonight."

He stared at her.

"There are computers for guests in the business center." He pointed down the hall. "You can probably find what you're looking for."

"Where can I get a bike?"

"A motorcycle?"

"No, a bike with pedals."

"The city's much too spread out for a bike."

"Oh." That was news to her. "Do you have a bus schedule?"

Melburn grimaced and handed her one.

She went straight to the computers and did her research.

Lucy's hunt for Romero began at eight o'clock. She walked into the aptly-named Havana Sky Bar wearing a blue, one-shouldered top, skinny black pants, and stiletto heels. The club outfit was Romero's favorite. She never told him she found it at the Fells Point Goodwill store.

The bar was carved into the side of a mountain and overlooked the glittering lights of Los Angeles. There was no roof, giving the impression the bar was illuminated by the overhead constellation of stars. She took a seat at the bar and yawned widely.

"Having trouble with the time zone change?" the bartender said, smiling. His bulging, unnatural muscles spilled from his clingy T-shirt.

She nodded.

"What can I get you?"

"A water, please."

"Wooder? I don't know what that is. How do you make it?"

"Turn on a faucet and fill up a glass."

"Oh, you mean *water*?" The bartender laughed. "Where're you from?"

"Baltimore."

"What's your name?"

"I'm looking for someone. Can you help me?"

"Maybe," he said. He rubbed the pad of his right thumb against the pads of the adjacent fingers.

She slid a quarter toward him.

He chortled as he slid it back to her. "Who're you looking for?"

"I'm looking for Romero Sanchez. He's tall and handsome, nice teeth. He looks like a movie star."

"This is LA! Every man in this city looks like a movie star."

Lucy considered her glass of water. The bartender had filled it from a faucet on the other side of the bar. She was by herself, in a strange place. Rohypnol, GHB, and ketamine came to mind. For some reason she didn't trust this guy. She pushed away the water.

"He has a lot of Roach tattoos."

The bartender stopped smiling. "No, I don't know him."

"Where do Roach gangsters hang?"

"Whoever you are, Ms. Wooder, go home to Baltimore."

He walked away.

No matter. Romero would never go to this bar. There was nothing Latino about it—just a bunch of plasticized white people walking around being beautiful.

She visited three more bars. No one knew Romero, or so they said. She was too tired to sort truth from lies. She'd try again tomorrow.

Sleep was fitful. Throughout the night, disturbing dreams shocked her awake. A puppy smashed and killed by a pizza pan. Her mother, lying on the grass by the boat lake, alone and cold. Twice during the night, she got out of bed and wrote on index cards.

Pizza

Boat Lake.

Chapter 26

October 24

Lucy awoke at four in the morning. She had nothing better to do than review her strategy for finding Romero. Random bar visits weren't going to work.

She didn't know LA. The city was huge. A person couldn't go anywhere without getting on a six-lane highway. Last night, she'd traveled at least fifty miles and only visited four salsa bars. Forget the bus. She needed someone who could drive her around with efficiency and double-park while she made her inquiries.

Another problem—the stilettos. Her feet were killing her. No matter how she dressed, she'd look out of place. Might as well be comfortable. Lucy put on jeans, a T-shirt, running shoes, and an Orioles baseball cap. She pulled her hair through the hole in the back of the cap.

It was still dark when she returned to the hotel's business center to generate another list of bars. When Romero was in Baltimore, he often dropped by Compression Connection for *pupusa*, his favorite Salvadoran meal. She decided to visit the bars serving *pupusa* for lunch, starting with the bars nearest Hollywood and working outward.

She went to the reception desk. Melburn was there.

"I need a driver, starting at eleven. Can you recommend someone?"

"One of our shuttle bus operators hires himself out as a personal driver."

"Call him."

Lucy passed the morning browsing inside Surveillance Spyware, the largest spy-equipment retail store in the world, according to the ad she saw in the *Los Angeles Times*. She wanted to buy a tiny, covert camera so she could secretly record her conversations with Romero.

The store was massive. There were nanny cams in coffee pots and clocks, recording devices tucked into everyday household items—air fresheners, computer flash drives, and tissue boxes. She considered buying the baseball hat with the pinhole-sized recorder implanted above the rim. *No, Romero's not dumb. He'll have me searched.*

The personal protection department was by far the largest. Stun grenades and pepper blasters. Taser guns disguised as pens, key chains, and lipstick cases. Three aisles over, Lucy found her heart's desire: a Flashbang bra holster. The holster attached to a women's bra, between the breasts, concealing the gun. Even under a T-shirt.

Lucy debated buying it. Wearing the holster in LA was out. Romero would find it in a second. Besides, she'd left her gun in Baltimore. She decided to buy the holster anyway—sometimes a woman needs to spoil herself.

"With practice, you can draw your gun in under three seconds," the saleswoman said.

"I'll take it."

At eleven sharp, Lucy met the driver in the hotel lobby. He was a sprite of a man, with feminine hands. His name was Fabio Varuna.

"I need to find someone. I may have to go to some shady parts of town. Are you willing to take me there?"

"Sure. Anywhere you wanna go."

"Good. How much?"

"Fifty an hour. Cash. In advance."

"All right. I'll pay you fifty at the top of every hour."

Fabio drove her to five Latino bars. No luck. It was now two thirty, and the lunch crowd had dwindled. There was one more bar on her list.

Lucy gave him the address.

"That's South Central. Gang territory. You don't wanna go there."

"You said you'd take me anywhere I wanted to go. If you're wimping out on me, give me back my money."

He took Interstate 110 to South Central. After a dozen turns, they were in a neighborhood similar to the unsavory parts of her hometown. Corner boys. Prostitutes. Homeless. Lucy saw Fabio's hands stiffen around the wheel. She could smell his fear.

They pulled in front of seedy-looking building, with no name.

"Here it is," he said. "Sure you wanna do this?"

"I'll be right back. Stay put."

Trash, broken bottles, needles, and cigarette butts covered the crumbling sidewalk. She stepped over a few shell casings. Right outside the building's entrance, she saw a man, in his twenties, straddling a bike—a Wabi Lightning SE fixed-gear bike, exactly like the one she had at home, the only difference being the GPS mounted on the handlebars.

"Cool bike," she said. "Does it have brakes?"

He regarded her with gray, expressionless eyes and said nothing.

She entered the building. It wasn't as scuzzy as it appeared from the outside. Large dance floor. Curved bar of polished wood. A small stage area for a band. Three men stared at her. She spoke to them collectively.

"I'm looking for Romero Sanchez. Do you know where I can find him?"

They exchanged glances and smiled at one another. One of the men slipped past Lucy and took a position blocking the door. She turned to face him. He was tall and lanky and had enough bling on his teeth to operate a jewelry store out of his mouth. A mosaic of intricate tattoos covered his face and neck, snakes woven into the design. Lucy recognized the gang symbols.

Vipers.

The gang was Roach's ferocious rival. Their competition for territory was behind much of the nation's gangland killings.

The bling-toothed man stroked Lucy's left arm with his fingertips. "Soft skin. Whatever you want with Romero, you can have with me."

"Paws off, Ass-breath!" she said as she tried to yank her arm away.

His fingertips turned into a cobra's grip around her arm.

Her skin tingled. The hair on her arms stood upright, atop of goose bumps, like flags on a pole. The two other men stepped closer. She was surrounded by three men who meant her harm. She stopped breathing. Everything slowed as time crawled. Her heart pounded with such force she expected blood to spurt from her eyeballs.

Her right hand clenched, with the knuckle of her middle finger raised slightly above the fist. She leaned away from Ass-breath, putting her weight on her right foot.

"What I want with Romero is to kill him," she said.

Ass-breath threw back his head and laughed, fully exposing his tattooed throat.

The time was right. She jabbed her knuckle into his Adam's apple. Arm straight. Full body weight behind it. Quick punch. Perfect hit. Just like Floater'd taught her. Ass-breath grabbed his throat and bent forward, gagging. She kneed him in the face. The other men stared in astonishment.

"Get that bitch!" she heard from behind the bar. "Bring her to me, so I can fuck her up."

The voice came from a man she hadn't seen. Must be the shot caller. Lucy hopped over Ass-breath's writhing body and ran outside. The bright sunshine blinded her. She squinted, barely able to see.

Where's Fabio?

No car. No Fabio.

She heard the thundering footsteps of the two men behind her. There was the Wabi bike, sitting there, with no lock. She grabbed the handlebars with both hands, ran beside it and mounted the bike as it picked up speed, a move she'd made thousands of times. She glanced over her shoulder and saw her pursuers falling away. No one could catch her on a bike. No one.

An engine fired up. They were getting into a car. A gray sports utility vehicle.

Where was she? She glanced at the GPS. The street names meant nothing to her. Interstate 110 was to her west. She remembered Fabio had made about a dozen turns from the 110. If she could somehow get to the interstate, she'd enter it by pedaling up the exit ramp and get on the 110 heading the wrong way. Pedal on the shoulder until the cops picked her up. There'd be a lot of explaining to do, but she'd be out of this mess.

There was a one-way street a block ahead, traffic heading east. She glanced behind her. The SUV was gaining. Only a half-block away. She reached the one-way street and turned west, the opposite way of traffic. They couldn't follow her driving the wrong way down a one-way street.

She pedaled west until she saw the SUV a half-block ahead on her left, waiting behind a stop sign on a side street. They'd looped around and were poised to grab her when she pedaled by. She pulled a U-turn, midblock, bringing traffic to a screeching stop. She pedaled east. The SUV bolted from the stop sign, turned right, and followed her. It was now two blocks behind.

The GPS told her the next intersection would bring her to a major thoroughfare. She turned right. It was a four-lane highway, two lanes in each direction. She made her way to the double yellow line and nestled in behind a bus. The pursuing SUV was four car lengths behind her. She saw an oncoming truck. She estimated she had five feet. Wide enough.

She pulled to the left and rode the yellow line, occupying the small space between the bus and the oncoming truck. The wind blew her baseball cap off her head. She was in daylight again, now in front of the bus. She took a left turn across oncoming traffic, onto a sidewalk, then a right turn down another one-way street, going the correct way.

Surprise! She found herself behind the SUV. The men hadn't yet noticed. The light ahead was green. On the right was a police car. She pedaled at leisure behind the SUV, taking her hands from the handlebars. She stretched, shook out her fingers, brushed the hair out of her face. And waited.

The driver looked into the rearview mirror. The passenger and driver snapped their heads around to see her. She held up her hands and saluted them with her middle fingers. The light turned red. The Vipers sailed through it. There was a short burst of the police siren. A moment later, the SUV was parked on the side of the road, getting a ticket.

Lucy laughed so hard she almost peed in her pants. She hadn't had this much fun since...she couldn't think of when.

She scanned while she cruised. Light traffic. No construction. No grates. No sand. She spotted a pedestrian one block up, on the right, waiting to cross the street. He was holding an umbrella. Odd. It was sunny.

She didn't see it happen until it was too late.

The umbrella, thrust into the spokes of her bike. The bike stopped. She didn't.

Good-bye teeth.

Chapter 27

October 24

Lucy's body catapulted from the bike seat. No helmet, no mouth guard, no protective gear of any kind. She crossed her arms in front of her face, an instinctive act of self-preservation. Her thighs rammed into the handlebars, but it didn't slow her velocity as she hurdled headfirst toward the pavement.

Something grabbed the back of her waistband, halting her forward trajectory. The man with the umbrella yanked her toward him, sideways from the bike. The momentum carried them both crashing to the street. As they fell, the pedestrian squeezed her head against his chest. He landed first. She landed on top.

Stunned, it took her a split-second to regain her senses.

Run!

Lucy sprang to her feet. The pedestrian grabbed her right ankle. Tripped her. She fell on her hands and knees. Tried to kick free of his grip. There was no escape. She'd have to fight. Her hands found loose gravel. She grabbed as much as her hands could hold. Her arms wound themselves to hurl the gravel into her assailant's face.

"Lucy!" the pedestrian said. "It's me! Peeps!"

She recognized the man holding her ankle. He'd driven Lucy and Romero to Pennsylvania the night Romero gave her the bracelet.

"Peeps?"

She crawled on top of him and pecked kisses on his mouth, his cheeks, and his forehead. "Oh, Peeps! Is it really you?"

"Get off me! Before we get run over."

Lucy encircled her arms around his waist as they walked together to a black Esplanade parked around the corner. Once inside, Lucy hugged him.

"Knock it off!" He pushed her away.

"Why'd you do that? Why'd you make me crash?"

"To stop your fuckin' bullshit before you dragged Romero into it." He pressed on the accelerator. "Where are you staying?"

"I want to see Romero."

Peeps backhanded her across the face, silencing her. She could taste blood gathering on her mouth. Her tongue slipped across her front teeth. They were still there. Peeps had split her bottom lip.

"Jesus! What was that for?" she said when she found her voice.

"You're not going anywhere near Romero. You're poison to him."

He entered the 110 heading south at eighty miles per hour. Peeps weaved in and out of traffic with ease.

"Where're you taking me?"

Peeps stared forward with clenched jaws.

"I'll find Romie no matter where you dump me. When I do, I'll tell him you hurt me."

"Go right ahead." Peeps laughed. "He hates you, you know. He'll ask me why I didn't kill you. Maybe I'll shove you out of the car right now."

He unsnapped her seatbelt with his right hand. They were doing eighty-five.

"You're not that stupid," she said. "There'll be an autopsy. Guess what the ME will find? A fetus! And the DNA will show it's Romie's baby. What kind of a fix will he be in then?"

"You're a lying bitch."

"Why do you think I'm going through all this? I need to do something about this baby. I have to talk to Romie first. He's the father, he gets a say. That's all I want."

Beats of sweat formed on Peep's upper lip, but Lucy knew he wasn't convinced. He needed another push.

"If Romie's not interested in the baby, I'll go back to Baltimore. I won't bother him again. All right?"

Peeps didn't respond, but stared at the interstate in front of him.

"Please," she said.

They drove in silence for the next five miles. Peeps turned onto the 405 and headed southeast. He drove for forty-five minutes, making several turns, before entering the city of Laguna Niguel. The roads were well kept, and the landscape blossomed with crimson flowers Lucy didn't recognize. Peeps pulled into the driveway of a single-family home on a cul-de-sac. The front yard displayed a massive garden of roses.

Peeps spoke in Spanish into his cell phone. He disconnected. "You stay here."

From the passenger seat, Lucy watched Peeps walk up the sidewalk. The front door opened. There was Romero, wearing jeans and a sleeveless T-shirt. Lucy watched as they spoke. She couldn't hear a word of the conversation, but Peeps was an expressive talker, telling the story with his hands. He told Romero about her altercation with Vipers, her bicycle chase through the streets of South Central. He re-enacted thrusting an umbrella into the spokes of the stolen bicycle, catching her as she flew over the handlebars. Peeps put a hand on his own stomach.

Romero glanced in her direction. With a gesture of his hand, he ended the conversation and followed Peeps to the car. His mouth was smiling; his eyes were not. They were dilated. He was amped up on something.

"Lucy, you're always full of surprises." He opened the passenger car door. "Come with me."

Romero led her through a gate to a backyard surrounded by a seven-foot fence. He watched as Peeps lifted Lucy's T-shirt, ran his hands down her back, between her breasts, down the outside of her legs, up her calves and thighs to her midpoint. Lucy stared straight ahead without blinking. Peeps removed a pouch from her ankle and emptied it. He showed Romero the cash, hotel key, and cell phone.

"She's clean." Peeps handed everything to Romero.

"Why the burn phone?" Romero said to Lucy.

"All my business contacts are in my smartphone. I was afraid I'd lose it, so I left it home. Got a pre-paid phone for emergencies."

Romero seemed satisfied with her answer and dismissed Peeps with a nod.

"Follow me," he said.

Peeps gave her a look that alarmed her more than anything that had happened that day.

October 24

Romero led Lucy to the kitchen. It was a large room, painted a cheery yellow with white trim. The tiled floor was a pattern of green, yellow, and white. A garden of potted herbs sat in front of a sunny bay window. There was a round yellow table with four matching chairs. He pulled out a kitchen chair and signaled for her to sit in it.

He joined her. Lucy began retching.

"Are you really pregnant?" he said, surprised.

Truth time. She braced herself for whatever would come next.

"No."

He didn't hit her, curse her, or threaten her. He simply watched as she mopped up the tears from her retching spell with the hem of her T-shirt. When she finished, he took her right hand and examined her palm. It was bloody.

"You're hurt."

"A little dinged up, that's all."

He left the kitchen and returned with a first aid kit. He cleaned her palm and applied a bandage. When he was finished, he kissed it.

"Give me your other hand."

He repeated the process.

"Take off your pants."

She didn't move. "Peeps already checked me for a wire."

"I know, I watched him."

Romero pointed to her knees. There was a wet blotch of red on each pant leg at the kneecap. She slipped off her pants, exposing bloody knees. He knelt in front of her and patched up her wounds, finishing with a kiss on each kneecap.

"Any other injuries?"

She shook her head.

"You forgot this one." He gently touched her mouth with a fingertip.

He dabbed the washcloth on her bottom lip. This time the finishing kiss was a soft graze across her mouth. She held the kiss, moved by his kindness.

Romero gave her a lifeless smile. His eyes were hard and cold. An understanding bolted through her—the Trojan was babysitting. Goosebumps of fear returned, and the hair rose on her arms.

"I'll be right back," he said.

He grabbed a bag of frozen peas from the freezer and handed it to her. She tore a corner of the bag open and began eating the peas, one by one.

"Want some?" she said.

He chuckled, his eyes now showing honest amusement. "The bag is for your face, knucklehead. Put it against your mouth. It'll help keep down the swelling."

"Oh."

Romero reached across the table and placed his right hand over her left. He caressed the top of her hand, the length of her fingers and finally, her fingertips.

"Why are you here, Lucy?"

His eyes blazed with frightening intensity. She tried to slide her hand away, but his touch was now a grip.

"The moment of truth has arrived. Tell me why you're here and don't lie. I'll know."

Lucy's focus on finding Romero had distracted her from preparing an answer to this obvious question. She needed time to think.

"I've never lied to you. Ever."

"You just said you were pregnant with my baby."

"I lied to Peeps, not you."

"You lied to him so he'd transmit the lie to me. You haven't answered the question." His hand was now squeezing hers. "Why are you here?"

"That's not true. I only told Peeps so he'd take me to you. I didn't expect him to tell you."

"Nice diversion, but you're avoiding the question." His hand squeezed hers to the point of pain. His other hand grabbed her around the neck. He pulled her head toward him until her face was inches from his. She could feel his fury breathing into her face.

"You're hurting me!" She dropped the bag of peas. Frozen peas bounced across the table and onto the floor.

"No more bullshit! Did McCormick send you?"

"No! Stop this!"

She strained to pull away. Romero's tight grip on her hand and neck paralyzed her in place. He stepped on her right foot, pinning it to the floor. Yanked her sideways from the chair. She couldn't save herself from falling. She was on her stomach, sprawled on the floor, Romeo straddling her back, clutching her hair, pulling her head backward. She was helpless.

He whispered into her ear, "I'm asking you the question one last time. You'll have five seconds to answer it. If you lie, if you hedge, if you don't answer—I'll smash your pretty face into the floor. I'll break your nose—I owe you a broken nose, remember? And I'll knock out those precious teeth."

Romero gripped her hair harder and pulled her head back until she thought her neck would snap. "Why the fuck are you here?"

Her options flashed through her brain. If she lied, Romero would know, and he'd break her nose, knock out her teeth. If she told the truth, Rick would indict her for obstruction of justice. There must be some sort of truth she could tell.

"I'm here because...my heart's...been broken!"

She choked back a single sob.

Romero released his grip and crawled off her. She went slack onto the floor.

"Get up." He pulled her upright by the forearm and steered her back to the kitchen chair. He sat and studied her while her hands trembled, and her eyes watered. She brushed away a tear with the heel of her hand.

"What does your broken heart have to do with me?" he said.

"I thought...if I saw you...I'd feel better."

"Do you think I'm an idiot? You flew across the country so I'd give you comfort for a broken heart? You expect me to believe that?"

She shook her head. "I don't expect you to believe anything I say, no matter what the truth is."

"I do believe you. You're a bad liar…always have been."

Romero slumped into his chair, looking morose and tired. He was coming down from his high.

"I don't have the energy to deal with you," he said. "Peeps'll be back soon. He'll drive you somewhere, I don't give a shit where…just so it's away from me. Lucy, come back here again, and I'll kill you."

She vowed to herself she wouldn't leave until she had her answer.

"May I use your bathroom? I have to pee."

He pointed down the hallway. "Do whatever it takes to get the fuck out of my house."

Lucy reached the hallway and stopped, confused. "Romie, where am I going?"

"To the bathroom, for crissakes."

The bathroom was large and clean and filled with a delicious, familiar scent. There was a long marble counter, with two sinks. A small mirror sat in the space between the sinks. The mirror held a razor and a small straw. There were two lines of cut cocaine. Romero had been snorting a line when he got the call from Peeps.

She froze in front of the vanity. All she could see were the parallel lines of the cocaine on the mirror. She had forgotten its beauty—the white, fluffy powder that, at that very moment, smelled like perfume. The craving surged in her. All she needed was a snort, and she'd be happy again. The coke would release her from the agony of her grief, just as it had released her from the guilt of Amber's crushed leg. The euphoria would last for only a few minutes, but it'd be worth it. A rush of sexual desire coursed through her. She wanted sex with Romero. Nothing was better than sex on coke.

Romero shouted her name from the kitchen. She didn't care. It was Lucy and the powder, with its sweet invitation. She reached for the straw, closed one nostril, and leaned over the table.

The door burst open. Romero slapped the straw from her hand, grabbed the mirror, and brushed the coke down the toilet.

"I'm sorry, Lucy, I'm sorry." He was gasping out his words. "I forgot this was here."

Lucy sat on the toilet with her face buried in her hands and wept. The sobs became more intense until she was gasping for breath. Tears and mucous poured down her face.

"I want it, Romie, I want it." She pleaded with him. "Just this once."

"I flushed it. It's gone."

"I still smell it! Why do I still smell it, if it's flushed? You can get more, I know you can. Let me have some. Please."

Romero reached over her and turned on the shower.

"Stand up, Lucy."

She stood. He undressed her and put her in the shower.

A cold rush of water stung her face. The shower curtain opened and Romero, now nude, stepped into the shower behind her. She turned to face him. He put his arms around her. She leaned against him and begged for coke.

"Shhhh…it's all right," he said. "I'll take care of you."

He tilted her head backward into the stream of shower water. After wetting her hair, he applied lilac-scented shampoo and massaged her scalp. When her hair was cleaned and rinsed, he took the bar of soap and lathered her back. He washed her arms, legs and breasts, with a touch that was gentle, loving.

After toweling her dry, he led her to his bedroom. There was a mirrored vanity with a cushioned chair. By gesture, he commanded her to sit in it. After re-bandaging her hands and knees, he dried her hair with a blow dryer, occasionally stopping to massage her neck and shoulders. Her muscles relaxed under the warmth of the hair dryer. When her hair was dry, he stroked it with a soft brush and moved her hair to one side. He kissed the nape of her neck. She shuddered.

"Are you cold?" he said.

"A little."

Romero pulled a sapphire-colored, lace nightgown from a drawer in the vanity and slipped it over Lucy's head. The nightgown smelled sweet, like lilacs. It felt slippery and silky.

He dabbed perfume on her neck. More lilacs. "This will help keep the smell of coke away."

There were photographs covering the vanity. She saw a photograph of Marcela and Romero taken in front of the Eiffel Tower. They were holding each other, giving the photographer joyful smiles.

Lucy touched the photograph. "She's so beautiful."

She saw Romero's reflection in the mirror. His eyes were glistening. "When did you go to Paris?"

"I took Marcela there on our honeymoon."

"Tell me about Paris."

"It's old, but vibrant. Cultured. Good food. Wonderful wines. Interesting fashions. You and your mother should go together. You should always see Paris for the first time with someone you love."

There was no change in his demeanor or facial expression.

"What did you say?"

"You should see Paris for the first time with someone you love. Take your mother."

She had her answer—Romero didn't kill her mother. The crushing guilt flowed away from her, replaced by a sense of weightlessness. Romero kissed her neck again. He walked to the bed and pulled down the sheets.

"Come to bed," he said.

She slipped between the sheets. They smelled fresh and clean. The bed was large. A king, she guessed. Comfortable, soft.

Romero climbed on top of her, his eyes hot with sex.

"I'll make you forget the coke," he said in a low murmur. "I'll make you forget the man who broke your heart."

He kissed her in the penetrating way that always made her body rise toward his. Not this time; there was no sexual desire, only the weight of his body on hers. The sheets felt heavy. Her arms felt heavy. She could barely lift them around his neck. Even breathing was an effort.

Romero parted her legs with his and nestled between them.

"Condom," she whispered.

He stretched for the drawer to his nightstand and opened it. He groaned.

"Don't go anywhere." He pecked a kiss on her forehead.

Lucy heard the door of the bathroom cabinet open and shut. A soft wind passed through the bedroom window. Was it the Santa Ana winds she'd read about? There was a palm tree outside of the bedroom window, its palms fluttering in the setting sun. Maybe her mother was in heaven sitting under a palm tree.

The bed moved. Romero sat on its edge, next to Lucy.

"Wake up." Romero shook her gently. "C'mon, babe, wake up."

She tried to. Couldn't.

Chapter 29

October 25

The morning sun seeped into Lucy's dream. Her mother was leaning over her, brushing hair from her face and kissing her forehead. The scent of sticky buns floated in the air. Bacon, too. Breakfast was the one meal her mother always made from scratch.

"Time to get up," her mother said in a voice as sweet as nutty caramel.

Lucy slowly emerged from her pleasant dream. The insistent voice no longer sounded like her mother's. It was deep and resonant.

Lucy's eyes shot open. "Mom?"

"No, babe, it's me."

Tears of disappointment filled Lucy's throat. She had to swallow them before she could ask where she was.

"You're in California, with me. Don't you remember?"

She sat up and looked across the room at the large, round wall clock. It was seven o'clock.

"The clock's wrong," Romero said. "It's eleven."

"In the morning?" She was incredulous.

"Yes, sleepyhead…in the morning." He smiled at her. "You've been out for seventeen hours. Get dressed and come into the kitchen." He pointed to the vanity chair. "Your clothes are over there. I washed them."

The kitchen buzzer sounded. Romero kissed her lips and went into the kitchen.

She found her clothes neatly folded on the chair, topped with a tooth-brush and a fresh bar of soap. Romero had somehow cleaned the blood from her jeans. Dressing was difficult. Pain shot through her neck and shoulders whenever she turned her head. Her back ached. Every muscle was stiff. She hurt all over, like the time she'd been doored on St. Paul Street.

This time the pain wasn't from an accident. Romero had hurt her. On purpose.

She tried to make sense of the night before. Romero had threatened to bash in her face, break her nose, knock out her teeth. Afterward, he saved her from a relapse. Cleaned her up. Let her sleep. Now he was making her breakfast. He must still care about her. Maybe he cared enough to help her find her mother's killer.

All she had to do was ask, she was sure of it. He'd use his wide net-work of ruthless criminals to get justice. There'd be no dithering around about the killer's constitutional rights. Self-incrimination, speedy trial, and search and seizure would mean nothing to Romero. Justice would be quick, efficient, and over.

Not really. There'd be a heavy price to pay for Romero's help. She'd be indebted to him. He'd suck her into his world, where drugs were close. She'd probably end up using again. Her life would be destroyed. No, she was going to find her mother's killer by herself. Without Romero. Without McCormick. And when she found the fuckin' beast who'd murdered her mother, she'd kill him herself. Then it'd be over.

The kitchen table was set with elegant placemats and napkins. Pink tea roses filled a crystal bowl in the center of the table. The sizzle of fry-ing bacon triggered a long rumble from Lucy's stomach. It was her first hunger pang in ten days.

"Good morning," Romero said. He was standing at the stove, wearing an apron over a dress shirt and pants. He dished food onto two plates. "Sit down. I hope you're hungry."

Romero set a plate in front of her—bacon, eggs, and a pecan sticky bun—her favorite meal. Next came a glass of orange juice and a cup of coffee. He joined her at the table. Within minutes, she consumed every-thing on her plate. Romero re-filled it. She cleaned that plate too. She said nothing while she ate except to ask for more food. When she was finished, she looked up from her plate to thank him. He was staring at her, upset and distressed.

"What's wrong?" she said. "Did I eat too much?"

"No, no…please eat as much as you want."

"No more, I'm stuffed. Those sticky buns were delicious. You and Mom should have a bake-off. "

He seemed pleased at the compliment.

"How's your mother?"

"She's good."

Lucy watched Romero's reaction to the mention of her mother. There was none, confirming he had nothing to do with killing her.

They sat together quietly. Lucy didn't feel like talking. She'd found the answer she was looking for and wanted to go home. She missed Baltimore.

Romero broke the silence. "Are you in trouble?"

"No, why would you think that?"

"The way you're acting—erratic. And you look like shit."

Anger roiled in her stomach.

"I look like shit because black and blue aren't my colors."

He half-smiled at her. "Now that's the Lucy I know. Welcome back."

"You shouldn't have hurt me. You shouldn't have done that."

"Jesus! It's not as if you have clean hands."

She studied her hands, turning them over as she did so. She glanced up at Romero to make sure she hadn't misunderstood him. He was grinning and shaking his head.

"I didn't mean that literally. I was pointing out you're not in a position to complain. You broke my nose."

"I was trying to save my life."

"And I was trying to save mine. McCormick—"

"Stop it! McCormick has nothing to do with this. I came here on my own."

"Because of a broken heart."

"That's right."

"Whatever trouble you're in, I can fix it. I'm a powerful man."

"I'm not in trouble."

"Like hell you're not!" Romero hooked her eyes with his. "Listen to me…I've always liked you. You know why? Because you'd tell me exactly what you thought. Not many people do. You've always been direct and honest. Now you come to me, strung out and secretive. All this drama isn't because some asshole broke your heart. What's happened?"

"I told you."

Romero threw a balled-up paper napkin at Lucy. She deflected it with her hand and seethed. No, she'd never ask for his help. He grabbed the plates from the table.

"If you can't trust me," he said, "I'm done with you. You hear me? Done."

"I want to go home."

He tossed the plates into the sink with a loud clatter. "You're an ungrateful bitch, you know that? I gave up Alvarado for you. You've never said a word of thanks."

"Me thank you? I saved you from murdering a man. You should've thanked me."

His expression told her she'd scored.

Romero stalked from the kitchen. He returned a few minutes later, now wearing a suit jacket. Everything about him was softer—his eyes, voice, and demeanor. He moved a kitchen chair closer to Lucy and sat down.

"I'm trying here, babe. I really am." He reached for her right hand and held it. "I'm more than fond of you. I'll help you, but you gotta be straight with me. That's the deal. I could find out what's going on with you in a nanosecond, but I'm not going to. It's up to you. If you leave here and change your mind, my offer's still open. Write about the weather on your blog. I'll be watching for it. Until then, leave me alone." He released her hand. "Before you go, we have some business to attend to. Did you tell anyone besides Peeps you were pregnant with my baby?"

"No. Why?"

"There are people who hate me. They'll hurt anyone, even my baby or the mother of my baby, to get to me. I need to know you're not vulnerable."

Lucy was horrified. "What kind of sick monster would hurt a baby to get to someone?"

"That's the world I live in," he said bitterly. "What's your answer?"

"No, Peeps was the only one I told."

"All right, we're finished here. I have things to do. I'm leaving. Peeps'll be here in thirty minutes to take you to your hotel...Lucy, think about what I've said."

He leaned into her face and kissed her lips. "I love you."

Lucy stared at the door for a full minute after it closed behind him.

"Liar! Liar!" she screamed. Romero didn't love her. Hurting and loving didn't mix. That's what her mother told her.

She leaned over the kitchen sink and rinsed Romero's kiss off her lips with the faucet water. She had the urge to smash the pile of dirty dishes sitting in the sink. Her conscience poked at her. Maybe she shouldn't have lied about being pregnant. She looked at her hands. Were they clean? Maybe she could clean up her conscience by cleaning up the house.

Before long, the dishes were stacked in the dishwasher, and the pans were hand-washed, dried, and put away. She neatened the bedroom and made the bed. What time was it? She didn't want to keep Peeps waiting. He was nobody to irritate.

The bedroom clock told her it was nearing nine. She remembered it was broken. Probably needed a battery. Maybe she could fix it and save Romero some trouble. She took the clock from the wall. She needed a flathead screwdriver. Where would Romero keep that? She rummaged through the kitchen drawers. No luck. She found a junk drawer with batteries, pens, pencils, and stray coins. There was a paperclip.

Within seconds, she'd removed the back from the clock. Her jaw dropped. A listening device was buried inside the clock. It looked exactly like the device she saw in Surveillance Spyware.

Her breathing became loud and ragged. Was someone listening to her? Could they tell she'd found the bug? She tried to control her breathing. Slow, rhythmic, steady. Her fingers trembled as she reassembled the clock and hung it on the wall.

Don't drop the fuckin' thing!

Were there any more listening devices? She checked Romero's computer mouse. Bugged. She found two bugs sewn into the seams of the sofa. Another in the kitchen curtains. A thought panicked her—was someone watching her search the house? Was there a video camera somewhere? She spun on her heels and looked at the coffee pot. Her knees shook as she realized her predicament.

Law enforcement was after Romero in a big way. McCormick was likely behind it. Romero was going down. Maybe she'd go down with him. It wouldn't be long before Rick knew she'd visited Romero. She hadn't said anything about her mother's homicide investigation, but Rick wouldn't care. He'd indict her, just like he said he would.

Should she warn Romero? That would guarantee her indictment. Every choice was bad.

She couldn't save Romero. Even if she told him about the bugs, the law would eventually catch up with him. It was only a matter of time. Romero had to save himself.

Silence was her only option. Maybe Peeps would find the bugs. Since he'd searched her, he'd search the house. He'd warn Romero. She could only hope. Peeps would be there in five minutes. The thought of getting back into a car with him made her uneasy. Why? It didn't matter why. She should listen to herself. Get out of there fast.

"Took a cab," she wrote on piece of paper. Put the note on the kitchen counter.

Fled.

October 26

The red-eye to Baltimore was quiet. The cabin was dim, illuminated by the soft glow of open laptops and overhead reading lights. The drone of the jet engines had lulled most of the passengers to sleep. The whispers of flight attendants occasionally interrupted the sounds of snoring.

Lucy was wide awake. She was well rested, nourished and, for the first time in more than ten days, feeling like herself. Her mother was right—a good meal and a night's rest can transform a person. She always said that.

The quiet of the cabin and Lucy's clear state of mind enabled her to think. Now that she excluded Romero as her mother's murderer, what was next? It made sense to start where the police had already been and work from there. How could she get information about the investigation from the police?

The Maryland Public Information Act popped into her mind. She could write to the government and request information. If the government refused to give it to her, she could file a lawsuit. Minerva said the lawsuit wouldn't pass the *red-face* test—a person can't get information about a pending criminal investigation unless the prosecutor agrees, and McCormick wouldn't. End of story.

The *red-face* test didn't apply to her; she didn't give a rat's ass what anybody thought. Rick could laugh at her. The judge could laugh with him.

So what? The worst that could happen was she'd end up exactly where she was now. Besides, shit happens—that's what Rick told her, a lifetime ago.

She had no idea how to make a request for information. What exactly was she asking for? Her Internet research on criminal investigations and forensics left her reeling. The information was too much, too conflicting, too hard to understand. Maybe she could learn forensics by binge-watching episodes of *Law & Order* and *CSI*. Who gets the request? That was the next question. State's Attorney's Office? Police Department? Santa Claus? She decided to start backward. Rick would never give her any documents—that was a given. Her request had to be good enough for the inevitable lawsuit.

The jet's wheels hit the tarmac. It was seven in the morning, BWI Airport.

Lucy sat for a moment on the front stoop of her house, inhaling the nippy air. It felt good; it smelled even better. She'd missed Baltimore's particular brand of pollution. When she opened her front door, she found a pile of mail littering her foyer. Most of it was bills. Bills she couldn't pay. Best to ignore the mail for now. She needed to focus on her information request.

Lucy unpacked and, on a whim, strapped on her Flashbang holster. She modeled it in front of her bedroom mirror. The holstered gun hanging between her breasts looked rather sexy, in her opinion. Drawing the gun from the holster was another matter; after four clumsy attempts, she realized she needed a lot of practice. She removed her gun and secured it.

As she pedaled to the courthouse on North Calvert Street, her bicycle felt good beneath her body. Relaxing, familiar and easy—like a faithful, old boyfriend. She practiced the track stand at the traffic signals and waved to her messenger friends as she zipped along the city streets.

Lucy entered the civil department and spotted two clerks at the counter, both named "Christine." The duplicate names had been the source of much confusion. Lucy had nicknamed them "Puddin'" and "Pop." Puddin' had skin the color of silky chocolate pudding. Pop had an effervescent personality. The nicknames stuck, to the gratitude of all who dealt with the Christines.

As soon as the women saw Lucy, they rushed from the counter and embraced her in a group hug.

"So sorry for your loss," Puddin' said.

"Such a terrible thing," Pop said.

"What can we do to help you?" they said together.

"Thanks, Puddin' Pop." She wiped her tears away with the back of her hands. "I'm looking for a lawsuit involving the Maryland Public Information Act."

"Any lawsuit in particular?" Pop said.

"I want to look at one you think's a winner."

"Massey & Henderson filed one this morning," Puddin' said. "They file a lot of MPIA suits and win most of them."

She handed Lucy the file and pointed to a nearby table. "You can go over there and read it."

Lucy studied the lawsuit as if were a textbook. The complaint referenced the MPIA, attached a copy of the request letter, named the state agencies involved, and stated that the agencies denied the request. She asked Pop to make a copy of the complaint. Now she had a template.

She spent the rest of the day watching crime shows and drafting her MPIA request. The final draft listed thirty-five documents, reports, and CitiWatch tapes. Tomorrow she'd do the easy part—make copies and deliver the request to the powers that be, including Appoline Mercer.

Mercer's gonna flip her shit.

Chapter 31

October 27

A loud knock on the office door drew Rick's attention from the search warrant affidavits piled on his desk.

"Come in." He expected to see Penelope Lundt.

The visitor wasn't Lundt, but Mercer. He compared her appearance with his mother's. They were the same age, sixty-one, but Mercer looked ten years younger. She was physically fit, well maintained, and wrinkleless.

Mercer tossed a large, brown envelope onto his desk.

"Don't give that girl jack shit. And find out who's behind this."

End of conversation. Mercer left, leaving only the echoes of high heels clicking on the hallway tile floor.

Rick examined the thick envelope. The return address belonged to Lucy Prestipino. He opened the envelope, curious. Inside was the most thorough MPIA request he'd ever seen. Who helped her? He hoped it wasn't one of Sanchez's attorneys.

He called her. Lucy picked up right away.

"Hello, Lucy. I haven't seen you around. Are you doing all right?"

"I'm managing, thank you…look, I know you're busy. You don't have to make small talk. Is there anything new in the investigation?"

"Not that I can share. I'm calling about your request for information. It's an amazing request. The best I've ever seen."

"You want to know who helped me. Is that why you're calling?"

"No, no. I want to discuss your request, to see what we can work out."

"You can tell that silver-tongued, botoxed snakehead I figured out how to do it on my own."

He smiled into the phone.

"I'm glad to know you don't consider me a silver-tongued, botoxed snakehead."

"I can't see you getting botox."

Rick laughed out loud, although he didn't mean to. "I'm glad to see you haven't lost your spark. When are you coming back to Loaves & Fishes? I miss you. We all do."

"I can't...not right now...the place reminds me too much of my mother. Excuse me."

He heard her blow her nose and clear her throat.

"I'm back. Sorry. Are you going to give me what I asked for? Yes or no?"

"No."

"Are you speaking for all the agencies or the State's Attorney's Office?"

"The other agencies will do what we say. Lucy, listen to me. Drop this. Let us concentrate on finding your mother's killer. Every minute we spend dealing with your MPIA request is a minute—"

"Can you put it in an e-mail?" Her voice cracked. "This is too hard to talk about."

"All right, I will. Take care of yourself."

She hung up without saying another word.

As soon as she disconnected, Rick wrote the e-mail she requested. He did his best to explain the public policy reasons behind the refusal to disclose. They were the same reasons he explained before, in his office, the day after her mother's killing. She was too distraught to understand. He wrote simply and directly, using language suitable for her level of education. It took him more than an hour.

⊷⊶

Lucy put the finishing touches on her lawsuit. When she was finished, she held the document in her hands and admired her work. She waited for Rick's e-mail so she could attach it to the lawsuit.

Over an hour passed before it arrived. The e-mail infuriated her. It didn't say anything more than what he'd told her in his office. Plus, he wrote it like she was some sort of dope. What an asshole.

No matter. Tomorrow, she'd file the lawsuit and ask for an emergency hearing. She'd also ask Puddin' Pop to expedite its processing. She had no doubt the hearing would be harder than drafting the lawsuit. Why worry about it now? One day at a time, just like she learned from AA.

Chapter 32

October 28

F iling the lawsuit was surprisingly easy—all it took was handing Puddin' the filing fee, the complaint, and the cover sheet. After Puddin' docketed and processed the lawsuit, Lucy asked her to expedite the hearing.

"That's up to the court, hon, but I'll do what I can."

The cold air hit Lucy's face as soon as she stepped from the courthouse. It was nine o'clock in the morning. The city appeared dark and depressing. Clouds blocked the sun with an endless blanket of gray. The smell of the air told her snow was on the way.

She practiced her track stands, knowing that within a few hours, she'd transform into a messenger mercenary, taking full advantage of the inevitable chaos that would result from even a trace amount of snow. She pedaled along West Pratt Street, heading toward Ground Zero, looking forward to seeing her posse. Except for Floater. He disapproved of her lawsuit. "Let the experts do their jobs," he said. "Don't get in their way."

As she biked past Café No Delay, she glanced through the front window, longing for a latte, a luxury now out of her budget. She caught a glimpse of Rick McCormick. He was holding a cup of coffee in one hand and a phone in the other. His expression was the usual intense frown. Lucy remembered the day she met his sister, Colleen. Why didn't he introduce her? It still pissed her off.

It made her mother mad, too. She ranted like an insane person. *Nothing I hate more than a man who mistreats a woman. Lowest form of scum on this Earth.* Lucy got a funny feeling in her stomach. She'd write down her mother's words as soon as she got to the next red light.

There was an ear-piercing shriek.

A woman was in the crosswalk, directly in front of the bike, pushing a stroller. Lucy jammed on her brakes. The bike slid across the intersection and bumped the stroller, jostling it. She jumped from her bike, letting it crash to the ground. "I'm sorry! I'm sorry! Is your baby all right?"

The woman lifted a tiny bundle out of the stroller and pressed it to her chest. Both the woman and baby were crying.

A man ran out of a fast food store. "I saw the whole thing! That messenger ran right into the stroller. She could've killed the baby!"

Someone grabbed her arm. "You stay put, young lady." The arm grabber was an obese man wearing a tattered coat smelling of alcohol.

Within minutes, a large crowd of pedestrians surrounded her, hurling disgust and hatred her way. She was terrified. The flash mob had agitated itself into a fury. She expected to be beaten or shot.

A forceful voice shouted at the crowd. "Step back! Make way."

Rick charged through the crowd holding his State's Attorney's badge above his head.

"Let go of her, sir," he said to the man holding Lucy's arm.

His voice and demeanor intimidated the crowd into disbursing. Only Lucy and the woman with the baby remained.

"Has anyone been hurt?" he said. "Do I need to call an ambulance?"

The woman shook her head.

"It was all my fault," Lucy sobbed out.

Rick pointed to an outdoor café closed for the winter. "Take your bike and wait over there."

She sat at a table as Rick talked privately with the woman. After a few minutes, Rick handed the woman his card. He walked into the busy intersection holding up his badge and let loose a deafening whistle that halted traffic in all directions. Still holding up his badge, he directed the woman to push her stroller across the street. Once he got traffic moving again, he sat at the table with Lucy. "They're both fine. She decided not to press charges."

"Thank you." Lucy wiped away a tear rolling down her cheek.

"What happened today? Didn't you see her?"

"Not until I was almost on top of her. I remembered something about my mother and stopped paying attention."

"What did you remember?"

Her face grew hot. How much should she tell him? She decided to lay it all out. Maybe he would see the murder investigation should be going in another direction.

"I remembered our last conversation. It was the day before she died. She called me. It ended up being a strange phone call."

"How so?"

"I was interested in this man—"

"Romero Sanchez?"

"No, no—this was after I broke up with Romero. It was someone I'd known for a few months. We were only friends, but I liked the guy. A lot. I thought he liked me, too. He was sending me those signals, you know? One day, I ran into him at a coffee shop. He was with his sister."

Rick's face fell.

"He ignored me—didn't introduce me. I know it sounds silly, but I was upset and told my mother. She went ballistic. Talked about men mistreating women. She went on and on. It was out of proportion to what I'd told her.

"When I remembered it today, I thought about how odd it was. Did something happen to her she'd never told me about? Maybe it had something to do with—"

Rick's face looked pained. "I'm sorry I didn't introduce you. It had nothing to do with you. I love my sister, but she's her own social network. Can you believe she has over a thousand friends on Facebook? If I introduced you, she would've posted it within minutes. Before long, the rumors would be flying. My family would have us engaged, then married, then with a bunch of kids. It'd be a runaway train. I wasn't in the mood for it. I didn't mean to hurt you."

"You're not hearing me. I'm not looking for an apology. My mother—"

"I hope you understand. Will you forgive me for my rudeness?"

"Yes, you're forgiven, okay? I need to tell you—"

"It's too early for you to go back to work." He spoke with a grave voice. "You have a dangerous occupation. You could hurt yourself, or someone else. You were lucky today. Take more time off."

She wanted to slap him. He didn't listen to her. Never did, never would. It was fruitless to keep trying.

"I need to tell you something," she said. "I filed an MPIA lawsuit today."

Rick stared at her. After a heartbeat, his rich voice exploded into a shout.

"Don't you know all this bullshit is sucking the life out of the investigation? You're taking resources away from finding your mother's killer. We have other crimes to solve and prosecute, other crime victims and grieving families we need to take care of. This isn't just about you."

Rick walked away. Snow began to flurry.

Lucy said a silent prayer for Detective Marlow, thankful the cop had ordered her to ride a bike with brakes.

Chapter 33

December 12

Lucy's stomach churned as she checked the time on her phone. In less than twenty-four hours, Rick would chew her up and spit her out, right on the courtroom floor.

She waited forty-five long days for the hearing. The lawsuit seemed so promising when she filed the complaint, but within days, Rick filed an answer and a motion to dismiss. The motion was short, to the point, and skewered the basis of her lawsuit. Now she understood the meaning of the *red-face* test.

The last forty-five days had been rocky. Minerva scoured all of Debbie's files and accounts. It turned out Debbie had no money—she'd been scraping by, weighed down by a mortgage and the home equity loan she obtained to finance Lucy's rehab. Debbie never opted for pension or death benefits, apparently choosing to eke out a few additional dollars from her paycheck. There was no life insurance or house equity. In fact, Lucy's childhood home was deeply underwater.

"Walk away from the house," Minerva said. "If you try to save it, you'll lose your own."

Lucy expected to lose her house anyway. She'd used the last of her savings to pay her utility bills. She couldn't pay the mortgage. What Lucy needed was income. She tried to jump start her messenger business, but couldn't concentrate. As soon as she picked up a courier package, she forgot where she was going with it or how to get there. More than once, she was waiting at a light when tears inundated her. Her reputation for reliability tanked, and her hard-won customer base fizzled away.

An argument with Floater, triggered by Joseph, nearly killed their friendship. Joseph came and went from AA meetings. Whenever he showed, he sat next to her, trying to have private conversations, asking if she needed a ride home. He was a pest. She couldn't tell Joseph to leave her alone—he saved her from a relapse. Floater came to her rescue. He arranged for others to sit by Lucy and artfully interrupted every conversation Joseph tried to start. One day Lucy exploded.

"Your anger is eating you alive," Joseph said during a meeting. "Forgive your mother's killer. That's the only way to find peace."

She almost spit in his face. "Forgive? Peace? Fuck you!"

Joseph walked out of the meeting and never came back. Floater was livid. "You can't act that way! Do you realize what you've done? You chased away an alcoholic from an AA meeting. He was only trying to help you—we all are. Get some professional help, dammit!"

Her rage infected her work life. She found a job at a fast food store and lasted three days. She was taking an order when she overheard a male customer, speaking in Spanish, talking to a curvaceous teenager about the size of her breasts. Lucy became incensed, screamed at him in Spanish, hurling the insults she intended to say when she first met Romero. This time she got it right—the Spanish was perfect.

"No, Lucy!" the teenager said. "He was just ordering a chicken breast sandwich!"

Moments later, she was fired in perfect English.

Despair drove Lucy to her bed. There were days when she couldn't get up. Today was one of them. She hid under her covers holding her father's picture against her cheek.

"Daddy," she whispered. "I need help with tomorrow's hearing. Please talk to God about making shit happen."

Her phone rang. She reached across the bed and answered it, praying there was a reprieve.

"Ms. Prestipino? This is Dr. Michaels."

Lucy was befuddled. "Who?"

"John Michaels, the veterinarian taking care of your mother's dog."

"Huh?"

"The dog is ready to go home."

"Is this some kind of sick joke? He's dead! Murdered along with my mother."

"Ms. Prestipino...may I call you 'Lucy'?" He spoke without waiting for an answer. "Lucy, I'm terribly sorry about your mother. And I'm sorry no one told you her dog is alive."

"Steppie's alive?"

"Yes, he's— "

Lucy dropped the phone. It bounced off the bed and onto the floor. The battery shot out. Once she retrieved the phone, it took her trembling fingers two minutes to slip the battery into place.

The phone rang.

"Lucy? It's Dr. Michaels again. We got disconnected."

"I'm sorry, I dropped the phone. Did you say Steppie's alive?"

"Yes, he's sitting on my lap right now. I imagine this is quite a shock. I'm glad to finally know his name. We've been calling him 'Fearless.'"

Her mouth was dry.

"I just learned you didn't know he was in my care. When I called the police to get your number, no one knew anything about the dog. My assistant, Maggie, was able to track you down from the funeral home. I don't know where the communication failed, but it did. Terribly so."

"Steppie's alive?"

"Yes, and he's doing great. Steppie has a long way to go, but he'll recover faster if he were in a loving home. Would you like to come get him?"

Lucy nodded, unable to speak. She cleared her throat. "Yes."

"Good! I'll give you the full run down when you get here. I'm in Roland Park. Do you know where it is?"

She knew exactly where it was. A thirty-minute drive would take her to the land of mansions and butlers and manicured yards. There were magical boutiques with shoppers wearing St. John's suits and Hermes scarves. It was hard for Lucy to believe Roland Park was part of Baltimore City.

"Yes, I know where it is."

"You need to have some soft food on hand. There's a little dog supply store right down the street from my office. It's called 'Happy Howlers.' Why don't you stop there before you come in? Tell the folks you need soft food for Fearless. They know who he is. He's a celebrity around the neighborhood."

When the conversation ended, Lucy confronted the transportation issue. She couldn't drive; she didn't even have her learner's permit. Anyone who could give her a ride was working. Dogs weren't allowed on busses. She had no money for a cab. Lucy could think of only one solution: drive Debbie's car without a license and hope she didn't get caught. A big risk, but she didn't care. Nothing was going to keep her from getting to Steppie. Not even the law. Thirty minutes later, Lucy arrived at Happy Howlers with a steering wheel slick with sweat.

Jingling bells on the front door welcomed her to a wonderland of dog products and services. Suede coats, strollers, nail polish, and boots. A grooming salon. Photography studio. There was even a dog party room. Lucy meandered through the aisles selecting an array of soft dog food. When she finished, she got in line behind a customer at the cashier's counter. Next to the register was a large jar, with a hand-written label, "Save Fearless." Money stuffed the jar.

"Want to make a donation for Fearless?" the cashier said to the customer. "He almost died trying to save his owner." She pointed to the jar. "This is for his medical care."

The customer pushed in a twenty-dollar bill.

Five minutes later, Lucy entered the office of John Michaels, DVM. The reception room was cozy and warmly lit. Dogs on leashes strained to meet her, unable to get traction on the linoleum floor. One dog, an aged mutt, was off leash and lounging on his back soaking up a sunbeam. Lucy bent down to pat his stomach.

"That's Dr. Michaels's dog," said a woman sitting behind the reception desk. "He's called 'The Old Gentleman.' He's blind and deaf, but he teaches us how to enjoy life."

The woman who spoke had luscious brown curls and hazel-green eyes. She was wearing scrubs decorated with dancing dogs and cats.

"Hi, I'm Maggie, Dr. Michaels's assistant," she said. "How can I help you?"

"I'm Lucy Prestipino. Dr. Michaels called me about— "

"You're here about Fearless! So glad to meet you. Follow me."

Maggie brought her into a small examining room. "Dr. Michaels will be here in a second. We're going to miss the little guy. What a sweet boy."

Dr. Michaels walked in holding a file. He was handsome, with a straight nose and a wide smile. She guessed he was in his late sixties, but it was hard to tell—his hair was the color of a UPS truck, without a speck of gray.

Behind his thick, wire-rimmed glasses were hazel eyes of compassion. He extended his hand and shook Lucy's.

"I'm so sorry for the miscommunication. I wondered why you hadn't been in touch with us."

"The police told me Steppie was dead."

"No one thought he was going to make it. He's one tough pooch. Your mother would've been very proud of him."

Lucy's eyes filled.

"Please accept my sympathy."

"Thank you...Dr. Michaels, how did Steppie end up here? He was shot in Patterson Park."

"I don't know the whole story. A young man brought him here. He was wearing a police uniform, but I think he might've been a recruit. He said he brought Steppie here because it didn't seem right to put the dog down after what he'd done to defend his owner. He'd gotten my name from friends on his tennis team at the L'Hirondelle Club. When he told me the story, I knew I had to try to save the dog."

"Do you know the recruit's name? I'd like to thank him."

"No, I never heard it. Let me tell you about Steppie. He's recovering from a third surgery and is still on pain medicine and antibiotics." He handed Lucy a bag of pills and a piece of paper. "Here's the medication schedule. Over the next two weeks, you're going to wean him off of the meds.

"Steppie is strong-willed. He hates taking pills. Put them in a bit of peanut butter and give him lots of water to wash them down. And always check to make sure he swallows the pills. He's a sneaky little pooch. Sometimes he eats the peanut butter and spits out the pills." Dr. Michaels chuckled for a moment and then became serious. "He doesn't have any front teeth. You'll have to grind up his food. It would be best if you could make his food yourself. There are lots of recipes for dog food on the web. It's fine to take him outside on a leash. He's pretty shaky now, but it won't take long before he starts chasing squirrels. Do you have any questions?"

"I have to go to court in the morning about my mother's case, and I don't have anyone to leave him with. Can I come back tomorrow to get him? Would that be all right?"

"That's fine."

Dr. Michaels opened his file. "Now for the business part. I want to discuss the bill with you."

He handed her a thick packet, twelve pages long. The only page Lucy focused on was the front summary page. The total was over twelve thousand dollars.

Lucy stopped breathing for thirty seconds before she could speak. "I can't pay it! I can't!"

She put her head on the examining table and heaved cries of anguish. The tears seemed to be bubbling up from her toes. She couldn't stop herself.

"You're not going to put him down if I can't pay, are you? You're not going to give him away to someone else?"

"No, no, of course not," Dr. Michaels said. "Now, now...please, don't cry. You don't owe anything. Donations paid the whole bill."

"I'm sorry, Dr. Michaels," Lucy said with embarrassment. "That happens all the time. It comes out of nowhere. I start crying and crying."

"There's no need to apologize. You're too hard on yourself." Dr. Michaels smiled at her. "Now let me go get our hero."

A few minutes later, he returned cradling Steppie in his arms. The dog was barely awake and drooling. Lucy winced when she saw the tracks of black stitches covering his stomach. Dr. Michaels handed him to Lucy.

"Steppie, Steppie," she whispered. She nuzzled her face against his. He licked her nose. She was sure the dog recognized her.

"Time for you to start your new life." She kissed him. "Time for both of us to start our new lives." She looked up. "Dr. Michaels, you've been so kind. Can you help me with one more thing?"

"What do you need?"

She explained, and he agreed.

Chapter 34

December 13

Lucy looked lovely.

When Rick entered the courtroom, he spotted her right away. She was sitting on a wooden bench in the spectator gallery, wearing the same dress she'd worn for the strong-arm trial. Her hair was pulled into the same messy bun, with the same wisps of golden hair framing her face. He'd never forgotten how she captured the hearts of jurors as she hobbled to the witness stand clunking her cast along the way.

Lucy must've been lost in thought. She didn't look his way until he spoke.

"Hello, Lucy. How are you?" He had the urge to tuck the rebellious hair strands back into her bun.

"I'm fine. And you?"

She isn't fine, and she doesn't care how I am.

Her face seemed different, somehow. Thinner, that's what it was. She'd lost weight. The eyes were different, too—still the intriguing blue and brown, but no longer as vibrant. She seemed older, weary.

Rick held the swing gate open for her as they moved from the gallery to the well of the courtroom. Lucy hesitated when she reached the two counsel tables.

"You sit on the left side," he said. "I sit on the right."

"Thank you." They took their respective seats.

He pulled the *Prestipino* file from his briefcase and positioned it in front of him, along with a yellow pad and pen. Lucy brought only a tiny black-and-white photograph. She sat ramrod straight in her seat, silent and motionless, with her hands clasping the photograph, and her ankles tucked under her chair.

Detective Campbell came through the door and summoned Rick to join him in the back of the courtroom. He was surprised to see Campbell; he hadn't asked him to be present. He was even more surprised when Campbell showed him the subpoena he'd just received from Lucy. A moment later, the courtroom clerk swept through the door, followed by the judge's law clerk and the bailiff.

The courtroom was quiet, except for the sounds of the clerk rustling papers and testing the courtroom's recording system. The judge was late. It was now nine thirty.

Rick tried to dam the usual flood of aggression that surged in him before a hearing. The *killer instinct*. Take no prisoners, scorch the Earth. That's what trial lawyers were supposed to do—advocate as forcefully and cleverly as permitted by law. From those best efforts, the truth would emerge, and justice would be done. That was the theory, anyway.

Like all theories, this one had its kinks. Arguing against a *pro se* litigant was tricky business. Advocating with too much force and cleverness could backfire; the attorney looks like a bully, and the judge feels compelled to protect the *pro se* litigant.

Rick watched Lucy, trying to imagine how Judge Bentley would perceive her. She looked vulnerable and a little dazed. He had to tread lightly. Maybe Lucy would refer to Mrs. Mercer as a "silver-tongued, botoxed snakehead." That'd be a game changer. He smiled. Lucy sure had a gift for insults.

"Something funny, Mr. McCormick?" she said.

Her cold voice sent a rush of hot blood to his face.

"All rise," the courtroom clerk said.

The Honorable Henry Susque entered the courtroom, trailed by a golden retriever. The judge took his seat at the bench. After circling for a few seconds, the retriever flopped on the floor by the jury box.

"Good morning, everyone," the judge said. "Judge Bentley is under the weather, so I'm stepping in for her. Please accept my apology for the delay. I had to review the pleadings. You may sit down."

Rick was unhappy with the turn of events. He disliked appearing before Susque. The judge had a quirky personality he didn't understand. The retriever was a perfect example. Who brings their dog into a courtroom? Judge Susque's hearings were riddled with his silly jokes, mostly directed at the attorneys. Rick could tolerate the eccentricities, but justice demanded consistency. Susque was as random as a winning lottery ticket.

"Will the parties identify themselves for the record," the judge said.

Rick stood and introduced himself. Lucy did the same.

"Do either of you have an objection to my dog being present?"

"No objection, Your Honor," Rick said, hiding his annoyance.

"What's your dog's name?" Lucy said. "Can I say 'hello'?"

"Ms. Prestipino, may I present Cassiopeia, dog extraordinaire. She's a retired comfort dog."

The judge nodded toward Lucy. Cassiopeia loped to Lucy and held up her paw. She shook it.

Rick clenched his teeth. Lucy'd won the judge's favor in less than thirty seconds.

"All right." The judge picked up the court's file. "Let's start with the motion to dismiss. Mr. McCormick, do you have anything to add? Otherwise, I'm going to hear from Ms. Prestipino."

It was a signal to Rick the judge agreed with the motion, but wanted Lucy to have her say.

"I have nothing to add."

"Do you have anything to subtract?"

"Excuse me?"

Lucy giggled. The judge smiled.

"Lighten up, Mr. McCormick. It was a joke. It's your turn, Ms. Prestipino. What do you want to say?"

Lucy stood, fingers touching the surface of counsel's table. "I know there are good reasons why police shouldn't reveal their investigations while they're still going on, but there's an exception. If it's in the public interest, which it is in this case. The police are on the wrong track, and the killer's getting away."

"Why do you think the police are on the wrong track?" the judge said.

"This is like the Chandra Levy case. You know...the one in DC?"

Rick knew the case well. In 2001, Chandra Levy, a Washington, D.C. intern, vanished from her apartment. The revelation of Levy's affair with a married congressman set off a media frenzy that overshadowed the investigation into her disappearance. More than a year later, a dog-walker discovered Levy's remains near a trail in Rock Creek Park. Over nine years passed before a jury convicted a Salvadoran immigrant of first-degree murder. The congressman had nothing to do with the murder. His political career was ruined.

"I'm familiar with the case," the judge said. "Why is this like the Chandra Levy case?"

"In that case, the investigators thought the congressman could've been responsible for Chandra's disappearance. While they were looking into that, the investigators didn't realize that someone was hunting and attacking women in Rock Creek Park. That's what's happening here. It started because I used to date Romero Sanchez. Have you heard of him?"

"Yes," the judge said flatly.

"Mr. McCormick warned me about Romero, and I broke up with him. After my mother was killed, everyone assumed Romero had something to do with it. The gang unit got involved. Now all they see is gang. Maybe my mother's murder was about something else."

"What do you think it was about?"

"I don't know…yet. You see, the day before my mother died, we had a peculiar phone call. She got angry over something silly. It was crazy, not like her at all. Now I wonder if that had something to do with her murder."

"Did you tell anyone about this peculiar phone call?"

She glanced at Rick. "I tried to tell Mr. McCormick, but he didn't listen. I guess because it didn't fit in with his gang theory."

Rick jumped to his feet. "That's not correct, Your Honor. This is the first I'm hearing about it."

"Don't you remember?" she said to Rick. "It was right after I had the bike accident with the stroller. When I tried to tell you, all you talked about was your sister."

The conversation came roaring back to him. Fuck.

"His sister?" the judge said. "Is this ringing a bell, Mr. McCormick?"

Rick wanted to evaporate. "Yes…that part of the conversation got lost somehow."

"I'm stuck on the sister part," the judge said with an edge in his voice. "Ms. Prestipino, do you have a personal relationship with Mr. McCormick?"

The courtroom became unnervingly quiet. Rick could feel everyone watching him, waiting for her answer.

"We used to volunteer at Loaves & Fishes. Sometimes we'd run into each other and talk. That's all."

Judge Susque gave Rick a hard and lengthy look. He then returned his attention to Lucy.

"How about Romero Sanchez? Do you have a relationship with him?"

"You mean, now?"

"Yes, now."

"Oh, no! No. It's over."

The judge flipped to a paper-clipped page in the court's file.

"Ms. Prestipino, I'm looking at the memorandum filed by Mr. McCormick. He states your breakup with Romero Sanchez was violent. You broke his nose. Is that true?"

Lucy seemed ready for the question. "Yes, it's true. Afterward, Romero called Mr. McCormick and gave him the identity of his wife's killer. He did that to protect me. Why would he protect me and then kill my mother?"

Rick was worried. Judge Susque was listening to her. She'd gotten some mileage out of the conversation about his sister. The Chandra Levy comparison was a clever touch. Rick made a tough decision—he would reveal some important information he'd withheld from the motion to dismiss. Lucy would be devastated. He didn't want to hurt her but...

"Mr. McCormick, is there anything you want to add along those lines?" Judge Susque must've been reading him.

"Prior to her mother's killing, Ms. Prestipino called the Crime Stoppers Hotline with a tip. The tip was that an undercover officer, posing as a friend of Sanchez, had been made. We believe Sanchez realized Ms. Prestipino was the source of this tip, felt betrayed, and killed her mother out of revenge."

An eerie silence descended on the courtroom. Rick glanced at Lucy. She was still standing. Holding onto the photograph. Hands shaking. Face ashen.

"Please sit down, Ms. Prestipino," the judge said. She did. The bailiff brought her a glass of water.

Rick watched her as the clock marked off sixty seconds. She kept swallowing, clearing her throat, and blinking. She opened her mouth to speak. Nothing came out. Her eyes watered. It was excruciating. She was crumbling before his eyes.

Cassiopeia put her head in Lucy's lap. She began stroking the dog.

Then something changed in Lucy. Rick could feel it. She stood up straight and leaned toward the judge.

"I want to call two witnesses."

Rick objected, intending to argue he hadn't received any notice of witness testimony. The judge cut him off with a wave of his hand.

"Overruled. Ms. Prestipino, call your first witness."

"Detective Campbell," she said.

Campbell took the witness stand. The judge asked him the preliminary questions.

"Go ahead," the judge said to Lucy.

"Detective Campbell, what's the name of my mother's dog?"

"You told me his name was 'Steppie.'"

"Is Steppie alive or dead?"

Campbell frowned. "He's dead."

"How'd he die?"

"He was shot at the time your mother was killed."

"That's all I want to ask Detective Campbell," she said.

"Any questions, Mr. McCormick?" the judge said.

Rick answered in the negative, and Campbell left the witness stand.

"The next witness is John Michaels," Lucy said. "He's out in the hallway."

Rick and Campbell exchanged *who-the-hell-is-he* looks.

The bailiff escorted Michaels into the courtroom. After the witness was sworn, the judge asked him to state his name and occupation.

"My name is John Michaels. I'm a veterinarian."

The judge motioned to Lucy to ask her questions.

"Dr. Michaels, do you know a dog named 'Steppie'?"

"Yes, I do."

"Is he alive or dead?"

"He's very much alive."

Rick's stomach hit the courtroom floor. Judge Susque was staring at the witness with a slack jaw.

"Am I hearing this right?" the judge said. "The victim's dog has been alive all this time?"

"I've been taking care of him for the last eight weeks."

"How did Steppie come under your care?" the judge said.

Dr. Michaels told the story of Steppie and the unidentified police recruit.

"How was your bill paid?" Lucy said.

"By donations, over twelve thousand dollars. Steppie's heroism was widely known in the neighborhood. Nearly every store posted donation signs. There were even a couple of fundraisers."

The judge's face turned as red as a steamed crab.

"Mr. McCormick?" the judge said. "Do you have any questions for Dr. Michaels?"

Rick ruled out questioning the witness. Who knew what would come out during cross-examination? This was a police fuck up; the less said the better. As embarrassing as the testimony was, it didn't take away from his legal argument.

"No questions."

Judge Susque thanked Dr. Michaels for his testimony and excused him from the courtroom.

"Well, we seem to have covered the merits of the complaint as well as the motion to dismiss, so I'm going to rule on the whole ball of wax," the judge said. "I'll hear your arguments now. Ms. Prestipino, you go first."

"For eight weeks, I thought Steppie was dead. Even though a whole neighborhood knew he was alive, the police didn't know. If they could make a big mistake like that, they could be making another big mistake in the investigation. Just like Chandra Levy.

"All I want is to look into my mother's murder myself. It's too late for me to get my own crime scene evidence. I won't get in the way of their gang investigation, I promise. They don't have to show me anything having to do with Romero or gangs. That's all I have to say."

"I'll hear from you now, Mr. McCormick."

"The State apologizes to Ms. Prestipino for the mistake concerning Steppie. But that doesn't change the reasons for not revealing the details of an ongoing criminal investigation. Disclosure could jeopardize the investigation, risk the admissibility of evidence collected, and thwart our ability to obtain a valid confession. Ms. Prestipino has demonstrated her difficulties with anger management—she broke Sanchez's nose. What will she do if she finds her mother's killer?

"Most important is the danger to Ms. Prestipino. Let's not lose sight of the fact we're dealing with a dangerous, ruthless gang. She could get hurt, raped, trafficked—even killed."

Judge Susque told them to sit.

"I'm ready to rule. I'm disturbed by the lack of communication between the victim's daughter, the prosecutor, and the police. I'm even more disturbed a whole neighborhood knew the victim's dog was alive—held fundraisers for his medical expenses—but the police and prosecution were clueless. Incredible! And cruel. Ms. Prestipino might have found comfort from the dog in her time of sorrow."

The judge glared at Rick and Campbell. "Ms. Prestipino is right. If the police could make such a grievous error about whether the victim's dog was dead or alive, there could be other grievous errors."

He turned his gaze to Lucy. "The State is also right. There could be very dangerous people responsible for your mother's killing. I don't want to allow you access to investigation documents only to read in the *Sun* that, as a result of my decision, you've been killed."

Judge Susque rubbed his head as if he had a headache. "Mr. McCormick, I am ordering that within twenty-four hours, you permit Ms. Prestipino to view all forensic and investigatory reports. This is to be done under your personal supervision. However, this will not include anything concerning Romero Sanchez, Roach, or any other gang. Ms. Prestipino may take personal notes, but may not receive copies. You are also to arrange for her to view the CitiWatch tapes."

"Ms. Prestipino, you cannot share any information about the investigation with anyone, directly or indirectly. If you do, I'll hold you in contempt. In addition, if you discover any information, have any ideas, thoughts, or conclusions, you are to tell Detective Campbell. Are there any questions about my decision?"

There were none, and the hearing ended.

Campbell stalked out of the courtroom. Rick heard the sound of rapid footsteps snapping on the hallway's marble floor. *Campbell's pissed. So am I.*

Rick approached Lucy. An apology was in order; what happened to Steppie was inexcusable. He stood in front of her for a few awkward moments.

"Can you leave first?" she said. "I need a minute."

Rick left without making his apology. He stole a glimpse at Lucy. She was sitting at counsel's table, pressing the photograph to her heart and sobbing.

This day was going to shit. It was time to face Ms. Snakehead.

Chapter 35

December 13

The day was shittier than he thought.

By the time he returned to the State's Attorney's Office, everyone knew he'd been beaten by a *pro se* opponent who didn't have a high school degree. It wouldn't be so bad if his colleagues kidded him about it. Instead, they treated him as if he'd been disbarred. *Sorry, Rick.* He heard that a dozen times.

He exchanged heated words with Campbell.

"Why didn't you tell me about your conversation with Lucy?" Campbell said. "She gives you information like that, and you talk about your sister? What the fuck?"

Rick counter-punched. "Why didn't you know the dog was alive? You're telling me there wasn't a single cop in the department who knew about a fundraiser for a *shot dog*?"

The argument with Campbell paled in comparison with the berating he endured from Mercer. She harped on the damage he caused to future prosecutorial efforts: "Now there's a judicial decision allowing public access to investigatory materials during a pending case. A roadmap for anyone who wants to use it—criminal suspects, defense counsel, the press."

"Do you want to file an appeal?" he asked.

"Don't be stupid. That's all we need—an appellate decision affirming Susque's decision. It'll bind every prosecutor throughout the State. Not worth the risk."

From there, she moved to a personal attack: "Any ASA who can't prevail in court against a drug addicted, alcoholic, high school dropout is inept."

He expected her to fire him, but she didn't. Instead, she went for his jugular: "I'm considering dissolving the gang unit. As far as I can tell, it's been a waste of taxpayers' money and a misallocation of resources."

As he walked to his office, his colleagues watched him as if he were a perp taking the walk.

Fuck this. I'm getting a job at Café No Delay.

Rick instructed Lundt to vet the *Prestipino* file and redact anything pertaining to Sanchez and gangs. He called the crime lab and Campbell to make sure the file was complete.

"Any updates, Ulysses?" Rick called the detective by his first name, hoping to thaw the ice between them.

"No, Mr. McCormick."

He waited all afternoon for Lucy to call, but the call never came. Did something happen to Steppie? His heart sank whenever he thought about the dog. Files got lost in the system. Inmates, too. But dogs? Lucy had every right to be furious.

It was time to face her. She lived nearby; close enough to hand-deliver the file and wait while she reviewed it. Tropical Storm Shit was still hanging over his office. It'd be nice to get away from its torrents until it passed—even if it meant clashing with Hurricane Lucy.

As Rick drove down Lucy's street, he called to tell her he was coming. She'd be angry if he just showed up; more fuel to the fire. No answer. He pressed on the doorbell. Sanchez popped into his mind. Broken nose.

"Rick?" She was holding a dog bowl and a baby spoon. "What're you doing here?"

Lucy looked distracted and upset. She walked away without waiting for his reply. He interpreted the open door as an invitation to come in. The house was cold, maybe sixty degrees. There was a carpet of unopened mail littering the floor.

"Don't mind this," she said. "I'm a little behind on my paperwork." She shoved the mail with her foot, making a path to a dog bed in the dining room.

"Come meet Steppie. He's being stubborn. Won't eat. All he wants is peanut butter."

The dog was nearly invisible as he lay, curled in a ball, on the white fleecy bed. Steppie opened a sleepy eye when Rick stroked the top of his head.

"I can't get him to eat," she said.

"Let me try."

He sat cross-legged on the floor next to the dog's bed. "C'mon, Steppie. We're going to try something new." He kissed the dog's head as he lifted him from his bed. Steppie was soon cradled in Rick's arms, staring up at his face.

"Watch the squirrel, Steppie." With his right hand, he dipped the spoon into the bowl of dog food and flew it around Steppie's head. "See the squirrel? See it?"

Steppie followed the spoon with his eyes, spellbound. When the dog's jaw dropped slightly, Rick slipped the spoon into his mouth. Steppie gummed the food and swallowed it.

"How'd you know to do that?" Lucy said.

"I used to watch my mother feed Colleen. She was a picky eater."

Rick fed Steppie until the dog turned his head away from the spoon. "I guess you're full." He gently returned Steppie to his bed. Lucy was smiling at him, her eyes expressing gratitude.

"Have you eaten?" she said. "I made a big pot of dog food. Want to stay for dinner?"

"Sure." He didn't care what it was—it smelled delicious.

It wasn't dog food, but beef stew. Steppie's share was ground into mush; the remainder was a chunky blend of meat, vegetables, and gravy. It tasted great.

He ate two full bowls of stew before he approached the subject of his visit. He began on a positive note.

"Have you ever thought of becoming a trial lawyer? You'd be terrific at it."

Lucy screwed up her face as if the idea was preposterous. "No way, it's kind of...boring, don't you think?"

He doubled over and howled until he saw her confounded expression. She hadn't meant it as a joke.

"I wasn't bored at all," he said, grinning. "Actually, I was quite terrified."

He opened his briefcase and handed her a thick file.

She put the file on the dining room table. "Ever seen *Xena: Warrior Princess*? There's a Xena marathon on TV. Want to watch it while I look at the file? If that's not your thing, some kind of sports is probably on."

"Xena sounds fine."

He stared at the television, but his mind was on Appoline Mercer. He couldn't understand her shift in attitude. They had a fine working relationship until she made him chief of the gang unit. The unit was doing well; the *Sun* wrote a complimentary article about the unit's new anti-gang, middle-school initiative. The Alvarado investigation earned the unit accolades. Even the Police Commissioner called to congratulate him. There wasn't a word of acknowledgment from Mercer. He decided to let it go, for now. He was too tired to think about it.

———————

Lucy's right hand was cramped, and she had a large callous on her middle finger. After two hours, she'd copied, word-for-word, only a quarter of the documents. At this rate, she wouldn't be done for another six hours.

She groaned when she came upon the DNA profile. There were columns of numbers, scientific terminology, and nonsensical information. If she copied it wrong, it wouldn't mean anything, even to an expert. As she toiled, she became aware of slow, rhythmic breathing, too loud to be Steppie's. She looked at Rick. He was sitting upright, with closed eyes, and his head listed forward. A brief snore convinced her he was asleep. She reached for her phone and began snapping pictures.

Click, click, click...

After every click, she glanced at Rick. He must've had a hard day because he didn't move a muscle. Within forty-five minutes, she was finished.

———————

Rick awoke with a start when Lucy covered him with a blanket.

"I'm sorry...I didn't mean to wake you," she said. "You looked cold."

He rubbed his eyes with his hands, embarrassed. "Oh, man, I must've fallen asleep. What time is it?"

"Nine o'clock." She lifted one side of the blanket, sat beside him, and covered herself. "This is my favorite episode."

Together they watched Xena battle warlords, struggle with decisions, and protect her friends. Rick's attention strayed to the deluge of mail on the floor.

"You can't ignore your mail. There could be something crucial in there."

"Like what? I've lost everything important to me. Nothing else matters."

"What about Steppie? He needs you. You have to take care of him. Feed him, give him a place to live. If you lose your house, where will you go? Most apartments don't take pets. He's been through so much. Don't make him move again, or start over with a new family. He's your best friend now."

Lucy was listening to him, maybe even agreeing with him, for the first time since he met her. Those crazy eyes focused on his face.

The next thing he knew, he was kissing her. He didn't remember thinking about kissing her, he just did it. Her lips were soft, and her breath was sweet. Her hair smelled terrific—like beef stew. Lucy didn't pull away, encouraging him to kiss her harder, deeper, longer. He found her tongue and caressed it with his. A lock of her beef stew hair tickled his cheek. His lips remained on hers while he brushed the lock away. His fingertips moved from her cheek, down her neck, and rested on her breast. She leaned back on the love seat, and he climbed on top of her, still kissing her lips. His other hand grasped her buttocks. He pressed her pelvis toward his, still kissing her. He took a breath.

"Rick," she gasped when her mouth was free. "Stop!"

He bolted off her and scrambled to the other side of the love seat.

"I don't know what came over—"

She placed her fingers over his lips. "Listen. Don't say you're sorry, you'll spoil it. You must've known I needed a nice kiss. When this is all over, maybe we can pick it up again—right where we left off. Anytime sooner would tangle everything up. It could turn into a real mess, don't you see?" She handed him the *Prestipino* file. "Good night."

＞＜

Lucy brought Steppie to bed with her. She lay on her side, with tucked knees. Steppie turned in circles, pawing the bed, and settled into the crux of her bent knee. The heat radiating from his body made her warm and comfortable.

For the first time in a while, she was proud of herself. The little voice inside her head warned her not to have sex with Rick, and she listened to it. It took longer than it should have to pull herself away, but she did it. A love affair with Rick would cost him his job. Ms. Snakehead would find out and fire him. She'd have to settle for the memory of his kiss. It was a great kiss; the best she'd ever had. Romero's kisses came close, but then, he didn't know who he was kissing.

Rick was right about Steppie. He was her friend, and he needed her. She'd take care of him, whatever it took. Nurture Steppie back to health. Get a job. Earn some money and pay her bills. No more tears. One day she'd figure out who killed her mother, she just knew it.

When I find him, I'll wait for the right time. Babysit him. And when he's good and comfortable, I'll say "Surprise!" and hit him with a Taser. He'll be helpless, and I'll do everything to him that he did to Mom. I'll use my gun to knock out his teeth and smash his cheekbone. I'll use a tire iron to crush his skull. I'll leave him in the rain somewhere, all alone. Then I'll see him in hell. It'll be so worth it.

Lucy was content as she drifted off to sleep.

Chapter 36

December 14

Lucy grabbed her broom and swept the mail—all eight weeks of it. She started in the foyer and worked her way through the living room toward the dining room. Once she'd swept the mail into a pile, she scooped it up with her hands and tossed it into her laundry basket, each fistful burning her hands like hot asphalt.

Her ears rang, and her heart pounded. Sweat dripped down her back. She was having a panic attack. How could she deal with all the mail? She sat on the love seat and focused on taking slow, measured breaths.

The rhythmic breathing alleviated the anxiety. Soon she was able to admire her clean floor; she'd almost forgotten the carpet was light blue.

"That's enough mail for today, Steppie."

The dog poked his head up from his nap. With woozy legs, he crawled out of his dog bed, stretched, and made his way to the laundry basket. He circled it. Sniffed it. When his investigation was complete, he lifted his leg and urinated on it.

"Steppie!" She shot off the love seat. "No! No! No!"

She snatched the dog and carried him outside, holding him at arm's length. Brilliant sunshine warmed the brisk cold day. She supervised while Steppie explored the sidewalk with his nose.

A solitary, involuntary chuckle erupted from her stomach. Maybe Steppie had the right idea—don't worry about the mail, just whiz on it. After a few minutes, she decided it was safe to bring him inside.

She knelt by the laundry basket, wearing plastic gloves and holding a sponge. A bucket of water and a trashcan were within easy reach. She started with the carpet and moved on to the mail. Most of it was soaked with urine.

"Jesus! How can so much pee come out of such a little dog?"

The first ten envelopes she grabbed were junk mail. She tossed them into the trashcan. As Lucy pulled the envelopes from the laundry basket, the mail became a cleaning task, rather than an overwhelming reading, sorting, and deal-with-it task. She hummed along, wiping envelopes and opening them. The stack of read mail got higher, and her sense of dread got lower.

The post office had forwarded the next envelope from her mother's address. It was bright pink, like a birthday card, and displayed a Hallmark gold seal. The card originated in Utah, sent by Mrs. Jason Hunter. Lucy didn't know any Mrs. Jason Hunter from Utah. She opened it. A check for two hundred dollars fell out. The card was blank, other than the signature. *XXXOOO, T-*

She remembered seeing another pink envelope. She rummaged through the basket and retrieved it. Same pink card, same sender. This time the envelope contained a check for three hundred dollars and a note.

> *Dear Debbie,*
> *Jason had a good month. Thanks so much for your patience.*
> *XXXOOO, T-*

Questions buzzed. Who is *T*? Why is *T* sending her mother checks? There was a telephone number on the check. Lucy checked her phone. It was eight o'clock in the morning, making it six o'clock in Utah. Too early for a phone call, her mother would've said. Lucy called anyway.

The phone rang seven times before an answering machine connected. "You have reached the Hunter residence. Please leave a message."

"Hello, my name is Lucy Prestipino. I'm calling—"

A sleepy voice interrupted her message. "Lucy? Is that you?"

"Yes, but who are you?"

The voice laughed softly. "Oh, Lucy, it's me, Tiffany Lotofsky."

Lucy was too shocked to say anything.

"Why are you calling?" Tiffany said. "Is your mother okay?"

"Mom passed away."

There was a gasp. Then silence.

The silence gave way to loud, heaving sobs. In the background, Lucy heard a male voice say, "What is it? What's happened?"

The male voice came on the line. "Who is this?"

"Lucy Prestipino. I'm a high school friend of Tiffany's. I told her my mother passed away."

"This is Jason, Tiffany's husband." His voice was thick. "When did this happen?"

"October fifteenth. I was going through my mother's mail and found Tiffany's cards. I would've called sooner, but I didn't know Tiffany was still in touch with her. I didn't even know where Tiffany was."

"This is a terrible shock. How'd your mother die?"

Lucy swallowed. "She was killed while walking her dog."

Jason coughed back his emotion. "Tiffany's very upset. I'll call you back when things settle down a bit."

It wasn't until the phone disconnected that she discovered Steppie sleeping on her lap. Lucy sat, mindlessly patting the dog. Touching his soft fur was soothing. The mutual affection drove away any thoughts of alcohol or drugs. An hour slipped by.

The phone rang. "Lucy, it's Tiffany."

"I'm sorry. I didn't mean to spring bad news on you. I don't understand any of this. Why do you send my mother checks? Why is your name Hunter? Why—"

"Your mother was good to me."

"I don't know what you mean," Lucy said, frustrated. "What're you talking about?"

"Do you remember when she hit Lance with the pizza pan?"

"Of course I do. Why?"

"That's when it started. She knew. She tried to warn me, tried to tell my parents. I didn't listen. My parents—they weren't good parents—not like your mother. They thought Lance was the greatest thing since sliced bread. When I got pregnant, they considered it a smart move on my part, him being a handsome football player and all. Your mother knew what he was.

"After she hit him with a pizza pan, she came over to my house, talked to me, talked to my parents. We were dreadful to her, kicked her out. She caught me by myself a few days later. She told me if I ever needed help, I could call her. Said she'd help me no matter what. Later, she did help, exactly like she said she would."

Tiffany wept. Lucy listened to her sobs without saying anything.

"About three years ago, I knew I had to get away from Lance. He put me in the hospital a couple of times. I was afraid to tell anyone. I lied to the hospital and the police. It took me a while to realize he was going to kill me one day. My parents were useless. I called your mother. She took me in, the kids too.

"I could've stood it for myself, but he started getting violent with the kids. I ran away. I didn't have any place to go. We stayed with your mother for a week. She insisted I go to the police and press charges. He ended up in jail. She gave me the money I needed to take care of myself until I could get a job, get therapy. She helped pay for my divorce lawyer too. Ten thousand dollars, in all.

"I went back to school. That's where I met Jason. We married a year ago. He's a good man. The kids love him. He's helping me pay back what I owe her. Your mother was wonderful to me. I can't believe she's dead."

"I didn't know any of this," Lucy said. "She never told me."

"Don't be mad at her. I begged her not to tell anyone. I was so ashamed. How could I have married a man like that?"

Tiffany cried again. While Lucy waited it out, she wondered how many other secrets her mother had kept.

"Lucy?"

"Still here."

"You know, she understood. Your mother knew exactly what to do. She never said, but I thought maybe she'd been through it herself. I hope you don't mind my asking…were your parents happy?"

"Yes, I know they were."

"Do the police know who killed her?"

"No."

"And you're trying to find out who did it, aren't you? I know you—that'd be something you'd do."

Lucy didn't answer.

"Promise me you'll be careful."

After disconnecting with Tiffany, Lucy re-read Judge Susque's order. She was supposed to tell Detective Campbell about any information she uncovered. Fat chance she'd tell that lying fucker a thing. Campbell had looked right into her face and said Javier wasn't police.

After the MPIA hearing, Campbell waited for her in the courthouse lobby. Told her how sorry he was about Steppie. Gave her a ride to Dr. Michaels's office. Lights and sirens, too. She never let on she thought he was a two-faced prick. Besides, she'd already told Campbell about her mother clobbering Lance with the pizza pan. Good enough.

Lucy held her father's photograph. Debbie had always spoken highly of him. Told her he was her advocate in heaven. Why make up lies for no reason? She could've just not said anything. Why would her mother keep a picture of her father if he abused her? No, they were happy together. She refused to spend any more time wondering about that.

Her mother's bedroom flashed into Lucy's mind. On the day Debbie was killed, Lucy found her bed unmade. Her father's picture was in the rumpled sheets. She must've slept with the picture. Did she pray to her father for help like Lucy did two days ago? Why did her mother need help?

She took two cards from her pile of blank index cards. On one card, she wrote *Tiffany*. On the other, she wrote *Dad's Picture*. She taped both cards to her dining room wall, next to the card marked *cell phone*, for no other reason than it felt right to put them there.

Now it was time to read the documents she'd fought for and won.

December 15

Six hours passed. Lucy found nothing helpful. Forensic technicians collected enough human genetic material from Steppie's mouth to produce a DNA profile. It was entered in the Combined DNA Index System. No hits.

Footprint impressions revealed a size ten sports shoe sold by Walmart. Too common to trace. Forensics needed the actual shoe to match the impressions.

No usable fingerprints.

She read summaries of interviews with confidential informants. Not a whiff of a connection between Roach and her mother's killing. Marlow canvassed the Patterson Park neighborhood three times. No one saw or heard anything.

For some reason, Sergeant Javier Rodriguez of the narcotics unit was helping with the investigation. Were drugs involved in her mother's murder? Did someone mistake her for a dealer and try to rob her? As she read more, it seemed to her Rodriguez was doing more footwork than drug-related investigation. He'd reviewed all of the CitiWatch tapes. His report stated the killing had taken place beyond the range of several cameras.

Lucy called Rodriguez. "Was my mother's killing drug-related?"

"No, Lucy."

"Why are you involved in the investigation?"

"You saved my life. I owe you."

Lucy pressed on through the documents. Public Works pried open every manhole cover within six blocks of Patterson Park. Investigators combed the sewers searching for the gun. Never found.

Police found a bandana at the scene. Blue and black, Roach colors. No DNA obtained from the bandana.

Lucy spotted a reference to a *red ball* on the ballistics report. She knew what that was: a high priority investigation. Her mother's murder was a red ball? Rick never told her. If he had, she would've backed off, for a little while anyway. Why was it a red ball?

She learned the answer when she read the ballistics report. The bullet that hit Steppie was a through and through. Investigators found it in a rock three feet from Steppie's body, too fragmented to obtain rifling characteristics.

The police recovered a .45 ACP cartridge casing. Digital images of the cartridge casing markings were submitted to NIBIN, the National Integrated Ballistics Information Network, for a computer comparison of other images in the system. There was a possible hit, later confirmed by a firearms examiner. Her mother's murder was linked to a crime in New York City.

Debbie and a New York City homicide detective were killed by the same gun, twenty-two years apart.

⁃⁃

Detectives Campbell and Marlow were already in the conference room when Rick arrived. Marlow greeted him verbally; Campbell barely acknowledged him. Rick sat next to Marlow, facing Campbell. He wasn't afraid to look Campbell in the eye and wanted Campbell to know it.

"What's the word from New York?" Rick said.

"NYPD has fired up its investigation of Detective Parks's killing," Marlow said. "I expect we'll be hearing from them soon."

The pen Rick held between his fingers tapped on his yellow legal pad, rapidly, as if it were counting his streaming thoughts.

"Doesn't mean Sanchez didn't—"

"I know what it means," Campbell said. "And I know what it doesn't mean—we don't have probable cause to arrest Sanchez. In fact, we have exactly squat connecting him to the Prestipino killing."

"Are you telling me you've given up? It's now a cold case?"

"It became a cold case as soon as you got involved."

"Excuse me?"

"You've been directing this investigation," Campbell said. "Not your job, but somehow it happened. You made it a gang case and sucked us in. We've lost time, maybe leads. Stay the fuck away from the investigation, and maybe we'll get somewhere."

"You're pissed because you fucked up the dog thing, which fucked up the hearing. Now you're blaming me."

"You gave up the identity of an undercover."

"I knew it was a possibility before the hearing," Rick said. "I got the okay from Tony Cola. By the way, Javier's out of undercover work. No harm done."

Marlow rapped her knuckles on the table. "This isn't getting us anywhere."

The sound of the knocking got their attention, but it was the stern maternal tone that quieted them.

"We're starting this conversation over," she said. "Rick, the case isn't cold. We're pursuing another direction. We're combing through Mrs. Prestipino's life to see if it yields any leads. Maybe Lucy's right. Maybe her mother's killing doesn't have anything to do with Roach."

Rick's stomach churned. Of course, Sanchez murdered Lucy's mother, issued a *luz verde*, green-lighted her. He had plenty of connections. It would've been easy for him to get a professional hitter. The notion of abandoning Sanchez as a suspect sickened him.

"We have to close the loop on Sanchez," Rick said. "He needs to be interviewed."

"How?" Campbell said. "He won't come in voluntarily. We'd have to arrest him. And we'd better have probable cause or his lawyer will sue us for false arrest and any other tort he can think of. Assuming we can find something to arrest him for, he'll lawyer up, won't say a thing. Even if we could get him to talk, we have nothing to interview him with, no leverage at all. It'll be fruitless. We'd end up looking like assholes."

Campbell was right. Sanchez was an intelligent, savvy man who wouldn't be tricked into making admissions. Premature questioning could backfire; he'd learn more about the investigation than the police would learn about his involvement. The risks of interviewing him outweighed the benefits.

"I have an idea," Marlow said. "Sanchez doesn't have to talk. We can learn a lot just by being in the room with him."

"What do you have in mind?" Rick said.

"He must feel some sort of bond with Lucy, whatever it is. Otherwise he wouldn't have told you about Alvarado. Let's get him in the box, show him the crime scene photos, one by one. Slowly...spike his curiosity. Once he's seen the photos, we'll announce the victim is Lucy's mother. Then sit back and watch his reaction. I'm betting it'll be crystal clear whether he had something to do with it. And we can do all this without asking any questions, with his lawyer sitting right there."

Both men smiled.

"First we have to find him," Rick said. "Any ideas where he is?"

"We haven't seen him in Baltimore since the altercation in Compression Connection," Campbell said. "He occasionally shows up in Fairfax, Virginia. Montgomery and Prince George's Counties, too."

"Each of those jurisdictions has a gang task force," Rick said. "I'll contact them. Ask them to keep a lookout for Sanchez. Arrest him if they can. Then we'll talk to him. See what happens." Rick paused, not sure he wanted to re-open the can of worms. "Detective Campbell, one last question...after the hearing, did you speak to Lucy?"

"Yes," Campbell said. "She fed me dog food."

"I got dog food too."

"Lucky dog."

With that, their argument was over.

⚊▬⚊

The worrywart grew in Lucy's throat.

She searched the Internet for information about the murder of NYPD Detective Thomas Parks. He'd investigated the gangland killing of the entire leadership of the Manhattan-based Vipers clique. The detective was convinced Roach was behind the mass murder. Parks was gunned down while barbequing in his own back yard.

The worrywart changed to fear, but not for herself. She feared for Rick.

December 20

Rick was looking forward to meeting Montgomery County ASA Deirdre Rappaport. She'd been the gang unit chief for only two months when Rick called her, explaining what he wanted. "Sure, we'll find a way to get acquainted with Mr. Sanchez," she said. Her voice was as sultry as a Washington, DC summer night.

She called four days later. Montgomery County police nabbed Sanchez for failing to stop for a pedestrian in a crosswalk. It was an incarcerable offense, eye-witnessed by PO III John Linthicum.

Rick glided down the new Intercounty Connector toward the Montgomery County Police Headquarters. The ICC was an expensive toll road with wide lanes and little traffic. The perfect combination lulled inattentive drivers into speed traps. Everyone had a story about getting caught on the ICC.

He set the cruise control at sixty. There was only a sprinkling of cars on the road, and his mind drifted. He was on Lucy's love seat, surrounded by the scent of beef stew, kissing her, touching her. She was reciprocating with joyful enthusiasm.

He didn't know why he kissed her like that, but he was grateful she'd had sense enough to disengage. She was nice about it, too. He didn't understand her at all. One minute she was kicking his ass, the next she was kissing his lips.

Thirty minutes later, Rappaport greeted Rick at police headquarters. He was disappointed—her voice was much younger than she was. Rappaport was in her mid-sixties, with a ready smile and smart-aleck, blue eyes.

"You're much younger than I thought you'd be," she said.

His immediate reaction to Rappaport was the opposite. She laughed from her belly. "My fellow prosecutors tell me I shouldn't tease out-of-county colleagues. But, you know, I just can't help it."

She introduced him to Officer Linthicum who gave him a rundown of the events leading to the arrest. Sanchez had driven from a parking lot near the Montgomery County Circuit Court. He paused at the four-way stop, looked both ways, and proceeded while a pedestrian was still in the crosswalk.

"As cool as they come," Linthicum said. "Very polite. Cordial. Kept his hands on the wheel. When I asked for his license and registration, he asked for permission to pull out his wallet and open the glove compartment. He wasn't the least bit perturbed when I arrested him."

Rick remembered Lucy's words from months ago. "What was he doing at the courthouse?"

Rappaport and Linthicum shrugged *I-don't-knows.*

"Deirdre," Rick said. "Were you in court, by any chance?"

"I was there on a heavy sentencing. Why?"

"There's speculation that one of Sanchez's duties with Roach is to evaluate gang prosecutors."

"The courtroom was packed. I didn't notice Sanchez." She grinned, eyes sparkling. "If I'd known he was going to be there watching me, I would've worn my Spanx."

Spanx? Rick had no idea what it was. He'd have to ask Colleen.

She returned to business. "Follow me. Sanchez and his attorney are waiting in an interview room. The lawyer is Emilio Vega. The video camera has been set up. Your detectives are here and ready to go. Campbell will be doing the talking. You and I will observe the interview from the technical services room."

If Sanchez was surprised by the sight of Campbell and Marlow, he didn't show it. His expression was one of mild amusement. He gazed at the detectives from his chair at the table, smiling patiently as if he were about to hear the punch line of a long-winded joke.

Vega flanked Sanchez. The attorney was rotund, at least three hundred pounds. Two chins spilled over his shirt collar. Still, he looked good in his suit. Rick gave mental accolades to the man's tailor.

"What's the charge?" Vega said, snapping his wrist to check the time.

"Failing to stop for a pedestrian in a crosswalk," Marlow said.

"So give him the citation."

"It's being prepared now."

"My client gets cuffed, arrested, and dragged down here to wait two hours for a citation anyone else would've gotten on the street." He was hissing his words, getting angrier by the moment. "Whatever game you're running, Mr. Sanchez isn't playing. I've instructed my client not to say a word. Save us all a lot of time, and give him the citation."

Sanchez looked toward the wall, apparently guessing the location of the hidden camera. "McCormick, I'm not talking to your detectives. But maybe I'll talk to you. Would you care to join us?"

It took Rick an instant to decide. He wanted to see Sanchez's face, up close and personal, when he saw the photographs of Mrs. Prestipino's dead body.

"Don't do it," Rappaport said. "He's up to something."

He ignored the warning.

Rick and Sanchez exchanged greetings in Spanish. The room was tiny and now crowded. Marlow stood, and Rick took her seat at the table.

Sanchez displayed his hands. They were handcuffed together as well as to the table. "A little heavy-handed, don't you think? Why didn't you simply ask me to come in?"

"Give me your contact information, and I'll do that next time."

Sanchez laughed. "Emilio, I told you he was funny, didn't I? Let me introduce you. Rick looks Latino, speaks Spanish, and can even dance a decent salsa. But he's a poseur. On the inside he's as Latino as the chair you're sitting in. Isn't that right, Rick?"

Rick had long ago come to terms with the disparity between the cultures of his birth and adoptive families. He flashed Sanchez the look he perfected in middle school: *you're a fuckin' asshole.* "Is that the best you have? You'll have to do better if you want to get under my skin. Shall we conduct business or trade insults?"

"My client isn't answering questions," Vega said.

"I won't ask any."

Campbell handed Rick a large brown envelope. He extracted ten photographs and lined them up, face down, on the table. When he was satisfied he'd provoked Sanchez's curiosity, he turned them over, slowly, one-by-one, starting with the establishment shots of the crime scene. Next came the photos of Mrs. Prestipino's body, close-ups of her bruised and bloodied face, shots of the broken teeth found near the body, and the post-mortem shots.

Sanchez glanced at the photos with bored, disinterested eyes, but he was no longer smiling. Rick met Sanchez's eyes with his own, and held them. He waited for him to ask the obvious question: *who is she?*

Minutes passed. Sanchez ignored the bait. Rick answered the unasked question.

"The homicide victim is Debbie Prestipino. Lucy's mother."

Sanchez gasped. It was nearly inaudible, but Rick heard it. Sanchez reached for a photograph. His attorney rebuked him with a sharp, "Romero!" He withdrew his hand.

"When did this—" Sanchez blurted.

He was silenced a second time by his attorney.

"October fifteenth of this year."

Vega swept his arm across the table, scattering the photographs onto the floor. "Enough of this bullshit!"

Sanchez lunged toward Rick but was thwarted by the handcuffs. "Coward! You piece of shit coward!"

"Romero," Vega said. "Don't say anything! Not a thing."

Vega turned toward Rick. "Give my client the goddamn citation. If you've got probable cause for any other charge, arrest him."

Sanchez glared at Rick, his eyes dark and lethal. "I never took you for a coward, McCormick. A small, gutless, pock-faced rat fuck. You're a pathetic piece of shit. Using a woman to do your dirty work."

What's he talking about?

Sanchez said, "How did you get her to—"

"Shut up!" Campbell said to Sanchez. He faced Rick. "We got what we came for. We don't have to listen to this crap."

"Wait!" Rick said. He was confused. What was he missing? Sanchez wasn't making sense.

"Did you threaten her?" Sanchez said. "Is that what you did, you cocksucker?"

"We're done here," Marlow said. She reached under Rick's arm and yanked him to his feet. He stood, planted in front of the table, staring at Sanchez, trying to understand what he was saying.

"No," Sanchez said. "Lucy's too tough for your lame-dick threats. You manipulated her, didn't you? Set her up."

"Lucy? Is that who you're talking—"

Marlow pulled Rick out of the interview room. Rappaport was waiting on the other side of the door and led the group to technical services. The videotape was still rolling as they watched Officer Linthicum hand the citation to Vega.

"We may have to send your client to traffic school," Linthicum said.

Vega began shouting, but Rick didn't hear the words. He was focused on Sanchez, who was still sitting in the chair, hands cuffed to the table.

"What just happened?" Rick said to Campbell.

"Lucy met with Sanchez," Marlow said. "He thinks you sent her."

Rick couldn't believe it. Lucy wouldn't have done that. He'd told her not to. She told Judge Susque she hadn't seen Sanchez since the fight in CC's. Vega was still shouting.

"Shut up, Emilio," Sanchez said.

The attorney shut up.

Sanchez looked into the camera and spoke directly to Rick, this time in English.

"A *luz verde* is too good for you, McCormick. I'm going to kill you slowly. I'm going to butcher your reputation, ruin your precious career. Every gangster and every lawyer will know Baltimore's gang prosecutor, the rising star, is nothing more than a cowardly piece of shit, a pussy, a bitch. You'll have to fight for every conviction you get."

Sanchez laughed. Smirking, contemptuous.

The core inside of Rick turned white hot. He charged to the door.

"No, you don't." Campbell blocked his path. "Don't you see what he's doing? He's goading you into asking him questions about Lucy. He won't answer without getting something from you. We got what we came for. Time to leave."

Rappaport placed her hand on Rick's arm. "Watch your back."

"Lucy's got more balls than you," Sanchez shouted into the camera as Rick was leaving.

Chapter 39

January 3

L*iar.*
The word had polluted Rick's brain for two weeks. It began like a small pocket of sludge swirling around the moorings of an Inner Harbor dock. The pocket drew more cigarette butts, more empty cans, and more debris until, two weeks later, it had swollen into a giant cesspool of toxic waste.

Lucy had made a fool out of him. Saw Sanchez despite his directive to stay away. Set him up for humiliation. He could still hear Sanchez's jeering voice.

Lucy's got more balls than you.

He considered indicting her for obstruction of justice, but ruled it out. She hadn't told Sanchez about her mother's killing; the crime scene photos took him by complete surprise. He couldn't have faked his reaction. Lucy'd played Sanchez, too. Chances were good Sanchez would come after her himself. Jail might be the safest place for her.

Rick dwelled on the MPIA hearing. Lucy lied to Judge Susque about her relationship with Sanchez. A perjury charge—now that was promising. He needed to read her exact words before determining whether she committed a crime. Perjured testimony had to be precise, an outright lie; no misunderstanding, no misinterpretation, no hedging. He could prove she'd gone to California and seen Sanchez. The transcript of the hearing would show she lied about it.

He'd ordered a transcript as soon as he returned from Montgomery County. Due to the holidays, it just arrived. Rick picked up a yellow marker and scanned the transcript for Lucy's exchange with Judge Susque.

> JUDGE: How about Romero Sanchez? Do you have a relationship with him?
> MS. PRESTIPINO: You mean, now?
> JUDGE: Yes, now.
> MS. PRESTIPINO: Oh, no! No. It's over.

Rick thumbed through the rest of the transcript, muttering, "Fuck! Fuck!" Judge Susque didn't ask her the operative question: when was the last time you saw or spoke to Romero Sanchez? Rick didn't ask it either. Lucy had no obligation to volunteer the information, only answer the question truthfully.

She'd outsmarted him, the lying bitch. He needed to purge her from his head. That's exactly what Campbell told him when they reviewed the videotape.

"Stop thinking about her! She's a career wrecker. She'll ruin you. We've had our disagreements, but you're an excellent prosecutor. You have a chance at a stellar career, you could go places. Don't blow it. Stay away from her, stay away from this case. I'll tell you if anything important turns up."

It was good advice, and Rick knew it. He thanked Campbell. Now if he could only wake up in the morning without Lucy's kiss lingering on his lips. He threw the transcript across the room.

There was a soft rap on his door. It was Lundt. She was doing well since he put her in charge of the gang-involved juvenile and misdemeanor cases. Able to negotiate plea agreements favorable to the State. Good conviction stats on cases she tried. She was developing a reputation as a tough, but reasonable prosecutor. Judges liked her. So did defense counsel.

"Come in," he said. "What's on your mind?"

Lundt took a seat, holding a foot-high pile of files on her lap.

"I don't know what's going on," she said. "For some reason, more and more defendants are filing motions and discovery requests, even in the most routine cases. Every case is being litigated like it's a death penalty case. I'm having trouble keeping up."

Rick looked at the pyramid of files on his desk. The dots connected. He'd ignored Sanchez's angry threat. *You'll have to fight for every conviction you get.* Rick blew it off as macho bluster; no one could have that much power. Yet, it seemed to be happening.

"Is there a particular gang filing an inordinate amount of paper?" Rick said.

"Roach."

"Probably a coincidence." Rick hoped it was true. "There's an ebb and flow to these things."

"Ebb and flow? It's more like a tidal wave. If it doesn't stop soon, Mrs. Mercer will have to hire a lot more prosecutors to keep this place afloat."

He wasn't concerned. Mercer would do exactly that. Criminal defendants had a Sixth Amendment right to a speedy trial. The Maryland rules had strict time limits for prosecution, and a heavy caseload was no exception. If need be, she'd let him borrow prosecutors from the violent crimes unit.

"Penelope, you're doing a great job. Keep doing what you're doing. If the work load gets too much for you, I'll ask Mrs. Mercer to divert some prosecutors our way."

Rick's phone rang. It was Alexander Stonegate, Assistant Public Defender. He cupped his hand over the receiver.

"Anything else?" She shook her head and left. Alex was calling about Marcello Rivera, a low-level gang hanger-on who robbed a tourist at the Inner Harbor. The prosecution had Rivera dead-to-rights: the CitiWatch camera recorded the robbery, and the tourist identified him without hesitation. The police caught him with the stolen wallet less than a block away from the crime scene. When confronted by detectives with the weight of the evidence against him, Rivera sobbed out his confession. A dunker.

Rick was amenable to a plea of simple assault. This was Rivera's first offense; no weapon involved, no one was hurt, no other exacerbating circumstances. Most importantly, the tourist didn't want to return to Baltimore to testify. Rivera had a constitutional right to confront his accuser. The case would get tossed without the tourist's testimony.

"I'm representing a dumb-ass," Alex said. "My client won't take the plea. I told him it's a good deal. He won't budge. He wants a jury trial. This morning I filed a demand for a bill of particulars. Motions to suppress are on the way. Maybe he'll plead out later, but for now, we're going to trial."

"Mind telling me his defense?"

"He claims his identical twin did it."

Rick rolled his eyes. It was this kind of bullshit that made Rick glad he was a prosecutor and not a public defender. Prosecutors could screen out lousy cases; public defenders couldn't screen out stupid, lying clients—they were stuck with them.

"You know how the saying goes," Alex said. "Prosecutors get the cream of the crop; public defenders get the cream of the crap."

"Yeah, I know…I'm looking forward to seeing the twin's birth certificate."

The men commiserated with a chuckle.

"Talk to your client again," Rick said. "We have information Roach defendants are under an order to paper up the files. It's a strategy to jam up the works in the State's Attorney's Office. We're just beginning to see it. It won't be long before it affects your office, too."

"You're kidding. Who can issue an order like that?"

"Romero Sanchez."

"Why would he do that?"

"Sorry, Alex. I'm not at liberty to say more. Tell your office to expect some pushback from us. Any Roach gang member who jerks us around with paper isn't getting a plea offer. And we'll seek the max under the sentencing guidelines."

"You intend to punish defendants for exercising their right to make the State prove its case?"

"No, we're exercising our full discretion for any defendant we believe is taking orders from Roach."

There was a long silence before Alex spoke. "There's a rumor floating around there's a vendetta between you and Sanchez over that bicycle messenger. The one who testified in the Coopersmith trial. I hope not. No girl is worth the troubles you're going to have if it's true."

Rick said nothing. He added the Rivera file to the pyramid.

⚊⚊

Three miles away in Canton, Lucy felt better. She ate the slow cooker meals she made for Steppie—stews rich with meat, vegetables, and whole grains. Every night, Steppie slept in the bend of her knee. He was warm and soft and lulled her to sleep with the sound of contented snoring. She awoke eight hours later feeling refreshed. There were no more nightmares, no more murderous fantasies.

The mail slot clanked. There was an envelope from Mercy Hospital—another polite letter informing her there were no records pertaining to Debbie Prestipino nee Debbie Tate.

Lucy had subpoenaed the records from every Maryland hospital. Her efforts yielded nothing. At least the letters from the hospitals were polite. She'd also subpoenaed the records from Maryland's shelters for battered women. Outraged phone calls flooded her phone. Privileged and confidential information, a lawyer would say, barking into the phone. She'd mail the lawyer the autopsy report. A few days later, someone from the shelter would call.

"Hon...this is off the record. We looked through our records. Your mother was never here. We hope you get the monster."

She talked to her mother's neighbors, friends, boss, and co-workers. Every conversation had the same result—no information. The MPIA documents held no clues. Mercy Hospital was her last hope.

Frustration filled her. Lucy practiced quick-drawing her Sig from her Flashbang holster. For some reason, it always calmed her. She endured much frustration since her mother died; now she could draw her gun in less than three seconds.

Steppie watched her practice until he pawed her leg.

"Know what?" she said. "We need to get out of this place. We're gonna try something new."

Lucy strapped a dog-sling against her chest with four holes facing outward. She slid Steppie into the sling, positioning him so his back was flat against her chest. He whimpered as she gently maneuvered each paw through a hole.

She tugged on the straps until she was confident Steppie was secure. Next came the goggles. The dog didn't complain when she slipped them over his eyes; he seemed more amazed than anything else. His head jerked from right to left and back again, as if he couldn't get enough of his new point of view.

"Ready to roll?"

She wheeled her bike through the front door onto the sidewalk. With her left foot on the pedal, she pushed off with her right

"Here we go!"

At first, Steppie was silent and still. She glanced down and found Steppie staring straight ahead, mouth open, tongue out. Lucy turned onto Boston Street and picked up speed. Steppie began to sing.

"Ooooooo," he howled.

She recognized the howl as an expression of exhilaration—freedom, joy, soaring spirits—the feeling she had whenever she was on her bike.

"Ooooooo," Lucy imitated.

They bayed together as she glided around corners and coasted down hills. Amused pedestrians waved and smiled as they sped through Fells Point, Little Italy and circled back to Canton.

She found herself in Patterson Park, standing next to her bike, staring at the boat lake. Lucy learned from the MPIA documents that police divers found Debbie's phone in the lake, about thirty feet from the water's edge. Why would it have been there? If it were stolen, the killer wouldn't have thrown it away—not without making a few calls first. No, her mother threw it there. That didn't make sense either. She would've handed it to the robber, no sweat.

Lucy's stomach flipped.

An hour later, they arrived home to the fragrance of lamb stew. The smell nauseated Lucy—she was sick of stew. Steppie wasn't sick of it at all; he slurped happily while she made the index card, *Phone in Boat Lake*. For reasons she didn't understand, she was inclined to post the card next to the one that said *Lance*.

Steppie heard the knock before she did. He bolted to the front door, yapping. It was five o'clock.

Unexpected knocks at the door spooked her. She holstered her Sig. Her heart raced as she peered through the door's peephole. She leaped backward, away from the door, as if she'd looked into the barrel of her own loaded gun.

Chapter 40

January 3

Romero Sanchez was on her front stoop.

Lucy folded over and put her head between her knees. She wanted every oxygen-rich blood cell to rush to her brain so she could think. Should she open the door? Romero knew she was inside; the lights were on, and Steppie was barking loud enough to split an eardrum. She couldn't let him inside—if Rick found out, he'd haul her in front of a grand jury. Why was Romero here? She had to know.

Lucy opened the door. Steppie shot out and rebounded against Romero's thighs. He leaped and spun until she snatched him by the collar.

"No! Get down!" She lifted the dog and pressed him against her chest as she stood in front of Romero on the front stoop.

"Hi," she said.

Romero broke open a wide smile that displayed his white teeth and dimples. He was wearing a black cashmere coat. A scarf the color of a robin's egg looped around his neck. He looked more handsome than she'd ever seen him.

He held a large Donvito's pizza box. Readers of the *Baltimore Sun* voted Donvito's the number one pizzeria in Little Italy. She could smell the cheese and pepperoni. It was her favorite pizza. Romero kept moving the box from one hand to another. It was steaming hot. Her mouth salivated.

"May I come in?" he said.

"No."

"No? Why not?"

"Whenever you're around, my life gets very complicated."

"I know exactly what you mean."

"Why are you here?"

"I thought you'd like to eat a pepperoni pizza."

"I would. You can leave it."

"Come on, babe, it's freezing out here."

Romero's mahogany eyes implored her. The allure of the pizza was irresistible. Lucy could hear a voice shouting inside her head. *Don't do it! Listen to yourself! You'll be sorry if you let him in!*

"Okay, you can come in. Only for a minute."

Romero put the pizza box on the coffee table in the living room. As soon as Lucy released the dog, he scampered to Romero to resume his enthusiastic greeting. Romero squatted and offered his hand for the dog to sniff.

"Who's this little guy?"

"Steppie."

Romero's smile vanished.

He knows.

She watched Romero's eyes as they surveyed the house. Half the furniture was gone. So was most of the décor. She stopped noticing the emptiness a long time ago.

"What's going on here?" he said.

"Getting ready to move. I'm gonna flip this place." That was the lie she told her posse. Flip it, make a profit, and buy another—onward and upward until she was a Baltimore land baroness. She lied because the truth was too hard to tell: short sale, if she was lucky; foreclosure, if she wasn't.

He gave her an intense look. "In this economy?"

"Small houses are in demand. Now's a great time for me to sell." The lies kept coming and coming. She almost believed them herself.

"Jesus, it's as cold in here as it is outside," he said.

"Keep your coat on."

"Let me take a look at you." Romero took her hands and held them out. He slowly turned her around. "You look good, babe, real good."

In an instant, his arms enfolded her shoulders in a tight embrace. He kissed the top of her head and nuzzled his face in her hair. His hands moved to her cheeks, and he cupped her face while he showered kisses on her forehead, cheeks, and lips.

"I've been so worried about you," he whispered between kisses. "Lucy, tell me the truth. Are you selling off your stuff? Do you need money?"

Not from him, she didn't. She stood straight and proud. Why should she feel humiliated? None of this was her fault.

"Of course not." Her voice was light, with a touch of offense. "Let's eat. I'm starved."

She stashed Steppie inside his crate. Lucy and Romero ate pizza side-by-side on the love seat. He didn't say much, but kept looking at her, smiling, as if he was thrilled to see her. He had a knack for making her feel important, and she fell in love with him because of it.

After they finished eating, Lucy took Steppie from his crate. She cuddled the dog in her arms, cooing and kissing him as she walked toward the love seat.

"You treat Steppie like he's a baby."

She smiled, knowing it was true.

"When the time is right, you're going to be a great mother."

Her eyes moistened. She blotted the tears on Steppie's fur before sitting next to Romero. The dog burrowed into the small space between them. Romero stroked the dog's head and after a few seconds, Steppie rolled onto his back, displaying the angry scars on his stomach.

"What happened to him?"

"He was shot."

Thirty seconds elapsed in silence.

"Why didn't you tell me?"

"I couldn't."

"It was McCormick, wasn't it? He thought I did it and threatened you with prosecution if you told me, didn't he?"

She patted the soft fur on Steppie's stomach instead of answering.

"So what does McCormick have on me? Why does he think I killed your mother?"

Steppie's eyes opened wide. He moved from his spot and climbed onto Lucy's lap.

"I don't want to talk about him. Is this why you came here? To talk about Rick?"

Romero shook his head. "No, no...You're hurting my feelings here, Lucy. When you came to see me, I didn't know about your mother. I thought you were there with some sort of an agenda, that maybe McCormick had gotten to you. I behaved badly. It took me a while to figure out something was horribly wrong. I didn't know what it was until a few days ago. Now I understand you were grieving your mother and came to me for comfort. I'm sorry I blew it."

Romero had everything right except the reason she went to see him. She didn't intend to correct him.

"I thought you knew everything that went on," she said.

"Look...I heard a woman in Baltimore was killed, and the police were looking at Roach. My people assured me it wasn't us. That was the end of it as far as I was concerned. I don't micro-manage my people. What's the status of the investigation?"

"It's pending."

"I know that." He sounded miffed. "Tell me specifics. Did they recover a gun? Was there DNA evidence? Did—"

"I can't tell you anything. There's a court order."

"A gag order? Against the victim's daughter? Unbelievable!"

"Why do you keep asking about this?"

"Because I'm interested, because I want to help. I can help you, you know. Want to find out who killed your mother? Just bring me up to speed."

She was tempted. Romero's gangsters could go where the police couldn't. They would do things the police wouldn't. The gun came to mind—the one used to kill a New York cop over twenty years ago. If Romero could find out what happened to the gun, the investigation into her mother's murder would get somewhere. She couldn't tell him about the weapon without violating Judge Susque's order.

"If you want to help, call Rick."

Romero's eyes turned black. "Fuck that asshole."

Steppie jumped from the love seat and scratched the front door.

"He needs to go out," she said.

The outside air smelled dank and musty. It told her rain was on the way. For several minutes, Steppie sniffed around, explored, and did everything but his business. Why did he want to go out? Another male who confused her.

"You're done, Steppie. Time to go inside."

The dog refused to budge.

"C'mon, let's go."

He planted his paws on the ground and pulled against the leash.

"Steppie! Now!"

He held his ground. Lucy picked him up and carried him into the house. As soon as she opened the door, she knew there'd be trouble. Romero was standing in the dining room, staring at the maze of index cards. He spun in her direction with eyes as black as his cashmere coat.

"You didn't come to me for comfort, did you? I was right. You had an agenda—hunting your mother's killer." He seized the crossed-off index card with his name on it and tore it from the wall. "I'm glad to see you eliminated me as a suspect."

She unhooked Steppie from the leash. The dog meandered over to the dining room and planted himself at Romero's feet.

"That asshole told you I killed your mother, and you believed him."

"No, I never believed it, not really. What if my mother was killed because of me? I had to know. Don't you get it?"

"No, I don't." He ripped up the card and threw the pieces on the floor. "I'd never do anything to hurt you."

He took a step toward Lucy and tripped over Steppie, landing with a crash on his hands and knees.

"Fuck!" he shouted.

Lucy rushed to Romero. "Are you all right? He gets under my feet all the time. I'm so sorry."

He pushed her away. "Do something about that fuckin' dog."

Rage swelled inside of her.

"Did you call him a *fuckin' dog*? He got shot fighting to save my mother. Bit the scumbag so hard his teeth broke off. He took a bullet! Steppie's brave. Who are you to call him a *fuckin' dog*? Have you ever done a brave thing in your life? Anything? Steppie's no *fuckin'*—"

"Lucy, stop!" He was standing in front of her. "You're right. Steppie's brave. A courageous dog. Brave like you, like your mother. I'm sorry. I didn't mean—"

"*Trojan*…a perfect name for you. You come to my door bearing a gift—a pizza! How stupid can I be? You came here to get informa—"

"Enough! I only wanted to check on you. To see how you were doing. I wanted to tell you, in person, how sorry I am for your loss. I got angry because you hurt me, Lucy, you—"

"You're sorry for my loss?" She covered her ears with her hands. "No! No! You can't say that to me. You're not allowed."

"What are you talking about?"

Steppie was barking. Ear-piercing, relentless barks.

"You can't say you're sorry. Not you...not you." She was screaming, needing to be heard over Steppie's barking. "I know you didn't kill my mother, but how many other people have you killed? You make a living at killing, at destroying lives with drugs and guns. For money. How many lives have you shattered?" Cells of fury exploded inside her. "And you know what happens to those left behind! That makes it so much worse. Marcela was murdered, the wife you claim you loved. You know the suffering, the nightmares, the regrets. You still didn't stop. You make me sick. You're—"

Romero grabbed her arms and shook her. "Stop it! Stop it!"

Steppie crouched, baring his toothless gums, snarling.

"You have no soul," she screamed. "There's no hope for you. You're going to hell. You'll spend eternity in—"

Romero face-slapped Lucy into silence.

Steppie leaped, throwing himself against Romero's right leg with a force that knocked him off-balance. The dog gnawed on Romero's ankles.

"Get off of me!" He flicked his leg, sending Steppie sliding across the carpet. The dog charged back, barking, growling. Romero shoved him away with his hand.

An odd sensation overtook Lucy. Everything slowed down. The sound of deep breathing filled the room. It drowned out Steppie's barking, Romero's shouting. The breathing was heavy, rhythmic. It belonged to Lucy. She was floating above the dining room table, watching herself in the living room.

Romero was backing away from her, holding his hands up, palms out. The anger was gone from his eyes. There was fear. She'd never seen him look afraid.

"Lucy, you don't want to do this."

Do what?

"Be careful, don't let the gun go off by accident."

She saw the barrel of her gun, pointing toward Romero. She held it with both hands. Decocker off. Hammer released. Chamber loaded. The gun was steady. She wasn't nervous. Her stance was perfect. All the practice paid off. She was close enough for a head shot. Couldn't miss. Funny thing was, she didn't remember reaching into her holster and taking out the weapon. Maybe this was a dream. She could pull the trigger and be sure.

"No one hurts Steppie," she said.

"I won't hurt Steppie. He's a good dog. A brave dog."

"Get out."

"I'm leaving." Romero backed toward the door. He opened it with one hand behind him while he faced her.

"Don't come back here, Romero. We'll catch up with each other in hell."

The door shut. He was gone.

Chapter 41

January 4

It was one o'clock in the morning. Lucy studied her wall of index cards, praying she'd see the answer. It was right there in front of her, she knew it; but all she could see were handcuffs and prison garb. She couldn't decide what to do.

One side of her wanted to stay mum. It was unlikely Rick would find out Romero now knew the details of the police investigation. Her other side urged her to tell Rick. Otherwise, he'd be a sitting duck for whatever Romero decided to do with the information. The only solution was to figure out who killed her mother. Her unlawful disclosure would become a moot issue. No, more like a mute issue—not worth talking about.

An hour passed, and Lucy's prayers weren't answered. Time to 'fess up. She punched in Rick's office number. He wouldn't be there, but if she left a message, she'd be locked into telling him what happened. There'd be no chickening out.

"McCormick."

She froze.

"Hello?" he said.

"Sorry… It's Lucy. I didn't expect you to answer. I just wanted to leave a message."

"I'm busy now. What's your message?"

"Can you come over tomorrow? I need to show you…something."

"You're supposed to call Campbell. Remember Judge Susque's order?" He was cryptic, cold.

"Detective Campbell will probably call you after I call him. I thought this would save a step."

Rick was quiet for so long she thought they'd disconnected.

"Can you come over? I'll make you some stew."

"No. Call Campbell."

"All right." She tried to stop the trembling in her voice. "Good night."

Steppie followed her upstairs and parked himself outside the bedroom door while she got ready for bed. Rick sounded angry. The last time they were together, he kissed her. They hadn't spoken since. What happened?

"C'mon, Steppie." She crawled into bed. The dog remained posted by the door, still guarding her, protecting her from Romero. She hadn't thought about Romero since slamming the door behind him. She began sweating and shaking and thanking God she didn't shoot him. In her mind's eye, she was on the witness stand explaining the killing to a jury.

Well, you see, he insulted my dog and the next thing I knew, I blew his head off.

At three thirty, her bedroom window rattled against a wailing wind. At four, she heard sleet clattering on the roof. Experience told her what would happen next; the sleet would encase the city, taking down the power lines and transforming the streets into skating rinks. Schools would close. There'd be a milk, bread, and toilet paper run on the grocery stores. Television news would present the weather as if it was the apocalypse. A metaphor for her life.

She fell asleep hoping Rick wouldn't be too mad about the index cards.

<hr />

The massive snowstorm shut down Baltimore City. The courts closed, giving Rick an unexpected free day. He could use the extra time to prepare for one of the upcoming trials, but he was sick and tired of thinking about criminals. He got a text message from Alex inviting him to a snowball fight—State's Attorneys vs. Public Defenders. Tempting. He imagined it turning into a flash mob with mass arrests. Who would prosecute, and who would defend? The *Sun* would have fun with that.

He kept thinking about Lucy's call. She'd been lying low since the MPIA hearing. She stopped harassing him about the investigation. Campbell and Marlow were working their asses off, but leads were drying up. The Prestipino homicide was turning cold. Maybe she'd stumbled onto something. There had to be more to it; she called at two in the morning.

Rick called Campbell. No, he hadn't heard from Lucy. Rick told him about the early morning call.

"I have no idea why she'd call," he said. "I'll drop by her place when I get a chance. It'll be a while. We're pretty busy here today."

A half hour later, Rick's curiosity got the better of him. He decided to visit Lucy. Rick heard a snowplow. Good, he'd be able to drive. She lived only two miles from him, but the weather was bitterly cold, and the sidewalks were icy. Walking would be nearly impossible.

What was truly impossible was freeing his car from the wall of ice and snow left behind by the plow. Walking was the only option. It took Rick forty-five minutes to trudge to Canton. Lucy's house looked cold and unwelcoming, obviously without power. He knocked on the door.

"What're you doing here?" she said.

"The court is closed. I thought I'd stop by."

She looked blank.

"You called me, remember? You said you wanted to show me something. Here I am."

"Oh. Give me a second."

Lucy put Steppie in his crate.

"What I want to show you is in the dining room."

He followed her until they were facing the wall of index cards. The cards were displayed in some sort of order not apparent to him. He estimated there were twenty-five cards. Each displayed only one or two words. *Lance, cell phone, boat lake, Colleen, autopsy.* Some cards had information excluded from Judge Susque's order: *bandana, NYPD Detective Parks, Roach, Vipers.*

"What does all this mean?" he said.

"It doesn't mean anything. Only words, shorthand for random thoughts. Whenever something strikes me as important, I make a card."

"What does Colleen have to do with this?"

"Nothing. It's shorthand for the conversation I had with my mother before she died."

"Take it down. I don't want my sister's name associated with a homicide investigation."

Lucy removed the card and handed it to Rick.

"Where'd you get the information about Detective Parks?" he said.

"From the documents you gave me."

Damn that Lundt! She didn't vet the documents like I told her to.

"Why are you showing me this?" he said.

"Someone saw the cards...by accident."

"Who?"

"Romero."

Rick had a fleeting vision of his hands around Lucy's neck, ringing it. Stupid, stupid girl. She'd put him in an untenable position. Now that he knew she violated the court order, he had to do something about it. He walked to the living room window, waving her away when she followed him.

The snow turned to sleet while he considered the Fifth and Sixth Amendments. He was in her home at her invitation. No arrest. No custodial circumstances. He could ask her all the questions he wanted without having to advise her of her rights. The trouble was, he couldn't testify about her statements as long as he was the attorney of record in the MPIA case or any prosecution brought against Lucy. That was fine by him; he was busy enough without adding this pile of crap to his plate. He was happy to step aside for another prosecutor.

"Let's sit down," he said. "Tell me how it happened."

She perched on the love seat next to him, her hands folded in her lap. "Yesterday, Romero came for a surprise visit. I forgot the cards were on the wall."

"You said a surprise visit. Did he appear at your door, uninvited?"

She nodded.

"Why'd you let him in?"

"At first I wasn't going to, but I gave in."

"Why? Did he threaten you in some way?"

"No...he had a pizza. Pepperoni, my favorite, from Donvito's. I was hungry."

He felt his jaw drop.

"Are you mad?" she said sheepishly.

"Did he ask about the investigation?"

"Uh-huh."

"What did he want to know?"

"At first he asked what you had on him. Then he asked the status of the investigation. Later he offered to help me find my mother's murderer, but he needed me to bring him up to speed."

"What did you tell him?"

"I didn't tell him anything. I said if he wanted to help, he needed to call you."

"And what did he say?"

"He wasn't interested."

"Answer the question. What exactly did he say?"

"He said, 'Fuck that asshole.' Why does he think you're an asshole?"

"How did he see the cards?"

"I went outside with Steppie. I forgot about the cards, and when I came back inside, he was looking at them."

"What happened then?"

"He saw the top card—the one where I crossed off his name. He was angry I ever thought he could kill my mother. We had an argument. He left." Her eyes watered.

"I'm curious. Chances were good I'd never find out about this. Why'd you tell me?"

"I didn't know what Romero was going to do. I didn't want you to be blindsided."

"The way I was blindsided by your secret trip to California?"

Lucy's eyes opened wide. "Wha—"

Rick stood. "I'm leaving now."

"Wait a sec—"

He walked to the door without turning around or acknowledging her. She grabbed his sleeve.

"Rick? What's gonna happen next?"

"My office will file a motion to hold you in contempt. We'll see where it goes from there."

For a heartbeat, she looked wounded. The wounds gave way to anger.

"You're not so different from Romero, you know. You bully. You manipulate. You...what was it you called it? You babysit. Is that what you were doing when you kissed me? If you know about my visit to California, then you know I didn't tell Romero anything. Nothing about my mother, nothing about the investigation. I didn't even tell him about the bugs. And, just so you know, when I kissed you back, it was for real. I can't wait to tell Judge Susque how you tried to seduce me into giving you information."

Bugs? Seduce?

She opened the door. "Get out. Do whatever you're going to do, but get the fuck out of here."

He paused at the doorway.

"Get out or I'm calling the police."

He spun to face her.

By then she was talking to 9-1-1. "There's someone in my house who won't leave. He's got a gun!"

Rick yanked open the door. Lucy pushed him through it.

———

Steppie whined in his crate as soon as the door slammed shut. Lucy cringed. She'd forgotten about the dog. All because of Rick. No wonder Romero thought he was an asshole. She was glad she scared the shit out of him. Served him right. She didn't actually call 9-1-1. She pretended to and it worked. The asshole got out of there in a hurry.

She let Steppie out of the crate. He stood on his hind legs and put his paws on her knees.

"You're such a good dog." She picked him up and hugged him. "Let's get out of here."

The outside temperature was warm enough to replace the sleet with dreary, rainy weather. They strolled down Eastern Avenue and into Patterson Park and before long, they were standing in front of the boat lake. Why did her mother throw the phone into the lake? It was a worthless, junkie phone.

The answer hit her: the phone had information. Information the killer wanted. Information her mother died protecting.

Lucy ran home, carrying Steppie in her arms. The answer was coming—she could almost see it.

January 5

*C*heckmate.

Rick's jaw ached from clenching his teeth. Taking action against Lucy was out of the question. Her testimony would embarrass him. Judge Susque would hit the roof. Accuse him of being unprofessional, maybe unethical. Susque might complain to Mercer or report him to the bar association. Why didn't he let Campbell talk to Lucy?

Lucy pretending to call 9-1-1, now that was a fine trick. He got two blocks from her house and called 9-1-1 himself. "This is ASA Sean Patrick McCormick. You just got a call from a woman in Canton claiming someone armed with a gun was inside her home. The call was made by an angry witness I was interviewing."

The 9-1-1 call taker kept him on the phone, getting additional information, until she said, "Mr. McCormick, we didn't get such a call." A few minutes later a radio car rolled up as he walked home. "Are you all right, Mr. McCormick?" a uniformed patrol officer said.

Rick's face got hot thinking about it. He fantasized about a new strategy to get rid of Sanchez. Encourage Lucy to date him. Give it six months, and he'd probably kill himself.

Yesterday's storm wreaked havoc on the court's trial docket. The court bumped Rick's trial for two months, giving him time to chew on his conversation with Lucy. What did she mean by *bugs*? It was eleven in the morning; eight, Los Angeles time. Assistant District Attorney Jill Sanders might be in her office.

Sanders had kept him abreast of the criminal proceedings against Luiz Alvarado. They shared any intelligence obtained on Romero Sanchez. Rick had sent her the video of his interview with Sanchez. He trusted her.

She answered on the first ring. After cordial greetings, Rick got to his point.

"Is there a wiretap on Sanchez?"

"Why are you asking?"

"Lucy Prestipino mentioned she saw bugs at his house."

"Is this the same Lucy whose name prompted Sanchez to go berserk during an interview?"

"One and the same."

"What did she say about bugs?"

"Not much. Only that she didn't tell Sanchez she saw them."

"And you're sure she wasn't talking about insects."

"I'm sure. She meant surveillance equipment."

"What kind of surveillance? What exactly did she see?"

"I don't know. She blurted it out. There was no chance for me to follow up."

"I don't know what Lucy's talking about. If our office had a wiretap, I would've been the one to have requested it. Maybe the feds have one. We're not always informed about these things. I'll call my contacts at the U.S. Attorney's Office and see if they know anything."

Rick gazed out of his office window onto East Baltimore Street. Yesterday's storm had passed, leaving the street speckled with pools of water. Water sprayed the air as cars drove through the puddles, sometimes landing on unfortunate pedestrians. Rick could see distant clouds separating from one another, driven apart by emerging sunshine.

He'd gotten only a few, fitful hours of sleep the night before, and he was dragging. It was time to fuel up on espresso. Later, he'd tackle the stacks of files covering his desk and wait for Jill to call back.

Café No Delay was jammed; the rest of the city had the same idea. Customers lined up outside the door, talking collectively about the storm, bonding over the common experience. As he waited, the sun emerged, prompting a whole new conversation among the crowd. Eventually, he reached the cashier. He walked away with a *Sun* paper and a double espresso. He snagged an empty table in the back.

Rick was contentedly enjoying his solitude when he heard an Irish brogue, "Top o' the morning to ye."

He looked up and did a double-take.

"I need to speak to you," said Sanchez. He was wearing gloves, a black skullcap and a hoodie. Sanchez pulled up a chair.

"Call my office and make an appointment," Rick said. "Like everyone else."

Sanchez threw his head back and laughed. "Funny guy. We should hang out."

Rick glared until the gangster spoke again.

"Our girl isn't doing well. Have you been to her house? She's losing everything."

"If you're talking about Lucy, she's her own girl."

"That she is." Sanchez smiled. "We need to protect her from herself."

"I've been trying to protect her since the day she met you."

"You drove her right to me, don't you see that?"

Rick ignored the question as absurd and asked his own. "Did you kill Mrs. Prestipino?"

"So direct. You could learn a thing or two from Lucy. Her interrogation techniques are much more artful. But to answer your question, of course I didn't. Why would you think so?"

"Where were you on October fifteenth?"

"I was in Magic Valley Hospital in Utah, getting a rhinoplasty." Sanchez let out an amused chuckle. "Lucy broke my nose, but I suppose you already knew."

Sanchez reached under his hoodie. Rick reached into his suit jacket.

"Relax, I'm not strapped," Romero said. "I'm retrieving some papers."

He slid them across the table to Rick. "Here's the name of the surgeon and a medical release allowing you to talk to him about my surgery. I trust you'll be discreet in your inquiries. Some of my colleagues might think it's a sign of weakness for a man to get his nose broken by a woman. Then again, they don't know Lucy."

Rick took the papers. "This doesn't exonerate you. You could've green-lighted Mrs. Prestipino."

"Why would I do that?

"You just said it—Lucy broke your nose. She humiliated you."

"Afterward I gave you Alvarado." His eyes were as dark as pitch. "Why would I then kill her mother?"

"I'm coming after you, Sanchez. I'll figure out your grand scheme and how Lucy fits into it. If you're here to convince me you're innocent, you've wasted your time."

The two men stared at one another across the table. Sanchez broke the silence first.

"I'm here to trade."

"Trade? What do you have to trade?"

"Information. In my pocket is the name of the man tasked by Roach with disposing the gun used to kill NYPD Detective Parks—the same gun that killed Lucy's mother. I'll give it to you, but only if you give me what I want."

"Which is what?"

"Your promise not to take any action against Lucy."

Rick had already ruled it out, but there was no reason to reveal that to Sanchez. He was going to bargain for what he really wanted. First, he'd allow Sanchez to make his pitch; he might spill something interesting.

"I'm listening," Rick said.

"I suspected Lucy's house was in foreclosure. Went online and checked the court records. Lo and Behold! What do I find? Her MPIA suit. She beat you in court. Got herself a court order. Only she accidentally violated it. How long did it take her to tell you? Less than twenty-four hours? She'd want to do the right thing. I'll bet you didn't advise her of her rights before you questioned her."

Rick said nothing.

"And now you're going to punish her, you mother fucker. How will you do it? Contempt? Obstruction of justice?"

Disdain gushed from Sanchez's mouth.

"You set her up," he said. "Planted the idea in Lucy's head I killed her mother. Threatened her about contacting me. Dribbled out information, but not too much—just enough to drive her mad. Did you forget this was the same woman who chased a strong-arm robber on a bike around Baltimore City? Of course, she was going to find out for herself if I killed her mother. It was totally foreseeable. So was your response."

"Stop your people from papering up our criminal prosecutions," Rick said.

"That's not on the table. I made you an offer. Your answer is either *yes* or *no*."

"No." Rick stood and grabbed his coat.

"You're a hard man, McCormick." Sanchez put his hand in his pocket and pulled out an index card. "If we don't have an agreement, I'll give this to Lucy. She'll take it—just like she took the pizza. She'll add it to her wall of index cards. Have you seen it?"

Rick sat down. "We have one exactly like it in the gang unit."

"I seriously doubt it. It's a masterpiece of deductive thinking. I believe she's only a few inspirations short of discovering who murdered her mother. Care to make a wager on whether she'll tell the police who it is? I'm betting she won't. She'll take care of business herself." Sanchez rubbed the index card between his fingers. "Are you sure you don't want the name?"

"How'd you get it?"

"I have some influence in Roach. I made inquiries."

"Risky business for you. Why're you doing this? What's Lucy to you?"

Sanchez leaned back in his chair and sipped his coffee. His eyes were damp. "I owe her. She stopped me from killing a man."

Rick's heart pounded. Was Lucy right? Did Sanchez want out of gang life? He bent low across the table so he could whisper.

"Get out of Roach. We'll protect you, we'll help each other."

Sanchez shook his head slowly. "You sound just like my wife." He grabbed a napkin from the table and quickly wiped his eyes. "Let's get back to business. I've made you an offer. Are you going to accept it or not?"

"Stop jamming up the State's Attorney's Office."

"No can do. That decision was made by someone with a higher pay grade than mine. I revealed it out of anger. Paid a heavy price, too."

Sanchez lifted the bottom of his hoodie. There were bandages covering his torso. "Two broken ribs. For the first time in ten years, I was disciplined. Take it as a compliment, Rick. And you can thank me later."

"Thank you? I don't under—"

"For the last time—are you in or out?"

"In."

Sanchez handed Rick the index card with a gloved hand. He left the coffee shop, taking his napkin and coffee cup with him.

Chapter 43

January 5

Rick tossed the rest of his espresso down his throat. He didn't understand why or how it happened, but Sanchez handed him a clue to solving two murders. He began walking to police headquarters to find Campbell and Marlow.

Within a block, he was sprinting. Headquarters was an uphill climb, only a quarter mile away, but Rick covered it in less than three minutes. It felt like a long three minutes; he was preoccupied with thoughts of Lucy. The signs of her financial distress were right in front of him. Missing furniture, dim lighting, cold house. He also hadn't appreciated the complexity of her index card chart. His anger at her disclosure blinded him from seeing what was there. Was Lucy close to solving her mother's murder? He worried Romero was right.

An unwanted thought crept into his brain. No, he didn't push Lucy into going to California; she'd done that on her own. Romero's accusation was preposterous. She was responsible for her own actions. The espresso soured in his stomach.

Rick pulled open the front door to police headquarters as Campbell and Marlow were coming out.

"Counsel," Campbell said. "I just left you a message."

"I was on my way to see you," Rick said, breathless. "We need to talk."

"How'd you make out with Lucy?" Campbell said.

Make out with Lucy? How'd he know?

"What?"

"I saw her this morning," Campbell said, sounding irritated. "She said she already talked to you. What're you doing? We agreed I'd be the one to interview her, isn't that right?"

"Before you bust my chops…hear me out. Do you have time now? We need to talk in private."

Interview room three was empty. The trio sat in metal chairs positioned around a matching metal table. The table was smaller than a card table and wobbly. Rick took out a business card, folded it in half, and slipped it under one of the legs of the table. His world was unbalanced. At least he could have a steady table.

"The police department thanks you," Campbell said. "That table's rocked since this place was built."

"You're wel—"

"God dammit!" Campbell said. "You keep getting in our way."

"Listen to me—"

"I was at Lucy's house first thing this morning. She was outside, getting on her bike. The dog was wearing goggles and strapped to her chest like a swaddled baby. Damnedest thing I ever saw. She wouldn't talk to me. The issue's *mute* as she called it. Put on her helmet and took off. Seemed upset. What the hell happened?"

Rick described his meeting with Lucy, including her index card chart. When Marlow heard Sanchez saw the chart, she shook her head and groaned.

"Are you telling us Lucy showed Sanchez the details of our homicide investigation?" Campbell said. "She violated Susque's order. What're you doing about it?"

"Nothing. Here's why." Rick handed the index card to Campbell.

"What is it?" Marlow craned over Campbell's shoulder. Written on the card was a single word: *Tiptoes.*

"It's the street name of the man Roach paid to ditch the gun used to kill Detective Parks. Sanchez gave it to me. Just now."

Campbell and Marlow looked flabbergasted. Rick told them about Sanchez's surprise appearance at Café No Delay.

"Why would he give you this?" Marlow said.

"In exchange for my agreement not to go after Lucy."

"She's been nothing but trouble to him," Campbell said.

"He said he owes her. Said she saved him from killing a man. Didn't say who—I'm guessing either Luiz Alvarado or Javier Rodriguez. He became quite emotional."

Rick inhaled. "Lucy once told me she thought Sanchez wanted out of Roach. I broached the subject with him, but he scoffed at the idea. My gut tells me she might be right."

"How do you know you're not being scammed?" Campbell said.

"I don't...but I'm willing to chance it."

Campbell studied the card, turning it over and over. He tossed the card on the table. "Chance it with your life? Sanchez threatened you. He could be drawing you in. Solving a cold murder of a cop? The perfect bait. You need to recuse yourself from this case. You're in too deep—with Lucy, with Sanchez. Talk to Mercer. Have her put in someone who can be more objective."

No way. This investigation is mine, and I'm going to see it through.

Marlow picked up the index card. "I'll pass this on to NYPD."

"Treat Sanchez as a confidential informant," Rick said. "Say nothing to anyone. Understood?"

Campbell and Marlow nodded their assent.

"Rick," Marlow said. "Ulysses could be right. Be careful."

———◆———

Rick usually had an "open door" policy to his office. Now he kept his door closed. He didn't want his colleagues to think he was a hoarder.

Prosecution files were stacked into a three-way wall that surrounded his desktop computer. More files filled his credenza and bookcase. Files were piled on the floor within arm's reach of his chair. Within each file, there were motions to dismiss, motions to suppress, jury trial demands, and discovery requests. It wasn't only Roach files—the litigation deluge had spread to other gangs. Gangs would slaughter each other over territory, but they apparently reached a consensus on one subject: get Rick gone.

There were twenty-five phone calls to return, including one from Judge Davis's chambers scolding him for failing to appear at the scheduled suppression hearing. The judge was furious. Appear in court at two o'clock this afternoon with an explanation, the message said, or the State's case will be dismissed. Appoline Mercer called three times. Jill Sanders called twice. He spent a minute prioritizing his return calls.

Rick called Sanders.

"Bottom line—there's no federal or state wiretap on Sanchez's property," she said. "Either Lucy's mistaken, or more likely, she's spinning you."

"She's too smart to make that kind of mistake. We've had our moments, but she's never lied to me. Something's wrong here."

"She didn't tell you about her visit to Sanchez, did she? I'm concerned you're being sucked into a dangerous situation by a pretty, clever girl for purposes that may be illegal or unethical. It's clear you have personal feelings for her, even if you refuse to admit it."

"Jill, it's me...you know me. How could you think—"

"I've seen it before. Three years ago, Roach manipulated one of our finest attorneys into obstructing justice. A brilliant prosecutor. Now he's disbarred, broke, and has a criminal record. Hear me on this—I'll do whatever it takes to prevent something like that from happening to you."

Rick was insulted, but he wouldn't let Sanders's paranoia stop him from what he had to do.

"All right, I understand. Don't worry." He used his most reassuring voice. "Let's switch topics for a moment. Has anyone ever approached Sanchez about turning state's evidence?"

"Why in the world do you think that would be productive?"

Rick was torn. How could he answer Sanders's question without telling her about his meeting with Sanchez? Telling her would only fuel her suspicion. Worse, if she blabbed to the wrong person, any hope Sanchez could be turned would be jettisoned.

"It never hurts to ask." His answer sounded ridiculous, even to him.

"Stop it!" Sanders shouted into the phone so loudly he had to hold the receiver away from his ear. "Absolutely ludicrous! To answer your question, I spoke to Sanchez. Marcela called the LAPD gang unit, asking for help, wanting to get her husband out of Roach. She talked to Detective Angela Delgado.

"Delgado arranged for Marcela to call me. She begged me to get her husband out of Roach. I later met with Sanchez, secretly. Asked him if he wanted out of the life, told him we'd work with him, protect him. He laughed in my face. 'You sound just like my wife,' he said. Two days later, Marcela was dead.

"I pleaded with Marcela to get away from Sanchez. She refused, saying her husband would never hurt her. Next thing, Marcela's hacked to pieces." Jill's voice cracked. "I'll always blame myself for not pressing harder."

Rick was silent.

"Lucy's given you the impression Sanchez is a redeemable guy, but he's a vile beast. Do you know how he became a shot caller? He put a baby girl in a hot car, in front of her mother, and made the poor woman watch her baby cook until she told him where her husband was. Roach killed him. She later jumped off the Golden Gate Bridge holding her baby. We couldn't prosecute Sanchez. Anyone who knew anything refused to cooperate. They were terrified.

"You'll never convince me Sanchez wasn't behind his wife's murder. I don't care if someone else copped to it. I'll do what I have to in order to protect you from that monster, I swear I will."

"Not necessary," Rick said, trying to appease her. "I promise. I appreciate your concern. And your honesty. Thank you."

Right before they disconnected, it occurred to Rick to clarify something Sanders had said.

"Jill, sorry. One more thing before we hang up. What exactly did Sanchez say to you? 'You sound just like my wife?' Is that what he said?"

Rick heard nothing but the phone disconnecting.

Chapter 44

January 5

Judge Marilyn C. Davis ran a tight ship. Contrary to many judges, a hearing scheduled before Davis for nine o'clock started promptly at nine o'clock. She didn't care if an attorney was on vacation, getting married, or attending his mother's funeral. Figure it out, she'd say, but be in my courtroom, on time and fully prepared. Her trials proceeded at warp speed. She expected attorneys to stipulate to all agreed-upon facts. Attorneys' trial objections had to be succinct. She shut down any grandstanding, blustering, or bickering by attorneys with an embarrassing rebuke. Rick always marveled how a judge, who stood a roly-poly five feet at most, could intimidate the most seasoned attorney.

To Rick's relief and surprise, Judge Davis was easily mollified. He apologized for his non-appearance at the suppression hearing, speaking for less than thirty seconds. He offered no excuses, was brief and to the point. Rick hoped his reputation as a reliable and efficient attorney would persuade Davis to cut him some slack.

"I'm denying the defendant's motion to dismiss," Davis said. "Mr. McCormick, get your calendar in order. I won't be so accommodating next time." She re-scheduled the suppression hearing for the following week.

Rick glanced at Judge Davis while he gathered his file. She smiled at him, but it was not a smile of approval. It struck Rick as a grim smile of sympathy. Like the kind you see at funerals.

As he hiked back to his office, he resigned himself to asking for help with his caseload. He'd almost blown a prosecution by failing to appear, first time ever. He'd talk to Mercer before day's end.

Rick stepped through the door of the State's Attorney's office. All eyes turned in his direction. They quickly looked down, or out the window, or past him.

"Good afternoon, Mr. McCormick," the receptionist said. "Mrs. Mercer is waiting for you in the conference room."

He found Mercer at the table, sorting through prosecution files. They were the same files that, as of that morning, covered his office. Mercer's laptop was stationed in front of her.

"Sit down," she said. He sat.

"Why didn't you return my telephone calls? I left three messages."

"I'm sorry. I had to wrap up something that was time sensitive. Afterward, I was in court."

She gazed directly into his eyes, without expression.

"Not much is more time sensitive than numerous messages left by your boss. I've received three disturbing telephone calls. The first was from Judge Davis. You failed to appear at a suppression hearing. Our office tried to find you, but you didn't return the calls. We couldn't send another ASA because you had the file. Judge Davis threatened to—"

"I just came from Judge Davis's courtroom. It's okay. She accepted my apology, as did opposing counsel. The hearing's been rescheduled for—"

"Mr. McCormick, it's by no means *okay*. What I was about to tell you, before you interrupted me, was that Mary Genzler, the rape victim, and her family were present in the courtroom. They traveled from North Carolina for the hearing. Took time off from work, arranged for childcare. Ms. Genzler left the courtroom distraught. I met with the family for over an hour assuring them our office cared about them, cared about the case, and we were fully committed to seeking justice. Not only did you embarrass me and this office, you risked the prosecution of a brutal rapist."

Rick looked away from Mercer, embarrassed. No one told him the victim was coming to the suppression hearing. "I'm sorry. I'll call Ms. Genzler and—"

"You'll do no such thing. I've reassigned the case to David Mendelsohn in the violent crimes unit."

Rick couldn't think of anything to say.

"The second disturbing call came from ADA Jill Sanders in LA. She told me about your unfounded belief Romero Sanchez is being wiretapped. She investigated and told you there were no such wiretaps. It turns out the idea was planted in your head by Lucy Prestipino. Ms. Sanders is gravely concerned you're being manipulated for purposes that are unknown at this time. I suspect the purpose has to do with what I'm about to show you."

Sanders called Mercer? He felt betrayed.

Mercer opened her laptop and turned it toward Rick. Within a few clicks of the keyboard, he was watching himself with Sanchez in the interview room of the Montgomery County Police Headquarters. He saw himself display the crime scene photos of Debbie Prestipino. Sanchez was nonchalant, cool, disinterested. The swagger evaporated when Rick identified the victim as Lucy's mother.

Mercer's mouth formed a tight line as they listened to Sanchez's threats.

> *A luz verde is too good for you, McCormick. I'm going to kill you slowly. I'm going to butcher your reputation, ruin your precious career. Every gangster and every lawyer will know Baltimore's gang prosecutor, the rising star, is nothing more than a cowardly piece of shit, a pussy, a bitch. You'll have to fight for every conviction you get.*

Mercer shut the laptop.

"And this is the result." She swept her arms over the stacks of files on the conference table.

Before he could respond, she spoke again, this time in a louder decibel. "I received a complaint from the Public Defender's Office about your plea and sentencing policy. Specifically, it's now the policy of the gang unit to refuse to discuss plea agreements and to seek the maximum sentence for any defendant who challenges evidence."

"That's not entirely correct. If I believe gang shot callers are directing a defendant to jam up the prosecution's case, I won't negotiate a plea and will seek the maximum sentence. That's my policy."

"Your policy? This is the Office of the State's Attorney. You seem to have forgotten *I'm* the State's Attorney. I'm the only one in this office who makes policy."

"Mrs. Mercer—"

She held up her hand, stop-sign style. "Following the MPIA hearing, I expressed my dissatisfaction with your performance. It's clear to me you do not have the judgment or experience to run a unit. Explain why I shouldn't fire you."

For a brief moment, Rick considered telling Mercer about his meeting with Sanchez. He knew she'd demand to know the details. Lucy's name would come up. So would her violation of Judge Susque's order. Mercer would be enraged. She'd go after Lucy. The deal with Sanchez would fall through, the opportunity lost. Rick ruled against telling Mercer about Sanchez. He'd have to come up with another explanation to save his job.

"If you fire me, Sanchez will have accomplished his purpose. You would have allowed a ruthless gangbanger to make a personnel decision that belongs to you and only you. If he gets away with this, where will it end? It'll end with Roach running this office."

Mercer's face turned scarlet. Rick braced himself. It crossed his mind she might slap him. She stood and leaned over the desk toward him.

"Mr. McCormick." Her voice was controlled and calm. "It'll end when I put a stop to this personal vendetta between you and Sanchez. I will not let this office get drawn into a testosterone-laden pissing contest."

She flicked open her phone. "Security, send someone to ASA McCormick's office. He'll be clearing out his personal belongings. Escort him out of the building when he's finished."

Chapter 45

January 6

The *New York Times.* The *Baltimore Sun.* Lucy loved how the newspapers felt in her hands, the way they smelled. Steppie dozed in her lap while she read the *Times*. She was fascinated by an article about the use of DNA fingerprinting to locate biological relatives. Private DNA companies were forming around the country to serve the ever-growing interest in genealogy. DNA profiling was being used to determine the probability of paternity, maternity, family relationships, eligibility for membership in Native American tribes, and immigration benefits.

A searcher could submit a DNA sample to a private, commercial company. The company would produce a DNA profile and compare it to the existing profiles in its database. There might be a familial relationship if the comparison revealed a sufficient number of repeating identical genetic sequences, called *alleles*, at specific locations on a chromosome, or loci. The probability of a familial relationship would be based on the number of identical alleles at each tested loci. Like the databases used for CODIS, the private databases were growing with every DNA sample submitted.

The article noted that Maryland's DNA Collection Act prohibits the police from using familial DNA searches to solve crimes. She wondered why. Constitutional issues concerning the right to privacy, it went on to explain.

Lucy picked up the DNA profile she got from the MPIA hearing. Who are you? Are you somehow related to me? Tiffany's words about Debbie came to mind.

She never said, but I thought maybe she'd been through it herself.

She re-read the autopsy report. Her eyes moved to the section entitled, "Internal Examination." The report indicated every system was normal except for the musculoskeletal system: fractures of the right 10th rib, right clavicle, and nose. The injuries were at least twenty years old. The report described the scars on Debbie's forehead and wrist. She'd also had a ruptured right eardrum.

The information wasn't news to Lucy. At one point or another, her mother explained each injury. Lucy had given the explanations to Marlow. "Tell me about the scar on your mother's wrist," Marlow said.

"My mother said she was at a party. She tripped over a glass table and fell through it."

"What about her broken clavicle?"

"She took a hard hit playing soccer as a kid."

"Broken rib?"

"Basketball."

"Nose?"

"Basketball again."

Marlow stopped pursuing the abuse angle when Lucy showed her the death certificates of her father and maternal grandparents. Even if Debbie had been abused, the possible suspects couldn't be Debbie's killer; they'd died long ago.

Lucy had accepted her mother's explanations without question. Now they sounded suspicious. Soccer? Basketball? For as long as she could remember, Debbie was never athletic. You have to be a person who liked the rough and tumble to play contact sports. That wasn't her mother; she was always fearful, hesitant. Hopscotch was the limit of her mother's physical risk-taking.

Could a private DNA company tell her if she was related to the man whose DNA profile she now held in her hands? It seemed a long shot, but she couldn't afford to eliminate any connection, no matter how unlikely, without checking it out. A search engine quickly took her to a list of DNA genealogy search companies. She selected KinKonnect DNA; it was the least expensive option and was located in Baltimore City. Lucy spoke to a customer service representative.

"This is a most unusual request," the representative said. "We collect the DNA from our customer and produce the profile. We then compare the profile with those in our database—not with a DNA profile we didn't produce. How do we know the profile you have is even accurate?"

"I'm willing to chance it," Lucy said. "You can put all kinds of limitations in your report if you want."

"Let's say we're willing to do it. If there's a match, we might not be able to tell you the degree of relationship. DNA testing looks at specific loci on each chromosome. You have twenty-three pairs of chromosomes; half of the pair is from your mother and half from your father. Your parents have twenty-three chromosomes that came from their parents, and so on and so forth. The further up the ancestral line we go, the fewer genetic sequences can be compared."

Lucy decided to take the shot. "Understood. What do I do next?"

"You have to decide what kind of DNA test you want. There's the mitochondrial DNA testing, the autosomal DNA STR testing, the—"

"Whoa!" Lucy was overwhelmed. "I want you to do the easiest and cheapest test first—then I'll decide from there."

The swipe along the inside of Lucy's mouth was quick, no more than a split-second. The technician holding the swab was a petite Asian woman who wore one-inch fingernails, four-inch heels, and a five-inch hair up-do.

"All done," the technician said. She scanned the paperwork. "We'll have the results in five days. I see here you want to pick up the report, is that correct?"

"Yes, along with the DNA profile I gave you."

Lucy pedaled home. The DNA testing depleted the last of the money she received from Tiffany. She hoped it was worth it.

Chapter 46

January 11

The envelope wasn't what Lucy expected. It was thin and ordinary. An envelope that could contain life-changing information ought to be thick and made from the finest, heavyweight paper. It should be sealed with wax, rather than a lick of a tongue on a gummed flap. If she hadn't picked up the envelope from KinKonnect DNA herself, she'd have thought it was junk mail destined for the recycle bin.

Steppie slept soundly in Lucy's lap as she sat at her dining room table. She opened the envelope, gingerly, half-expecting anthrax to spill from it. The report contained all manner of limitations to its conclusion, each related to the fact the lab was comparing Lucy's DNA profile to a profile it hadn't produced. It was corporate cover-your-ass stuff, as far as Lucy was concerned. She knew the crime lab's profile was accurate.

The report was a jumble of numbers, listed under columns labeled *Locus, PI, Allele Sizes.* The operative sentence didn't appear until the end of the report, right above the notarized signature of the Ph.D. who verified the correctness of the results.

> *The unidentified subject of the provided DNA Profile is not excluded as the biological father of Ms. Prestipino. Based on testing results obtained from the analysis of the DNA loci listed, the probability of paternity is 99.9999%.*

"Give me a fuckin' break!" She threw the report across the table and watched it flutter to the floor. Steppie leaped from her lap.

"My father? Seriously? He's dead!"

She rummaged through a pile of documents and found her father's death certificate. After thirty minutes and three telephone transfers, she reached Dr. Michael Linwood, Director, KinKonnect DNA.

"Your company screwed up. In an ass-backward way, your report said the man in the DNA profile I gave you is my father. My father's dead. I have his death certificate. I want my money back."

There was a long pause before Dr. Linwood responded.

"Ms. Prestipino, there are risks to ancestral searches based on DNA. One such risk is the discovery of family secrets."

"What're you talking about? What family secrets?"

"Perhaps the man who raised you, the man you believe is your father, is not your biological father."

Linwood's words hit her like shards of glass.

"No, that can't be…it can't be…I have a birth certificate that says you're wrong."

"The paternity stated on a birth certificate isn't always accurate."

"That would mean…my mother lied."

"I'm truly sorry. Sometimes this happens. I can refer you to some counselors who—"

She disconnected. What a waste of money. Back to the chart of index cards.

After Lucy's altercation with Rick, she'd ripped down her chart, but not before scanning them into her computer. It took her an hour to re-print the cards. No more wall charts, she decided. She wanted to gather the cards in a hurry in case of unexpected visitors.

She spread the cards on the dining room table, hoping a pattern would emerge. She ordered them by date, by common words, by subject matter. Once, she closed her eyes and organized them randomly. Hours passed. No matter how she arranged the cards, she found no clues. The index cards weren't getting Lucy anywhere but frustrated. Time for a break.

She read the *Baltimore Sun* obituaries. Nothing noteworthy—no lessons to be learned, no lives to inspire. Moving on to the sports section, she read about the Baltimore Ravens. They were going to the NFL playoffs; the city was ecstatic. She worked her way through the remainder of the paper. Nothing interesting.

Maybe the *New York Times* would have something worth reading. Out of habit, she began with the obituaries. Her mother taught her an informed citizen needed to read at least two newspapers. It made perfect sense to her at the time, but now she wondered: why a New York newspaper? Debbie could've read the *Washington Post*—it had the same political leanings as the *Times*, and its news was closer to home. And why the focus on obituaries?

Lucy grabbed two index cards and began a column.

NY police officer shot

Cartridge casings

She wrote out two more cards and added them to the list: *New York Times, Obituaries*

All the while, she was playing whack-a-mole with the paternity report. It kept popping up in her mind, and she'd smack it down. Her conversation with Dr. Linwood gnawed at her. *The paternity stated on a birth certificate isn't always accurate.*

Lucy panted. Her hands trembled while she made a new index card. It was barely legible. *Birth certificate.* Where should she put it? It didn't fit in the New York column. She was born in Maryland. She recalled the struggle to get the birth certificate. Her mother's resistance. Their bitter argument.

She remembered who'd found the birth certificate—Romero, a criminal. What if he hired someone to produce a fake birth certificate? If the birth information was wrong, it was because she'd given it to him.

Mercy Hospital. Her fingers tapped out her intuition on her laptop. There was no Mercy Hospital in New York City. Dead end. She persisted. Soon she was studying the history of New York Hospitals. She found Our Lady of Mercy Hospital Medical Center. It merged with Montefiore Medical Center in 2008. The hospital was located in the Bronx. Bingo.

I was born at Mercy Hospital, all right, but not the one in Baltimore.

Debbie had been protecting her own lies. Once Lucy saw the original birth certificate, the jig would be up. Her mother would be forced to tell the truth.

A theory formed in Lucy's mind. Her parents lived in the Bronx. Debbie escaped from domestic violence. Took Lucy with her. Hid in Baltimore.

Her mother religiously read the *New York Times*, hoping to one day see her father's obituary. She didn't live to see that obituary. He found her first. And killed her.

Why now? He was gone for over twenty years. He needed something Debbie wouldn't give him. The cell phone? Is that why she threw it in the boat lake? Debbie was protecting something in it; the only thing the dinosaur phone had were phone numbers.

She turned cold.

The phone had Lucy's number. Debbie died protecting her daughter.

She couldn't grasp the concept that her father had killed her mother. It was easier to imagine what he looked like. Probably tall and lean. Blond hair, blue eyes. None of those physical attributes came to Lucy from her mother.

What about the other attributes? The ones you couldn't see. Like her addictions. She'd read that inclination to addictions could be genetic.

With the suddenness of a violent bike crash, she hated herself. The thought of her father's genes being part of her DNA made her want to slash her wrists and rip off her skin. Anything to rid herself of his repulsive chromosomes.

Her imagination played a movie.

She's standing next to her father, side-by-side, their arms around each other's waists. They're posing in front of a camera. Father and daughter, long lost but found again. She's holding a serrated kitchen knife in her free hand. Plunges it into him. Twice, once in each lung. As he slowly suffocates, she kicks him in the ribs. Crunch. She stomps on his clavicle. Snap. She can't think of any parting words other than *Adios*. After he's dead, she calls 9-1-1. Makes herself an Irish car bomb. Chugs it down. Takes a long drag from a joint. Mellows out until the police arrive.

Chapter 47

January 12

Colleen galloped down the front steps when Rick pulled into their parents' driveway. She was trailed by two small boys, Terence and Alonzo. They were biological brothers, five and seven years old, respectively. They'd been placed with Rick's parents by the Montgomery County Department of Social Services. Rick knew the drill; after the mandatory six-month period of post-placement supervision, there'd be a final adoption hearing. A judge's signature would expand the McCormick family from four to six. He would gain two little brothers.

"Hey, you!" Colleen gave Rick a hug.

The boys stood in front of Rick; Terence with a smile and Alonzo with suspicion. He'd met them six times before. Terence took to him quickly; Alonzo remained aloof and uncertain, no matter what he did to win his friendship.

"Don't take it personally," his mother said in her trademark soft voice. "Alonzo's been through a lot. It'll take time, but it'll happen. You'll see."

"And if it doesn't?"

"We'll do our best by him."

Rick squatted so he was eye-level with the boys. "Happy birthday, Alonzo! Want a special piggyback ride? You can hop on too, Terence."

Terence climbed onto Rick's back. Alonzo watched, but said nothing.

"He doesn't talk much," Terence said.

"No problem," Rick said, more to Alonzo than to Terence. "You know, when Colleen first came to our family, she didn't say much either. Now she won't stop yapping."

Colleen grinned.

"Let's go inside," she said. "Mom's baking Alonzo's cake. Dad's out buying some fancy wine. He's been taking classes at the L'Academy de Cuisine. Learning to cook is his latest project." She took Alonzo's hand and followed her brother into the house.

Beef stew. Its odor smacked Rick in the face and turned his stomach. Lucy served him beef stew the night he kissed her. Everything went to shit after that.

"Rick, are you all right?" Colleen said. "You look kinda sick."

"I'm fine. It's nice to be home."

He walked into the kitchen, still wearing Terence on his back, and hugged his mother. Catherine McCormick had short gray hair, vivid blue eyes, and an infectious smile. She was married for thirty-four years to Rick's father, Jack McCormick. She introduced herself as Jack's "bride" or "trophy wife," depending on the circumstances.

"Stew smells great," he said, suppressing his gag reflex.

"Tell your father. It's his stew. I'm stirring the pot until he gets back."

Catherine placed a step stool by the kitchen counter. "Alonzo, want to frost your birthday cake?"

On the counter was an unfrosted cake, a bowl of vanilla icing, food coloring, multi-colored sprinkles, candles, and a spatula. Catherine tied an apron around the child.

"It's your cake," she said. "You can decorate it any way you want."

The sheer joy and wonder on Alonzo's face warmed Rick's heart.

He heard a commotion coming from the foyer. Jack had returned home, increasing the decibel level with his pounding footsteps and boisterous greetings. Terence jumped from Rick's back.

Seconds later, Jack walked peg-legged into the kitchen with Terence wrapped around his right leg. He kissed Catherine and gave Rick a bear hug. Jack leaned over Alonzo's shoulder and pointed to the cake. "You missed a spot, Lonny. Make sure you cover it up nice and thick."

Rick chuckled. There weren't any bare spots anywhere; on the cake, the counter, the step stool, or Alonzo's face.

"Terence, I want to talk to Rick," Jack said, peeling Terence from his leg.

Rick followed his father to the library. It was a simple room; a desk with a computer, two white Ikea bookshelves, and two chairs. Artwork created by Alonzo and Terence papered the walls.

"Haven't seen you in a while," Jack said. "How's life been treating you?"

Rick had been fired, humiliated, and probably rendered unemployable as an attorney, at least in Baltimore City and surrounding counties. His dreams of becoming a U.S. Attorney were demolished.

He wanted to spill out his troubles, but not today. The McCormick family gathered to celebrate Alonzo's seventh birthday. Alonzo never had a birthday party or a birthday cake. It was his day to be the center of the family's attention.

"Good. Real good."

Rick asked the question that had been on his mind for months.

"Why'd you and Mom do it? Start a new family. You had an empty nest. You could've traveled, done anything you wanted. Why'd you start over?"

Jack smiled. "The social worker asked us that, too. Short answer—we're selfish. When Colleen left for school, things were too quiet. We missed the hustle-bustle of kids coming and going. We missed helping with home-work, going to high school games, watching a homecoming float being built in our driveway. All that stuff. We weren't ready to give it up, not yet. We thoroughly enjoyed the parenting ride and didn't want it to end."

After dinner and cake, it was poker time. Jack dealt the cards and called the game. Five card stud, nothing wild. Each player had ten cookies, the McCormick version of poker chips. Catherine divided the family into teams. "We're going to teach our new players how to play."

Rick was Alonzo's partner. He knew it was his mother's way of giving Alonzo another chance to get comfortable with Rick. Alonzo proved to be a good poker player. He had an excellent memory and quickly under-stood the game.

Rick showed the dealt hand to Alonzo. "What do you think? How many cards should I throw back?"

Alonzo took the cards and organized them. Two queens, two jacks, and a deuce. He pulled out the deuce. "This one."

"Good job. Before long, you'll be beating all of us—even Colleen."

"No way," Colleen said. "That'll never happen. I'm *Colleen, Princess of Poker.* No one will conquer me." She then stood and waved her fork

246 • Ellen Ann Callahan

like a scepter. She fumbled the fork. It bounced on the floor and landed near Rick's foot.

"What're you trying to do," he said, "kill your opponents?"

He leaned down to fetch the fork. As he handed it to Colleen, he discovered she was eating a cookie—one of his. She gave him a sly smile. Terence and Alonzo giggled.

"Colleen's sneaky," Alonzo said. "She fights dirty."

Fights dirty?

"What did you say?" Rick said.

Alonzo's eyes widened.

"He was joking." Catherine said quietly.

"I know, I know." Rick leaned against the back into his chair. "It's...sorry..."

He couldn't complete the sentence because he couldn't complete his thought. *Fights dirty.* The phrase ricocheted inside his head like a rubber super ball. It collided with another thought bouncing around in his head. *You sound just like my wife.* Sanchez had said it to Rick and to Jill Sanders. He had to figure it out—it was bugging the hell out of him. *Bugs?*

Click.

Rick slapped the table. "It was right in front of me all the time!" He laughed. His family stared.

He extended his hand toward Alonzo. "Alonzo, my man, I owe you. I've been trying to figure something out for days, something really important. You gave me a giant clue. You helped me solve the puzzle. Can I shake your hand in thanks?"

Alonzo took his hand.

Chapter 48

January 12

For a moment, Lucy believed she'd downed the Irish car bomb.
It was morning. She woke up on the bathroom tile floor, her hair caked with vomit. The smell triggered her memory of the night before. She spent most of it retching. Her teeth were chattering, and her clothes were soaked with the tears she'd cried.

She felt a warm spot in the crux of her knee. It was Steppie, her new friend. The friend who never lied to her. Even her mother lied to her. Raised her to believe she was the daughter of Gary Prestipino. No, her father was a violent animal who'd murdered the mother of his child.

Her whole life, her mother lied to her, all the while intolerant of any untruth that came from Lucy's lips.

Liar! Hypocrite! Bitch!

Steppie whimpered. She raised herself from the floor and took the dog outside. It was a dank and misty morning. The rain fell like bits of city grit on her cheeks. She surveyed her street. It looked different somehow. Everything did. It had all changed. She'd changed, too. Lucy didn't know who she was anymore.

She lingered on the front step. After Steppie finished, he crawled into her lap. She patted him aimlessly while she contemplated her next steps. First, she had to give her mother's killer a name. Thinking of him as her father revolted her. A thug, a brute, a murderer.

Pop! Pop! Pop! That would be the sound of her gun when she shot him. She decided to call him "Pops."

Now that Lucy knew who killed her mother, she had to find him. How would she do that without knowing his name or where he lived? It seemed logical to start at the beginning—New York City, where she was born. Maybe his name was in the hospital records or on her birth certificate. No, if her mother was hiding from Pops, she would've changed her identity—Lucy's, too. How could she get her birth certificate without knowing basic identifying information? Besides, Pops didn't strike her as a stand-up man who'd admit paternity.

Could he still be in New York? Maybe he was entrenched in New York, the way she was in Baltimore. Why would he come to Baltimore to find her and then go back to New York? He must know where she is—if Dr. Michaels could find her through the funeral home, so could Pops.

Looking for him in New York was another long shot, but she didn't know where else to aim. Where in New York should she look? She had no idea. After mulling it over, she decided looking for him was the wrong approach. She'd get him to come to her. How?

She remembered the New York bicycle messenger she met three years ago at the Baltimore Bike Messenger GangBang Race. She loved the alleycat race—an unsanctioned, body-bashing, biking competition throughout the neighborhoods of Baltimore City.

She met the New York messenger during the post-race celebratory consumption of Natty Bohs. He spit the beer onto the street, inches from Lucy's feet. "This tastes like piss!"

"Shut your mouth," she said. "Talking trash about Natty Boh is the same as dissing the Star Spangled Banner or Edgar Allen Poe."

He laughed and introduced himself. *Lights-Out* was his name—a nickname earned by the numerous times he'd been rendered unconscious. She spent the afternoon showing Lights-Out her favorite places in Baltimore. That night, while they were in bed, he whispered the decimal value of Pi between slow, languid kisses. She found the mathematical sweet talk oddly erotic. She replied by moaning comparisons of granite and solid surface countertops. Lights-Out might be addled, but she had a sweet spot for him.

Somehow, he learned about her mother's death. "Call me if you ever need me," was hand-written on the sympathy card. Lucy needed him.

She called, hoping his words were not empty syllables used to appease a vague sense of manners.

"Lucy," he said. "How are you holding up?"

"I'm calling for a favor."

"Anything. I owe you. Did you know I started my own messenger company? You inspired me, you having your own company. I've got twenty-five people working for me. It's called Piece of Pi Courier Service."

"Piece of Pie? What does that even mean?"

"Pi—like three point one four. It means nothing, but customers remember it. So, what can I do for you?"

She told him she recently learned her father was somewhere in New York. It was urgent she find him. "The trouble is, I don't know his name… it's a complicated family situation. A lot of drama I don't want to bore you with."

"What do you want me to do?"

"Would you hang some posters for me?"

"Sure thing. How many?"

"Depends on how much it'll cost."

"Let's see…you being an old friend…if it's all right with you, I'll have my messengers put them up near every pickup and delivery address. That way I don't have to charge you for a separate delivery. How about a dollar a poster to cover costs?"

"How about fifty cents?"

"You're killing me here. You win…but only because of your sexy dissertation on countertops. You know, that came in handy—I bought a house and put in some new ones. Granite. Come to New York, and we'll christen them. I'll explain how airplanes fly. Bernoulli's Principle."

"Sorry. I'll have to take a rain check from Principal Bernoulli."

"Too bad. Back to the operative question. How many posters?"

"A thousand."

She heard him gasp.

"Jesus! What do you need from the guy? A body part or something?"

"Something like that."

"A thousand posters—that kind of number adds complications. My people would have to duck the cops. The mayor is trying to clean up the city. I could get a big fine for littering."

"I'll throw in a case of Natty Boh."

"The negotiations are going backward."

Lucy exhaled deeply into the phone. After a few heavy breaths, she moaned, "3.141592653589—"

"Okay, I'll do it."

Designing the poster was harder than Lucy expected. Her name and address couldn't be on it—she didn't want every bonehead in New York pestering her, especially the litter-conscious mayor of New York City.

After two hours, she was pleased with her work. She e-mailed the poster to a New York copy shop with instructions to produce a thousand. "Someone from Piece of Pi Couriers will pick them up," she said.

Lucy held a hard copy of the poster in her hand.

> *Dear Pops,*
> *I was 21 before I learned about you. We need to talk. Come visit. You know where I live. Your daughter, born May 1, Mercy Hospital, New York City.*

Afterward, Lucy took Steppie for a bike ride. She pedaled to a liquor store and bought one Guinness stout, a bottle of Bailey's Irish cream, and a bottle of Jameson Irish whiskey. She found a corner boy and bought a joint.

Nothing more to do but wait for Pops.

January 13

Roach killed Marcela, Rick was certain of it. She'd called the police, and begged for help. Later, she spoke to Jill Sanders. Get my husband out of the gang, she pleaded. Roach knew about the call. Knew she was pressuring Romero to leave the life. Roach had bugged their home. Heard it all.

Roach fought dirty. It was ruthless. Capable of anything. Discipline was savage, especially against those deemed traitors. Marcela betrayed Roach. She'd convince her husband to betray the gang if she wasn't stopped. Roach stopped her by killing her.

Roach tricked Sanchez into believing it was a revenge killing. He'd screwed the wife of Luiz Alvarado. Alvarado, in a fit of jealous rage, killed Marcela with a machete. Sanchez believed that's what happened, but Rick didn't.

Rick wanted to tell Sanchez he'd been played by Roach. Use it to convince him to turn state's evidence, to testify against the gang, to crush it. Rick's career would be saved. No, not just saved—propelled into the legal stratosphere. He smiled with self-satisfaction until he realized it was only a theory. He needed proof.

He could tell Sanchez about the surveillance, but it wouldn't be enough. Sanchez would think law enforcement planted the bugs. He'd accuse Rick of deceit, payback for getting him fired. Rick had to come up with more before he approached Sanchez.

He had to answer the first question first. Why would Luiz Alvarado slaughter a woman, knowing he'd end up with a life sentence? It had to be money. It was always money. Where'd the money go? Alvarado didn't have it. He was in prison for the rest of his life.

Rick called Alexander Stonegate. At first, the conversation was awkward. Alex was defensive, apparently waiting for Rick to blame him for getting fired.

"Rick," Alex said. "Shit hit the fan around here when you refused to negotiate pleas."

"I know, I know. I stand by the decision. Mercer disagreed, and I got canned, simple as that. No hard feelings. I hope we're still friends."

"Of course we are. If you're calling about a job with the PD's office, I can't help you. You're *persona non grata* around here."

"That's not why I'm calling…I'm calling about Luiz Alvarado."

"I don't represent him anymore." The reserve was back in Alex's voice. "My representation was limited to the extradition proceedings. The case is over. I can't discuss him with you. Attorney-client privilege, remember?"

"I'm not interested in the legal representation or any communications between you and your client. Just your impression of him, if you're willing to share it. When you met him, did you take him for a man who was capable of committing a savage crime, especially against a woman?"

"No, but when it comes to matters of the heart, people are capable of anything. Where are you going with this? And why? You don't work for the State's Attorney's Office anymore."

"I'm scratching an itch. Something's off about this whole thing."

"Luiz's wife said that, too. When he turned himself in, she called me. Said her husband couldn't have done such a thing. He was a lazy, momma's boy and didn't give a shit about his family. Sanchez did more for her kids than her husband ever did. Luiz knew for months his wife was sleeping with him. Didn't seem to mind at all. She also said Luiz wasn't brave enough. If Marcela screamed, he would've run away with his tail between his legs. Maybe Luiz reached a breaking point and snapped. Maybe it was a territorial thing. I don't know. Now, it's your turn to answer a question. Does this have anything to do with Sanchez?"

"Indirectly."

"Directly or not, I'm worried about you. Take some time off. Get out of Baltimore. Get away from Lucy, Sanchez, Roach, the whole rotten bunch. Walk away."

"Thanks for the advice. I owe you a beer."

Momma's boy. He had to find her. Mrs. Alvarado went to Bon Secours Hospital for surgery on a broken hip. That was in September. Where did she go after discharge? Certainly not back to her home on Langston Street. She'd lived alone and wouldn't have been able to take care of herself.

He called Bon Secours. After several transfers, he ended up speaking with Ms. Rollins in the medical records department.

"Hello, I'm looking for Juanita Alvarado," Rick said. "Mrs. Alvarado was in your hospital last September because of a broken hip. Can you tell me where she went after she was discharged?"

"I need a HIPPA release signed by Mrs. Alvarado. The fee for the records is fifty cents a page. Once I get the release, I'll call you and tell you how much the total is. You can pay when you pick up the records."

"I don't want her records. I want to know where she is."

"I understand, sir. If she were ever here…and I can't even tell you that… but if she were, the records would state where she went after discharge. I need a signed HIPPA release to give you the information."

"Let me understand this," he said through clenched teeth. "I need to find her and have her sign a HIPPA release so you can then give me the records that tell me where she is?"

"Yes, sir."

Rick muttered impatient curses to himself.

"Look, mister. Why don't you just go to the post office and ask for an address correction? You know her last address, don't you?"

"Her street, not the house number."

"If she's old enough to break a hip, she'd have a landline instead of a cell phone. Look her up in the phone book."

Rick felt like an idiot for not thinking of that himself. Twenty minutes later, he stood at the counter in the post office. He asked the clerk for an address correction. She instructed him to fill out an envelope with Mrs. Alvarado's full name and address, along with his return address.

"You should get this back in the mail in a day or so," she said. "A sticker will be on the envelope with the new address."

"Is there any possibility I could get this today? Whenever it's convenient for you. I'd be happy to wait."

The clerk looked him over. "You're Attorney Rick McCormick, aren't you?"

"Yes."

"I know you don't remember me. I was robbed at gunpoint two years ago. You prosecuted the case and made sure the creep got jail time. I'll get the address for you right now, as a thank you."

Rick was happy that, at least in one person's eyes, he wasn't some inept idiot attorney. Within five minutes, the clerk returned to the counter and handed him the envelope with the new address.

Momma Alvarado resided in The Fairview in Queenstown, Maryland. He assumed it was some sort of home for senior citizens. He checked his phone. It was one thirty. Queenstown was about two hours away. He had time to visit The Fairview, ask for a tour, and find out the financials.

When Rick entered the grounds of The Fairview, his first reaction was one of disconnect; the campus had the look and feel of a university, but most of the students had gray hair. Some walked with canes; some were in wheelchairs.

The Fairview was one-hundred thirty acres of lush expanse located in Queen Anne's County, along the shore of the Chesapeake Bay. As he traveled down a driveway that seemed never-ending, he could see the majestic spans of the Chesapeake Bay Bridge on the horizon. There were walking paths, dotted with benches that meandered around a small lake. A pergola was perched by the lake, covered in dormant wisteria vines. The view was spectacular.

A tall, dark-haired woman met him at the reception desk. She introduced herself as the on-duty Admissions Advisor. Her name was Dr. Irene Simpson. She led him to her office and offered him a cup of coffee. They spoke across her desk, with Rick facing a wall of awards, diplomas, and credentials.

"How can I help you?" she said.

Rick explained his parents were aging. He wanted information so they could begin planning their retirement years. It was better to do the research sooner than later, when they might be pressured by a parental health emergency. His family knew Juanita Alvarado, and she was happy living at The Fairview.

"Oh yes, Mrs. Alvarado. A lovely lady. She recovered fully from her broken hip. I'm happy to report she's doing well in our assisted living facility."

So much for HIPPA.

"That's wonderful news," he said.

Dr. Simpson asked for more particulars about his parents' health and abilities, and he replied with vague information.

"The Fairview is a continuing care facility. Many residents stay for years. Our residents typically start out in independent living. They move into more care as they age and their health declines."

She explained the meal plans, medical staff, and security.

"Would you like a tour?"

"Not at this time. It would be helpful if you explained the cost."

She handed him a thick brochure. "We have different plans, depending on the kind of deposit residents pay upon admission. For example, under the refund plan, the deposit is $100,000. If the resident dies within sixty months of admission, the resident's estate gets a partial refund, amortized over the length of the admission. Under the flat plan, the deposit is $70,000, but there is no refund. The amount of the monthly fee depends on the level of care needed by the resident. For example, independent living is $2,000 per month."

"What's the monthly fee for assisted living?"

"$3,500."

"Do you accept Medicaid?"

"No."

Rick heard enough. He asked for, and received, a copy of a blank admission contract and the current fee schedule.

"Nice meeting you." He shook her hand good-bye.

He wasn't sure what shocked him more. That Luiz Alvarado was serving a life sentence so his mother could live in a luxurious senior facility or that anyone, including Sanchez, could be that valuable to Roach. What did Sanchez do for Roach? He must be much more than a shot caller. Maybe the question wasn't what he did, but what he knew.

Rick had enough to talk to Romero. Now he needed to find him. How?

I'll get Lucy to help.

Chapter 50

January 13

It was a good day, so far.

Lights-Out called to announce *Mission Accomplished*—one thousand posters now papered New York City and its boroughs. A few minutes later, the mail brought her a fortuitous surprise—a Members Elite credit card. She called customer service and activated the card, almost unable to suppress her giggles and snorts. Now she had a sparkly silver card with a $25,000 credit limit. Why the card was sent to her was a mystery she didn't plan to solve.

As soon as she disconnected from the bank, she called Manhattan Liquors in New York City. Yes, they sold National Bohemian beer and yes, they could deliver it to the office of Piece of Pi Courier Service. Lucy paid for it with her spanking new credit card.

Inspired by her run of good luck, she tried to use the card to redeem her home from foreclosure. No luck there, but she still had $24,975 to spend. Maybe she'd go to Paris and take Steppie with her. They'd dine together in a fine restaurant near the Eiffel Tower, savoring exotic cheeses and bread.

"We should do Paris before Pops shows up," she said to Steppie.

A car door slammed. Footsteps. A knock on her door.

Pops is here already?

She stashed Steppie into his crate, brushed her hair with her fingers, and looked through the peephole.

Rick McCormick.

She pretended she wasn't home. Clearly, he wasn't fooled; the knocking became louder and more insistent. She heard him shout, "Lucy, open the door!" Her phone rang. Two text messages chirped on her phone. The phone rang again. The final shout was, "Damn it!" Finally, there was quiet.

"Dickhead," she muttered. She let Steppie out of the crate.

Lucy enjoyed thirty minutes of peace before the knocking and the phone calls resumed. The mail slot creaked open. A piece of pepperoni pizza fell through the slot and landed face down on the foyer floor. Steppie darted for it. Lucy pried the pizza from Steppie's mouth, opened the door, and threw the pizza into Rick's face.

"Get out! Get out! And take that fuckin' pizza with you!"

"I need to reach Romero. It's an emergency."

She stared at the marinara sauce dribbling down Rick's chin. A pepperoni clung to his right shoulder. He was holding a box from Donvito's Pizzeria.

"I didn't know how to get your attention. I have to talk to you. Please let me come in."

"All right, you can come in. The pizza stays outside."

Rick came inside, sans the pizza. He began to sit down.

"Don't make yourself comfortable. Say what you want to say and leave."

She stood in front of him, jaw squared, hands on hips.

"Tell me about the bugs you saw in Romero's place."

"You think I'm going to answer your questions? After you said you'd file for contempt against me? What happened? Need more evidence? Taking a second shot?"

"No one's going to file for contempt."

"When did you decide that?"

"Right after I spoke with you."

She wanted to slap him. "Why didn't you tell me? You left me twisting like a fish on a hook, worrying every time I heard a knock on my door I'd be dragged away in handcuffs. You're—"

"I was angry at you. You lied to me. You went to California, behind my back, and saw Romero, after I specifically told you not to talk to him."

"I didn't lie. I—"

"You lied by omission. You set me up to be humiliated."

"So you decided to punish me? Teach me a lesson? My mother's been murdered, and you're worrying about being embarrassed?" Lucy's eyes watered with fury. "How can you be so...petty? You're a small man, McCormick."

Steppie pawed her leg. She picked him up and wiped her tears on his fur.

"Lucy—"

"I'm going upstairs to clean myself up. When I come back, you'll have five minutes to say your piece."

The shower water was as hot as she could bear it. She stood in the shower's stream, and the water pounded her face. She wanted Romero in the shower with her, washing her hair, soaping her body. He'd make her feel better. He always did.

She dried herself, threw on some jeans and a T-shirt.

Steppie began barking loud, relentless yaps that penetrated her eardrums. She heard the dog tearing around the house. She ran down the stairs but stopped midway. Rick was holding his phone, directing a small beam of light onto the floor, urging Steppie, "Get it! Get it!" Steppie was chasing the beam, cutting this way and that, trying to catch the elusive prey. Lucy was sure she could see a smile on the dog's face. She let out a hearty laugh.

"Steppie's a great dog," Rick said. He dropped to his knees and stroked Steppie on the stomach. "You've taken amazing care of him. The last time I was here, he looked half-dead. I didn't think he'd make it."

She descended the rest of the steps and sat on the love seat. "Why haven't you asked your law enforcement buddies about the bugs?"

"I did. There are no law enforcement wiretaps in Romero's home."

Her heart skipped a beat. "If I answer your questions, are you going to hurt me with the information?"

"No, no, I promise. Nothing you say to me will come back on you."

She thought it over for a moment and decided to answer.

"Romero's bedroom clock was slow. He told me Peeps—that's his driver—was gonna get it fixed. Later, Romero left to do something, and I was by myself in the house. I thought the clock had a dead battery. It would've been silly for me not to fix it, right? When I took the back off the clock, that's when I saw it."

"How'd you know what it was?"

"I went to a spyware store before I saw Romero. I wanted to record my conversation with him, in case he confessed to something. I decided against it. Good thing because Peeps searched me. I'd probably be dead if I was wearing anything. Anyhow, as soon as I saw it in the clock, I knew what it was. Then I looked around the house and found all kinds of bugs. I thought police put them there. I freaked and took off."

"Did you tell Romero?"

Lucy shook her head. "No, no. Like I said, I thought it was police. I didn't want to get into trouble. You know, I listened to you about that. I didn't tell Romero anything about anything. So, if it wasn't police, who was it?"

"I believe it was Roach."

"Roach? Why?" Lucy could feel her intestines twisting themselves into a knot.

"I don't have all the answers yet. When you told me about the bugs in Romero's house, I called a colleague in LA District Attorney's Office. Her name is Jill Sanders. Jill said no law enforcement agency had a wire-tap on Romero, including the feds. She also said Marcela had called her and asked for her help in getting Romero out of Roach. Two days later Marcela was killed.

"So I started thinking, 'What if Roach was worried about Romero and put in its own surveillance?' They would've heard Marcela's conversation with Jill. We know Marcela was pressuring Romero to get out of the gang. Roach would've heard that, too. Maybe Roach green-lighted Marcela and made it look like a revenge killing. All to keep Romero from betraying Roach."

Rick stood and paced back and forth in front of her. His voice resounded, and his hands gestured. He was making a closing argument—as if she were a one-woman jury.

"So why would Alvarado do it, I asked myself," he said. "The word on Alvarado is he's no family man. He knew about Romero's relationship with his wife and never objected. Alvarado's relationship with his mother is another story. He's a caring and devoted son.

"Momma Alvarado used to live in an impoverished neighborhood on Baltimore's west side. Now she lives in The Fairview in Queen Anne's County. It's a beautiful community for seniors, right on the Chesapeake Bay."

Lucy understood where he was heading. "How much does this place cost?"

He handed Lucy the brochure. "Get this—the cost of admission is $100,000. Residents also pay a monthly fee. $3,500 for assisted living, which is where she's been for the last four months."

Lucy gripped the brochure so tightly it crinkled into a paper ball. What Rick said was too horrible, too despicable, too loathsome. She threw the crumpled-up brochure across the living room.

"How can you stomach being around such evil? You can do and be anything—why do you choose to be around evil? Why?"

Rick took both her hands with his. "Because I want to stop it. I want to protect the good people from the evil ones. Will you help me?"

"How?"

"Get me in touch with Romero."

"What will happen if I do?"

"I'll tell him what I told you. I'll ask him to help me destroy Roach. He'll probably refuse, but I have to try. Do you know how to reach him?"

She closed her eyes tightly and nodded. "When I was in California, he knew something was wrong, but I wouldn't tell him. He said if I wanted his help, I should write about the weather on my blog. He's not going to call. We parted on bad terms."

"How bad?"

"Bad enough that I don't want him back in my life."

"Will you give it a try? Just a blog entry, that's all I'm asking."

Lucy sighed and opened her laptop. "Is there anything in particular you want me to say?"

"Type this—'Weather is stormy. Windy enough to rock the cradle.'"

She posted the words. "What does it mean?"

"I'm warning Romero he's in danger. 'Rocking the cradle' is an old mobster expression for making someone feel relaxed before you kill him."

Her hand flew up to her mouth to stifle her gasp. "You think Roach is going to kill him?"

Before he could answer, her phone rang.

"Tell him to get away from his house and call you back on a prepaid phone," Rick said.

She followed the instructions. Romero disconnected.

Twenty minutes passed. Lucy jumped when her phone rang.

"Don't hang up," she said. "I'm handing the phone to Rick McCormick."

She could hear only one side of the conversation. Rick was holding back, telling Romero only that he was in danger of betrayal from inside the gang. She studied his facial expressions hoping to glean Romero's reactions. Ninety seconds into the conversation, she no longer had to guess. A stream of angry words, in Spanish, blasted from Rick's phone. He was sputtering, unable to say more than two words in a row.

Lucy snatched the phone. "Romie, it's me."

Romero said nothing.

"I have something on my mind I have to say. It doesn't have anything to do with what Rick said. It's personal. After my mother died, I pretty much lost my mind. I did a lot of crazy stuff. I think I've found my mind again. Not all of it, but enough to know I need to make amends. I'm sorry I told Peeps I was pregnant."

"Jesus Christ!" Rick said. He jumped off the love seat and began talking to himself. "I don't believe this," he said again and again.

"What's going on?" Romero said.

"Rick's upset. I didn't tell him much about my trip to California. Will you forgive me?"

"How could you believe I killed your mother? If you want my forgiveness, you explain that to me."

The only way to explain it was to blame Rick. That would ruin everything.

"You don't have to say anything," Romero said. "I know exactly what happened. You knew right away it wasn't me. You told McCormick, but he didn't believe you. He was so sure, so convincing. After a while, you quit listening to yourself and listened to him. You got all twisted around. You stopped believing what you knew was true."

What Romero said was precisely right. How'd he know?

"He's twisting you around now," Romero said. "Trying to twist me. Don't you know that?"

"I'll tell you what I know," she said. "I know you're under surveillance because I saw the bugs. Saw them with my own eyes. All this time I thought it was police. That's why I didn't tell you. I wasn't worried about you because if Peeps searched me, he'd search your house, too. Right? I figured he'd find them right away. So I'll ask you—does Peeps search your house for surveillance?"

He didn't answer.

"Check the house yourself. Look in the bedroom clock, the mattress, the sofa, your computer mouse—that's where I saw them. If police put them in, Peeps would've found them and told you. If you find bugs, then you'll know Roach put them there. You'll also know Peeps isn't your friend."

Ten seconds elapsed before he spoke. "I hope you know Rick isn't your friend. From the beginning, he's tried to keep you away from me. Now it suits him to put me back in your life. Think about that."

He disconnected.

Lucy tossed the phone on the love seat. She curled her feet under herself and stared into the distance with her arms crossed in front of her.

"Great strategy," Rick said. "Good thinking about getting him to check—"

"Don't talk anymore. Don't say a thing."

They passed the next hour in silence. She didn't look at Rick once.

Lucy's phone rang. It was Romero. He was breathless, choking on his words.

"Do you trust McCormick?" he said.

"Enough to listen to what he has to say. Talk to him. In person, not on the phone. Then decide what to do. If you want to meet with Rick, tell me. I'll arrange it. It'll be in a safe place. I'll protect you both. Neither one of you will know where you're meeting until the last minute."

"You want me to do this, don't you?"

"I want you to live. That's what I want."

"Arrange a meeting."

"Get yourself to Pittsburgh. Call me when you're there."

An hour after Rick left, she blogged, "Hooray! Only six months to go until I get my driver's license. So many places to go and things to see! I wish I had it now."

Chapter 51

January 15

At noon, Lucy exited the Baltimore beltway onto Interstate 70 and headed west to Deep Creek Lake, aptly nicknamed "Maryland's Best Kept Secret." Few people knew about the four-season resort, despite the diligent publicity efforts. This secrecy suited her fine; she liked the quiet remoteness of the community. Even the three-hour drive from Baltimore was pleasant.

In the beginning of her drive, the interstate was thick with traffic from the cities; Baltimore, then Frederick, then Hagerstown. Once past Hagerstown, the traffic lightened, and she could admire the farmlands and rolling hills as they slowly transformed into ever-higher mountains.

I-70 split, and Lucy bore left onto Interstate 68. In the distant west, she could see a giant gash in the Allegheny Mountains, known as "Sideling Hill," where the interstate sliced through the mountain range. Her car shifted into a lower gear as it climbed the east side of Sideling Hill. When she reached the crest, she pulled into the rest area and purchased a small coffee from the bank of vending machines.

She sat in her car, sipping her coffee, and glowed in the beauty of the infinite vista. The sun was brilliant, the visibility clear, and the traffic sparse. She envisioned herself biking down Sideling Hill. It'd be easy. She could coast down the west side of the mountain, on the shoulder, for over two miles before the interstate flattened out. She didn't know the grade, but it was steep enough to need a runaway truck ramp. No worries if her brakes burned up; she could bail onto the sandy truck ramp. Getting back to her car wouldn't be a problem. At the bottom of Sideling Hill, there was an exit leading to a gas station. She could hire a tow truck to drive her back to the rest area. All and all, a doable plan. This might be her last chance before Pops showed up.

Lucy removed the bike from the car rack and checked its tires and brakes. Satisfied everything was in working order, she slipped on her protective gear—pads, helmet, sunglasses, and mouth guard. She walked her bike to her start point and scanned the road before her. No hazards in sight. Perfect. Familiar tingles sparked her spine.

She launched with a shout, "Woo-hoo!"

The wind was bitter cold against her face. Tears streamed down her cheeks; not from the cold, but from the freedom. Lucy glanced at her speedometer. Twelve miles per hour. The speed limit was sixty-five. She pedaled and picked up speed. Now she was traveling at thirty. It felt good, safe. She pedaled harder. Forty-five miles per hour. It was the fastest she'd ever traveled on a bike. Elation. Delight. Heaven.

Flashing lights. A Maryland State Police vehicle was pacing her. No sirens. The bike's front wheels shook. The shakes convinced her to slow down. After coasting a mile, she eased to a stop. The police vehicle parked behind her with its lights flashing.

She removed her helmet and mouth guard. As the trooper walked toward her, she sized him up; young, serious, and as clean cut as freshly mowed grass.

"I'm Trooper James Bittinger, Maryland State Police. Do you know why I stopped you?"

"No, sir." She knew why, but she wasn't going to admit anything.

"Please remove your sunglasses," he said.

He looked at her pupils. Experience told her he was assessing her level of sobriety. He made no comment about her mismatched eyes.

"Hand me your driver's license."

She reached into a pants pocket and pulled out her license. She'd received it yesterday, by express mail, from Romero. It claimed to be effective as of January eighth. Trooper Bittinger studied the license. Lucy prayed it would pass for the real thing.

"You've only had your license for a week?"

"Yes, sir."

The trooper asked her to walk heel to toe. She complied easily. Count backward from eighty-eight. She made no errors. Lift your right foot six inches in front of you and keep it there, looking only at your raised foot. She executed the task perfectly. Watch my pen. She watched the pen as it moved back and forth in front of her eyes.

"Where's your car?" he said.

"At the rest stop on Sideling Hill."

"I'll drive you to your car." He opened the door. "Get in."

"Can you take my bike, too? Otherwise, I'll have to stop and get it. That could be a dangerous situation."

He sighed.

The trooper attached the bike to the rack on the front of his vehicle. He looped around the interstate and parked next to her car in the Sideling Hill rest stop.

He unhooked the bike. "Put your bike away. Then get into your car and wait for me. I'm getting something from the machines. Want anything?"

She shook her head. A few minutes later, Bittinger returned to his car with a cup of coffee. He flipped through a thick book, typed on his computer, and called on his radio. Would the trooper discover her fake driver's license? She was nearly apoplectic.

He emerged from his vehicle and stood beside her driver's window. "I don't know what to do about you." He handed Lucy her driver's license. "Give you a ticket or take you in for a psych evaluation."

Lucy exhaled. Romero was good. Somehow, her fake license was in the MVA database.

Bittinger took off his sunglasses and focused his eyes on her. They were cobalt blue. For some reason, she was pleased. Until that moment, she hadn't realized how tired she was of brown-eyed men.

"How about letting me go?"

"Not an option."

"A warning? I have a perfect driving record."

"For all of a week? Now that's something to be proud of. No, I'm going to ticket you." He handed her a citation for riding a bike on a controlled access highway.

She signed the citation. "Maybe you can give me on-the-spot probation before judgment." Some of her posse had gone to traffic court and gotten a PBJ. No conviction, no points.

Bittinger's flat, patient voice disappeared. He spoke softly, but the words stung like she'd biked into a hornet's nest.

"Miss Prestipino, maybe you think this little antic you pulled is funny, some story to tell your friends. Thirteen motorists called 9-1-1. Our emergency communications staff could've been prevented from handling calls that were more important. The drivers who reported you were distracted. They could've had accidents.

"This highway is a major route west for truckers—eighteen-wheelers hauling big loads—lumber, turbines, even houses. Seeing someone biking on the interstate is startling. Any one of them could've hit their brakes, jackknifed, or lost their load. People could've been killed. *You* could've been killed. Did you think about any of that before you got on your bike?"

"No." She felt like crying in shame.

"What were you thinking?"

"I was thinking about all the times I've been over this hill in a car. About how much fun it'd be to pedal down it. Imagine! Two miles downhill. No stops, no pedestrians, no manhole covers, no doors that could fly open. Just a straight shot. Today the sun is bright, illuminating every hazard. I thought I could fly. I jumped on my bike and flew so fast I listened for my own sonic boom. I thought I might be able to touch heaven and maybe someone there. A person never knows when a day like this might come around again. That's what I was thinking."

He studied her for a while before he spoke. "I want your word you won't do this again."

"You have it, I promise. I'm sorry."

"You can go now."

Lucy drove off, wishing her car had another gear called *slink.*

Ninety minutes later, Lucy exited the interstate and took the winding back roads to Deep Creek Lake. Her final stop was the house she'd rented for the weekend, using her shimmering credit card. The lakefront house was a three-bedroom chalet secluded in the woods on the southern side of the lake. Every home on the lake had a name; this house was called "Hearts Afire."

The lakeside of the house had a large deck, about forty feet from the ground. Lucy looked over the deck's railing and saw the lake peeking through the thick woods surrounding the house. The leafless treetops hovered over the deck. Come summer, the tree leaves would cover the deck like a canopy. As soon as she spotted the hot tub, she dashed inside and put on her bathing suit.

She slid into steaming water, closed her eyes and leaned against the hot tub wall. The warm water relaxed her. Before long, her feet rose to the surface. She floated on her back with her limbs outstretched. Her worries slipped away. The mountain air was frigid on her face. Her breath drifted above her. She closed her eyes and nearly fell asleep. Bits of stinging on her face interrupted her semi-conscious state. It was snowing.

She longed for her mother. They were supposed to go to Deep Creek together. Now her mother was gone. Murdered. Lucy's thoughts drifted to Pops.

The idea of killing the man appealed to her in a way she didn't understand. It would be justice, for sure. In her mind's eye, she could see herself pointing her gun at him. He'd be asking for forgiveness, begging for mercy. She'd pretend he was persuading her. Rock the cradle. Sing him a lullaby, like her mother did when she was a little girl. She would smile at him. Sweetly.

Pop! Pop! The first shots would be in the leg. He'd scream and fall to the ground, helpless, pleading. She'd drop a concrete block on his chest. Listen to his ribs and clavicle snap. Kick him in the eardrum until blood oozed down his skull and puddled beneath his head. Knife time. She'd slice his wrist and forehead, giving him the same scars he'd given her mother. Concrete block again; this time on his face. And if that didn't kill him, she'd empty the rounds into his body, blowing him apart into a million pieces. He'd end up like Humpty Dumpty. No one could put him together again.

By the time she finished her daydream, her jaws were aching from her gritted teeth. "I've got to stop thinking like this," she said to the bubbles in the hot tub. "It can't be good for me."

She sat up. It was time to get cracking on her to-do list. The frigid air hit her shoulders. Brrrr. She resisted the urge to duck her face into the water, knowing it'd be unbearably cold when her warm, wet face hit the air again. Next time she was hot-tubbing with a snorkel.

After unpacking her bags, she drove ten miles to the city of Oakland, the seat of Garrett County. She stopped at Walmart to buy groceries, two men's bathing suits, and a snorkel. The snorkel eluded her.

A voice across the aisle said, "Can I help you find something, Miss Prestipino?"

It belonged to Trooper Bittinger.

"Am I under surveillance or something?"

"I live here."

"Let me guess. You live in Bittinger." Bittinger was a small town, northeast of the lake.

"Correct. You're quite the detective, aren't you?"

"I can't detect where the snorkels are."

"Snorkels? The lake's mostly frozen."

"Don't be silly! It's for snorkeling in the hot tub."

He smiled. His teeth were crooked, just like hers.

Near the entrance of Walmart was a family hair salon. Lucy decided to get her first professional haircut and use her new credit card. Soon she was sitting in a black swivel chair wearing a plastic cape. The stylist's name was Grace. Her hair was auburn, highlighted with pink and blonde streaks. The short, spikey haircut emphasized her hazel eyes and freckles.

"Doing something special tonight?" Grace said.

"I'm seeing an ex-boyfriend and a non-starter boyfriend. I want to look good."

"Both at the same time?"

"Yes."

"Where's this happening?"

"Black Bear."

"I'll make you look fabulous."

Chapter 52

January 15

Rick walked into the Black Bear Tavern and Restaurant at eight thirty in the evening. Lucy had said nine, but he arrived early, wanting to scope out the surroundings before meeting Romero. When he entered through the main door, he found two more doors: the right door led to the *Tavern*; the left to the *Nite Club*. He peered through the nightclub door and saw a dance floor and a couple of bars. A flyer advertised that live music from *Advection Fog* would begin at ten. There were several young men on the stage setting up instruments.

Lucy's instructions were to meet inside the tavern. He took the *Tavern* door and found himself inside a sports bar. Wooden stools with red, vinyl seats surrounded a horseshoe-shaped bar in the center of the tavern. Wood-veneered tables were scattered around the bar, each decorated with a metal basket holding food condiments. Large, flat-screen TVs hung on the walls between neon-lighted beer advertisements. Rick heard a background mix of country and rock music from what he guessed was satellite radio.

Four customers sat at the bar. They were dressed in variations of a theme: flannel shirt, jeans, and a hat that was either red or camouflage. The hair was long, and the race was white. Rick felt conspicuously out of place—a Latino wearing dress pants and a long-sleeved white shirt.

He found a table in the back, away from the bar. The bartender, wearing long hair, jeans, and flannel, approached Rick and handed him a menu.

"If you're hungry, I recommend the Crabby Black Bear burger."

Rick replied he was expecting someone; he'd order later.

A clean-shaven, muscular man in his twenties entered the restaurant. He wasn't wearing the style of the day, but corduroys and a sweater. The patrons at the bar sang out a chorus of "Hey, Jimmy!" Jimmy slid onto a stool and drank the bottle of Pepsi the bartender set in front of him. He gave Rick a friendly nod.

It was quarter to nine when the tavern door opened again. Romero.

"*Hola.*" Romero joined him at the table.

They spoke in Spanish, exchanging polite greetings. Rick was nervous. He sensed the anxiety radiating from Romero. After the greetings, they said nothing. Rick followed Romero's gaze to Jimmy.

"Is he one of yours?" Romero said.

"No."

Romero's eyes narrowed. "I'm not stupid. He's a cop." He stood.

"Sit down! He doesn't have anything to do with me. If he's a cop, it's a coincidence."

"This is a set up!"

"Shut up and sit down, for Christ's sakes."

Romero's eyes widened. Rick turned to see what had caught his attention. There was Lucy, standing in the doorway, smiling at Romero. Something about her was different; Rick couldn't put his finger on it. She looked good, that's for sure.

Lucy waved to them, prompting Romero to sit down. She glided past the bar toward the table, but Jimmy interrupted her path by speaking to her. Lucy knew the cop.

"He's one of Lucy's," Romero said.

She sat at the table.

"You look gorgeous," Romero said. "A vision."

Rick thought so too, but he'd missed the opportunity to say it first. Saying it now would sound silly.

Lucy flushed at the compliment. "Thanks."

She leaned over to them and whispered, "What's wrong with you two? You're wigging out the locals. This is a resort. Smile. You look like a couple of terrorists plotting to blow up the Deep Creek Dam. Talk and smile. That's an order."

Romero nodded toward Jimmy. "Lucy, do you know him?"

"Unfortunately, I do," she said with a shamefaced smile. "He's a state trooper. He gave me a ticket on my way up here."

Romero shot her an irritated scowl. "You got a ticket? After all my trouble? Let me see it."

Her smile disappeared. "No. None of your business."

"Under the circumstances, I'd say it was my business."

"What circum—oh, I get it. You think this is some sort of trap. All right, you can see it. I don't want to hear about it, not a single word." She turned to Rick. "You either."

Lucy handed Romero the ticket.

"Riding a bike on a controlled access highway?"

She snatched the ticket from his hand. "Look, I figured you two would be hungry and tired when you got here. Tomorrow's going to be a hard day. I thought it'd be good if we met here and had a nice dinner. If you'd rather spend the time in a sour funk, go right ahead. Not me."

She walked over to the game tables. Rick could hear her racking up pool balls.

What trouble had Lucy caused Romero? Rick found it oddly satisfying to know Romero wasn't immune from Lucy's ability to irritate.

"Tell me about the ticket," Rick said.

"She was biking on I-68, going down something called 'Sideling Hill.'"

"Sideling Hill? Jesus! It's a major trucking route. Steep. At least a six percent grade. It's got a runaway truck ramp."

A few minutes later, Lucy came back, followed by Jimmy.

"Jimmy wanted to meet you. These are my friends, Rick McCormick and Romero Sanchez. This is Trooper James Bittinger."

Jimmy pulled up a chair. "Welcome to Deep Creek."

"I have a question," Romero said. "Why didn't you lock her up?"

"I would have," Rick said.

"These are your friends?" Jimmy said to Lucy.

"We run hot and cold." She turned to Jimmy. "I'm going to contest the ticket."

"Good luck with that," Rick said to Jimmy. "She beat me in court."

"You're a lawyer?" Jimmy said.

"Rick's an Assistant State's Attorney with Baltimore City," she said.

Rick didn't want to mislead a cop. "Former ASA."

"What do you mean *former*?" she said.

"Office policy disagreement," Rick said.

"Did you have something to do with that?" she said to Romero, her eyes flashing.

No answer.

Lucy threw down her napkin and left the table.

"Is she a lawyer, too?" Jimmy said.

Rick rolled his eyes. "Ha! She doesn't even have a high school diplo—"

"That's not what I asked you," Jimmy said.

Jimmy and Romero glared at Rick. He struggled to recover. "I mean, it's ironic she beat me—"

"What brings you to Deep Creek?" Jimmy's friendly tone was gone.

"We're discussing an important matter, trying to hammer out an agreement," Romero said. "Lucy suggested we come to this peaceful place."

"What does Lucy have to do with this?"

"She knows us both," Rick said. "It was her idea we meet. She's a… facilitator."

"This is a nice town, with nice people," Jimmy said. "There won't be any trouble, understand?"

Rick clenched his jaw. Jimmy thought he was a thug. That was true about Romero but not him; he didn't want to be lumped together with a low-life gangster.

"This is a beautiful place," Romero said, smiling widely. "I can see why you're so protective of it. Don't worry about us. We may disagree with each other, but we won't cause any trouble." The charm oozed out of him.

"I'm glad we understand each other." Jimmy left the table.

"You disrespected her," Romero said. "You're a little shit, you know that?"

The tavern door opened, and a company of young women trooped in. Rick watched each woman as she scanned Romero. He witnessed the alluring smiles, flirtatious eyes, and the swaying hips. The display of naïve seduction made Rick sick. Any one of them would have sex with Romero, if he wanted it. While Rick was ruminating, he missed the opening notes of Steppenwolf's "Born to Be Wild" when they sounded from the speakers.

Romero leaped to his feet and darted between customers toward the pool table. When he found Lucy, he pulled her into his arms. Rick watched

Lucy and Romero dance slowly to the energetic song, her head buried in his shoulder. He stroked the back of her head tenderly and brushed his lips against her hair. She wiped her cheeks with her fingertips.

Rick ordered tequila.

When the song ended, Lucy pulled away from Romero. He handed her a handkerchief. She smiled, dabbed her eyes, and kissed him on the cheek. Lucy headed off in the direction of the women's restroom.

"Nice save," Rick said when Romero returned to the table. Rick slid a shot of tequila toward him. They clanked their glasses together and swallowed their shots.

Rick headed to the bar. The bartender looked up from the beer mug he was filling from a tap. "What would you like?"

"Can you get a Latino station on your radio?"

"I can, but I'm not putting it on. That's not what my customers want to hear."

Rick pulled some bills from his wallet. "I'll give you fifty bucks if you play Latino music for fifteen minutes."

"You got it."

As Latino music poured from the speakers, customers exchanged befuddled looks. Rick snagged Lucy as she headed toward the table.

"My turn to dance with you."

She winced. "I don't want to."

"Why not?"

"I'm a bad dancer. I don't want to embarrass myself."

"If you can bike, you can dance. Come on, live a little."

Lucy shrugged and followed him to a space between two tables.

"I'm going to teach you how to salsa. We'll stand side-by-side so I can show you the steps."

She looked around the room at the other customers, her face grimacing and flushing pink.

"Don't look at them," he said. "Look at me. Okay, stand with your feet together."

He put his left foot forward, rocked back on his right, moved his left foot back to the starting point, paused, and repeated the steps, this time starting with a backward step on his right foot.

"It's an eight-count, but counts four and eight are pauses. Let's try it together."

She stood beside him and repeated the steps with ease.

"You're doing great, Lucy!" Rick heard the surprise in his own voice. Why in the world did she think she was a bad dancer?

"Now we'll try it as partners," he said.

They stood facing each other, her right hand in his. They danced the eight-count without misstep. He caught the glimmerings of a smile on her face.

"Let's try this," he said.

He showed her the basic S-turn. Soon they were able to execute the turn into a cross-body lead 180. The crowd was now watching. Each dance step was more intricate than the one before. Patrons smiled with approval as Rick twirled her using complicated footwork. One song blended into another. Lucy kept up with him, laughing with pleasure. When the set was over, Rick bent forward and kissed Lucy's hand. The crowd broke into appreciative applause.

"That was so much fun!" she said, fanning herself. "I need some water. I'll catch up with you in a sec."

Romero had a shot of tequila waiting for Rick at the table. "Do you have any idea how many times I tried to get Lucy to dance? She never would."

One of the women who'd flirted with Romero came to the table. She barely acknowledged Romero when she asked Rick to dance. Rick mentally thanked his mother. During those dark high school days of bad skin, Catherine insisted he take dance lessons. "Girls won't notice your skin if you know how to dance," she said. His mother was right. If he could snag a single dance, the girls lined up for his company. He never went home from a dance floor alone.

The music returned to country rock. "No thanks," Rick said to the woman. "Not my genre. Maybe another time."

Lucy bounded back to the table carrying three glasses of water. "Hey, I'm ready for another dance."

Her exuberant demeanor vanished. Lucy said nothing as she stared at the empty shot glasses on the table. Her incredulous expression told Rick what she was thinking. *What the hell are you doing? We're here to eat, you dumbass. I turn my back for a minute, and you're drinking shots with Romero. Do you want to be hung over when you tell him that Roach murdered his wife?*

Rick felt the color rise to his face. Romero must've been receiving his own telepathic scolding—he wasn't looking at Lucy, but past her, toward the door.

"I'm bushed," Romero said, tossing money on the table. "Let's go."

Without a word, the trio put on their coats and walked in a line around the tables toward the exit. Jimmy was at the door, waiting for them. He handed Lucy a business card. "I don't know what's going on here, but if you run into trouble, call me."

Chapter 53

January 16

Rick smelled coffee coming from somewhere. He found himself lying on a bed, tangled up in two blankets. His head pounded, and his jaws ached. He'd had another restless night. He tracked the scent of coffee until he reached the kitchen. Coffee mugs, orange juice, and blueberry muffins were on the table along with plates and napkins. Anxiety toyed with his stomach. No food for a while. He'd take a chance on the coffee.

The sliding glass door opened. Lucy poked her head inside.

"Get your coat and come outside. The sun's about to come up."

He complied and sat with her on the deck.

"Thanks for last night," she said, smiling. "I've always wanted to learn how to dance, but never had the nerve."

The coffee hadn't kicked in. All he could manage was a tired, "You're welcome."

"Here it comes!" she said.

At that moment, the sun emerged over a distant mountain. It was a blazing fireball hurling ribbons of pink and orange across the gray-blue sky. Lucy's skin glowed rosy, and her hair glinted gold. She was the most beautiful woman he'd ever seen. When Rick saw the breath steam from his mouth, he wondered if Lucy had taken his breath away.

"Are you all right?" she said.

"Yeah…just a little slow this morning."

They sat quietly for ten minutes.

Lucy spoke first. "What's gonna happen to Romero?"

"Depends on him. If he decides to come in, he'll meet with prosecutors and investigators. They'll make him Queen for a Day. He'll tell them everything he knows with the understanding that whatever he says during the proffer session won't be used against him. A written agreement will be negotiated—probably along the lines that Romero will testify in exchange for witness protection and minimum jail time. How good a deal he gets depends on what he knows."

"If he decides to come in," Lucy said.

"If."

Romero opened the sliding glass door. He was showered and shaven, every hair in place. He smiled at Lucy, apparently feeling better than Rick.

"Lucy, you look as fresh as dew on a daffodil," Romero said.

Her skin glowed rosier. Soon the trio was watching the sun ascend. A herd of deer traipsed through the woods near the lake's edge. Otherwise, the woods were still.

"Lucy, I want to talk to Rick privately."

Without a word, Lucy slipped into the kitchen. Rick could see her through the sliding glass door peeling carrots.

"All right, Rick. Tell me why I'm here."

Rick spent the next twenty minutes outlining his investigation, starting with Lucy's discovery of the surveillance equipment inside Romero's house. Rapid puffs of steam came from Romero's mouth. His forehead glistened with sweat.

"Roach green-lighted Marcela," Rick said when he finished.

"You're a liar! A fuckin' liar!" Romero hurled his coffee cup at Rick, barely missing his head. The cup bounced off the railing onto the deck. Coffee sprayed the deck, immediately forming into frosty droplets.

Lucy rushed through the sliding glass door.

"Fuckin' lies! All of it!" Romero paced around the deck, overturning chairs in his path. "That Fairview admission? It means shit. She's got family. She could've inherited the money, won the lottery."

"Romie," Lucy said, in a voice as comforting as a warm latte. "Sit down."

He sat in an Adirondack chair.

"I want you to look at this." She handed him a large manila envelope. She stood behind the chair and gently ran her fingertips through his hair while he scanned the envelope's contents.

"What am I looking at?"

"These are Mrs. Alvarado's admission records. She went to The Fairview the day before Luiz turned himself in." She continued to stroke Romero's hair.

"How did you get—" Rick said.

"I subpoenaed them in our MPIA case."

"What? Our case has nothing to do with—"

"Shush!"

Rick shushed.

"Did you ever ask Roach to help you find Luiz?" she said to Romero. "You spent months looking for him. Roach's connections could've found him in days."

"Leadership refused...fuckin' around with a soldier's wife...they'd warned me. We're not wasting resources hunting down a soldier because you couldn't keep your dick out of his wife's pussy. That's what they said."

"They allowed a soldier to slaughter your wife without punishment?" Lucy said. "Does that make sense? What would you've done?"

Romero was eerily quiet. He sat motionless and watched the deer forage for bits of greenery. The frozen lake glittered under the rising sun.

"This setting reminds me of your eyes," he said.

Lucy continued to stroke his hair, her eyes now brimming with tears. "You know what Rick told you is true. You've known it since you found those bugs. Now you have to decide."

"What should I do?"

"You can't go back—they'll kill you. There are only two choices. You can disappear and hope Roach or the law never finds you. Or you can make a deal."

"They're not going to let me walk. I've done too much. No matter what protection they promise me, once I'm in prison, I'm a dead man."

Lucy was still behind him, caressing his hair. "Right now, you're not on some street, making an on-the-spot, life-and-death decision. You're in a safe place. You can think...play things out. Why don't you see what they offer? Then decide. Rick told me your deal depends on how much you know. Do you know much?"

"They could bring the mother of all RICO actions with what I know."
She leaned down and kissed his cheek. "Come inside, Romie. It's cold out here."

———

Lucy wanted to do two things before she went home; drive along the lake's seventy-mile shoreline and visit the Mountain Lake Renewal Center. She wanted to say good-bye to both, not knowing what the future held.

Now was as good a time as any to say her good-byes. Romero had asked her to leave the house. "I have things I need to discuss with Rick, ugly things," he said. "I don't want you to hear them." She left reluctantly, remembering the coffee cup Romero had thrown at Rick.

The lake was as beautiful as ever. Most of it was frozen, but pools of water peeked though a few unfrozen spots. The water was an iridescent blue and reflected the bright cumulous clouds drifting across the sky.

Lucy drove past a road she'd never seen before, Stepping Stone Drive. She thought of Steppie. Did he miss her? Probably not. Dr. Michaels's office was kenneling him. Steppie'd barked and spun as soon as he pranced into the veterinarian's reception area.

When she completed her tour of the lake, she drove to the Mountain Lake Renewal Center. Cars filled the parking lot. It was visitation day. Once a month, families could visit their loved ones—the substance-addicted children who resided at the center for treatment. Debbie had visited her on each and every visitation day.

She walked toward the office of Mary Donnelly, the center's director, feeling odd and unsteady. This visit was supposed to be a happy reunion. Instead, memories of struggles and hurt flooded her.

"Lucy?"

It was Dr. Donnelly, who hadn't changed at all in six years. The director was smartly dressed and perfectly coiffed, despite her seventy years. Lucy liked Dr. Donnelly. She was a fair disciplinarian who tolerated no nonsense from the patients.

Lucy gave her a big smile. "I was in Deep Creek for the weekend. I thought I'd stop by to say 'hello,' but I forgot it was a visitation day. I know you're awfully busy."

"Never too busy for you, dear." Dr. Donnelly gave her a hearty hug. "You're looking splendid."

"Thanks, and you haven't changed a bit."

"Let's walk and talk. I'd like to show you our new addition. Tell me about yourself."

Lucy told her about her house and her courier business, omitting the facts that her house was in foreclosure, and her business was gone.

"How's your mother? I so admire her."

Lucy expected the question. She'd prepared herself to tell the truth; now she couldn't. Dr. Donnelly would whisk her into the office and counsel her. Lucy would weep, shriek, and rip out her own hair. It was visitation day; histrionics wouldn't do. Other patients and families needed the director.

"Mom's fine."

After a few minutes, Lucy said, "Dr. Donnelly, you…this place…saved me. I've been clean for six years. I wanted you to know…and to thank you."

Dr. Donnelly hugged her a second time. "This job can get very discouraging. When one of our success stories returns to visit, it keeps me going for a long time."

They said their good-byes, and Lucy walked through the lobby toward the exit.

"Lucy!" a male voice called.

Across the lobby was a large L-shaped sofa crammed with people. In front of the sofa was a coffee table. Two visitors sat on the table. Two more people shared a freestanding chair. Four people stood.

She spotted Jimmy Bittinger, waving. He sat in the middle of the sofa, apparently wedged in. He struggled to free himself. Once he was standing, he tried to get around the table. His path was blocked. The two people sitting on the table scooted over, making a space between them. Jimmy jumped over the table.

"Lucy!" he said when he made his way to her. "What're you doing here?"

"Are you sure I'm not under surveillance?"

He laughed. "Come meet my family."

They walked together to the crowd. He greeted his mother first. "Mom, this is the girl I was telling you about. Lucy Prestipino. Lucy, this is my mother, Ruth Bittinger."

Before Lucy could say *How do you do,* Jimmy said, "Hey, everyone, I want you to meet someone."

The crowd stood.

"This is Lucy. Lucy, this is my father, James Bittinger…my brothers and sisters—Luke, Zachary, Matthew, Henry, Iris, and Grace. This is Marsha—she's married to Luke. And this is Susan, married to Matthew. This is my grandmother, Beth Ann Bittinger."

Each took turns shaking Lucy's hand. Every blood relative had a shade of red hair, ranging from Jimmy's blondish-red to Grace's auburn. She recognized Grace as the stylist who'd cut her hair.

"Did you tell Jimmy I was going to Black Bear?" Lucy said. "I wondered why he was there."

"I hope you don't mind. I thought Jimmy would like you."

The family sat, making space for Lucy to sit between Jimmy and his mother, Ruth.

"Are you applying for a job here?" Jimmy said, "I heard Mountain Lake is looking to hire people."

Two lies, in the same place on the same day, was one too many.

"No. I was a patient here. I came to say 'hi' to Dr. Donnelly."

The Bittinger family exchanged glances and became quiet.

After a few seconds, Ruth said, "How long ago were you here?"

"Six years ago. I came when I was fifteen."

She picked up Lucy's hand and rubbed it against her cheek. Lucy's hand became wet from Ruth's tears.

"God sends us angels when we need them," Ruth said.

"I don't understand, Mrs. Bittinger."

"We have another son, Nathaniel. He's our youngest boy, sixteen. He's here for the second time. Had a relapse a month ago. He's having a difficult time. We're so worried about him." A tiny tear streamed down Ruth's right cheek. "Here, out of nowhere, you walk in at the exact right moment. You're beautiful and healthy—showing us it's possible to beat the drugs, giving us hope. That's what makes you an angel."

Jimmy's father placed a loving hand on Ruth's shoulder.

"I've done a lot of things I'm ashamed of," Lucy said. "I'm not an angel."

"Today, at this moment, you're an angel to me."

Chapter 54

January 16

Rick was impressed with Lucy's foresight. Before she left the house, she placed two bathing suits on the kitchen table. She must've known Romero would suspect wires. She was agreeable about leaving the house when asked, only wanting twenty minutes to finish making a sweet potato casserole. When Romero joked she was making a last meal for the condemned, she shamed him into shutting up.

"Don't be a jerk. Look, I've always wanted to make a full-blown turkey dinner, but my mother took charge of Thanksgiving. This turkey dinner is for me, not you." She put the turkey in the oven with instructions: "Start basting when the timer goes off."

Lucy left the house, taking Romero's charm with her. He turned morose and sour.

"How do I know this place isn't wired?"

"You don't. Nothing's stopping you from leaving...other than the prospect of getting taken out by your own gang."

Rick held up the bathing suits and nodded toward the hot tub. "Lucy left these."

As Romero eased himself into the steaming water, Rick saw the tattoos covering Romero's torso, arms and legs. Gothic letters spelling R O A C H were inked across his chest, intertwined with lifelike images of roaches feasting on squirming vipers. Swarms of roaches crawled down his forearms. More of the same mutilated his legs. It was grotesque. Romero was muscular and fit, but his body was deformed under the weight of disturbing images. How could a woman bear to be touched by a man who looked like that? How could Lucy?

Romero grinned at Rick's reaction to the tattoos.

"I gave you a name," Romero said, the grin vanishing. "What's the status of the murder investigation?"

"How would I know? The police haven't told me anything and they won't. You made sure of that."

Romero slid across the hot tub seat until his back was in front of a jet. "It wasn't my idea. Roach wanted you gone."

"Why?"

"You were too good, McCormick. Once you got a little more experience, you'd be unstoppable. You would've cost Roach too much money, in terms of defense counsel expenses and lost opportunities for future growth. Your middle school initiatives were already working. Putting crime scene photo pop-ups on Roach web sites was a stroke of genius. Our supply of corner boys and hoppers in West Baltimore was shrinking. You got green-lighted."

Rick's stomach muscles knotted, squeezing the breath from his lungs. He sank under the water to hide his fear until he could collect himself. A few seconds later, he surfaced and shook the water from his head.

"So why aren't I dead?"

Romero lounged against the hot tub, his long arms stretched across the rim. "I persuaded Roach leadership that killing a prosecutor was old-school gang shit. Too visible, too much public outrage. I didn't think it was in Roach's interest to kill you. So I checked you out, watched you in court. You're ambitious, but your real weakness is macho pride. I convinced the leadership we could get you out of the way by forcing you to fail. I knew you'd never cave no matter how overwhelmed you got. Your boss is ambitious. Mercer needs her stats to get reelected. She'd never back you up if it would fuck up her reelection. A perfect storm. You'd get fired. Simple. No killing, no press, no investigations." Romero smiled. "Consider it a compliment."

Rick shivered. The air was colder. The sky changed from sunny to milky white.

"Is this the same shit you pulled on that prosecutor in LA?" Rick said.

"Yeah…In your case, it turned out to be unnecessary." Romero faced him wearing a malevolent grin. "You would've flamed out on your own. I was fooled by your performance in court. Charming, commanding, amiable. Outside the courtroom…well, let's just say you're not a people person. Lucy's a perfect example. All she wants is respect, but you never figured that out. Your career wouldn't have gotten far even if we'd left you alone."

Anger surged inside of Rick. He was trying to save Romero's life and was getting thanked with a game of mind-fuck. Well, he wasn't going to play.

"What've you decided?" Rick said.

"I've taken Lucy's words under advisement. I'll decide after I've heard the deal that's offered."

"You said you know everything. What do you know?"

"I'm not giving you any sneak previews without a lawyer."

"If you want me to smooth the path for you, give me something to tell people. How do you know what you know?"

Romero scooped up some foam that had accumulated on the water and tossed it from the hot tub.

"Roach isn't some crap operation, disorganized cells wreaking havoc for small change. It's run like a closed corporation. We have a board of directors and officers. We sell franchises—all those sects and cells police chase after are franchisees. We supply them with products to sell, and they pay us hefty franchise fees. We have vice presidents in charge of any vice you can imagine."

"What's your position with Roach?"

He scooped out another handful of foam.

"President. I run the day-to-day operations."

The hair rose on Rick's neck. His heart hammered so loudly he was sure Romero could hear it, maybe even see it pounding through his chest. He was sitting in a hot tub, half-naked and unarmed, with the man who ran the most ruthless gang in the country. Was Jill Sanders right? This could be a set up. Would Lucy come back to find him hacked to pieces?

"I have no interest in harming you," Romero said. "You're a fuckin' asshole, but you mean something to Lucy."

"What does she mean to you?"

"I've never put a name to it…respite, I suppose. When I'm with her, I don't think about Roach. I can pretend I have a normal life."

Romero slid deeper into the hot tub. The water covered his shoulders. "It took a lot of effort to see her. Roach security is never far behind me. Whenever I came to Baltimore, I'd give them the slip. It set off a brouhaha. Eventually leadership came around. They saw Lucy was good for me. They acquiesced to having only Peeps protect me when I came to Baltimore. What an idiot I am! He didn't protect me—he spied on me. Leadership must've known about Lucy's mother. They kept it from me."

Rick said nothing.

"I'll be killed if I go to prison."

"The U.S. Marshals Service has never lost a cooperating witness under its protection. Depending on what you know, you could be out of prison in time to start a new life. Get remarried, have children."

"That means nothing to me." Romero turned his upper body and spit on the deck. "I had a vasectomy when I was seventeen."

Rick was flabbergasted, both by the information and the fact that Romero told him.

"Seventeen? You were a kid."

"Old enough to know any baby of mine would be born with a death warrant. Those were Peeps's exact words."

Rick stayed silent. Romero wanted to talk.

"Been to LA?" Romero said.

"Several times. Not a favorite place."

"Don't blame you. It gets hot in LA, scorching hot. You open your front door and get hit in the face with a furnace blast. There are street signs everywhere—don't leave pets in cars. It was one of those oven-hot days. At least a hundred degrees, probably more. The sun so bright it hurt your eyes to go outside. I was washing my car when I got the call to come to the corner of Strathmore and Cedar."

Romero shivered. He reached for the hot tub controls and turned up the water's temperature.

"The Vipers' local shot caller was Hernandez Santos. He got into a beef with Roach, and they were looking for him. I don't even remember what it was about. Maybe I never knew. I was just a soldier then, and no one explained things to soldiers. You followed orders.

"When I got to the corner, Carolyn Santos was standing there, outside her car, surrounded by Roach. She was holding a baby—a pretty, little girl. The baby was all dressed up, like Carolyn was going around the neighborhood showing her off. You know how women do. The baby was wearing one of those tiny pink hairbands around her head. She looked real cute. Dark hair, chubby, happy thing. Lots of curls. I guessed she was three months old.

"My lieutenant introduced me, 'This is Santos's wife and baby,' he said. 'Find out where he is, any way you can.' I knew it was a test. If I refused, I'd be punished. I could handle that, but I knew Roach would stop protecting Marcela."

The water's temperature climbed to one-hundred-three degrees. Romero shivered and cranked up the heat.

"Carolyn wasn't a beautiful woman, but nice-looking enough. Strong. I could see it in the way her jaw was set. When I asked her where her husband was, she stared at me with defiant eyes. Lucy's eyes. I know you've seen them—fierce, determined.

"I knew Carolyn would eventually give it up. I'd have to beat the shit out of her. Break her jaw, knock out her teeth, blind her. I couldn't do it. She was a good woman. Her baby began to fuss. I had an idea—an easier way. I could get the information without hurting Carolyn. I took the baby from her arms and put her in the car seat. I shut the car door. I told Carolyn the baby wouldn't come out until she told me where her husband was. Every mother protects her child, right? I thought she'd give it up right away. I wouldn't have to hurt her. It'd be done, simple."

Romero ducked under the water, now one-hundred-five degrees. Rick was lighted-headed and nauseated. He lowered the temperature. A minute passed. Romero remained under the water. What was he doing? Rick was about to yank him up when Romero surfaced, breathless and red-eyed. He stared at the filter bobbing on the water for another minute before he spoke.

"It wasn't simple. Five minutes passed. The baby was sweating, crying. Ten minutes. Carolyn screamed, begged for me to let the baby out, but she wouldn't give up her husband. My lieutenant was standing there, waiting to see me cave. I couldn't, I couldn't risk Marcela. It went on and on. The baby was suffering, I couldn't stand it. I prayed to God that Carolyn would break. It was a choice—the baby or Marcela. God, help me, I prayed. The baby started vomiting and choking. Carolyn fell to her knees and begged me, promised to blow me for the rest of my life, anytime, anywhere. Finally, she broke and told me where to find her husband. Peeps laughed afterward. He said, 'Any baby of yours is going to be born with a death warrant.' I knew it was true.

"Roach killed Santos an hour later. Carolyn later jumped off the Golden Gate Bridge holding her baby. It began my ascendancy in Roach. I was known as a creative problem solver. Rivals called me a ruthless sociopath."

Romero looked upward. It was snowing. There was a half-inch of snow on the deck.

In the next moment, Rick heard gagging. Romero leaped out of the hot tub and ran to the deck's railing. He leaned over and vomited until nothing but clear liquid dribbled out.

"Oh God! Oh God!" he cried as he wretched up nothing. He banged his head on the deck railing, twice, with sickening thuds. Romero stood up straight and gazed out toward the lake, motionless, calm, as if he'd just made a momentous decision. An alarming intuition swept over Rick; Romero wanted to kill himself. He was about to jump from the deck. Rick bolted for Romero and grabbed his right forearm to pull him away from the railing.

Romero's fist was in his face before he saw it. Pain exploded in his left cheek. Blood spilled down his cheek and onto the deck. He was lying on the deck, on his side, stunned, but aware enough to see Romero charging toward him. He couldn't get traction in the snow to get on his feet. He turned on his back and watched Romero advance. Muscles. Weight. Strength. Romero had the advantage in every way. Rick reached for something, anything to defend himself. He found the coffee cup Romero had thrown at him.

Romero loomed over him, poised to strike. "Motherfucker."

Rick swung the coffee cup in a perfect arc until it collided squarely into Romero's jaw. Romero staggered backward, losing his footing on the slippery deck. He twisted and turned, arms waving, trying to regain his balance. The deck shook when he landed, hitting the hot tub on the way down.

Rick was on his feet. Fists in a knotted ball. He now had the advantage. One solid punch was all he needed. He'd aim for the teeth. Didn't care if it cut up his knuckles. He'd get rid of that shit-eating grin. He rushed toward Romero, who was sprawled on the deck, grabbing at the hot tub, slip-sliding, trying to get to his feet. Rick primed to release his punch.

No. He would not strike a suicidal man.

"Stop it! I don't want to fight with you."

Romero stopped struggling. He slumped to his hands and knees, rolled onto his back, and lay in the snow. He looked as wet, cold, bruised, and bloody as Rick. Rick staggered to the Adirondack chair, holding on to the deck's railing to keep from falling on the slick deck. He grabbed the towel hanging on the back of the chair and made his way back to Romero.

"Sit up," Rick said.

Romero complied. Rick wrapped the towel around him. He helped Romero to his feet and led him inside the house. Rick poured two cups of coffee. They sat at the kitchen table, shivering and spent. The oven timer went off.

"What're we supposed to do?" Rick said.

"I'll take care of it." Romero basted the turkey and returned to the table.

"Why'd you hit me?" Rick said. "I'm trying to help you."

"Like hell you are. You're trying to help yourself. That punch was payback for blindsiding me with the crime scene photos of Lucy's mother. Payback for showing Lucy pictures of my butchered wife. Payback for making Lucy believe I could've murdered her mother. You're a low-life rat bastard."

"I believed you killed Lucy's mother, I surely did. I was wrong. I'm sorry about that, but not the rest of it."

"At the railing...you knew what I was thinking. Why'd you stop me?"

"It's not in me to stand by and watch a man kill himself, no matter how much I detest him. What about Lucy? I don't understand why, but she cares for you. If you're still thinking along those lines...don't, just don't. She's had enough losses in her life. She'd find a way to blame herself. She's been a good friend to you. Don't put that on her."

Romero was quiet.

"What did you mean when you said the choice was between the baby and Marcela?"

Anguish swept across Romero's face.

"I'm going to clean up," was his answer.

Chapter 55

January 16

Rick's abrasions stung under the shower's stream. The fight lasted only a few seconds; he was cut and bruised from head to toe. He was grateful for the snow—the slick deck had leveled the fighting field. Otherwise, he'd have been no match for Romero.

As he dried himself, he heard someone walking around the kitchen, shutting cabinets, rummaging for pots and pans. Lucy was back. He was glad. Romero listened to her; she'd close the deal.

Rick entered the kitchen as nonchalantly as he could. Lucy was making corn pudding.

"Smells great," he said.

She glanced up from the pudding and smiled. Momentarily.

"Oh, my God! What happened to you?"

He faked an embarrassed grin. "Slipped on the deck. It was the snow. Turned the deck into a skating rink. You should've seen us trying to get from the tub to the door. Total slapstick."

He could see from her face she knew he was lying. She yanked open the sliding glass door. Trampled snow covered the deck from one end to the other.

"Where's Romie?"

"Right here," Romero said. He walked through the kitchen to the sliding glass door. "Be careful out there. It's slippery."

She saw the gashes on Romero's forehead and an angry cut along his jawline.

"You were fighting! I should've listened to myself. I knew something like this would—"

"Knock it off!" Romero said so forcefully Rick jumped. "It's not your fault."

"You're not responsible for everything that goes wrong," Rick said. "So quit thinking like that."

Lucy stared at them. "Wow. It looks like you've reached common ground on something."

Her attention turned toward the hallway. Rick followed Lucy's gaze to Romero's suitcase.

"You're leaving?" Rick said.

"Yes."

"Why?" Lucy said. "You're not even going to try to make a deal?"

"It has nothing to do with a deal." Romero stood in front of her and held her shoulders with his hands. "I'm not as brave as you. Simple as that. If you see truth on the other side of a plate of glass, you'll dive through it, face first. You don't care about the pain, the blood. You don't care about the scars. You face it down, no matter what the truth brings. I'm not like that."

"What're you going to do?" she said.

"Disappear. Vanish."

"Will I ever see you again?"

"No."

Lucy sat at the kitchen table, looking crestfallen.

"Rick," she said. "I want you to leave the house. Just for a little while."

"Why?"

She paused a beat. "I want to say good-bye to Romero."

Rick threw up his hands. "You want to fuck him? Is that want you want?"

Romero's eyes lit up.

"I want to say good-bye. How I do so is none of your business."

"Jesus Christ! How naïve can you be? He's a monster! He told me—"

"McCormick!" Romero said. "Whatever I told you is privileged. Attorney-client privilege."

"Bullshit! I'm not your lawyer."

"You led me to believe you were."

"You know I didn't. You—"

"If you violate the privilege, I'll file a complaint with the bar association. You'll be finished as a lawyer."

"What's going on?" Lucy said.

"I won't be part of your machinations," Rick said to Romero. "Lucy, get your coat. We're leaving."

"No," she said.

Romero opened the front door. He made a grand, sweeping gesture for Rick to get out.

"I've done everything I can to keep you from harm," Rick said to her. "If you don't come with me now, I'm done...finished with you. Make up your mind."

"I'm staying."

Rick snatched his coat, wishing he'd taken that one last punch to Romero's shit-eating grin. Romero was still holding the door. Rick paused as he passed in front of him.

"Wherever you go, you'd better take Lucy with you. She's as good as dead as soon as Roach realizes you're gone."

Romero slammed the door behind Rick.

⸺

Lucy saw the hot-sex light vanish from Romero's eyes. What did Rick say to him?

"What is it?"

Romero didn't answer, apparently preoccupied.

She stood on her tiptoes in front of Romero and kissed the gashes on his forehead, the cut on his chin, the hollow in his throat. She grazed his mouth with hers and lingered on his lips. Her tongue slid across his teeth. He tried to circle his arms around her, but she pushed him away, allowing her space to unbutton his shirt. She took a half step backward when she saw the bruises on his torso. Romero covered her mouth with his to catch the gasp escaping from her lips.

"Come to bed," she said when Romero released her mouth.

Lucy led him to the upstairs bedroom. She removed her clothes and pulled down the sheets. She held out a soft brush.

"Will you brush my hair?"

He sat on the edge of the bed, next to her, brushing her hair, stroking it. He nuzzled the back of her neck and caressed her breasts. She lay on top of him and kissed every bruise, every tattoo. He told her he loved her, he missed her. When he said he was sorry, a sob slipped from his mouth.

"Shhhh…" she said.

Lucy made love to him with all her might. Romero climaxed and slept soundly, with her head on his shoulder and her legs intertwined with his. She stroked Romero's chest while she prayed to Marcela Sanchez. "Help me, Marcela. Help me save your husband's life."

Fifteen minutes passed.

Romero cried out, "No! No!" He bolted upright in the bed, still asleep, sweat pouring down his face. He was panting between sobs.

"Wake up, Romie!" Lucy shook him gently. "You're having a bad dream."

"What should I do, *mi amada*?" he choked out.

She looked into Romero's eyes.

"Are you asking me or Marcela?"

He looked away.

"I'll answer for both of us," she whispered. "Our advice would be the same. Kill Roach. Kill them all. Your whole life has led you to this time and this place. You can get rid of Roach. Only you can do it. You're the only one smart enough, strong enough, brave enough. Save others from the tears you have cried. I love you, *mi amada*. Never forget that."

"How can you love me? I'm a monster."

"Maybe you were, but not now."

He leaned back on the bed and stared at the ceiling, saying nothing. She waited.

"I can't do this unless I know you'll be safe," he said.

"Tell me what you want."

"As part of any deal, I'm going to demand protection for you. Promise me you'll cooperate."

"Protection? I don't need protection. I can take care of myself."

"Listen to me, *mi amada*! You can't take care of yourself against Roach. No one can. Roach knows who you are and where to find you. They'll snatch you up, torture you until I agree to stop talking. They'll release what's left of you and welcome me back with open arms. Then one day, after they've made me feel comfortable and secure, they'll kill me. And they'll kill you."

"What does protection mean, exactly?"

"Your name will be changed, and you'll be relocated. You'll have to start a new life."

She wept. "You're asking too much."

"If you don't promise me, I'll disappear. I'll go somewhere where there aren't any newspapers, television, or computers. I don't want to learn about your murder. Will you promise?"

"Only if you promise me something."

"What is it?"

"You'll fix this thing with Rick's job. And don't say you didn't have anything to do with it. I know you did."

"I don't know how to fix it."

"Someone's going to ask you why you're doing this. Tell them it was because of Rick. That's all you have to say, and it'll turn out right. Promise?"

"I promise."

"I want to pick my new name and where I live. They'll agree if you tell them it's a deal killer if they don't."

"What do you want your new name to be?"

Lucy thought a while. "I've always liked the name 'Happy'—you know, like Happy Rockefeller. Maybe if I say it enough times, it'll seep into my soul and I'll be happy, right? My last name—well, I love my AA sponsor. I used to pretend he was married to my mother, that we were family. His last name is Holiday—that's the name I want."

"You want your name to be 'Happy Holiday'?"

"Yes."

Romero smiled and cupped her face in his hands. "It's time for you to leave. I can't do this with you here. There are too many horrific things I'll have to talk about it." He kissed her.

She caressed the gash on his jaw. "Rick'll be back. He left without his suitcase. I'm not leaving you two alone together."

"Call Jimmy Bittinger. Ask him to stay until the feds come."

"I'll have to tell him what's happening."

"Tell him what you need to."

She called Jimmy. He needed only a short explanation. "Funny," Lucy said after she disconnected. "He didn't seem surprised at all."

Chapter 56

January 16

Rick pommeled the steering wheel with his fists when he realized he'd left the house without his suitcase. He had to go back, but when? Not now, for sure. He didn't want to interrupt them *in flagrante delicto*. What a pair. He was happy to be rid of them both. They were going to end up dead. He was beyond caring.

As he drove down Garrett Highway, there was a sign on the left— *Trader's Coffee House*. He parked and entered, bells chiming as he opened the door. The shop had the feel of Café No Delay. Coffee-colored walls accented with dark orange. Tables and chairs. A fireplace. Leather sofa. A good place to pass the time until it was safe to return to the house. He paid for a newspaper and a coffee and took a seat in a comfortable, oversized lounge chair.

A tall, lanky blonde brought him the coffee. "Let me know if you need anything else."

He didn't. All he wanted was to ruminate about Lucy. Romero had sucked up to her. Called her *beautiful* and *brave*. She ate it up. What a fool! The thought of Lucy fucking that animal made him want to vomit.

Rick was furious with himself. Romero had suckered him. While they were in the hot tub, it seemed odd Romero was revealing so much information. Now he realized why—Romero didn't want him to tell Lucy about the baby. It was too horrible. She'd ditch him if she knew. Romero probably figured Rick already knew about it. Now he was muzzled by the attorney-client privilege. He could argue the privilege didn't exist, but the circumstances were ambiguous. Romero made sure of that. Should he tell Lucy and risk his license to practice law?

He swam in his pot of stew for the next two hours. Lucy needed to know. Fuck his law license. He'd get a new career if he had to. He punched in her number on his phone. The call went to voice mail.

Rick drove to Hearts Afire, wishing he'd brought a gun.

As soon as Rick turned into the driveway, he spotted the state police vehicle. He tore from his car into the house. The kitchen and living room were empty. No one on the deck. No sounds other than a distant television.

"Lucy!" he shouted.

Bittinger appeared in the hallway outside the television room. "She's fine."

"Where is she?"

"She left. Romero sent her home."

"Where's Romero?"

"Watching television."

"Why are you here?" Rick said.

"Romero's decided to turn state's evidence. Lucy didn't think you and Romero should be alone together. From the looks of you, she was right. The state police will be keeping Romero company until the U. S. Marshals arrive."

It took him a moment to absorb the information. He opened the door to the television room and saw Romero, lounging on the sofa, watching *Xena: Warrior Princess.* Romero gazed at him but said nothing.

"Why'd you change your mind?" Rick said.

Romero shrugged a non-answer.

"I'm not your lawyer. I'm not going to represent you in this."

"I already have a lawyer. Minerva Wilson James."

"Minerva? How do you know her?"

"By reputation only. She's an excellent attorney. It seems she owes Lucy a favor. For what, I don't know. Minerva's coming tomorrow morning."

Rick had a thousand questions, but none came to mind. He stood speechless, staring at Romero, Bittinger, and *Xena: Warrior Princess.*

The trooper touched him on the arm. "Follow me."

They went into the kitchen.

"I understand Lucy helped you arrange this meeting so you could talk to Romero," Bittinger said. "You've done that. Is there any reason for you to stay?"

Rick wanted to see how it turned out. No—the real reason was to make sure he got credit for bringing Romero in. That'd be the only way he could salvage his career.

Bittinger spoke while Rick pondered. "I don't see how your presence at this point does anything but complicate matters. You've done a good thing here. Don't screw it up by staying too long."

"All right, I'll leave."

"Anything I need to know?"

"Romero's volatile. He's charming one minute, violent the next. He may be suicidal. For a moment, I thought he was going to jump off the deck. When I tried to pull him away from the railing, he coldcocked me. We fought. I thought he might kill me. All I can say is, 'Watch yourself.'"

"Thanks for the warning. Eat something, get your things. Then leave."

Rick took one bite from the sweet potato casserole and put down his fork. He didn't want to eat; he wanted to get the hell out of there. Once out the door, he'd never look back.

He began packing his suitcase. His bedroom shared a wall with the television room. Xena was speaking, and Romero and Bittinger were talking over her. Their conversation was easy, smooth. Rick couldn't figure out who was charming whom. He listened as he packed. The topic was *Xena: Warrior Princess.*

"This is Lucy's favorite show," Romero said. "She was raised on it."

"If you ever tell anyone this, I'll deny it. I used to watch it with my kid sister. My parents thought I was a terrific big brother for spending time with my sister. Truth is—it gave me an excuse to watch Xena. You have family?"

"Used to."

Rick closed his suitcase and continued listening.

"Romero, I hope you don't mind my asking…but I don't get it. You're a good-looking man. Smart. Charming. The ladies like you. You have everything. How'd you get mixed up with Roach?"

Rick sat on his bed and waited for Romero's answer. It came a full minute later.

"I had everything except parents with legal immigration status. They lived in El Salvador during the civil war. They paid a fortune to coyotes to get them out. They ended up in LA and started a new life. I was born in LA, so I was a US citizen. Marcela, too. Her parents were undocumented. We grew up living next door to one another. When I was thirteen and she was eleven, our parents were deported. We stayed behind. Our parents said, 'No matter how hard it will be, it will still be better than growing up in El Salvador.'

"Marcela went to a foster family. I went into a group home. I lasted two months and took off. I found Marcela. She ran away with me. We lived together, on the streets, making our way. I was big, even as a thirteen-year-old. I passed myself off as sixteen and got jobs. I was able to support us and even send money to our parents. We've lived off the grid. No one bothered us; we didn't bother anyone.

"Overnight, it seems, everything went to shit. Marcela hit puberty. She grew up, filled out, became beautiful. She got noticed by a Viper shot caller. When she ignored him, he turned up the heat. 'Take care of me, Marcela,' he said, 'and I'll take care of Romero. LA can be a dangerous place.' I was afraid for her. I couldn't fight the Vipers by myself. I was still hurting over the fact the government shipped my parents back to El Salvador. Didn't trust anyone. I didn't know where to get help. I joined Roach in exchange for Marcela's protection. That fuckin' Viper shot caller disappeared.

"At first Roach was subtle. Sent us to school. Made sure we had food, a place to stay. We became part of a family again. Thanksgiving, Christmas—something right out of a Norman Rockwell painting. God, how we'd missed being in a family. Didn't know how much until we had one again. Before long, I was protecting my new family. I became a criminal and for what? Roach murdered my wife."

Rick heard Romero sob, followed by Jimmy's voice.

"You're doing a courageous thing here. I'll pray it works out for you."

"I'm beyond prayers."

"I don't believe that."

Rick heard the theme music for Xena. Another episode was starting.

"Xena, the vicious warlord, redeeming herself through good works and friendships," Romeo said. "Do you believe in it?"

"Do I believe in redemption? Yes, I do."

"Since I've known Lucy, she's been seeking redemption. I never understood what for."

"That's between Lucy and God."

"You're a man of faith?" Romero said.

"I try to be."

"You'd be good for Lucy. When this is over, you should look her up. She'd make a wonderful wife."

"I mean no disrespect, but I'm not taking dating advice from a gang member. I don't even take dating advice from my own mother."

Romero laughed out loud.

Rick knocked on the door. "I'm taking off now." He crossed the room and extended his hand. "Good luck, Romero."

Romero ignored him.

———

It was after dark when Lucy arrived in Baltimore. The Canton neighborhood was tucked in for the night. She cruised the streets surrounding her house, scanning for rental cars or those with New York license plates. There were none. The hunt for a parking space was brief; there was a spot directly in front of her house.

She ripped down the hand-written sign she'd posted on her front door, "Gone down the ocean." Once inside, she gathered the mail from the foyer floor and settled into her only living room chair. It was seven.

Tomorrow she'd pick up Steppie. She imagined patting him, rubbing his chest, and scratching the top of his head. His absence made the house quiet and creepy. Lucy didn't spook easily, but she was moved to holster her gun.

Lucy's stomach growled. She thought about her turkey dinner. After making the abundant meal, she'd left without knowing how it tasted. What a bite. Actually, what a non-bite. Her refrigerator was nearly empty, but she'd been able to scrape a meal together with less. Cheese, eggs, leftover vegetables. An omelet.

There was a polite rap on the door.

She looked through the peephole. Joseph. He was dressed up, looking rather dapper. She opened the door.

"Are you in trouble?"

It was the same question Joseph had asked her when he'd rescued her from Poe's.

"I hope not," he said. "I'll find out soon enough."

"What're you doing here?"

"You invited me." He handed her one of the posters. "I'm your father."

C h a p t e r 5 7

January 16

L ucy stared at Joseph, silent and dumbfounded. This had to be a joke. The man was too old to be her father.

"Aren't you going to invite me in?"

She opened the door wider. When he stepped into the foyer, the over-head light shined on his taffy-colored hair. The streaks of yellow hair matched the yellow of hers. She had his lean physique. His eyes told her this was no joke. Crystal blue—like her left eye.

Arithmetic swirled inside her head. Joseph had to be at least fifty. That would make him thirteen years older than her mother. Debbie was fifteen when Lucy was born, putting him in his late twenties. There was no denying the math. Her father was a woman abuser and a murderer. Now she could add child molester to his resume.

The poster wouldn't stop shaking in her hands.

"You should sit down," he said.

She sat at the kitchen table, half-dazed. Joseph joined her.

"Why didn't you say anything?" she said, tears in her voice. "At Poe's. All those AA meetings. You never said a thing."

"I've been searching for you for so long. Years, actually. When I first spotted you across the street from Poe's, I praised God—I'd finally found you! I was crushed when I saw your eyes. My baby girl had two blue eyes.

• 300

I was thrown off by your brown eye. It wasn't until your mother…died, I found out it was really you."

"What about after she died?" she said. "You knew then who I was, but you still didn't say anything. I was falling apart. I needed you. You said nothing."

"I tried to! So many times I lost count. At the meetings, you avoided me. And that damned sponsor of yours kept getting in the way. Do you remember the last thing you said to me? 'Fuck you!' What was I supposed to do?"

She hit the table with her hands. "You were supposed to tell me straight out who you were—not hang around me like some sort of pervert."

"Pervert!" He recoiled in disgust. "How was I supposed to tell you *straight out*? Your mother's death. An awful thing. You were going through such a bad time. I couldn't pop into your life and announce I was your father. I thought it would go better if you got to know me first. It didn't work out that way, did it? You cussed me out."

"So you gave up on me."

"No. I decided to give it more time. Try again a little later. In the meantime, I wanted to help you. I knew you needed money, so I had my bank send you a credit card. I guaranteed payment. I didn't know what else to do."

Joseph slumped into in his chair and put his hands in his lap. He had a look about him that was both passive and desperate.

A million questions swam in the swamp of Lucy's emotions. Automatically, she began her relaxation exercises. Deep breaths. In. Out. In. Out. She spent a minute breathing deeply.

"I appreciate the credit card. And I'm sorry I cursed at you. That was totally rude. Will you forgive me?"

Joseph nodded, tears forming in his eyes.

"May I call you 'Pops'? That's what I've been calling you in my head all this time."

"Yeah, that's fine."

"You wanted me to get to know you," she said. "Tell me about yourself. Are you married?"

"No."

"Ever been?"

"Twice."

"I'm sorry. It was the alcohol, wasn't it?"

"It was a lot of stuff, alcohol included."

"Do you have other kids?"

"Three. I'm not in touch with them. You're my last hope of having a family."

Lucy reached over and put her hand on his. "I'm here, Pops."

He looked at her with watery eyes.

"What do you do for a living?" she said.

"I paint."

"You're an artist?"

Joseph shook his head. "No, I paint houses. I have my own company. In New York."

"We're both business owners. I guess I got my entrepreneurial spirit from you."

He smiled slightly and sat a bit straighter.

"My messenger business keeps me busy twenty-four-seven. How are you able to take time off to come to Maryland?"

"I have a crew. I do the estimates, they do the painting. Once I have a few jobs going, I can take off until they finish."

"I could learn a lot from you," she said. "Maybe you could teach me."

"I'd like that."

Lucy strategized. Where does one start when lulling a murderer into a confession? With food, of course.

"Would you like something to eat? I was about to fix dinner."

"That would be nice."

As she stood at the counter breaking eggs, she sensed him assessing her. Her hands shook as she grated the cheese, not from fear, but from rage. She considered shortcutting this dance. Open the utensil drawer, pull out the eight-inch chef's knife, plunge it into his throat. He wouldn't see it coming. Trouble was, he'd be dead before she got the answers she needed.

She plated the omelets and put them on the table, along with utensils and napkins.

"Smells wonderful," he said. "You're a good cook, like your mother." He filled his fork and paused. "I'm sorry for your loss. Truly, I am. Has there been any progress in the investigation?"

"The police are clueless."

"No one should have to go through what you're going through." Joseph swallowed his forkful of omelet. "Did your mother speak poorly of me?"

"No. She never mentioned you at all. I didn't know about you until after she died."

"How'd you find out?"

"I was going through her papers and found my birth certificate. It said I was born in New York. All Mom's lies came to light after that."

A concoction of deception, truth, and guesses. Did he believe it?

"What lies?" he said.

"My whole life, she lied. She told me I was born at Mercy Hospital. I thought she meant Mercy Hospital in Baltimore. She mislead me on purpose, I know it. She hid my birth certificate from me. Told me my father was Gary Prestipino. Another lie."

Tears of anger seeped from the corners of Lucy's eyes. If only her mother had told the truth, she'd be alive today. Lucy would've seen to it.

"I'm glad you found me," he said.

"You found me first, didn't you? How?"

"I have a bookkeeper. His name's Walter. He knows someone who works for New York Vital Records. Walter said people lose birth certificates all the time. They want to get a passport or something, can't find their birth certificate, and ask Vital Records for another one. Walter asked his contact to keep a lookout for any request from you or your mother.

"Last fall, my prayers were answered. Your mother wrote asking for a birth certificate with your new name. Your name used to be Josephine. That's how I found out she lived in Baltimore. I still couldn't find you. Your name wasn't on any public record I could find—not even a driver's license."

Lucy was thunderstruck. Everything she owned was in the name of her business; her house, bank accounts, loans. There was never enough income to open a retirement account or file a personal tax return. She had no idea she'd been living under the radar.

"Did you ask Mom where I was?"

He shifted his posture almost imperceptibly. "No."

A lie. He'd telegraphed it.

"How'd you meet her?"

"I saw her at Penn Station. She'd just come off a bus from somewhere—I never knew where. All she had was a backpack. She looked lost so I asked her if she knew where she was going. We started talking, and I bought her some lunch. I felt sorry for her, told her she could stay with me until she got settled. I got her a job. She took care of my apartment and cooked for me. I was working nights. Then she got herself pregnant."

"What kind of job?"

"As a dancer. She liked to dance."

Lucy knew the story. She saw pimps troll the bus stations in Baltimore for vulnerable runaways. Her mother ended up dancing in a tittie bar or worse.

"How come your name isn't on my birth certificate?" She guessed that part, but cast the question to see what it caught.

"I wasn't sure I was the father. When I saw your blue eyes, I knew I was. I meant to add my name to the birth certificate, but when you came home from the hospital, things were chaotic. New baby and all. I didn't mean to disrespect you or your mother. It got away from me."

"Pops—"

"Don't ask me any more questions. This is too painful. I don't want to relive it."

Good, she wanted it to hurt—as much as a needle plunged into his eyeball. She was going to keep needling him with her questions.

"Why'd you leave us?"

"I didn't leave you! She left me."

True.

"Why?"

"I hate to speak ill of the dead, especially your mother. Here's the truth—she was a nitwit of a mother. When you and Sabrina—that was the name she told me when I met her—she lied about that, too—when you came home from the hospital, she didn't know how to take care of you. I had to show her what to do.

"I don't want to hurt you, but she didn't want you. Said she was too young for a baby. I told her to grow up. A week after you were born, she snuck off to an adoption agency. Wanted to give you away, can you believe it? I put the nix on that. No way would my blood be raised by strangers."

Lucy was shocked. "I don't believe you!"

"I have the papers to prove it. Right in my pocket. Want to see them?"

"You bet I do." Lucy thrust out her hand, palm up.

Joseph grabbed some papers from his back pocket and placed them in her hand. It was a document from an adoption agency, entitled "Medical

History and Background Information." The form was partially completed in her mother's handwriting.

"I caught your mother filling this out and set her straight."

"I still don't believe it," Lucy choked out.

"I couldn't believe it either. What mother doesn't want her baby? We worked it out and were happy for about four months. One day, she disappeared. Into the wind she went. Took you with her. She stole a lot of money from me. I looked for her, but gave up after a while."

No body shift, at all. He wasn't lying. She could see the truth in his eyes and hear it in his voice. There was more to the story for sure, but the basics were there.

She'd been gripping the tabletop with her hands while Pops told this truth. When he finished, she put her forehead on her hands and wept.

Chapter 58

January 16

Rick's gas tank was a quarter full as he drove on I-70 past Hagerstown. The weather was a drizzly mess. A quarter tank would probably get him home, but he didn't want to chance it in the nasty weather. He pulled into the next gas station. The wind and rain blew in his face as he pumped gas. His mind drifted to summer. The beach. Ocean City. Seagulls. The smell of french fries. He was playing in the sand, making castles. Colleen was laughing. She poured a bucket of water over his head.

A wave of anxiety ripped him from his daydream. His heart pounded. Sweat dripped down his sides from his armpits. What just happened? *Shake it off! Think!* To clear his head, Rick bought a cup of coffee from the gas station's mini-mart.

Rick's daydream ate at him as he drove onto the interstate. What was it about the daydream that made his heart race? Ocean City. Colleen. Sand castles. Water. Seagulls. Bucket. He turned it over in his mind until he entered the Baltimore beltway. The weather worsened; the rain poured down in buckets.

Buckets, that was it. Then he put it together.

"Why'd you do such a reckless thing?" he asked Lucy when he questioned her about her ticket. She answered, "Always wanted to." The morning after they danced at Black Bear, she thanked him. "I've always wanted to learn how to dance, but never had the nerve." Thanksgiving dinner—her mother always made it. She'd put Romero in his place, "I'm making it for me, not you."

Lucy knew who killed her mother.

She was going to confront him.

She'd been working on a bucket list.

He pressed on the accelerator and headed toward Lucy's house.

———

Lucy had no idea how long she'd been crying when she lifted her head from the table. Joseph was staring at her with the helpless look men get when they see a woman cry. She picked up a napkin, dried her eyes, and blew her nose.

"Why'd you tell me all that?" she said. "It wasn't necessary."

"You needed to know what your mother was."

"You're right, I need to know the truth...all of it."

"I was the only one who really cared about you. You have no idea how much I've worried about you all these years."

Her tears flowed again.

"I'm all alone," she said.

"Not anymore."

"I need you, Pops, but you can't lie to me. Ever. My whole life's been based on lies. Promise you'll tell me the truth. No matter how bad it is."

"I promise. We're a team. We'll stand by each other, help each other."

She nodded through her tears and gave him half a smile. "I love you, Pops."

"I love you, too." Joseph leaned over and kissed her forehead. The overhead light shined directly on his face. The slight yellow tint of his skin seemed brighter. Addicts, alcoholics, recovering or not, sometimes wore that color. Hepatitis C.

"You don't look so good. Are you sick?"

"I have a bad liver. Been sober for ten years, but I'm paying for my indulgences. That's one of the reasons I wanted to find you. To tell you, so you don't make my mistakes."

"Is there anything I can do?"

"You can be my daughter until I pass. We need to make up for lost time."

Her eyes watered. "You're going to leave me, too?"

"Maybe not. I'm on the transplant list for a liver. If one comes to me in time, I could be saved."

"What about my liver? I guess not, I only have one, right?"

He perked up. "That's right. A person has only one liver. But you can donate a part of yours. It's called a 'living donation.' It'd probably take because we're blood relatives. It'd be safe for you."

"You can have my liver, all you want of it."

"You'd do that for me?"

"You're my father. You just said it—we're a team, we'll help each other."

Now it was Joseph's turn to weep. "You have a good heart."

"Promise me you'll tell me the truth. I have so many questions."

"Of course I will. I already promised you."

Lucy looked at the kitchen clock. "Oh, no!"

She reached for her phone on the kitchen counter. "I'm supposed to go out tonight. He's supposed to come by at ten. I'd rather spend the time talking to you. I'm going to head him off. Excuse me a second."

He gave her an appreciative smile.

Lucy dialed 9-1-1. She spoke before the call taker could say *Police, Fire, or Rescue?*

"Hi, it's Lucy. I'm so sorry, something's come up. I can't go out tonight. Can you come by tomorrow instead? Even later tonight would be better than now. Give me a little more time, okay?...Great...You're a doll."

She silenced her phone and pretended to disconnect. She slid the phone behind the coffee pot on the counter.

"Pops, why did you kill my mother?"

Chapter 59

January 16

"Kill your mother?" Joseph said. "I didn't kill your mother!" "Don't lie to me! I know you did it. I have a DNA report that proves it. If you want any part of my liver, don't lie to me. Ever. Why'd you kill her?"

He bawled. "I didn't mean it…it was an accident—"

"Stop crying! Tell me what happened."

"All I wanted was to talk to you. That's all. I saw Sabrina walking the dog. I said, 'Good morning.' She recognized me right away. Told me to get away from her. I said I only wanted to meet my daughter. She said she'd kill me if I tried. The next thing I knew, she was holding her cell phone. She was about to call the cops.

"I realized your number would be in her phone. If I could get the phone, I wouldn't need her to tell me where you were. I told her to give it to me. She said 'go fuck yourself' and took off running. The dog attacked me. Bit my ankles, wouldn't let go of my pants leg. Determined little fucker."

She studied him as he spoke. His story was too smooth, as if he'd rehearsed it in his mind, trying to justify what he'd done.

"I kicked him off. He kept coming back." Joseph shook his leg to demonstrate. "I shot him in self-defense. I ran after Sabrina. All I wanted was the phone. I caught up with her, and you know what she did? She threw the phone into the lake! I jumped for it, but it flew over my head. I watched it land in the water. It wasn't until I heard the splash that I saw Sabrina on the ground. I must've knocked her over when I went for the phone. I tried to help her, but she was dead."

Joseph was wailing now, punctuating every sentence with loud gulps of air.

"It was her fault. If she just told me where you were, if she just gave me her phone, none of this would've happened. It was an accident, and she caused it. It was her fault."

Police vehicles blocked the streets around Canton. Rick ditched his car on Eastern Avenue and ran. He got within two blocks of Lucy's house when a police officer halted him.

"I'm looking for Detective Sylvia Marlow," Rick said.

The officer recognized Rick and pointed to the SWAT Mobile Command Truck stationed on the corner of the next block. Rick saw Marlow speaking to a man dressed in SWAT gear, minus the helmet. The conversation appeared intense, focused. Another woman stood with them. Rick didn't recognize her.

Marlow spotted Rick and waved him over. She introduced him to Captain Wayne Chandler, Commander of the Special Operations Division, and to NYPD Detective Melanie Gilbert. Gilbert was investigating the killing of Detective Parks.

"Lucy's been taken hostage?" Rick said.

"We haven't yet determined what the situation is," Chandler said. "We're gathering intelligence to make an assessment. I'm told you know her pretty well. I have some questions."

"I'll help any way I can," Rick said.

"About twenty minutes ago, Lucy called the Emergency Communications Center," Sylvia said. "She pretended she had a date, and asked her date to come later. Didn't hang up. Left the phone on, but silenced it. She's having a conversation with her mother's killer. We're listening to it in real time."

"Who—"

"Joseph Kistler, her biological father," Gilbert said. "Detective Campbell and I interrogated Walter Devon AKA Tiptoes. Twenty-some years ago, Kistler and Devon were hoods operating out of the Bronx, specializing in *dispositions*. Local gangsters hired them to get rid of things. Guns, in particular. They eventually went their separate ways, until a couple of years ago.

"That's when Kistler hired Devon to find his daughter. She was born in New York City but disappeared with her mother when she was an infant. Devon bribed a clerk in New York Vital Records to notify him if anyone contacted the agency in connection with Lucy's birth certificate. Eventually, Mrs. Prestipino wrote to Vital Records stating Lucy's name had been changed and asking for a revised birth certificate. She enclosed an eighteen-year-old court order out of Maryland. That's how Kistler found Debbie Prestipino."

"Kistler just confessed to killing her," Marlow said.

"Maryland State Police reported Mrs. Prestipino owned a Sig P232 semi-automatic pistol," Chandler said. "Does Lucy have it now?"

"I don't know," Rick said. "She once mentioned having a gun. I've never seen it."

Gilbert handed Rick one of Lucy's posters. "On approximately January thirteenth, a thousand of these posters appeared throughout New York City. The NYPD wanted to cite the responsible party for littering. They learned a local messenger company distributed them. Further investigation revealed Lucy hired an old messenger friend to post them."

"As of at least three days ago, Lucy knew who killed her mother," Chandler said. "Did you know that?"

"Of course not."

"It appears she lured her mother's killer to her home," Chandler said.

"What exactly are you asking me?"

"Is Lucy capable of premeditated murder?" Chandler said.

"No," Rick said, not sure he was telling the truth.

"But she's capable of breaking her gangster boyfriend's nose," Chandler said.

"That was self-defense."

"And kicking a prosecutor in the shin," Chandler said. "If Lucy would do that to someone who made her mother cry, what will she do to the man who killed her?"

Chandler turned away before Rick could reply.

Rick inched closer to the command truck so he could listen to the 9-1-1 call. What was going on in the kitchen? Was she going to kill her father with her gun? Rick could hear muffled sounds of crying in the background. Who was crying? He watched Chandler signal his team to move into position. They crept in a single-file snake line toward the house.

He leaned against the command truck. His knees could no longer hold him. She'd tried to tell him Romero didn't kill her mother. He didn't listen. Why? Because he was a pig-headed idiot, that was why. Now she was going to get herself killed.

Rick wasn't a religious man, but he began praying.

Chapter 60

January 16

Joseph was heaving sobs.

"I told you to stop crying." Lucy's patience was running thin. "How'd you know she walked the dog in Patterson Park?"

"When I found out where she lived, I followed her for a couple of days. I wanted to talk to her there because it was quiet and peaceful."

"And isolated."

"No, no! That's not why."

"Why'd you bring a gun?"

"It's Baltimore City! I brought it for protection."

"Did you kill a New York cop with that gun?"

Joseph instantly turned off the waterworks. "How'd you know about—"

"Answer the question."

"No!" He shook his head vigorously. "Roach killed him. They hired me to get rid of the gun. It was a nice gun, so I kept it."

"Who in Roach killed him?"

"Lucy—"

She removed his plate and tossed it into the sink. "Get out."

"Tommy Gun. That was his street name. He liked military guns. That's all I know."

"Do you have it with you?"

He nodded.

"Give it to me. Ever since my mother died, I've been afraid of guns."

Joseph removed the gun from his shoulder holster and handed it to her. "Be careful. It's cocked and locked."

She held the weapon between the tips of her right thumb and pointer finger, as if she were carrying a dead rat.

"What kind of gun is this?"

"Colt M1911."

He put his head in his hands and resumed his weeping. She moved to a spot behind him and put her left arm around his neck. "Shhh," she whispered as she hugged. "It's all right, Pops."

It wasn't all right. Rage overwhelmed her, worse than any craving she'd ever experienced. *Kill him! Kill him!* He was a pathetic little shit. No better than the roaches she'd told Romero to exterminate. An abhorrent abuser, child rapist, and murderer. She'd be doing humanity a service if she killed him. Serving a lifetime in prison would be worth it.

She stood and clutched the grip of his gun. A perfect head shot.

Joseph was right. It was a nice gun.

Lucy looked past Pops through her front window. She caught a glimpse of movement outside. What was that? The street was unusually quiet. No cars driving by, no neighbors walking dogs. Something was going on. *Police!* This was her last chance to kill Pops. Now or never.

"Please forgive me," Joseph said. "I know you loved your mother. I loved her, too. More than any other woman I've ever known. I never meant for it to happen. Your mother was an angel."

The violent voice inside Lucy's head gave way to a softer one. It was calm and sweet. "You're an angel," it said to her. "You gave us hope."

Where had she heard that before? The question distracted her from her rage.

Seconds passed before she remembered. She'd heard the words at Mountain Lake Renewal Center earlier today. Mrs. Bittinger spoke them. How would that lovely woman feel if Lucy blew Joseph's head off? Hopeless, that's how. She visualized her own mother, the courageous woman who escaped from her abuser, taking her baby girl with her. She nursed Lucy through the addictions and risked everything to make sure Lucy had a decent life. All that sacrifice would be for nothing if Lucy pulled the trigger.

What about her own dreams? Having a family, being a wife and mother. That'd be impossible if she spent her life in jail.

Joseph was holding his head in his hands. Sniveling. He was a coward of a man. A liar and manipulator. Of course her mother loved her. Why else would she have protected her all these years from this pitiful excuse for a human being? Fuckin' low-life prick. Why should she waste her life for the momentary satisfaction of killing him?

Her mother was talking to her.

Just because you want to, doesn't mean you have to.

Lucy didn't know if the 9-1-1 operator was on the line. She hoped so.

"Pops, I'm disarming the gun," she said for the benefit of the police. "I don't want a loaded gun in my house." She removed the magazine and the round in the chamber. "Okay, that's done. I'm putting your gun on the counter by the toaster."

Lucy poured two glasses of milk and opened a box of chocolate chip cookies. She placed the snack on the table and sat. "Have some dessert. It's good for the soul."

Joseph nibbled on a cookie.

"Why'd you plant the bandana?"

Joseph shifted in his seat. "What bandana?"

"Oh, c'mon! The blue-and-black one. The one with Roach colors."

"I don't know about any bandana."

"You're lying. You've been doing good here, telling the truth. Keep going with it. Or our relationship is over."

He hesitated and let out a breath. "After your mother died, I dropped it."

"To throw off the investigation."

"Yes." Joseph looked bewildered and depleted.

"Why'd you have it in the first place?"

He didn't answer. Lucy knew he'd never admit to planning a murder. She'd gotten all the truth she was going to get.

"I'm tired," she said. "You look exhausted, too. Let's call it a night. Can you come back tomorrow? I'll fix you a big dinner. Steak, potatoes, gravy. And we can talk about getting started on the liver donation. Does that sound good?"

He nodded, his eyes wet.

"No more tears, you hear? Everything'll be all right."

Joseph reached for his gun.

"Do you need to take that?" she said. "I'm afraid I'll never see you again. If you leave your special gun here, at least I'll know you'll come back. Okay?"

She escorted him to the front door and smiled to herself. Her murdering father was about to walk right into handcuffs. Lucy had barely opened the door when Joseph slammed it shut.

"Cops! Outside!" Joseph's cell phone rang. He answered, listened a moment, and smashed the phone against the living room wall.

By then, Lucy was on the other side of the dining room.

"They called on my cell phone!"

He gave Lucy an intense look. "It was you, wasn't it? You told them!"

Why not tell him the truth? At least she'd get some satisfaction from seeing the expression on his face. He couldn't get to his gun. Besides, it wasn't loaded. If he tried to punch her, well...he'd get a lot more than he bargained for.

"No, Pops. It was you. You told them."

"How did I do—"

"The police heard everything. My cell phone's been on."

"You lied to me? The whole time you've been lying to me?"

"Yeah, every single word I said was a lie—especially the part about giving you some of my liver."

Joseph's mouth dropped open. He stood as if paralyzed. After a few seconds, Lucy heard him breathing again.

"Lucy, do you understand what you're saying? I'll die if you don't help me."

She smiled. "Good riddance."

"How can you say that? I'm your father!"

"The thought of you being my father makes me sick."

Joseph placed his hands together into a prayer position.

"Please, I'm begging you...don't let me die. I want to live."

"You should've thought of that before you murdered my mother."

"You're killing me!"

"I hope so."

She could feel the detonation waves of fury heading her way.

"You got only one way out," she said. "Open the door and turn yourself in. Maybe Maryland will give you a liver while you're in jail."

Joseph pitched forward. At first Lucy thought he'd fainted or was having a heart attack. She saw him raise the cuff of his pants. He stood straight, now holding a gun. A revolver. "You lying bitch! Just like your mother."

He pointed the gun at her. She stared in disbelief.

My own father's going to kill me?

She dove for cover behind the dining room table. Gunfire. Zinging bullet. The drywall rained down around her. She pulled out her Sig. Fired back.

Joseph screamed.

The front window shattered. A canister flew through air. Landed on the living room floor. Rolled toward Lucy. What's that? She'd seen something like it at the spy store.

Oh shit! A stun grenade.

Explosion. A blast of searing light. Smoke. Her head felt like it was blowing apart. High-pitched ringing pealed through her brain. Blackness everywhere. Couldn't see. Couldn't hear. Couldn't think. The smoke tasted like chemicals. She was gagging. Which way was up? Got on her hands and knees. Searched for her gun using her fingers. Nowhere. Found the dining room table. Tried to hoist herself up. She fell, smashing her mouth on the table's edge.

Lucy lay on her back and stared at the blackness.

A cloth covered her mouth. Joseph was trying to smother her. She flailed at him, still blinded.

"Police," a voice said. "Stay still. You're hurt."

The fog began to clear. Everything was blurry. She could make out a shape and color. He looked like a giant bear. A black bear, like the one she once saw at Deep Creek. This bear had large, insect eyes and fur as thick as tarpaulin.

The bear took off his helmet and goggles. "You're safe now."

He gently held the cloth to her mouth. She swept the inside of her mouth with her tongue. Her front teeth were gone.

A woman took the bear's place. "I'm Rosalie. I'm a paramedic, and I'm going to take care of you. Understand?"

She was the same paramedic who'd cared for Lucy when she'd crashed her bike on East Lexington Street.

Lucy spit the blood from her mouth. She tried to form the words without her front teeth.

"Remember me?" she garbled out.

"Sure do, hon. We need to stop meeting like this."

———

Rick watched as Joseph Kistler was removed from the house on a stretcher and loaded into an ambulance. Lucy had shot him in the leg. Kistler's injuries were serious but not life-threatening.

A second stretcher followed. This one carried Lucy. Rick ran toward it.

"Lucy!" he shouted. "Lucy!"

He didn't know what he'd say when he reached her. Maybe he'd tell her he loved her. No, that's something he should say at a calmer time—after a fine dinner, flowers. Right now he wouldn't say anything at all. He'd hug her tightly, if she'd let him. He prayed she would.

"Hold it!" said a man dressed in SWAT gear. "Don't come any closer."

SWAT maintained a perimeter around Lucy's stretcher as paramedics wheeled her to the ambulance. Photographers jockeyed around the protective wall of police. All Rick could see was Lucy's right hand, cuffed to the stretcher's rail.

He called his best friend, Assistant Public Defender Alexander Gatestone.

"It's Rick. I'm calling for a favor."

Chapter 61

January 30

The telephone calls began exactly two weeks after Lucy's arrest. The first was from Ronald Bartow, the U.S. Attorney for the Central District of California.

"I'm very pleased to speak with you, Mr. McCormick. I understand you were instrumental in turning Romero Sanchez. My office has a robust gang unit. I could certainly use someone with your talents. I'd like you to come to LA so we can discuss your joining my team."

Rick was speechless. After regaining his composure, he agreed to an interview the following Tuesday. After he disconnected, he stared at his cell phone. Why did Bartow think he had any influence over Romero?

Rick called Jimmy Bittinger.

"I got a call from a U. S. Attorney inviting me to a job interview. He was under the impression that I...and I'll quote him here...'was instrumental in turning Romero Sanchez.' Do you know anything about that?"

"Yes, I do. After you left Deep Creek, Romero asked me to stay with him through the proffer session. There was a slew of law enforcement at the house. My presence wasn't needed. I think he liked having me around. The details of the proffer session are confidential, so I can't tell you much. Suffice it to say Romero credited you with his decision to turn state's evidence."

"Why? The guy hates me."

"I think the 'why' is a 'who.' I'm guessing while you were gone from Hearts Afire, Lucy convinced Romero to go forward with the proffer session. They must've negotiated some kind of an agreement between them, and getting your job back was part of it."

"What did she agree to in exchange?"

Bittinger hesitated before answering, as if he were searching for a way to answer without compromising the confidentiality of the proffer session.

"Romero looked out for Lucy in a way that required her cooperation. You'd approve, I'm certain of it."

Bittinger's hesitation told him pressing for more details would be fruitless.

"There are a couple of things I want to tell you," Bittinger said. "The investigators and attorneys were spellbound during Romero's proffer. He was a great witness. Smart, articulate. He must have a photographic memory. Banks, account numbers, players. You name it, he knows it. At some point, there's going to be an international Roach take-down."

"What's the second thing?"

"Romero loves her, he really does. When you look back on this, try to remember it from that perspective."

"Does Lucy love him?"

"I have no idea. I seem to understand criminals better than women."

"I hear you on that."

Within the next few days, Rick received calls from the U.S. Attorneys for Maryland, Virginia, Illinois, and Florida. He could work anywhere in the country. The more he thought about his choices, the clearer it became he wanted to be with Lucy. Maybe they could decide together which offer to accept. She must want to get out of Baltimore, away from the sorrow and the bad memories.

He called her several times. There was no answer and no return calls. He sent her texts and e-mails. One day she replied by e-mail.

Rick -
I'm sorry I haven't gotten back to you. I need some time to be by myself, to think about things. I've been following your advice—can you believe it? I've been going to grief counseling and to a bereavement group. It's helping, like you said it would.

Thanks for getting Alexander Gatestone to represent me. He's a very kind man and a fine attorney, too. Alex is giving Ms. Snakehead all kinds of grief, but he's polite about it. It's giving her conniptions. I'm learning a lot from him.

I hope you're okay. Alex said things are going good for you. I'm glad.

Lucy

Rick was heartened by Lucy's e-mail. Things were looking up. If she needed space, he'd give it to her. He decided to keep an eye on her from a distance.

Twice a week he checked the court's criminal file to determine the status of Lucy's prosecution. Mercer had shown no restraint; she'd indicted her on attempted first-degree murder. He called Alex occasionally. "She's a trip, man," Alex would say.

Two weeks later, on a Friday afternoon, Alex called him.

"Lucy has an appointment with Judge Susque on Thursday afternoon at two. If there's anything you want to say to her, that'd be a good time. You could wait for her in the hallway outside the judge's chambers and catch her on the way out."

"Thanks, Alex. I'll be there. So what's the deal with the appointment? Pretty unusual for a judge to meet with a criminal defendant."

"It has nothing to do with the criminal case. That's over."

"The criminal case is over? What happened?"

"The charge was dismissed."

The following Monday, Rick got a call from Daniel Rubenstein, U.S. Attorney for the Southern District of New York.

"Can you come to Manhattan on Thursday?" Rubenstein said. "On Friday I'm leaving for a two-week conference. I'd like to talk to you before I go, if I could."

Rick agreed. This was his dream job. He'd meet with Lucy later and do it up right. Surprise her with a limo. Flowers. Dinner at the finest restaurant in Baltimore. He'd tell her how much he loved her, how much he wanted her to be part of his dream. Rick smiled, thinking about it.

Chapter 62

March 1

It was Thursday.

Lucy was nervous while she waited in Judge Susque's chambers. She kept her hands folded in her lap, trying hard to conceal her jitters. She concentrated on her breathing, taking deep, regular breaths. She must've been breathing louder than she realized; the judge's secretary looked up from her computer screen and gave Lucy a warm smile.

The nameplate on the secretary's desk said "Terri Ann Wasilifsky." Her posture was straight, and her bearing was regal. She had a no-nonsense-allowed demeanor, dispatching phone calls with polite efficiency. An enormous African violet sat in a crystal bowl on her desk. The plant was as elegant as its caretaker.

"How'd you get your violet to grow so big?" Lucy said.

"I water it once a week or so. The secret's the florescent light it's sitting under."

Wooder. The judge's secretary was from Highlandtown. The realization filled Lucy with hope. Maybe Ms. Wasilifsky was a hot mess in high school. If she had transformed herself into a swan, Lucy could too.

She pulled an envelope from her purse. "May I put this with your outgoing mail?"

"Of course. I'll see it goes out today."

The secretary's phone buzzed.

"You can go in now."

When Lucy entered the judge's conference room, he shook her hand with both of his. Cassiopeia, the comfort dog, wagged her tail.

"Good afternoon," he said. "Let's sit at the table."

He pulled out a chair for her. "Have you been taking care of yourself?"

Lucy nodded. "I've been going to AA meetings every day. I've started grief counseling. I also meet with Children of Homicide Victims Bereavement Group once a week. It's helping. I know it's gonna to take a while, but I'm getting better, I can feel it."

"Good, Lucy. I have great faith in you. I know you'll accomplish much in your life."

The judge picked up a file on the table.

"I granted the State's motion to open your adoption file. I thought you might want to look at it. It's under seal, but you can review it here in chambers if you'd like."

A raven-haired woman entered the room, holding books Lucy recognized were part of the Maryland Annotated Code.

After the judge introduced them, he explained, "Diana Nicholson is with the Maryland Attorney General's Office. She's an expert in the field of adoption. I thought she could answer any questions you might have as you read the file."

Lucy smiled with gratitude. The judge left the conference room.

"I suggest you start from the back of the file and work forward," Nicholson said. "The paperwork is filed in reverse chronological order."

She flipped to the back of the file and read a document entitled Petition for Adoption and Change of Name. Her stepfather had filed the petition when she was three. It stated that her birth father was Joseph Kistler and gave his address in New York. Gary Prestipino petitioned to adopt Lucy, terminate Kistler's parental rights, and change her name from Josephine Jenkins to Lucy Prestipino. Debbie had joined in the petition and consented to the adoption.

There were numerous exhibits attached to the Petition including health statements, wage verification, and her parents' marriage certificate. The last exhibit was Lucy's birth certificate. She was born at Mercy Hospital in New York City. The slot for the father's name was blank. The mother was Sabrina Jenkins, age fifteen.

The next document was a motion to waive service.

"What's this?" she said.

"Your stepfather asked the court to allow the adoption to go forward without telling your biological father about it. It's an unusual request. The reasons are explained in your mother's affidavit."

Lucy read her mother's hand-written affidavit. Some of the words were smeared and blurry. It started with an oath and a statement of personal knowledge. Debbie wrote:

> When I was fourteen years old, I ran away from home. My mother and father were not good people. I had no family who could take me in. I was afraid if I went to the police, I would end up in a group home. I took a bus to New York City. I wanted to be a dancer. My real name was Debbie Tate. I called myself Sabrina Jenkins when I went to New York. I thought it would be safer.
>
> I met Joseph Kistler at Penn Station as soon as I came off the bus. He was handsome and kind. He told me he was also a runaway. He said he was seventeen. He bought me a meal. When I told him I had no place to go, he invited me to stay at his apartment. I slept there, and the next morning I cleaned his apartment and did his laundry. Joseph liked that and said if I kept his place nice, I could stay there as long as I wanted.
>
> One morning, he made me breakfast and said we were celebrating our one-week anniversary. He made me some mimosas. I didn't know what they were, but they tasted good. I got dizzy. Afterward, he had sex with me even though I was crying, and I didn't want to. He later convinced me having sex was my idea. He said he loved me, and I was pretty.
>
> We began having sex regularly. After a while, he changed. He told me I needed to fix myself up, and I wasn't earning my keep. I tried my best to make him happy. He beat me a couple of times when I didn't do what he said. He got me a job as a stripper. I had to give him my pay for rent. Joseph was an addict and used the money to pay for his drugs. I didn't run away because he took care of me, and I loved him.
>
> I later found out I was pregnant. When I told Joseph, he said the baby wasn't his and told me to have an abortion. I

wouldn't do it. Joseph's friend, Walter, told him not to push me into an abortion because I was underage and could call the police on him. When the baby came, she looked like Joseph, and he was happy. He named her Josephine.

I was too young to care for a baby. I told Joseph I wanted to place Josephine for adoption. He punched me in the face and broke my nose. He also punctured my eardrum. He said he would never let me give his baby away. He said he would kill me if I ever brought it up again. I believed him because he had friends in gangs. I overheard him talk about helping a gang cover up the murder of a policeman.

One day a girl named Jennifer came to the apartment. She had a baby by Joseph. She told me he was twenty-five years old. I found out he had three other children and didn't support any of them. She showed me where he hid his money and then took some so she had money for her baby.

I waited for my chance and stole his money and ran away. I did it to save my baby. I hid from him. I went to Pennsylvania and got help from a women's shelter. I went back to using my real name because I never told Joseph what it was.

I am afraid to tell Joseph about the adoption. I know he will find me. He will take Josephine away even if he has to kill me and my husband to do so.

By the time Lucy finished reading the affidavit, her hands were trembling, and her eyes were streaming tears. No wonder her mother was always afraid.

"I know this is hard to read," Nicholson said.

"Why didn't my mother tell me?"

"I don't know. Maybe she was ashamed. Maybe she was afraid you'd think less of her. There are a lot of maybes. I wish I had answers for you, but I don't. I'm sorry."

Lucy dried her eyes and resumed reading the file. She read the court's order denying the motion to waive service. "Why didn't the court do what my stepfather asked?"

"The judge had to follow the law. An adoption would have terminated your father's parental rights. The U.S. Constitution protects those rights and requires due process before a court can terminate them. The details of due process vary from state to state. Under Maryland law, if an adoption petitioner knows where a parent is, the petitioner has to serve the parent with a show cause order."

"What if the parent has disappeared?"

"Service is made by publishing a notice in a paper. These days, the notice is also posted on a special website. None of that applied here; your mother knew how to find your father, so the law required he be served with a show cause order."

"Why? He raped my mother and abused her. He was a child molester!"

"He had a right to object to the adoption and get a chance to tell his side of things. If he objected, the court would've had a hearing to determine if the adoption was in your best interest. But your father couldn't object if he didn't know."

"Aren't there any exceptions? She was afraid of him."

"The only exception is if the parent consents to the adoption. Some states have additional exceptions. Not Maryland."

Lucy's stomach roiled. She wasn't a lawyer, but something about this service requirement didn't sit right with her.

The last page in the file was an order denying the adoption, but granting the change of name.

"If the judge denied the adoption, how could he change my name?"

"A name change doesn't terminate parental rights, so the court has more leeway. I suspect the judge was very sympathetic to the situation and wanted to do what he was allowed under the law."

Lucy closed the file and leaned back in her chair, exhausted.

"Do you have any questions?" Nicholson said.

"Only the ones you can't answer."

Nicholson handed Lucy her business card. "Call me if you think of any when you go home. By the way, Detective Marlow is waiting to see you."

"She is?" Lucy hadn't seen Marlow since her arrest. She didn't know whether to be pleased or worried.

"I'll send her in," Nicholson said as she departed.

Marlow greeted Lucy with a hug. "How are you holding up?"

Lucy gave the now-standard answer about counseling, the bereavement group, and getting better. She ended with, "What're you doing here?"

"The investigation turned up some information you need to have."

Lucy shook her head. "I can't bear to hear any more."

"Your mother would want you to know what I'm about to tell you. During Kistler's police interrogation, he admitted entering your mother's house a few minutes after killing her. He used the outside key to get in. Kistler was looking for anything that might tie him to the murder. He found her 'Important File' and took it. The NYPD found the file when searching Kistler's apartment."

Marlow handed the file to Lucy. "You need to look at it."

She saw the deed to the house, her mother's Last Will & Testament, a list of bank accounts and investments, and a life insurance policy.

"Look at the face page of the policy," Marlow said. "Debbie was insured for a million dollars, double indemnity in the event of accidental death or homicide. You are the sole beneficiary. The U.S. Marshals Service has taken care of the paperwork. The life insurance proceeds are now in an account with your new name."

Lucy's chest muscles contracted, squeezing the breath out of her lungs. When her lungs refilled with air, she wept, choking between sobs, "I don't want the money, I don't want it. I want my mother. Detective Marlow, bring her back to me. How could Mom think she could take care of me with insurance, when all she had to do was tell me the truth? Why didn't she tell me? Answer me that, and I'll give you all the money. Tell me, please tell me."

Marlow wrapped her arms around her. "I know you don't want the money. I know you'd do anything to get your mother back. Don't be angry with her. I can't explain why she kept secrets from you, but I do know one thing. She loved you with her whole heart. She did her very best to take care of you. This insurance money is part of that. Honor your mother. Take the money and tuck it away. One day, you'll have your own little girl. If you don't want to use the money for yourself, save it for her."

Lucy nodded while she blew her nose. "Thank you, Detective Marlow. Thank you for everything."

"It's almost three. The Deputy U.S. Marshal is probably here. Dry your eyes. Say 'farewell' to Lucy Prestipino in style. She's a good girl, as smart as they come. I'm going to miss her a lot."

They walked out of Judge Susque's chambers arm and arm. Out in the hallway, a middle-aged man wearing a U. S. Marshals uniform was waiting for them. He introduced himself as Deputy Marshal Peter Etchers.

"I'll take it from here, Detective."

Lucy kissed her friend on the cheek and watched her until she entered the elevator.

"Ms. Holiday," Etchers said. "Ready to start your new life?"

Happy Holiday took a deep breath and stood as tall as her frame would let her. "Let's go."

———

It was Friday afternoon before Rick returned to his apartment. He was elated. The interview had gone well. In less than two weeks, he'd begin his new job with the gang unit in the U. S. Attorney's Office for the Southern District of New York. As soon as he unpacked, he'd call Lucy. He rehearsed his words. He had a lot to tell her and he had to say it right.

He inserted a key into his mailbox and was surprised to find a hand-written envelope. It was from Lucy. Rick opened the envelope and found a letter.

> *Dear Rick,*
>
> *I wish I could have told you these things in person, rather than in a letter. This came up too fast for me to meet up with you. Anyway, I'll be seeing the Deputy U.S. Marshal this afternoon, and he'll take me to my new life. It's scary, but I'm ready to be someone other than Lucy Prestipino from Highlandtown. Not many people get a chance to start completely over.*
>
> *I'm glad to have known you. One day, I'll read in the paper you've been sworn in as a U.S. Attorney, or a judge, or maybe the FBI Director. Some things I just know, and this is one of them.*
>
> *Thank you for helping me through this awful time. I know I tested your patience. I hope one day, you'll be able to think well of me. I'll always remember how you taught me to dance. Dancing is such a joyful thing, and I never knew it. I'm going to dance every chance I get.*
>
> *And your kiss—that was the best kiss I ever got. I'll hold the memory of your kiss in my heart forever.*
> *Love, Lucy*

Rick re-read the letter a dozen times. Witness protection? He couldn't believe it. There must be a mistake. He called Alex.

"I got a letter from Lucy. What's going on? It sounded like she went into witness protection."

"Didn't you talk to her yesterday?"

"No, I had a job interview in Manhattan with the U.S. Attorney. Yesterday was the only day he was available. I thought I'd catch up with Lucy when I got back. I just found her letter."

"She's on the wing. Gone."

"Why didn't you warn me about the witness protection?"

"I couldn't, you know that. I shouldn't even be telling you about it now."

"Where'd she go? What's her new name?"

"I don't know. Even if I did, I wouldn't tell you. Sorry, man."

Rick disconnected. He read the letter again and berated himself aloud. "I shouldn't have put it off. I should have told her how I feel."

I'll find you Lucy. I swear I will.

Chapter 63

June 1

It was her 22nd birthday. Happy Holiday was used to her new name, but the new birthday threw her. May first, her old birthday, came and went without fanfare, or acknowledgment. Starting a new life was hard; getting rid of an old one was even harder.

She'd forgotten about her Sideling Hill citation, until this morning when she looked at her cell phone calendar. "Court," it noted. She decided, just for today, she'd go back to being Lucy Prestipino. Lucy, even after she vanished, wasn't going to be known as some low-life who 'failed to appear' for court. She didn't intend to tell Deputy Etchers about her temporary *Lucy* persona, either. He'd go ballistic. He was annoyed enough over the fact she'd made her new home in Deep Creek.

"Protected witnesses don't begin new lives in old residences," he said. "I don't know how you managed to pull this off."

She didn't care what Etchers thought. Romero bargained for her protection, and the bargain allowed her to pick her own name and to live anywhere she wanted.

Not only did Etchers disapprove of her new hometown, he ridiculed her new name.

"Happy Holiday? How're you supposed to blend into a community with a name that sounds like a stripper's?"

She liked Etchers. He was smart and capable but had the irritating habit of telling her how to run her life. He reminded her of Rick—only older, bigger, and more profane. Rick. How was he doing? He was probably relieved she was out of his hair.

Lucy scanned the one o'clock docket posted outside the courtroom in the Washington County District Court. There were about twenty-five cases; her name and citation number were not among them. She went to the clerk's office.

"I can't find my name or the citation number on the bulletin board," she told the counter clerk.

"Madam Clerk," said a voice behind her. "It's been taken care of."

Lucy smiled.

"Trooper James Bittinger." She turned around. Jimmy's eyes were blue and sparkling.

"Ms. Holiday. It's nice to see you again. I've been waiting here all morning hoping you'd show up."

She was delighted. "What did you mean, my citation's 'been taken care of?'"

"When I saw it on today's docket, I figured you forgot to tell the U.S. Marshals Service about it. I called them and *poof!*—the citation disappeared."

"You have magical powers. That's good to know."

Jimmy grinned. "I like your new look."

Her hair was brown and short. She intended to get a pixie style, but her hair had sprung into unruly curls when it was cut. Tinted contacts turned her eyes brown, both of them. Dental implants had given her straight, white teeth.

"I heard you bought the old Harvey place," Jimmy said.

"That's right. I've been fixing it up. How's your brother, Nathaniel?"

"He's back home from rehab. Doing well."

Jimmy was floundering for words. A few seconds passed before he said, "Let's go into the courtroom. It's empty. We'll have more privacy."

She followed him through the courtroom doors and sat on a wooden bench. Jimmy sat beside her.

"Lucy...um, Happy—shoot, it's going to take some doing for me to get used to that."

"You can call me Lucy, for today anyway. I'm letting her visit for a bit."

"By the way, I like your new name. A little goofy, but it sure fits you." He chuckled a little and then cleared his throat. "I wanted to say how sorry I am about your mother. About all of it. If you ever need anything, you can call on me. You can call on my family. We'll help you in any way we can."

Lucy stared into his eyes, feeling her own eyes water. She didn't want to cry. It'd been three days since she last cried, and she didn't want to break her streak. Her throat closed, and she couldn't say anything.

"I probably did the wrong thing here, bringing this up now," Jimmy said. "I know today's your birthday—well, your new birthday, and I've gone and spoiled it."

She choked out, "No, you didn't." Speaking the words freed up her throat. "You've made my birthday special. How'd you know about it? And my name, too? No one's supposed to know."

"After you left Hearts Afire, Romero asked me to stay with him. I heard everything, including the witness protection deal he made for you."

"How is he?"

"I haven't seen him since the proffer session, so I can't say how he's doing now. The session was hard on him. He had a lot to face up to. He turned himself inside out doing it. I know you were the one who convinced him to turn state's evidence. And you did it while enduring great personal sorrow. That's something you can be proud of for the rest of your life. I know your mother's proud of you."

"I guess you heard about my father."

"Yes."

"Why do you think my mother never told me about him? All those years of secrets and lies. I keep looking for an answer. No one has one."

Jimmy was quiet for a long time. Finally, he spoke. "Maybe she wasn't ready to tell you. Or maybe she thought you weren't ready to hear it. I think she was waiting for the right time, but she never got the chance. The chance was stolen from her."

A great weight lifted from Lucy's soul. Of course, her mother would've waited. Lucy was a substance abuser, a juvenile delinquent. Who knew what she would've done if she'd known the truth about her father when she was a teenager? The knowledge could've ruined her life—the life her mother had worked so hard to save and protect.

"Thank you, Jimmy."

He handed her a handkerchief. She didn't realize she was crying. She'd start another streak tomorrow.

"My family has been planning a birthday party for you. Will you come? They'd understand if you don't want to, but I hope you will."

"Okay."

"Good! It's at my parents' house. I've got cases on the one o'clock docket. If you don't mind waiting, you can follow me. I'll make sure to get you where you need to go."

Lucy believed him. Some things she just knew.

Acknowledgments

I am deeply indebted to my family and friends for their encouragement, enthusiasm, and love while I pursued my lifelong dream of writing a novel.

Thanks to my sisters, Kate Donvito and Maggie Callahan, and my brother of blessed memory, John Michael Callahan, for a goldmine of treasured memories, family lore, and yet-to-be written novels.

Thanks to my law school mates, Sue Schenning, Jane Sheehan and Sally Swann. For thirty-plus years, we've shared stories of life and law. Some of them made their way into this novel.

Thanks to my instructors and fellow writers at The Writer's Center, Bethesda, Maryland. Without their feedback, I'd still be writing like a lawyer.

Thanks to my friend, Jack Kenneally, for his Irish wit and wry sense of humor. Sometimes my characters surprised me when Jack's words came out of their mouths.

Thanks to my first readers: Corlyn Krinsky, Sharon Rosenthal, Sue Schenning, Susan Blumen, Maggie Callahan, Kate Donvito, and Donna Crockett-Gilkerson. My special thanks goes to Ginny Prestipino Westrick who endured my dreadful first efforts.

Thanks to Dawn Dowdle, Sharon Pickerel, and Kathryn Johnson who helped me transform my original tome into a book.

I consulted with many professionals. Their willingness to share their knowledge and time never ceased to amaze me. Any mistakes of fact, law or procedure are mine.

Thanks to Richard Snook, owner of Wabi Cycles, Los Angeles, California. Even though Mr. Snook understood Lucy Prestipino was a fictitious character, he helped me select her bicycle, albeit one with brakes.

Thanks to Donna Crockett-Gilkerson, P.T., for sharing her expertise in orthopedic rehabilitation.

Thanks to Sue Schenning, Associate Professor of Forensic Studies, Stevenson University, and former Deputy State's Attorney for Baltimore County, for sharing her expertise in criminal law and procedure.

Thanks to Dave Rosenthal, Senior Assistant Attorney General, Office of the Attorney General for the District of Columbia, for sharing his expertise in gangs and trial tactics.

Thanks to Kimberly Clements, District of Columbia Department of Forensic Sciences, Crime Scene Sciences Division, who answered my endless forensic, investigatory, and DNA questions.

Thanks to Detective Michele Smith, Montgomery County Police, Major Crimes Division, Homicide Section, and the instructors at the Montgomery County Police Citizen Academy, for teaching me the fundamentals of police work.

Thanks to Eric and Adriana Larios, for their Spanish translations.

Thanks to Scott Higham and Sari Horwitz, whose fascinating and heartbreaking book, *Finding Chandra: A True Washington Murder Mystery*, inspired Lucy Prestipino's courtroom argument.

Thanks to my dear children, Katie and Michael, who answered my recurring question, in its many variations: how would a twenty-something describe, think, do, or say _____? Their answers were always enlightening and laced with humor. Thanks to Katie, my ever-patient guru for all things relating to Word and formatting.

How can I possibly thank Ron Crockett, my loving husband of over thirty-seven years? Ron encouraged me through my inevitable periods of self-doubt, acted as a sounding board for my evolving plotlines, rescued me whenever my limited computer skills failed, cheered me on with unbridled enthusiasm, and never stopped believing in me.

About the Author

Ellen Ann Callahan is an author and freelance writer. Her articles and essays have appeared in *Maryland Life Magazine, The Washington Post, Washington Family Magazine,* and *Chicken Soup for the Breast Cancer Survivor's Soul.* She was an adoption attorney until she retired to pursue the writing life. She lives with her husband in Deep Creek, Maryland. For more information, visit www.EllenAnnCallahan.com